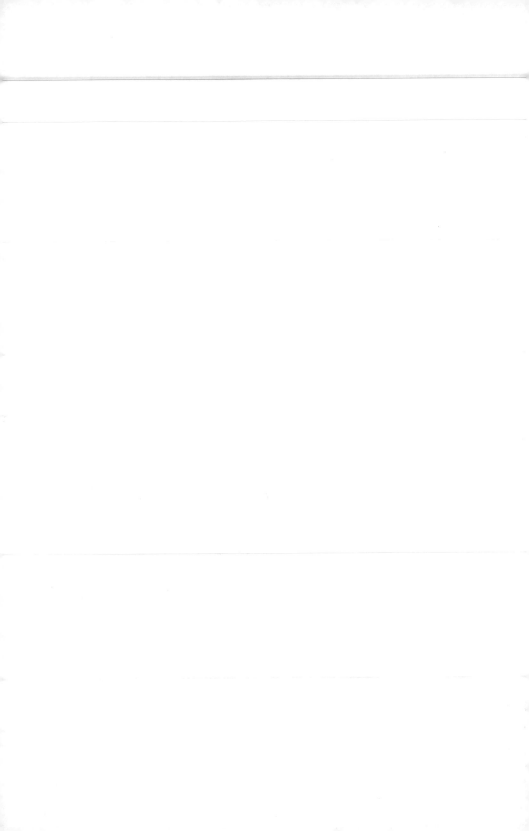

HALF A WAR

ALSO BY JOE ABERCROMBIE

HALF A KING
HALF THE WORLD

HALF A WAR

JOE ABERCROMBIE

HARPER
Voyager

HarperCollins*Publishers*
1 London Bridge Street,
London SE1 9GF

www.harpercollins.co.uk

Published by Harper*Voyager*
An imprint of HarperCollins*Publishers* 2015
1

A catalogue record for this book
is available from the British Library

ISBN: 9780007550265

Typeset in Minion by Palimpsest Book Production Limited,
Falkirk, Stirlingshire

Printed and bound in Great Britain by
Clays Ltd, St Ives plc

Find out more about HarperCollins and the environment at
www.harpercollins.co.uk/green

For Teddy

The man who stands at a strange threshold
Should be cautious before he cross it,
Glance this way and that:
Who knows beforehand what foes may sit
Awaiting him in the hall?

From Hávamál, the Speech of the High One

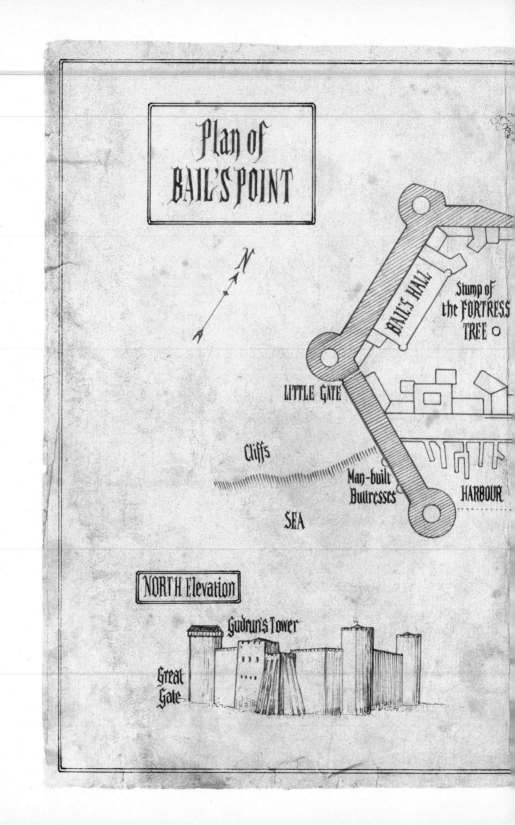

Plan of
BAIL'S POINT

N

BAIL'S HALL

Stump of
the FORTRESS
TREE

LITTLE GATE

Cliffs

Man-built
Buttresses

HARBOUR

SEA

NORTH Elevation

Gudrun's Tower

Great
Gate

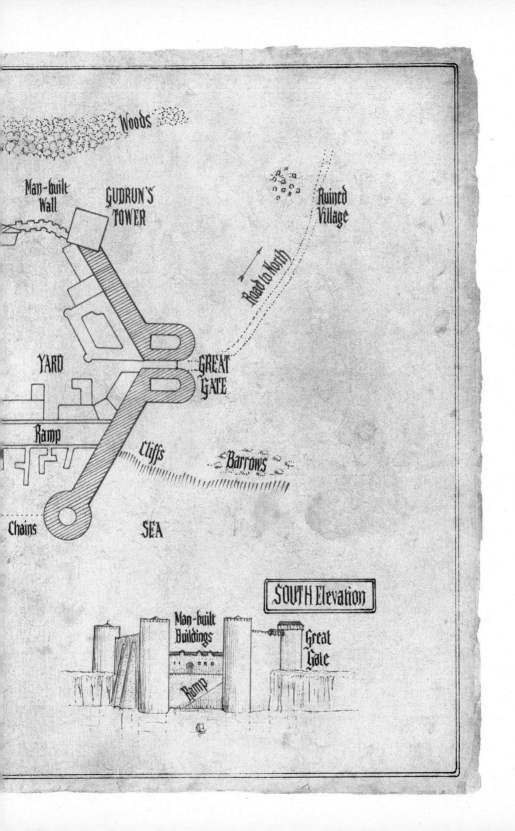

Rangbeld R.

Lunungad

Smoloo

VANSTERLAND

THE TA...

Ordbec

Hemenholm

Divine River

VULSGARD

Royetock

SAGENMARK

Amwend

Skefte

SHATTERED

GETTLAND

THORLBY

SEA

Skanelorra

Stokom

Heliun

Vistanger

Shaltveyr

THROVENLAND

SHENDS

Weska R.

Kanot

YALETOFT

Bail's Pt.

SKEKENHOUSE

Kuskilde

Skoder R.

Reerskoft

YUTMARK

N
HAULS
Denied R.
Serniriv
Denied R.
KALYIV
Hadorst
Shomel
Zatyr
GOLDEN SEA
Akhman
Sankar
FIRST of CITIES
Camnan
Istas
SEA of DREAMS
Ulsareen
Ostrisa
Jis
EMPIRE OF THE SOUTH

I

WORDS ARE
WEAPONS

THE FALL

'We have lost,' said King Fynn, staring into his ale.

As she looked out at the empty hall, Skara knew there was no denying it. Last summer, the gathered heroes had threatened to lift the roof-beams with their bloodthirsty boasting, their songs of glory, their promises of victory over the High King's rabble.

As men so often do, they had proved fiercer talkers than fighters. After an idle, inglorious, and unprofitable few months they had slunk away one by one, leaving a handful of the luckless lurking about the great firepit, its flames guttering as low as the fortunes of Throvenland. Where once the many-columned Forest had thronged with warriors, now it was peopled with shadows. Crowded with disappointments.

They had lost. And they had not even fought a battle.

Mother Kyre, of course, saw it differently. 'We have come to terms, my king,' she corrected, nibbling at her meat as primly as an old mare at a hay-bale.

'Terms?' Skara stabbed furiously at her own uneaten food. 'My father died to hold Bail's Point, and you've given its key to Grandmother Wexen without a blow struck. You've promised the High King's warriors free passage across our land! What do you think "lost" would look like?'

Mother Kyre turned her gaze on Skara with the usual infuriating calmness. 'Your grandfather dead in his howe, the women of Yaletoft weeping over the corpses of their sons, this hall made ashes and you, princess, wearing a slave's collar shackled to the High King's chair. *That* is what I think "lost" would look like. Which is why I say *come to terms.*'

Stripped of his pride, King Fynn sagged like a sail without a mast. Skara had always thought her grandfather as unconquerable as Father Earth. She could not bear to see him like this. Or perhaps she could not bear to see how childish her belief in him had been.

She watched him swill down more ale, and belch, and toss his gilded cup aside to be refilled. 'What do you say, Blue Jenner?'

'In such royal company as this, my king, as little as I can.'

Blue Jenner was a shifty old beggar, more raider than trader, his face as crudely chiselled, weathered and cracked as an old prow-beast. Had Skara been in charge he would not have been allowed on her docks, let alone at her high table.

Mother Kyre, of course, saw it differently. 'A captain is like a king, but of a ship rather than a country. Your experience might benefit Princess Skara.'

The indignity of it. 'A lesson in politics from a pirate,' Skara muttered to herself, 'and not even a successful one.'

'Don't mumble. How many hours have I spent teaching you the proper way for a princess to speak? For a queen to speak?' Mother Kyre raised her chin and made her voice echo effortlessly from the rafters. 'If you judge your thoughts worth hearing, pronounce them proudly, push them to every corner of the chamber, fill the hall with your hopes and desires and make every listener share them! If you are ashamed of your thoughts, better to leave a silence. A smile costs nothing. You were saying?'

'Well . . .' Blue Jenner scratched at the few grey hairs still clinging to his weather-spotted scalp, evidently a place unknown to combs. 'Grandmother Wexen's crushed the rebellion in the Lowlands.'

'With the help of this dog of hers, Bright Yilling, who worships no god but Death.' Skara's grandfather snatched up his cup while the thrall was still pouring, ale spilling across the table. 'They say he lined the road to Skekenhouse with hanged men.'

'The High King's eyes turn north,' Jenner went on. 'He's keen to bring Uthil and Grom-gil-Gorm to heel and Throvenland . . .'

'Is in the way,' finished Mother Kyre. 'Don't slouch, Skara, it is unseemly.'

Skara scowled, but she wriggled her shoulders up the chair a little anyway, closer to the board-stiff, neck-stretched, horribly unnatural pose the minister approved of. *Sit as if you have a knife to your throat*, she always said. *The role of a princess is not to be comfortable.*

'I'm a man used to living free, and I'm no lover of Grandmother Wexen, or her One God, or her taxes, or her rules.' Blue Jenner rubbed mournfully at his lopsided jaw. 'But when Mother Sea whips up the storm, a captain does what he must to save what he can. Freedom's worth nothing to the dead. Pride's worth little even to the living.'

'Wise words.' Mother Kyre wagged her finger at Skara. 'The beaten can win tomorrow. The dead have lost forever.'

'Wisdom and cowardice can be hard to tell apart,' snapped Skara.

The minister clenched her jaw. 'I swear I taught you wiser manners than to insult a guest. Nobility is shown not by the respect one is given by the highest, but the respect one gives to the lowly. Words are weapons. They should be handled with proper care.'

Jenner waved any suggestion of offence gently away. 'No doubt Princess Skara has the right of it. I've known many men far braver'n me.' He gave a sad smile, displaying a crooked set of teeth with several gaps. 'And seen most buried, one by one.'

'Bravery and long life rarely make good bedfellows,' said the king, draining his cup again.

'Kings and ale pair up no better,' said Skara.

'I have nothing left but ale, granddaughter. My warriors

have abandoned me. My allies have deserted me. They swore fair-weather oaths, oak-firm while Mother Sun shone, prone to wilt when the clouds gather.'

That was no secret. Day after day Skara had watched the docks, eager to see how many ships the Iron King Uthil of Gettland would bring, how many warriors would accompany the famous Grom-gil-Gorm of Vansterland. Day after day, as the leaves budded, then the leaves cast dappled shade, then the leaves turned brown and fell. They never came.

'Loyalty is common in dogs but rare in men,' observed Mother Kyre. 'A plan that relies on loyalty is worse than none at all.'

'What then?' asked Skara. 'A plan that relies on cowardice?'

Old, her grandfather looked as he turned to her with misty eyes and brewer's breath. Old and beaten. 'You have always been brave, Skara. Braver than I. No doubt the blood of Bail flows in your veins.'

'Your blood too, my king! You always told me only half a war is fought with swords. The other half is fought here.' And Skara pressed one fingertip into the side of her head, so hard it hurt.

'You have always been clever, Skara. Cleverer than I. The gods know you can talk the birds down from the sky when it pleases you. Fight that half of the war, then. Give me the deep cunning that can turn back the High King's armies and save our land and our people from Bright Yilling's sword. That can spare me from the shame of Grandmother Wexen's terms.'

Skara looked down at the straw-covered floor, face burning. 'I wish I could.' But she was a girl seventeen winters old and, Bail's blood or no, her head held no hero's answers. 'I'm sorry, Grandfather.'

'So am I, child.' King Fynn slumped back and beckoned for more ale. 'So am I.'

'Skara.'

She was snatched from troubled dreams and into darkness, Mother Kyre's face ghostly in the light of one flickering candle.

'Skara, get up.'

She fumbled back the furs, clumsy with sleep. Strange sounds outside. Shouting and laughter.

She rubbed her eyes. 'What is it?'

'You must go with Blue Jenner.'

Skara saw the trader then, lurking in the doorway of her bedchamber. A black figure, shaggy-headed, eyes turned to the floor.

'What?'

Mother Kyre pulled her up by her arm. 'You must go *now*.'

Skara was about to argue. As she always argued. Then she saw the minister's expression and it made her obey without a word spoken. She had never seen Mother Kyre afraid before.

It did not sound like laughter any more, outside. Crying. Wild voices. 'What's happening?' she managed to croak.

'I made a terrible mistake.' Mother Kyre's eyes darted

to the door and back. 'I trusted Grandmother Wexen.' She twisted the gold ring from Skara's arm. The one Bail the Builder once wore into battle, its ruby glistening dark as new-spilled blood in the candlelight. 'This is for you.' She held it out to Blue Jenner. 'If you swear to see her safe to Thorlby.'

The raider's eyes flickered guiltily up as he took it. 'I swear it. A sun-oath and a moon-oath.'

Mother Kyre clutched painfully hard at both of Skara's hands. 'Whatever happens, you must live. That is your duty now. You must live and you must lead. You must fight for Throvenland. You must stand for her people if . . . if there is no one else.'

Skara's throat was so tight with fear she could hardly speak. 'Fight? But—'

'I have taught you how. I have tried to. Words are weapons.' The minister wiped tears from Skara's face that she had not even realized she had cried. 'Your grandfather was right, you are brave and you are clever. But now you must be strong. You are a child no longer. Always remember, the blood of Bail flows in your veins. Now go.'

Skara padded barefoot through the darkness at Blue Jenner's heels, shivering in her shift, Mother Kyre's lessons so deep-rooted that even fearing for her life she worried over whether she was properly dressed. Flames beyond the narrow windows cast stabbing shadows across the straw-scattered floor. She heard panicked shouts. A dog barking, suddenly cut off. A heavy thudding as of a tree being felled.

As of axes at the door.

They stole into the guest-room, where warriors had slept shoulder to shoulder a few months before. Now there was only Blue Jenner's threadbare blanket.

'What's happening?' she whispered, hardly recognizing her own voice it came so thin and cracked.

'Bright Yilling has come with his Companions,' said Jenner, 'to settle Grandmother Wexen's debts. Yaletoft is already burning. I'm sorry, princess.'

Skara flinched as he slid something around her neck. A collar of twisted silver wire, a fine chain clinking faintly. The kind the Ingling girl who used to bind her hair had worn.

'Am I a slave?' she whispered, as Jenner buckled the other end about his wrist.

'You must seem to be.'

Skara shrank back at a crash outside, the clash of metal, and Jenner pressed her against the wall. He blew his candle out and dropped them into darkness. She saw him draw a knife, Father Moon glinting on its edge.

Howls now, beyond the door, high and horrible, the bellows of beasts not the voices of men. Skara squeezed her eyes shut, tears stinging the lids, and prayed. Mumbling, stuttering, meaningless prayers. Prayers to every god and none.

It is easy to be brave when the Last Door seems tiny for its distance, a far-off thing for other folk to worry about. Now she felt Death's chill breath on her neck and it froze the courage in her. How freely she had talked of cowardice the night before. Now she understood what it was.

A last long shriek, then silence almost worse than the noise had been. She felt herself drawn forward, Jenner's breath stale on her cheek.

'We have to go.'

'I'm scared,' she breathed.

'So am I. But if we face 'em boldly we might talk our way free. If they find us hiding . . .'

You can only conquer your fears by facing them, her grandfather used to say. *Hide from them, and they conquer you.* Jenner eased the door creaking open and Skara forced herself through after him, her knees trembling so badly they were nearly knocking together.

Her bare foot slid in something wet. A dead man sat beside the door, the straw all about him black with blood.

Borid, his name. A warrior who had served her father. He had carried Skara on his shoulders when she was little, so she could reach the peaches in the orchard under the walls of Bail's Point.

Her stinging eyes crept towards the sound of voices. Over broken weapons and cloven shields. Over more corpses, hunched, sprawled, spreadeagled among the carved columns after which her grandfather's hall was called the Forest.

Figures were gathered in the light of the guttering firepit. Storied warriors, mail and weapons and ring-money gleaming with the colours of fire, their great shadows stretching out across the floor towards her.

Mother Kyre stood among them, and Skara's grand-father too, ill-fitting mail hastily dragged on, grey hair still wild from his bed. Smiling blandly upon his two prisoners was a slender warrior with a soft, handsome face, as careless as a child's, a space about him where even these other killers dared not tread.

Bright Yilling, who worshipped no god but Death.

His voice echoed jauntily in the vastness of the hall. 'I was hoping to pay my respects to Princess Skara.'

'She has gone to her cousin Laithlin,' said Mother Kyre. The same voice that had calmly lectured, corrected, chastised Skara every day of her life, but with an unfamiliar warble of terror in it now. 'Where you will never reach her.'

'Oh, we will reach her there,' said one of Yilling's warriors, a huge man with a neck like a bull's.

'Soon enough, Mother Kyre, soon enough,' said another with a tall spear and a horn at his belt.

'King Uthil will come,' she said. 'He will burn your ships and drive you back into the sea.'

'How will he burn my ships when they are safe behind the great chains at Bail's Point?' asked Yilling. 'The chains you gave me the key to.'

'Grom-gil-Gorm will come,' she said, but her voice had faded almost to a whisper.

'I hope it will be so.' Yilling reached out with both hands and ever so gently eased Mother Kyre's hair back over her shoulders. 'But he will come too late for you.' He drew a sword, a great diamond in a golden claw for a pommel, mirror-steel flashing so bright in the darkness it left a white smear across Skara's sight.

'Death waits for us all.' King Fynn took a long breath through his nose, and proudly drew himself up. A glimpse of the man he used to be. He looked about the hall and, through the columns, caught Skara's eye, and it seemed to her he gave the slightest smile. Then he dropped to his knees. 'Today you kill a king.'

Yilling shrugged. 'Kings and peasants. We all look the same to Death.'

He stabbed Skara's grandfather where his neck met his shoulder, blade darting in to the hilt and back out, quick and deadly as lightning falls. King Fynn made only a dry squeak he died so fast, and toppled face forward into the firepit. Skara stood frozen, her breath held fast, her mind held fast.

Mother Kyre stared down at her master's corpse. 'Grandmother Wexen gave me her promise,' she stammered out.

Pit pat, pit pat, the blood dripped from the point of Yilling's sword. 'Promises only bind the weak.'

He spun, neat as a dancer, steel flickering in the shadows. There was a black gout and Mother Kyre's head clonked across the floor, her body dropping as though it had no bones in it at all.

Skara gave a shuddering gasp. It had to be a nightmare. A fever-trick. She wanted to lie down. Her eyelids fluttered, her body sagged, but Blue Jenner's hand was around her arm, painfully tight.

'You're a slave,' he hissed, giving her a stiff shake. 'You say nothing. You understand nothing.'

She tried to still her whimpering breath as light footsteps tapped across the floor towards them. Far away, someone had started screaming, and would not stop.

'Well, well,' came Bright Yilling's soft voice. 'This pair does not belong.'

'No, lord. My name is Blue Jenner.' Skara could not comprehend how he could sound so friendly, firm and reasonable. If she had opened her mouth all that would have come out were slobbering sobs. 'I'm a trader carrying the High King's licence, lately returned up the Divine River. We were heading for Skekenhouse, blown off course in a gale.'

'You must have been fast friends with King Fynn, to be a guest in his hall.'

'A wise trader is friendly with everyone, lord.'

'You are sweating, Blue Jenner.'

'Honestly, you terrify me.'

'A wise trader indeed.' Skara felt a gentle touch under her chin and her head was tipped back. She looked into the face of the man who had just murdered the two people who had raised her from a child, his bland smile still spotted with their blood, close enough that she could count the dusting of freckles across his nose.

Yilling pushed his plump lips out and made a high, clean whistle. 'And a trader in fine goods too.' He brushed one hand through her hair, wound a strand of it around his long fingers, pushed it out of her face so that his thumb tip brushed her cheek.

You must live. You must lead. She smothered her fear. Smothered her hate. Forced her face dead. A thrall's face, showing nothing.

'Would you trade this to me, trader?' asked Yilling. 'For your life, maybe?'

'Happily, lord,' said Blue Jenner. Skara had known Mother Kyre was a fool to trust this rogue. She took a breath to curse him and his gnarled fingers dug tighter into her arm. 'But I cannot.'

'In my experience, and I have much and very bloody . . .' Bright Yilling raised his red sword and let it rest against his cheek as a girl might her favourite doll, the diamond pommel on fire with sparks of red and orange and yellow. 'One sharp blade severs a whole rope of cannots.'

The lump on Jenner's grizzled throat bobbed as he swallowed. 'She isn't mine to sell. She's a gift. From Prince Varoslaf of Kalyiv to the High King.'

'Ack.' Yilling slowly let his sword fall, leaving a long red smear down his face. 'I hear Varoslaf is a man a wise man fears.'

'He has precious little sense of humour, it's true.'

'As a man's power swells, his good humour shrivels.' Yilling frowned towards the trail of bloody footprints he had left between the columns. Between the corpses. 'The High King is much the same. It would not be prudent to snaffle a gift between those two.'

'My very thought all the way from Kalyiv,' said Jenner.

Bright Yilling snapped his fingers as loudly as a whip-crack, eyes suddenly bright with boyish enthusiasm. 'Here is my thought! We will toss a coin. Heads, you can take this pretty thing on to Skekenhouse and let her wash the High King's feet. Tails, I kill you and make better use of her.' He slapped Jenner on the shoulder. 'What do you say, my new friend?'

'I say Grandmother Wexen may take this ill,' said Jenner.

'She takes everything ill.' Yilling smiled wide, the smooth skin about his eyes crinkling with friendly creases. 'But I bend to the will of one woman only. Not Grandmother Wexen, nor Mother Sea, nor Mother Sun, nor even Mother War.' He flicked a coin high in the hallowed spaces of the Forest, gold flashing. 'Only Death.'

He snatched it from the shadows. 'King or peasant, high or low, strong or weak, wise or foolish. Death waits for us all.' And he opened his hand, the coin glinting in his palm.

'Huh.' Blue Jenner peered down at it, eyebrows high. 'Guess she can wait a little longer for me.'

They hurried away through the wreckage of Yaletoft, flaming straw fluttering on the hot wind, the night boiling over with screaming and pleading and weeping. Skara kept her eyes on the ground like a good slave should, no one now to tell her not to slouch, her fear thawing slowly into guilt.

They sprang aboard Jenner's ship and pushed off, the crew muttering prayers of thanks to Father Peace that they had been spared from the carnage, oars creaking out a steady rhythm as they slid between the boats of the raiders and out to sea. Skara slumped among the cargo, the guilt pooling slowly into sorrow as she watched the flames take King Fynn's beautiful hall and her past life with it, the great carved gable showing black against the fire, then falling in a fountain of whirling sparks.

The burning of all she had known dwindled away, Yaletoft a speckling of flame in the dark distance, sailcloth snapping as Jenner ordered the ship turned north, towards Gettland. Skara stood and looked behind them, into the past, the tears drying on her face as her sorrow froze into a cold, hard, iron weight of fury.

'I'll see Throvenland free,' she whispered, clenching her fists. 'And my grandfather's hall rebuilt, and Bright Yilling's carcass left for the crows.'

'For now, let's stick to seeing you alive, princess.' Jenner took the thrall collar from her neck, then wrapped his cloak around her shivering shoulders.

She looked up at him, rubbing gently at the marks the silver wire had left. 'I misjudged you, Blue Jenner.'

'Your judgment's shrewd. I've done far worse than you thought I might.'

'Why risk your life for mine, then?'

He seemed to think a moment, scratching at his jaw. Then he shrugged. 'Because there's no changing yesterday. Only tomorrow.' He pressed something into her hand. Bail's armring, the ruby gleaming bloody in the moon-light. 'Reckon this is yours.'

NO PEACE

'When will they be here?'

Father Yarvi sat slumped against a tree with his legs crossed and an ancient-looking book propped on his knees. He might almost have seemed asleep had his eyes not been flickering over the writing beneath heavy lids. 'I am a minister, Koll,' he murmured, 'not a seer.'

Koll frowned up at the offerings about the glade. Headless birds and drained jars of ale and bundles of bones swinging on twine. A dog, a cow, four sheep, all dangling head-down from rune-carved branches, flies busy at their slit throats.

There was a man too. A thrall, by the chafe marks on his neck, a ring of runes written clumsily on his back, his knuckles brushing the bloody ground. A fine sacrifice to

He Who Sprouts the Seed from some rich woman eager for a child.

Koll didn't much care for holy places. They made him feel he was being watched. He liked to think he was an honest fellow, but everyone has their secrets. Everyone has their doubts.

'What's the book?' he asked.

'A treatise on elf-relics written two hundred years ago by Sister Slodd of Reerskoft.'

'More forbidden knowledge, eh?'

'From a time when the Ministry was fixed on gathering wisdom, rather than suppressing it.'

'Only what is known can be controlled,' muttered Koll.

'And all knowledge, like all power, can be dangerous in the wrong hands. It is the use it is put to that counts.' And Father Yarvi licked the tip of the one twisted finger on his withered left hand and used it to turn the page.

Koll frowned off into the still forest. 'Did we have to come so early?'

'The battle is usually won by the side that gets there first.'

'I thought we came to talk peace?'

'Talk of peace is the minister's battlefield.'

Koll gave a sigh that made his lips flap. He perched himself on a stump at the edge of the clearing, a cautious distance from any of the offerings, slipped out his knife and the chunk of ash-wood he'd already roughly shaped. She Who Strikes the Anvil, hammer high. A gift for Rin, when he got back to Thorlby. If he got back, rather than ending up dangling from a tree in this glade himself. He flapped his lips again.

'The gods have given you many gifts,' murmured Father Yarvi, without looking up from his book. 'Deft hands and sharp wits. A lovely shock of sandy hair. A slightly over-ready sense of humour. But do you wish to be a great minister, and stand at the shoulder of kings?'

Koll swallowed. 'You know I do, Father Yarvi. More than anything.'

'Then you have many things to learn, and the first is patience. Focus your moth of a mind and one day you could change the world, just as your mother wanted you to.'

Koll jerked at the thong around his neck, felt the weights strung on it click together under his shirt. The weights his mother Safrit used to wear as a storekeeper, trusted to measure fairly. *Be brave, Koll. Be the best man you can be.*

'Gods, I still miss her,' he muttered.

'So do I. Now still yourself, and attend to what I do.'

Koll let the weights drop. 'My eyes are rooted to you, Father Yarvi.'

'Close them.' The minister snapped his book shut and stood, brushing the dead leaves from the back of his coat. 'And listen.'

Footsteps, coming towards them through the forest. Koll slipped the carving away but kept the knife out, point up his sleeve. Well-chosen words will solve most problems but, in Koll's experience, well-sharpened steel was a fine thing for tackling the others.

A woman stepped from the trees, dressed in minister's black. Her fire-red hair was shaved at the sides,
runes tattooed into the skin around her ears, the rest
combed with fat into a spiky fin. Her face was hard,
made harder yet by the muscles bunching as she
chewed on dreamer's bark, lips blotchy at the edges
with the purple stain of it.

'You are early, Mother Adwyn.'

'Not as early as you, Father Yarvi.'

'Mother Gundring always told me it was poor manners
to come second to a meeting.'

'I hope you will forgive my rudeness, then.'

'That depends on the words you bring from
Grandmother Wexen.'

Mother Adwyn raised her chin. 'Your master, King
Uthil, and his ally, Grom-gil-Gorm, have broken their
oaths to the High King. They have slapped aside his hand
of friendship and drawn their swords against him.'

'His hand of friendship weighed heavily upon us,' said
Yarvi. 'Two years since we shook it off we find we all
breathe easier. Two years, and the High King has taken
no towns, has won no battles—'

'And what battles have Uthil and Gorm fought? Unless
you count the ones they fight daily against each other?'
Adwyn spat juice out of the corner of her mouth and
Koll fiddled uneasily at a loose thread on his sleeve. She
struck close to the mark with that. 'You have enjoyed
good luck, Father Yarvi, for the High King's eye has been
on this rebellion in the Lowlands. A rebellion I hear you
had a hand in raising.'

Yarvi blinked, all innocence. 'Can I make men rise up hundreds of miles away? Am I a magician?'

'Some say you are, but magic, or luck, or deep-cunning will change nothing now. The rebellion is crushed. Bright Yilling duelled Hokon's three sons and one by one he cut them down. His sword-work is without equal.'

Father Yarvi peered at the one fingernail on his withered hand, as if to check it looked well. 'King Uthil might disagree. He would have beaten these brothers all at once.'

Mother Adwyn ignored his bluster. 'Bright Yilling is a new kind of man, with new ways. He put the oath-breakers to the sword and his Companions burned their halls with their families inside.'

'Burned families.' Koll swallowed. 'There's progress.'

'Perhaps you have not heard what Bright Yilling did next?'

'I hear he's quite a dancer,' said Koll. 'Did he dance?'

'Oh, yes. Across the straits to Yaletoft where he paid the faithless King Fynn a visit.'

Silence then, and a breeze rustled the leaves, made the offerings creak and sent a twitchy shiver up Koll's neck. Mother Adwyn's chewing made a gentle squelch, squelch as she smiled.

'Ah. So your jester can spin no laughs from that. Yaletoft lies in ruins, and King Fynn's hall in ashes, and his warriors are scattered to the winds.'

Yarvi gave the slightest frown. 'What of the king himself?'

'On the other side of the Last Door, with his minister.

Their deaths were written the moment you tricked them into your little alliance of the doomed.'

'On the battlefield,' murmured Father Yarvi, 'there are no rules. New ways indeed.'

'Bright Yilling is already spreading fire across Throvenland, preparing the way for the High King's army. An army more numerous than the grains of sand on the beach. The greatest army that has marched since the elves made war on God. Before midsummer they will be at the gates of Thorlby.'

'The future is a land wrapped in fog, Mother Adwyn. It may yet surprise us all.'

'One does not have to be a prophet to see what comes.' She drew out a scroll and dragged it open, the paper scrawled with densely-written runes. 'Grandmother Wexen will name you and Queen Laithlin sorcerers and traitors. The Ministry will declare this paper money of hers elf-magic, and any who use it outcast and outlaw.'

Koll started as he heard a twig snap somewhere in the brush.

'You shall be cut from the world, and so shall Uthil and Gorm and any who stand with them.'

And now the men appeared. Men of Yutmark from their square cloak buckles and their long shields. Koll counted six, and heard two more at least behind him, and forced himself not to turn.

'Drawn swords?' asked Father Yarvi. 'On the sacred ground of Father Peace?'

'We pray to the One God,' growled their captain, a

warrior with a gold-chased helmet. 'To us, this is just dirt.'

Koll looked across the sharp faces and the sharp blades pointed at him, palm slippery around the grip of his hidden knife.

'Here is a pretty fix,' he squeaked.

Mother Adwyn let the scroll fall. 'But even now, even after your plotting and your treachery, Grandmother Wexen would offer peace.' Dappled shade slid across her face as she raised her eyes towards heaven. 'The One God is truly a forgiving god.'

Father Yarvi snorted. Koll could hardly believe how fearless he seemed. 'I daresay her forgiveness has a price, though?'

'The statues of the Tall Gods shall all be broken and the One God worshipped throughout the Shattered Sea,' said Adwyn. 'Every Vansterman and Gettlander shall pay a yearly tithe to the Ministry. King Uthil and King Gorm will lay their swords at the feet of the High King in Skekenhouse, beg forgiveness and swear new oaths.'

'The old ones did not stick.'

'That is why you, Mother Scaer, and the young Prince Druin will remain as hostages.'

'Hmmmmmm.' Father Yarvi lifted his withered finger to tap at his chin. 'It's a lovely offer, but summer in Skekenhouse can be a little sticky.'

An arrow flickered past Koll's face, so close he felt the wind of it on his cheek. It took the leader of the warriors silently in the shoulder, just above the rim of his shield.

More shafts flitted from the woods. A man screamed.

Another clutched at an arrow in his face. Koll sprang at Father Yarvi and dragged him down behind the thick bole of a sacred tree. He glimpsed a warrior charging towards them, sword high. Then Dosduvoi stepped out, huge as a house, and with a swing of his great axe snatched the man from his feet and sent him tumbling away in a shower of dead leaves.

Shadows writhed, stabbing, hacking, knocking at the offerings and setting them swinging. A few bloody moments and Mother Adwyn's men had joined King Fynn on the other side of the Last Door. Their captain was on his knees, wheezing, six arrows lodged in his mail. He tried to stand using his sword as a crutch, but the red strength was leaking from him.

Fror slipped into the clearing. One hand gripped his heavy axe. With the other he gently undid the buckle on the captain's gold-trimmed helmet. It was a fine one, and would fetch a fine price.

'You will be sorry for this,' breathed the captain, blood on his lips and his grey hair stuck to his sweating forehead.

Fror slowly nodded. 'I am sorry already.' And he struck the captain on the crown and knocked him over with his arms spread wide.

'You can let me up now,' said Father Yarvi, patting Koll on the side. He realized he'd covered the minister with his body as a mother might her baby in a storm.

'You couldn't tell me the plan?' he asked, scrambling up.

'You cannot give away what you do not know.'

'You don't trust me to act a part?'

'Trust is like glass,' said Rulf, swinging his great horn bow over his shoulder and helping Yarvi up with one broad hand. 'Lovely, but only a fool rests lots of weight on it.'

Hardened warriors of Gettland and Vansterland had surrounded the clearing on every side, and Mother Adwyn cut a lonely figure in their midst. Koll almost felt sorry for her, but he knew it would do neither of them the least good.

'It seems my treachery was better than yours,' said Yarvi. 'Twice, now, your mistress has tried to cut me from the world, yet here I stand.'

'Treachery is what you are known for, spider.' Mother Adwyn spat purple bark-juice at his feet. 'What of your sacred ground of Father Peace?'

Yarvi shrugged. 'Oh, he is a forgiving god. But it may be wise to hang you from these trees and slit your throat as an offering, just in case.'

'Do it, then,' she hissed.

'Mercy shows more power than murder. Go back to Grandmother Wexen. Thank her for the information you have given me, it will be useful.' He gestured towards the dead men, already being trussed by the feet to be hung from the branches of the sacred grove. 'Thank her for these rich offerings to the Tall Gods, no doubt they will appreciate them.'

Father Yarvi jerked close to her, lips curled back, and Mother Adwyn's mask slipped, and Koll saw her fear.

'But tell the First of Minsters I piss on her offer! I swore an oath to be avenged on the killers of my father. A sun-oath and a moon-oath. Tell Grandmother Wexen that while she and I both live, there will be no peace.'

NEVER BLOODY ENOUGH

'I'll kill you, you half-haired bitch!' snarled Raith, spraying spit as he went for her. Rakki caught his left arm and Soryorn his right and between them they managed to wrestle him back. They'd had plenty of practice at it, after all.

Thorn Bathu didn't move. Unless you counted the jaw muscles clenching on the shaved side of her head.

'Let's all just calm down,' said her husband, Brand, waving his open palms like a shepherd trying to still a nervous flock. 'We're meant to be allies, aren't we?' He was a big, strong cow of a man, no edge to him at all. 'Let's just . . . just stand in the light a moment.'

Raith let everyone know how much he thought of that idea by twisting far enough free of his brother to spit in Brand's face. He missed, sadly, but the point was made.

Thorn curled her lip. 'Reckon this dog needs putting down.'

Everyone's got their sore spots, and that tickled Raith's. He went limp, let his head drop sideways, showing his teeth in a lazy grin as his eyes drifted across to Brand. 'Maybe I'll kill this coward wife of yours instead?'

He'd always had a trick for starting fights, and wasn't half bad at finishing them either, but nothing could've made him ready for how fast Thorn came at him.

'You're dead, you milk-haired bastard!'

Raith jerked away, near-dragging his brother and Soryorn down in a shocked tangle together on the dockside. Took three Gettlanders to drag her off – the sour old master-at-arms, Hunnan, the bald old helmsman, Rulf, and Brand with his scarred forearm wrapped around her neck. All strong men, straining at the effort, and even then her stray fist landed a good cuff on the top of Raith's head.

'Peace!' snarled Brand as he struggled to wrestle his thrashing wife back. 'For the gods' sake, peace!'

But no one was in the mood. There were others growling insults now, Gettlanders and Vanstermen both. Raith saw knuckles white on sword hilts, heard the scrape as Soryorn eased his knife free of its sheath. He could smell the violence coming, far worse than he'd planned on. But there's violence for you. It rarely keeps to the patch you mark out for it. Wouldn't be violence if it did.

Raith bared his teeth – half-snarl, half-smile – the fire coming up in his chest, the breath ripping hot at his throat, every muscle tensing.

Could've been a battle for the songs right then on the rain-damp docks of Thorlby if Grom-gil-Gorm hadn't come shoving through the angry press like a huge bull through a crowd of bleating goats.

'Enough!' roared the King of Vansterland. 'What shameful pecking of little birds is this?'

The hubbub died. Raith shook off his brother, grinning his wolf's grin, and Thorn tore free of her husband, growling curses. No doubt Brand had an uncomfortable night ahead, but it had all worked out well enough to Raith's mind. He'd come to fight, after all, and wasn't too bothered who with.

The glaring Gettlanders shifted to let King Uthil through, his drawn sword cradled in his arm. Raith hated him, of course. A good Vansterman had to hate the King of Gettland. But otherwise he seemed very much a man to admire, hard and grey as an iron bar and every bit as unbending, renowned for many victories and few words, a mad brightness to his sunken eyes that said he had only a cold space where the gods usually put a man's mercy.

'I am disappointed, Thorn Bathu,' he grated out in a voice rough as millstones. 'I expected better from you.'

'I'm all regret, my king,' she growled, glaring daggers at Raith, and then at Brand, who winced like daggers from his wife was far from a novelty.

'I expected no better.' Grom-gil-Gorm raised one black brow at Raith. 'But at least hoped for it.'

'We should let 'em insult us, my king?' snapped Raith.

'A little insult must be suffered if one is to maintain an alliance,' came Mother Scaer's dry voice.

'And our alliance is a ship on stormy seas,' said Father Yarvi, with that honeyed smile of his that cried out for a headbutt. 'Sink it with squabbling and we surely all will drown alone.'

Raith growled at that. He hated ministers and their two-tongued talk of Father Peace and greater good. To his mind there was no problem you couldn't best solve by putting your fist through it.

'A Vansterman never forgets an insult.' Gorm wedged his thumbs among the knives bristling from his belt. 'But I have a thirst upon me, and since we are the guests . . .' He drew himself up, the chain made from the pommels of his beaten enemies shifting as his great chest swelled. 'I, Grom-gil-Gorm, Breaker of Swords and Maker of Orphans, King of Vansterland and favourite son of Mother War . . . will go second into the city.'

His warriors grumbled bitterly. An hour they'd wasted arguing over who'd go first and now the battle was lost. Their king would take the place of less honour, so they'd have less honour and, gods, they were prickly over their honour.

'A wise choice,' said Uthil, narrowing his eyes. 'But expect no gifts for making it.'

'The wolf needs no gifts from the sheep,' said Gorm, glowering back. King Uthil's closest warriors swaggered past, gilded cloak-buckles and sword-hilts and ring-money gleaming, swollen to new heights of undeserved arrogance, and Raith showed his teeth and spat at their feet.

'A dog indeed,' sneered Hunnan, and Raith would've

sprung on the old bastard and knocked his brains out on the docks if Rakki hadn't hugged him tight and crooned, 'Calm, brother, calm,' in his ear.

'Blue Jenner! Here's a surprise!'

Raith frowned over his shoulder and saw Father Yarvi drawn aside by some old sailor with a brine-pickled face.

'A welcome one, I hope,' said Jenner, clasping hands with Rulf like they were old oarmates.

'That depends,' said the minister. 'Have you come to take Queen Laithlin's gold?'

'I try to take any gold that's offered.' Jenner glanced around like he was about to show off some secret treasure. 'But I've a better reason for being here.'

'Better than gold?' asked Rulf, grinning. 'You've changed.'

'Far better.' Jenner guided someone forward who'd been hidden at his back, and it was like someone stabbed Raith right through his skull and all the fight drained out.

She was small and slight, swamped by a weather-stained cloak. Her hair was a wild tangle, a cloud of dark curls that twitched and shifted in the salt breeze. Her skin was pale, and chapped pink round her nostrils, and the bones in her cheeks showed so fine and sharp it seemed they might snap at a harsh word.

She looked straight at Raith with big eyes dark and green as Mother Sea on a storm-day. She didn't smile. She didn't speak. Sad and solemn she seemed, and full of secrets, and every hair on Raith stood up. No axe-blow to the head could have knocked him quite so senseless as that one glimpse of her.

For a moment Father Yarvi's mouth hung foolishly open. Then he shut it with a snap. 'Rulf, take Blue Jenner and his guest to Queen Laithlin. Now.'

'You were ready to do murder over who went first, now you don't want to go at all?' Rakki was staring at him, and Raith realized Gorm's men were strutting in after the Gettlanders, all puffed up near to bursting to make up for going second.

'Who was that girl?' Raith croaked out, feeling giddy as a sleeper jerked from an ale-dream.

'Since when were you interested in girls?'

'Since I saw this one.' He blinked into the crowd, hoping to prove to both of them he hadn't imagined her, but she was gone.

'Must've been quite a beauty to draw your eye from a quarrel.'

'Like nothing I ever saw.'

'Forgive me, brother, but when it comes to women you haven't seen much. You're the fighter, remember?' Rakki grinned as he heaved up Grom-gil-Gorm's great black shield. 'I'm the lover.'

'As you never tire of telling me.' Raith shouldered the king's heavy sword and made to follow his brother into Thorlby. Until he felt his master's weighty hand holding him back.

'You have disappointed me, Raith.' The Breaker of Swords drew him close. 'This place is full of bad enemies to have, but I fear in Queen Laithlin's Chosen Shield you have picked the very worst.'

Raith scowled. 'She doesn't scare me, my king.'

Gorm slapped him sharply across the face. Well, a slap to Gorm. To Raith it was like being hit with an oar. He staggered but the king caught him and dragged him closer still. 'What wounds me is not that you tried to hurt her, but that you failed.' He cuffed him the other way and Raith's mouth turned salty with blood. 'I do not want a dog that yaps. I want a dog that uses its teeth. I want a killer.' And he slapped Raith a third time and left him dizzy. 'I fear you have a grain of mercy left in you, Raith. Crush it, before it crushes you.'

Gorm gave Raith's head a parting scratch. The sort a father gives a son. Or perhaps a huntsman gives his hound. 'You can never be bloody enough for my taste, boy. You know that.'

SAFE

The comb of polished whalebone swish-swish-swished through Skara's hair.

Prince Druin's toy sword click-clack-scraped against a chest in the corner.

Queen Laithlin's voice spilled out blab-blab-blab. As though she sensed that if she left a silence Skara might start screaming, and screaming, and never stop.

'Outside that window, on the south side of the city, my husband's warriors are camped.'

'Why didn't they help us?' Skara wanted to shriek as she stared numbly at the sprawling tents, but her mouth drooled out the proper thing, as always. 'There must be very many.'

'Two and a half thousand loyal Gettlanders, called in from every corner of the land.'

Skara felt Queen Laithlin's strong fingers turn her head, gently but very firmly. Prince Druin gave a piping toddler's war-cry and attacked a tapestry. The comb began to swish-swish-swish again, as though the solution to every problem was the right arrangement of hair.

'Outside this window, to the north, is Grom-gil-Gorm's camp.' The fires glimmered in the gathering dusk, spread across the dark hills like stars across heaven's cloth. 'Two thousand Vanstermen in sight of the walls of Thorlby. I never thought to see such a thing.'

'Not with their swords sheathed, anyway,' tossed out Thorn Bathu from the back of the room, as harshly as a warrior might toss an axe.

'I saw a quarrel on the docks . . .' mumbled Skara.

'I fear it will not be the last.' Laithlin clicked her tongue as she teased out a knot. Skara's hair had always been unruly, but the Queen of Gettland was not a woman to be put off by a stubborn curl or two. 'There is to be a great moot tomorrow. Five hours straight of quarrelling, that will be. If we get through it with no one dead I will count it a victory for the songs. There.'

And Laithlin turned Skara's head towards the mirror.

The queen's silent thralls had bathed her, and scrubbed her, and swapped her filthy shift for green silk brought on the long voyage from the First of Cities, nimbly altered to fit her. It was stitched with golden thread about the hem, as fine as anything she had ever worn, and Skara had worn some fine things. So many, and so carefully arranged by Mother Kyre, she had sometimes felt the clothes wore her.

She was surrounded by strong walls, strong warriors, slaves and luxury. She should have felt giddy with relief. But like a runner who stops to rest and finds they cannot stand again, the comfort made Skara feel dizzy-weak and aching-raw, battered outside and in as if she was one great bruise. She almost wished she was back aboard Blue Jenner's ship, the *Black Dog*, shivering, and staring into the rain, and thrice an hour crawling on grazed knees to puke over the side.

'This belonged to my mother, King Fynn's sister.' Laithlin carefully arranged the earring, golden chains fine as cobweb that spilled red jewels almost to Skara's shoulder.

'It's beautiful,' Skara croaked out, struggling not to spray sick all over the mirror. She scarcely recognized the haunted, pink-eyed, brittle-looking girl she saw there. She looked like her own ghost. Perhaps she never escaped Yaletoft. Perhaps she was still trapped there, Bright Yilling's slave, and always would be.

At the back of the room she saw Thorn Bathu squat beside the prince, shift his tiny hands around the grip of his wooden sword, murmur instructions on how to swing it properly. She grinned as he whacked her across the leg, the star-shaped scar on her cheek puckering, and ruffled his pale blonde hair. 'Good boy!'

All Skara could think of was Bright Yilling's sword, that diamond pommel flashing in the darkness of the Forest, and in the mirror the pale girl's chest began to heave and her hands to tremble—

'Skara.' Queen Laithlin took her firmly by the shoulders,

fixed her with those hard, sharp, grey-blue eyes, jerking her back to the present. 'Can you tell me what happened?'

'My grandfather waited for help from his allies.' The words burbled out flat as a bee's droning. 'We waited for Uthil's warriors, and Gorm's. They never came.'

'Go on.'

'He lost heart. Mother Kyre persuaded him to make peace. She sent a dove and Grandmother Wexen sent an eagle back. If Bail's Point was given up, and the warriors of Throvenland sent home, and the High King's army given free passage across our land, she would forgive.'

'But Grandmother Wexen does not forgive,' said Laithlin.

'She sent Bright Yilling to Yaletoft to settle the debt.' Skara swallowed sour spit, and in the mirror the pale girl's stringy neck shifted. Prince Druin's little face was crumpled with warrior's determination as he hacked at Thorn with his toy sword and she pushed it away with her fingers. His little war-cries sounded like the howls of pain and fury in the darkness, coming closer, always closer.

'Bright Yilling cut Mother Kyre's head off. He stabbed my grandfather right through and he fell in the firepit.'

Queen Laithlin's eyes widened. 'You . . . saw it happen?'

The dusting of sparks, the glow on the warriors' smiles, the thick blood dripping from the tip of Yilling's sword. Skara took a shuddering breath, and nodded. 'I got away disguised as Blue Jenner's slave. Bright Yilling flipped a coin, to decide whether he would kill him too . . . but the coin . . .'

She could still see it spinning in the shadows, flashing with the colours of fire.

'The gods were with you that night,' breathed Laithlin.

'Then why did they kill my family?' Skara wanted to shriek, but the girl in the mirror gave a queasy smile instead, and muttered a proper prayer of thanks to He Who Turns the Dice.

'They have sent you to me, cousin.' The queen squeezed hard at Skara's shoulders. 'You are safe here.'

The Forest that had been about her all her life, certain as a mountain, was made ashes. The high gable that had stood for two hundred years fallen in ruin. Throvenland was torn apart like smoke on the wind. Nowhere would be safe, ever again.

Skara found she was scratching at her cheek. She could still feel Bright Yilling's cold fingertips upon it.

'You have all been so kind,' she croaked out, and tried to smother an acrid burp. She had always had a weak stomach, but since she clambered from the *Black Dog* her guts had felt as twisted as her thoughts.

'You are family, and family is all that matters.' With a parting squeeze, Queen Laithlin let go of her. 'I must speak to my husband and my son . . . to Father Yarvi, that is.'

'Could I ask you . . . is Blue Jenner still here?'

The queen's displeasure was palpable. 'The man is little better than a pirate—'

'Could you send him to me? Please?'

Laithlin might have seemed hard as flint, but she must have heard the desperation in Skara's voice. 'I will send him. Thorn, the princess has been through an ordeal. Do not leave her alone. Come, Druin.'

The thigh-high prince looked solemnly at Skara. 'Bye bye.' And he dropped his wooden sword and ran after his mother.

Skara was left staring at Thorn Bathu. Staring up, since the Chosen Shield towered over her. Plainly she had no use for combs herself, the hair on one side clipped to dark stubble and on the other twisted into knots and braids and matted tangles bound up with a middle-sized fortune in gold and silver ring-money.

Here was a woman said to have fought seven men alone and won, the elf-bangle that had been her reward glowing fierce yellow on her wrist. A woman who wore blades instead of silks and scars instead of jewels. Who ground propriety under her boot heels and made no apologies for it, ever. A woman who would sooner break a door down with her face than knock.

'Am I a prisoner?' Skara meant it as a challenge, but it came out a mouse's squeak.

Thorn's expression was hard to read. 'You're a princess, princess.'

'In my experience there's not much difference between the two.'

'I'm guessing you've never been a prisoner.'

Contempt, and who could blame her? Skara's throat felt so closed up she could hardly speak. 'You must be thinking what a soft, weak, pampered fool I am.'

Thorn took a sharp breath. 'Actually I was thinking . . . of how it felt when I saw my father dead.' Her face might have had no softness in it, but her voice did. 'I was thinking what I might have felt to see him killed. To see him killed in front of me, and nothing I could do but watch.'

Skara opened her mouth, but no words came. It was not contempt but pity, and it choked her worse than scorn.

'I know how it feels to wear a brave face,' said Thorn. 'Few better.'

Skara felt as if her head was going to burst.

'I was thinking . . . standing where you're standing . . . I'd be crying a sea.'

And Skara heaved up a great, stupid sob. Her eyes screwed shut, and burned, and leaked. Her ribs shuddered. Her breath whooped and gurgled. She stood with her hands dangling, her whole face hurting she was crying so violently. Some tiny part of her fussed that this was far from proper behaviour, but the rest of her could not stop.

She heard quick footsteps and was gathered up like a child, held tight, held firm, the way her grandfather had held her when they watched her father burn on the pyre. She clung to Thorn, blubbering into her shirt, howling half-words not even she understood.

Thorn did not move, made no sound, only held Skara for a long time. Until her shuddering stopped. Until her sobs calmed to whimpers, and her whimpers to jagged breaths. Then, ever so gently, Thorn eased her away, pulled out a scrap of white cloth and, even though her own shirt was soaked with slobber, dabbed a tiny speck

on the front of Skara's dress, and offered it to her. 'It's
for cleaning my weapons but I reckon your face is a good
deal more valuable. Maybe more dangerous too.'

'I'm sorry,' whispered Skara.

'No need.' Thorn flicked at the golden key around her
neck. 'I cry harder than that every morning when I wake
up and remember who I married.'

And Skara laughed and sobbed at once and blew a
great snotty bubble out of her nose. For the first time
since that night she felt something like herself again.
Perhaps she had escaped from Yaletoft after all. As she
wiped her face there was a hesitant knock at the door.

'It's Blue Jenner.'

When he shuffled hunched into the room there was
something reassuring in his shabbiness. At a ship's helm
or in a queen's chambers he was the same man. Skara
felt stronger at the sight of him. That was the man she
needed.

'You remember me?' asked Thorn.

'You're a hard woman to forget.' Jenner glanced down
at the key around her neck. 'Congratulations on your
marriage.'

She snorted. 'Long as you don't congratulate my
husband. He's still in mourning over it.'

'You sent for me, princess?'

'I did.' Skara sniffed back her tears and set her shoulders. 'What are your plans?'

'Can't say I've ever been much of a planner. Queen
Laithlin's offered me a fair price to fight for Gettland but,
well, war's young man's work. Maybe I'll take the *Black*

Dog back down the Divine . . .' He glanced up at Skara, and winced. 'I promised Mother Kyre I'd see you to your cousin—'

'And you kept your promise, in spite of the dangers. I shouldn't ask you for more.'

He winced harder. 'You're going to, then?'

'I was hoping you might stay with me.'

'Princess . . . I'm an old raider twenty years past my best and my best was none too pretty.'

'Doubtless. When I first saw you I thought you were as worn as an old prow-beast.'

Jenner scratched at the side of his grizzled jaw. 'A fair judgment.'

'A fool's judgment.' Skara's voice cracked, but she cleared her throat, and took a breath, and carried on. 'I see that now. The worn prow-beast is the one that's braved the worst weather and brought the ship home safe even so. I don't need pretty, I need loyal.'

Jenner winced harder still. 'All my life I've been free, princess. Looked to no one but the next horizon, bowed to no one but the wind—'

'Has the horizon thanked you? Has the wind rewarded you?'

'Not hugely, I'll confess.'

'I will.' She caught his calloused hand in both of hers. 'To be free a man needs a purpose.'

He stared down at his hand in hers, then over at Thorn.

She shrugged. 'A warrior with nothing but themselves to fight for is no more than a thug.'

'I've seen you tested and I know I can trust you.' Skara

brought the old raider's gaze back to hers and held it. 'Stay with me. Please.'

'Oh, gods.' The leathery skin around Jenner's eyes creased as he smiled. 'How do I say no to that?'

'You don't. Say you'll help me.'

'I'm your man, princess. I swear it. A sun-oath and a moon-oath.' He paused for a moment. 'Help you do what, though?'

Skara took a ragged breath. 'I said I would see Throvenland free, and my grandfather's hall rebuilt, and Bright Yilling's carcass left for the crows, remember?'

Blue Jenner raised his craggy brows very high. 'Bright Yilling has all the High King's strength behind him. Fifty thousand swords, they say.'

'Only half a war is fought with swords.' She pressed her fingertip into the side of her head, so hard it hurt. 'The other half is fought here.'

'So . . . you've a plan?'

'I'll think of something.' She let go of Blue Jenner's hand and looked over at Thorn. 'You sailed with Father Yarvi to the First of Cities.'

Thorn frowned at Skara down a nose twisted from many breakings, trying to work out what moved beneath the question. 'Aye, I sailed with Father Yarvi.'

'You fought a duel against Grom-gil-Gorm.'

'That too.'

'You're Queen Laithlin's Chosen Shield.'

'You know I am.'

'And standing at her shoulder you must see a great deal of King Uthil too.'

'More than most.'

Skara wiped the last wetness from her lashes. She could not afford to cry. She had to be brave, and clever, and strong, however weak and terrified she felt. She had to fight for Throvenland now there was no one else, and words had to be her weapons.

'Tell me about them,' she said.

'What do you want to know?'

Knowledge is power, Mother Kyre used to say when Skara complained about her endless lessons. 'I want to know everything.'

FOR BOTH OF US

Raith woke with a mad jolt to find someone pawing at him.

He grabbed that bastard around the throat and slammed him against the wall, snarling as he whipped his knife out.

'Gods, Raith! It's me! It's me!'

Wasn't until then Raith saw, in the flickering light of the torch just down the corridor, that he'd got his brother pinned and was about to cut his throat.

His heart was hammering. Took him a moment to work out he was in the citadel in Thorlby. In the corridor outside Gorm's door, tangled with his blanket. Just where he was meant to be.

'Don't wake me like that,' he snapped, forcing the

fingers of his left hand open. They always ached worst just after he woke.

'Wake you?' whispered Rakki. 'You would've woken the whole of Thorlby the way you were shouting out. You dreaming again?'

'No,' grunted Raith, sitting back against the wall and scrubbing at the sides of his head with his nails. 'Maybe.' Dreams full of fire. The smoke pouring up and the stink of destruction. Mad light in the eyes of the warriors, the eyes of the dogs. Mad light on that woman's face. Her voice, as she shrieked for her children.

Rakki offered him a flask and Raith snatched it from him, rinsed out his mouth, cut and sore inside and out from Gorm's slaps, but that was nothing new. He sloshed water into his hand, rubbed it over his face. He was cold with sweat all over.

'I don't like this, Raith. I'm worried for you.'

'You, worried for me?' Gorm's sword must've been knocked clear in the scuffle, and Raith took it up, hugged it to his chest. If the king saw he'd let it lie in the cold he'd get another slap, and maybe worse. 'That's a new one.'

'No, it isn't. I've been worried for you a long time.' Rakki glanced nervously towards the door of the king's chamber, let his voice drop soft and eager as he leaned forward. 'We could just go. We could find a ship to take us down the Divine and the Denied, like you always talk of. Like you used to talk of, anyway.'

Raith nodded towards the door. 'You think he'd let us just go? You think Mother Scaer would wave us off smiling?' He snorted. 'I thought you were supposed to be the clever one. It's a pretty dream, but there's no going back. You forgotten what things were like before? Being hungry, and cold, and afraid all the time?'

'You're not afraid all the time?' Rakki's voice was so small it brought Raith's anger boiling up and chased the terror of his dreams away. Anger was the answer to most problems, when it came to it.

'No I'm not!' he snarled, shaking Gorm's sword and making his brother flinch. 'I'm a warrior, and I'm going to win a name for myself in this war, and enough ring-money we'll never be hungry again. This is my right place. Fought for it, haven't I?'

'Aye, you've fought for it.'

'We serve a king!' Raith tried to feel the same pride he used to. 'The greatest warrior in the Shattered Sea. Unbeaten in duel or battle. You like to pray. Give thanks to Mother War that we stand with the winners!'

Rakki stared at him across the hallway, his back against Gorm's war-scarred shield, his eyes wide and glistening with the torchlight. Strange, how his face could be so like Raith's but his expression so different. Sometimes seemed they were two prow-beasts carved alike, forever stuck to the same ship but always looking opposite ways.

'There's going to be killing,' he muttered. 'More than ever.'

'Reckon so,' said Raith, and he lay down, turning his back on his brother, hugging Gorm's sword against him and drawing the blanket over his shoulder. 'It's a war, ain't it?'

'I just don't like killing.'

Raith tried to sound like it was nothing, and couldn't quite get there. 'I can kill for both of us.'

A silence. 'That's what scares me.'

CLEVER HANDS

K oll tapped out the last rune and smiled as he blew a puff of wood-dust away. The scabbard was finished, and he was good and proud of the outcome.

He'd always loved working with wood, which kept no secrets and told no lies and having been carved never came uncarved. Not like minister's work, all smoke and guesses. Words were trickier tools than chisels, and people changeable as Mother Sea.

His back prickled as Rin reached around his shoulder, tracing one of the lines of runes with a fingertip. 'What does it mean?'

'Five names of Mother War.'

'Gods, it's fine work.' Her hand slid down the dark wood, lingering on the carved figures, and animals, and trees, all flowing one into another. 'You've got clever hands, Koll. None cleverer.'

She slipped the chape she'd made onto the scabbard's point, bright steel hammered to look like a serpent's head, fitting his work as perfectly as a key fits a lock. 'Look at the beautiful things we can make together.' Her iron-blackened fingers slid into the gaps between his wood-browned ones. 'Meant to be, isn't it? My sword. Your sheath.' He felt her other hand sliding across his thigh and gave a little shiver. 'And the other way around . . .'

'Rin—'

'All right, more dagger than sword.' He could hear the laughter in her voice, could feel it tickling his neck. He loved it when she laughed.

'Rin, I can't. Brand's like a brother to me—'

'Don't lie with Brand. Problem solved.'

'I'm Father Yarvi's apprentice.'

'Don't lie with Father Yarvi.' He felt her lips brush his neck and send a sweaty shudder down his back.

'He saved my mother's life. Saved my life. He set us free.'

Her lips were at his ear now, her whisper so loud it made him hunch his shoulders, the weights rattling on their thong around his neck. 'How did he set you free if you can't make your own choices?'

'I owe him, Rin.' He could feel her chest pressing against his back with each breath. Her fingers had curled round to grip his hand tight. She was as strong as he was. Stronger, probably. He had to shut his eyes to think straight. 'When this war's done I'll take the Minister's Test, and swear the Minister's Oath, and I'll be Brother Koll, and have no family, no wife— ah.'

Her hand slid down between his legs. 'Till then what's stopping you?'

'Nothing.' He twisted around, pushing his free hand into her short-chopped hair and dragging her close. They laughed and kissed at once, hungrily, sloppily, stumbling against a bench and knocking a clutch of tools clattering across the floor.

It always ended up this way when he came here. That was why he kept coming.

Slick as a salmon she twisted free of him, darted to the clamp and snatched up her whetstone, peering down at the blade she was working on as if she'd done nothing else all morning.

Koll blinked. 'What are—'

The door clattered open and Brand walked in, Koll marooned in the middle of the floor with a great tent in his trousers.

'Hey, Koll,' said Brand. 'What're you doing here?'

'Came to finish the scabbard,' he croaked, face burning as he turned quickly back to his table and brushed some shavings onto the floor.

'Let's see it.' Brand put an arm around Koll's shoulder. Gods, it was a big arm, heavy with muscle, rope scar coiling up the wrist. Koll remembered seeing Brand take the weight of a ship across his shoulders, a ship that had been on the point of crushing Koll dead, as it happened. Then he wondered what it'd be like getting punched by

that arm if Brand found out everything his sister and
Koll were up to. He swallowed with more than a little
difficulty.

But Brand only pushed the stray hair out of his face
and grinned. 'Beautiful work. You're blessed, Koll. Same
gods as blessed my sister.'

'She's . . . a deeply spiritual girl.' Koll shifted awkwardly
to get his trousers settled while Rin stuck her lips out in
a mad pout behind her brother's back.

Gods, Brand was oblivious. Strong and loyal and good
humoured as a cart-horse, but for obliviousness he set
new standards. Probably you couldn't be married to Thorn
Bathu without learning to let a lot of things drift past.

'How's Thorn?' asked Koll, aiming at a distraction.

Brand paused as if that was a puzzle that took consid-
erable thought. 'Thorn is Thorn. But I knew that when
I married her.' He gave Koll that helpless grin of his.
'Wouldn't have it any other way.'

'Can't be the easiest person to live with.'

'I'll let you know if it happens. She's half her time with
the queen and half the rest training harder than ever, so
I tend to get her asleep or ready to argue.' He scratched
wearily at the back of his head. 'Still, I knew that when
I married her too.'

'Can't be the easiest person not to live with.'

'Huh.' Brand stared off into space like a veteran still
struggling to make sense of the horrors he'd seen. 'She
surely can cook a fight from the most peaceful ingredi-
ents. But nothing worth doing is easy. I love her in spite
of it. I love her because of it. I love her.' And his face

broke out in that grin again. 'Every day's a new adventure, that's for sure.'

There was a harsh knocking at the door and Brand shook himself and went to answer. Rin mimed blowing a kiss and Koll mimed clutching it to his heart and Rin mimed puking all over her work-bench. He loved it when she did that.

'Good to see you, Brand.' Koll looked up, surprised to see his master in Rin's forge.

'Likewise, Father Yarvi.'

You get a special kind of kinship when you take a long journey with a man, and though Brand and Yarvi could hardly have been less alike they hugged each other, and the minister slapped the smith's broad back affectionately with his withered hand.

'How are things in the blade business?' he called to Rin.

'Men always need good blades, Father Yarvi,' she said.

'And the word business?'

'Men always need good words too.' The minister traded his smile for the usual sternness when he looked at Koll. 'I had a feeling you'd be here. It's past midday.'

'Already?' Koll pulled his apron off, got caught in the straps, tore free and tossed it down, slapping the wood dust from his hands.

'Usually the apprentice comes to the master.' The tip of the minister's elf-metal staff rang against the floor as he walked over. 'You are my apprentice, aren't you?'

'Of course, Father Yarvi,' said Koll, shifting guiltily away from Rin.

Yarvi narrowed his eyes as he glanced from one of them to the other, plainly missing nothing. Few men were less oblivious than he. 'Tell me you fed the doves.'

'And cleaned out their cages, and sorted the new herbs, and read twenty more pages of Mother Gundring's history of Gettland, and learned fifty words in the tongue of Kalyiv.' Koll's endless questions had always driven his mother mad, but studying for the Ministry he had so many answers he felt his head was going to burst.

'The food of fear is ignorance, Koll. The death of fear is knowledge. What about the movements of the stars? Did you copy the charts I gave you?'

Koll clutched at his head. 'Gods, I'm sorry, Father Yarvi. I'll do it later.'

'Not today. The great moot begins in an hour and there is a cargo that needs unloading first.'

Koll looked hopefully at Brand. 'I'm not much at shifting boxes—'

'Jars. And they need shifting very carefully. A gift from the Empress Vialine, brought all the way up the Denied and the Divine.'

'A gift from Sumael, you mean?' said Brand.

'A gift from Sumael.' Father Yarvi had a faraway grin at the name. 'A weapon for us to use against the High King . . .' He trailed off as he stepped between Koll and Rin, balanced his staff in the crook of his arm and with his good hand lifted up the scabbard, turning it to the light to peer at the carvings.

'Mother War,' he murmured. 'Mother of Crows. She Whose Feathers Are Swords. She Who Gathers the Dead.

She Who Makes the Open Hand a Fist. Did you carve this?'

'Who else is good enough?' asked Rin. 'Scabbard's just as important as the blade. A good sword's rarely drawn. It's this folk'll see.'

'When you finally swear your Minister's Oath, Koll, it will be a loss to wood-carving.' Yarvi gave a weighty sigh. 'But you cannot change the world with a chisel.'

'You can change it a little,' said Rin, folding her arms as she looked up at the minister. 'And for the better.'

'His mother asked me to make him the best man he could be.'

Koll shook his head frantically behind his master's back, but Rin was not to be shut up. 'Some of us quite like the man he is,' she said.

'And is that all you want, Koll? To carve wood?' Father Yarvi tossed the scabbard rattling down on the bench and put his withered hand on Koll's shoulder. 'Or do you want to stand at the shoulder of kings, and guide the course of history?'

Koll blinked from one of them to the other. Gods, he didn't want to let either of them down, but what could he do? Father Yarvi set him free. And what slave's son wouldn't want to stand at the shoulder of kings and be safe, and respected, and powerful?

'History,' he muttered, looking guiltily at the floor. 'I reckon . . .'

FRIENDS LIKE THESE

R aith was bored out of his mind.

Wars were meant to be a matter of fighting. And a war against the High King surely the biggest fight a man could ever hope for. But now he learned the bigger the war, the more it was all made of talk. Talk, and waiting, and sitting on your arse.

The high folk sat around three long tables set in a horseshoe, status proclaimed by the value of their drinking cups – the Vanstermen on one side, the Gettlanders opposite, and in the middle a dozen chairs for the Throvenmen. Empty chairs, because the Throvenmen hadn't come, and Raith wished he'd followed their example.

Father Yarvi droned on. 'Seven days ago I met with a representative of Grandmother Wexen.'

'I should have been there!' Mother Scaer snapped back.

'I wish you could have been, but there was no time.' Yarvi showed his one good palm as if you could never find a fairer man than he. 'But you did not miss much. Mother Adwyn tried to kill me.'

'I like her already,' Raith whispered to his brother and made him snigger.

Raith would sooner have bedded a scorpion than traded ten words with that one-fisted bastard. Rakki had taken to calling him the Spider, and no doubt he was lean and subtle and poisonous. But unless you were a fly, spiders would let you be. Father Yarvi's webs were spun for men and there was no telling who'd be trapped in them.

His apprentice was little better. A lanky boy with scare-crow hair, a patchy prickling of beard no particular colour and a twitchy, jumpy, blinky way about him. Grinning, always grinning like he was everyone's friend but Raith was nowhere near won over. A look of fury, a look of pain, a look of hatred you can trust. A smile can hide anything.

Raith let his head hang back while the voices burbled on, staring up at the great domed ceiling of the Godshall. Quite a building, but aside from setting them on fire he didn't have much use for buildings. The statues of the Tall Gods frowned down disapprovingly from on high and Raith sneered back. Aside from the odd half-hearted prayer to Mother War he didn't have much use for gods either.

'Grandmother Wexen has proclaimed us sorcerers and traitors, and issued a decree that we are all to be cut from the world.' Father Yarvi tossed a scroll onto the table before him and Raith groaned. He'd even less use for scrolls than gods or buildings. 'She is set on crushing us.'

'No offer of peace?' asked Queen Laithlin.

Father Yarvi glanced sideways at his apprentice, then shook his head. 'None.'

The queen gave a bitter sigh. 'I had hoped she might give us something we could bargain with. There is scant profit in bloodshed.'

'That all depends on whose blood is shed and how.' Gorm frowned darkly towards the empty chairs. 'When will King Fynn lend us his wisdom?'

'Not in a thousand years,' said Yarvi. 'Fynn is dead.'

The echoes of his words died in the high spaces of the Godshall to leave a shocked silence. Even Raith pricked up his ears.

'Mother Kyre gave up the key to Bail's Point in return for peace, but Grandmother Wexen betrayed her. She sent Bright Yilling to Yaletoft to settle her debts, and he killed King Fynn and burned the city to the ground.'

'We can expect no help from Throvenland, then.' Sister Owd, Mother Scaer's fat-faced apprentice, looked like she might burst into tears at the news, but Raith was grinning. Maybe now they'd get something done.

'There was one survivor.' Queen Laithlin snapped her fingers and the doors of the Godshall were swung open. 'King Fynn's granddaughter, Princess Skara.'

There were two black figures in the brightness of the

doorway, their long shadows stretching out across the polished floor as they came on. One was Blue Jenner, looking every bit as shabby and weatherworn as he had on the docks. The other had made more effort.

She wore a dress of fine green cloth that shone in the torchlit dimness, shoulders back and shadows gathered in the hollows about her sharp collarbones. An earring spilled jewels down her long neck and, high on one thin arm, a blood-red gem gleamed on a ring of gold. The dark hair that had floated in a ghostly cloud was oiled and braided and bound into a shining coil.

Gods, she was changed, but Raith knew her right away. 'That's her,' he breathed. 'The girl I saw on the docks.'

Rakki leaned close to whisper. 'I love you, brother, but you might be reaching a bit high.'

'I must give thanks.' She looked pale and brittle as eggshell, but Skara's voice rang out strong and clear as she turned those great green eyes up at the looming statues of the Tall Gods. 'To the gods for delivering me from the hands of Bright Yilling, to my hosts for giving me shelter when I stood alone. To my cousin Queen Laithlin, whose deep-cunning is well known but whose deep compassion I have only lately discovered. And to the Iron King Uthil, whose iron resolve and iron justice is whispered of all around the Shattered Sea.'

King Uthil raised one grey brow a fraction. A proper show of delight from that old bear-trap of a face. 'You are welcome among us, princess.'

Skara gave a deep and graceful bow to the Vanstermen. 'Grom-gil-Gorm, King of Vansterland, Breaker of Swords,

I am honoured to stand in your long shadow. I would tell you how tales of your great strength and high weapon-luck were often told in Yaletoft, but your chain tells that story more eloquently than I ever could.'

'I thought it eloquent indeed.' Gorm fingered the chain of pommels cut from the blades of his dead enemies, looped four times around his trunk of a neck. 'Until I heard you speak, princess. Now I begin to doubt.'

It was all just words. But even Raith, who could flatter no better than a dog, saw how carefully each compliment was fitted to the vanities of its target like a key to a lock. The mood in the Godshall was already brighter. Enough vinegar had been sprayed over this alliance. Skara offered honey, and they were eager to lap it up.

'Great kings,' she said, 'wise queens, storied warriors and deep-cunning ministers are gathered here.' She pressed a thin hand to her stomach and Raith thought he saw it trembling, but she caught it with the other and carried on. 'I am young, and have no right to sit among you, but there is no one else to speak for Throvenland. Not for myself, but on behalf of my people, who are helpless before the High King's warriors, I beg that you allow me to take my grandfather's seat.'

Maybe it was that she stood on neither side. Maybe that she was young and humble and without friends. Maybe it was the music of her voice, but there was some magic when she spoke. No one could have rammed a word in on the end of a spear a moment before, now this room of bristling heroes sat in thoughtful silence.

When King Uthil spoke, it came harsh as a crow's call

after a nightingale's song. 'It would be churlish to refuse a request so gracefully made.'

The two kings had finally found one thing they could agree on. 'We should be begging you for seats, Princess Skara,' said Gorm.

Raith watched the princess glide to the high chair King Fynn would have taken, walking so smoothly you could have balanced a jug of ale on her head. Blue Jenner somewhat spoiled the grace of it by dropping onto the seat beside her as if it was an oarsman's sea-chest.

Gorm frowned towards the old trader. 'It is not fitting that the princess be so lightly attended.'

'I won't disagree.' Blue Jenner flashed a gap-toothed grin. 'Believe me when I say none o' this was my idea.'

'A ruler should have a minister beside them,' said Mother Scaer. 'To help pick out the lesser evil.'

Yarvi frowned across the hall at her. 'And the greater good.'

'Precisely. My apprentice Sister Owd is well versed in the languages and laws of the Shattered Sea, and a deep-cunning healer besides.'

Raith almost laughed. Blinking gormlessly sideways at her mistress, Sister Owd looked about as deep-cunning as a turnip.

'That is good,' said Gorm, 'but the princess must be as well guarded as she is advised.'

Laithlin's voice was icy. 'My cousin has my warriors to protect her.'

'And who will protect her from them? I offer you my own sword-bearer.' Gorm's weighty hand slapped down on Raith's shoulder, as shocking as a stroke of lightning, and struck his laughter dead. 'My own cup-filler. I trust my life to him every time I drink and I drink often. Raith will sleep outside your door, princess, and guard it faithfully as any hound.'

'I'd sooner have a nest of snakes outside her bedchamber,' snarled Thorn Bathu, and Raith was no happier. He could've gazed at Skara all the long day, but being ripped from the place he'd fought for and made her slave was nowhere near so pleasing.

'My king—' he hissed, as angry voices were raised all about the room. For years Raith and his brother had served their king together. That he could be so easily tossed aside was like a knife in him. And who'd watch over Rakki? Raith was the strong one, they both knew that.

Gorm's hand pressed heavier. 'She is Laithlin's cousin,' he murmured. 'Almost a Gettlander. Stick close to her.'

'But I should fight beside you, not play nursemaid to some—'

The great fingers squeezed so crushing hard they made Raith gasp. 'Never make me ask twice.'

'Friends! Please!' called Skara. 'We have too many enemies to argue with each other! I gratefully accept your advice, Sister Owd. And your protection, Raith.'

Raith glanced around the hall, feeling all those cold eyes on him. His king had spoken. He'd no more say than a dog does in his master's hunt.

The legs of his chair shrieked as he stood and numbly unslung Gorm's great sword from his shoulder. The sword he'd been cleaning, polishing, carrying, sleeping with for three years. So long he felt lop-sided without its weight. He wanted to fling it down, but couldn't bring himself to do it. In the end he set it meekly beside his chair, gave his astonished brother a parting pat on the shoulder, and in one moment went from a king's sword-bearer to a princess' lapdog.

His scraping footsteps echoed in the disapproving silence and Raith dropped numbly into a chair beside his new mistress, thoroughly beaten without even getting the chance to fight.

'Shall we return to the business of war?' grated out King Uthil, and the moot lurched on.

Skara didn't so much as glance at her new pet. Why would she? They might as well have come from different worlds. She seemed to Raith as sharp and perfect as a relic made by elf-hands. As calm, and confident, and serene in this high company as a mountain lake under the stars.

A girl – or a woman – with no fear in her.

BAIL'S BLOOD

S kara had hardly been more scared when she faced
Bright Yilling.

She had not slept an instant for the endless
ploughing over of what to say and how to say it, weighing
Mother Kyre's lessons, remembering her grandfather's
example, muttering prayers into the darkness to She Who
Spoke the First Word.

She had not eaten a scrap of breakfast for the endless
nervous churning of her guts. She felt as if her arse was
about to drop right out, kept wondering what would
happen if she let blast a great fart in the midst of this
exalted company.

She clung white-knuckle-tight to the arms of her chair
as though it was adrift on a stormy sea. Angry faces
swam from the gloom of the Godshall and she struggled

to study them as Mother Kyre had taught her. To read them, to riddle out the doubts and hopes and secrets behind them, to find what could be used.

She closed her eyes, repeating her grandfather's words over and over in her thoughts. *You were always a brave one, Skara. Always a brave one. Always a brave one.*

The young Vansterman, Raith, was hardly lending her confidence. He was striking, all right. Striking as an axe to the throat, his face pale and hard as chiselled silver, a deep nick cut from one battered ear, his forehead angrily furrowed, his short-clipped hair and his scarred brows and even his eyelashes all white, as if all sentiment had been wrung out of him and left only cold scorn.

They might as well have come from different worlds. He looked tough and savage as a fighting dog, calm and disdainful in this deadly company as a wolf at the head of his own pack. He would have seemed in his right place smirking among Bright Yilling's Companions, and Skara swallowed sour spit, and tried to pretend he was not there.

'Death waits for us all.' King Uthil's grinding voice echoed at her as if he stood at the top of a well and she was drowning at the bottom. 'The wise warrior favours the sword. He strikes for the heart, confounds and surprises his enemy. Steel is the answer, always. We must attack.'

A predictable rattling of approval rose from Uthil's side of the hall, a predictable grunting of disgust from Gorm's.

'The wise warrior does not rush into Death's arms. He

favours the shield.' Gorm laid a loving hand on the great black shield Raith's twin carried. 'He draws his enemy onto his own ground, and on his own terms crushes him.'

King Uthil snorted. 'What has favouring the shield won you? In this very hall I challenged you and from this very hall you skulked like a beaten dog.'

Sister Owd worked her way forward. Her face reminded Skara of the peaches that used to grow outside the walls of Bail's Point: soft, round, blotched with pink and fuzzed with downy hair. 'My kings, this is not helpful—'

But Grom-gil-Gorm boomed over her like thunder over birdsong. 'The last time Gettlanders and Vanstermen faced each other your famous sword went missing from the square, Iron King. You sent a woman to fight in your place and I defeated her, but chose to let her live—'

'We can try it again whenever you please, you giant turd,' snarled Thorn Bathu.

Skara saw Raith's hand grip the arm of his chair. A big, pale hand, scarred across the thick knuckles. A hand whose natural shape was a fist. Skara caught his wrist and made sure she stood first.

'We must find some middle ground!' she called. More of a desperate shriek, in truth. She swallowed as every eye turned towards her, hostile as a rank of levelled spears. 'Surely the wisest warrior uses shield and sword together, each at the proper time.'

It seemed hard to argue with, but the moot found a way. 'Those who bring ships should speak on the strategy,' said King Uthil, blunt as a birch-club.

'You bring only one crew to our alliance,' said King Gorm, fondling his chain.

'It's a good one,' observed Jenner. 'But I can't argue it's more than one.'

Sister Owd made another effort. 'The proper rules of a moot, laid down by Ashenleer in the depths of history, give equal voice to each party to an alliance, regardless of . . . regardless . . .' She caught sight of her erstwhile mistress, Mother Scaer, giving her the frostiest glare imaginable, and her voice died a slow death in the great spaces of the Godshall.

Skara had to struggle to keep her voice level. 'I would have brought more ships if my grandfather was alive.'

'But he is dead,' answered Uthil, without bothering to soften it.

Gorm frowned across at his rival. 'And had betrayed us to Grandmother Wexen.'

'What choice did you leave him?' barked Skara, her fury taking everyone by surprise, herself most of all. 'His allies should have come to his aid but they sat bickering over who sat where while he died alone!'

If words were weapons, those ones struck home. She seized the silence they gave her, leaned forward and, tiny though they looked, planted her fists on the table the way her grandfather used to.

'Bright Yilling is busy spreading fire across Throvenland! He puts down what resistance remains. He paves the road for the High King's great army. He thinks himself invincible!' She let Yilling's disdain chafe at all the tender pride gathered in the room, then added softly, 'But he has left his ships behind him.'

Uthil's grey eyes narrowed. 'A warrior's ship is his surest weapon, his means of supply, his route of escape.'

'His home and his heart.' Gorm combed his fingers carefully through his beard. 'Where are these boats of Bright Yilling's?'

Skara licked her lips. 'In the harbour at Bail's Point.'

'Ha!' The elf-bangles rattled on Mother Scaer's tattooed wrist as she swatted the whole business away. 'Safe behind the great chains.'

'The place is elf-built,' said Father Yarvi. 'Impregnable.'

'No!' Skara's voice echoed back from the dome above like a clap. 'I was born there and I know its weaknesses.'

Uthil twitched with annoyance but Laithlin set her hand ever so gently on the back of his clenched fist. 'Let her speak,' she murmured, leaning close. As the king looked at his wife his frown softened for an instant, and Skara wondered if he truly was a man of iron, or only one of flesh like others, trapped in the iron cage of his own fame.

'Speak, princess,' he said, turning his hand over to clasp Laithlin's as he sat back.

Skara craned forward, pushing her words to every corner of the chamber, striving to fill the hall with her hopes and her desires and make every listener share them, the way Mother Kyre had taught her. 'The elf-walls cannot be breached, but parts of them were destroyed by the Breaking of God and the gaps closed by the work of men. Mother Sea chews endlessly at their foundations.

To shore them up my grandfather built two great buttresses by the cliffs on the southwest corner. So great they nearly touch. A nimble man could climb up between, and bring others after.'

'A nimble madman,' murmured Gorm.

'Even if a few could get in,' said Uthil, 'Bright Yilling is a tested war-leader. He would not be fool enough to leave the great gates unguarded—'

'There is another gate, hidden, only wide enough for one man at a time, but it could let the rest of your warriors into the fortress.' Skara's voice cracked with her desperate need to persuade them, but Blue Jenner was at her side, and a finer diplomat than he appeared.

'I may not know much,' he said, 'but I know the Shattered Sea, and Bail's Point is the lock on it and the key to it. The fortress controls the Straits of Skekenhouse. That's why Grandmother Wexen was so keen to take it. Long as Bright Yilling holds it he can strike anywhere, but if we can take it from him . . .' And he turned to Skara, and gave her a wink.

'We win a victory for the songs,' she called, 'and bring the High King's chair itself under threat.'

There was a low muttering as men turned over the chances. Skara had caught their interest, but the two kings were restless bulls, hard indeed to yoke to one purpose.

'What if the ships have been moved?' grated out Uthil. 'What if you misremember the weaknesses of Bail's Point? What if Yilling has learned of them and guards them already?'

'Then Death waits for us all, King Uthil.' Skara would win no battles with meekness, not against such opponents as these. 'I heard you say we must strike for the heart. Yilling's heart is his pride. His ships.'

'This is a gamble,' murmured Gorm. 'There is much that could go wrong—'

'To win against a stronger opponent you must *risk*.' Skara thumped the table with her fist. 'I heard you say we must meet the enemy on our own ground. What better ground could there be than the strongest fortress in the Shattered Sea?'

'It is not my ground,' grumbled Gorm.

'But it is mine!' Skara's voice cracked again but she forced herself on. 'You forget! The blood of Bail himself flows in my veins!'

Skara felt them teeter. Their hatred for each other, and their fear of the High King, and their need to look fearless, and their lust for glory, all balanced on a sword's edge. She almost had them but at any moment, like doves flying to familiar cages, they might lurch back into their well-ploughed feud and the chance would be lost.

Where reason fails, Mother Kyre once told her, *madness may succeed.*

'Perhaps you need to see it!' Skara reached down and snatched the dagger from Raith's belt.

He made a desperate grab at her but too late. She pressed the bright point into the ball of her thumb and slit her palm open to the root of her little finger.

She had expected a few delicate crimson drops, but Raith clearly kept his knife well-sharpened. Blood spattered the table, flicked across Blue Jenner's chest and into Sister Owd's round face. There was a collective gasp, Skara the most shocked of anyone, but there could be no retreat now, only a mad charge forward.

'Well?' She held up her fist in the sight of the Tall Gods, blood streaking her arm and pattering from her elbow. 'Will you proud warriors draw your swords and shed your blood with mine? Will you give yourselves to Mother War and trust to your weaponluck? Or will you skulk here in the shadows, pricking each other with words?'

Grom-gil-Gorm's chair toppled over as he rose to his full great height. He gave a grimace, and his jaw muscles bulged, and Skara shrank back, waiting for his fury to crush her. Then she realized he was chewing his tongue. He spat red across the table.

'The men of Vansterland will sail in five days,' growled the Breaker of Swords, blood running into his beard.

King Uthil stood, the drawn sword he always carried sliding through the crook of his arm until its point rested before him. He took it under the crosspiece, knuckles whitening as he squeezed. A streak of blood gathered in the fuller, and worked its way down to the point, and spread out in a dark slick around the steel.

'The men of Gettland sail in four,' he said.

Warriors on both sides of the room thumped at the tables, and rattled their weapons, and sent up a cheer at seeing blood finally spilled, even if it was far from enough to win a battle, and most of it belonging to a girl of seventeen.

Skara sat back, suddenly dizzy, and felt the knife plucked from her hand. Sister Owd slit the stitching in her sleeve and ripped away a strip of cloth, then took Skara's wrist and deftly began to bandage her palm.

'This will serve until I can stitch it.' She looked up from under her brows. 'Please never do that again, princess.'

'Don't worry— ah!' Gods, it was starting to hurt. 'I think I've learned that lesson.'

'It is a little soon to celebrate our victory!' called out Father Yarvi, stilling the noise. 'We have first to decide who will do the climbing.'

'When it comes to feats of strength and skill my standard-bearer Soryorn is unmatched.' Gorm put his hand through the garnet-studded collar of the tall Shend thrall beside him. 'He ran the oars and back three times on our voyage from Vansterland, and in stormy seas too.'

'You will find no one as swift and subtle as my apprentice Koll,' said Father Yarvi. 'As any man who has seen him swarm up the cliffs for eggs will gladly testify.' The Gettlanders all nodded along. All except the apprentice himself, who looked almost as queasy as Skara felt at the notion.

'A friendly contest, perhaps?' offered Queen Laithlin. 'To see who is the better?'

Skara saw the cunning in that. A fine distraction, to keep these restless rams from butting each other before they met their enemy.

Sister Owd set Skara's bandaged hand gently down on the table. 'As an equal partner in the alliance,' she called, 'by ancient law and long precedent, Throvenland should also be represented in such a contest.' This time she refused to meet Mother Scaer's chilling eye, and sat back well pleased with her contribution.

Skara was less delighted. She had no strong or subtle men, only Blue Jenner.

He raised his bushy brows as she glanced over at him, and muttered, 'I find stairs a challenge.'

'I'll climb for you,' said Raith. Skara had not seen him smile until then, and it seemed to light a flame in that cold face, his eyes glinting bold and mischievous and making him seem more striking than ever. 'Got to be better'n talking, hasn't it?'

CHANCES

'We haven't had a chance to talk,' said Blue Jenner.

'I'm not much of a talker,' grunted Raith.

'Fighter, eh?'

Raith didn't answer. If he had to he'd answer with his fists.

'It's up to me to make sure the princess stays safe.'

Raith nodded towards the door. 'That's why I'm out here.'

'Aye.' Jenner narrowed his eyes. 'But is she safe from you?'

'What if she's not?' Raith stepped up to the old raider, teeth bared, right in his face so he was just about butting him. Had to show he was the bloodiest bastard going. Let them see weakness it'll be the end of you. 'How would you stop me, old man?'

Blue Jenner didn't back off, just raised his lined hands. 'I'd say "whoa, there, lad, old fool like me fight a young hero like you? I don't think so!" And I'd back right down soft as you like.'

'Damn right,' growled Raith.

'Then I'd nip to my crew and get six big fellows. Middle oars, you know, used to pulling but light on their feet. And when it got dark two of 'em would wrap you up real nice and warm in your blanket.' And he gave the blanket over Raith's shoulder a little brush with the back of his hand. 'Then the other four would bring out some stout timbers and beat that pretty package till it had nothing hard in it. Then I'd deliver the slop left over back to Grom-gil-Gorm, probably still in the blanket 'cause we wouldn't want to get mess all over Princess Skara's floor, and tell the Breaker of Swords that, sadly, the boy he lent us was a shade too prickly and it didn't work out.' Jenner smiled, his weathered face creasing up like old boots. 'But I'd rather not add to my regrets. The gods know I got a queue of the bastards. I'd sooner just give you the chance to prove you're trustworthy.'

It was a good answer, Raith had to admit. Clever, but with iron in it. Made him look a clumsy thug, and he didn't like to look that way. Subtle thug was better. He shifted back, gave Jenner a little more room and a lot more respect. 'And what if I'm not trustworthy?'

'Give men the chance to be better, I find most of 'em want to take it.'

Raith hadn't found that at all. 'You sure, old man?'

'Guess we can find out together, boy. You want another blanket? Could get cold out here.'

'I've dealt with colder.' Raith would've loved another blanket but he had to seem like nothing could hurt him. So he drew the one he had tight around his shoulders and sat down, listened to the old man's footsteps scrape away. He missed Gorm's sword. He missed his brother. But the cold draught and the cold stones and the cold silence were much the same.

He wondered if the dreams would be too.

HOW TO WIN

'When I ring the bell, you climb.'

'Yes, my queen,' croaked Koll. There were few people in the world he was as much in awe of as Queen Laithlin and most of them were here, now, watching. It felt like half the people of the Shattered Sea were rammed into the yard of the citadel in the shade of the great cedar, or crammed at the windows, or peering down from the roofs and the battlements.

King Uthil stood on the steps of the Godshall, Father Yarvi leaning on his staff at his right hand, Rulf beside him, scratching at the short grey hair above his ears, giving Koll what was no doubt meant to be a reassuring grin. Opposite, on a platform carefully built to just the same height, stood Grom-gil-Gorm, zigzag lines of gold forged into his mail glittering in the morning sun, his white-haired shield-bearer kneeling by him, Mother Scaer with her blue eyes fiercely narrowed.

Rin had found a way in, just as she always did, on a roof high up on Koll's left. She waved like a mad woman as he looked up, flailing her open palm around for luck. Gods, Koll wished he was over there with her. Or better yet in her forge. Or better yet in her bed. He pushed the idea away. Brand was standing right beside her, after all, and might not stay oblivious forever.

Queen Laithlin raised one long white arm to point towards the top of the cedar, gold glinting on the highest branch. 'The winner is the one who brings Princess Skara back her armring.'

Koll shivered from his toes to the roots of his hair, trying to shake free of the tingling nerves. He glanced up at the mast that stood rooted in the yard beside Thorn, carved from foot to head by his own hands on the long journey to the First of Cities and back.

Gods, he was proud of that mast. The carving he'd done on it, and his part in the story it told. There'd been brave deeds in plenty on that voyage, and he had to be brave now. He was sure he could win. What he wasn't sure of was whether he wanted to. For a man reckoned clever, he got wedged in a lot of stupid corners.

He gave one of those sighs that made his lips flap. 'The gods have a silly sense of humour.'

'They surely do.' Gorm's ex-cup-filler, Raith, frowned about at the crowd. 'When I got on the boat in Vulsgard I never thought I'd end up climbing trees.' He leaned close, as if he'd a secret to share, and Koll couldn't help leaning in with him. 'Nor playing nursemaid to some skinny girl.'

Princess Skara stood between a wide-eyed Sister Owd and an unkempt Blue Jenner, seeming as perfect and brittle as the pottery statues Koll had stared at in the First of Cities, long ago, trying to work out how they were made.

'Life is too easy for very pretty people,' he said. 'They get all manner of advantages.'

'I assure you it's as hard for us beauties as anyone,' said Raith.

Koll looked round at him. 'You're a good deal less of a bastard than I took you for.'

'Oh, you don't know me that well yet. Taking this damned seriously, ain't he?'

Grom-gil-Gorm's Shend standard-bearer had stripped to the waist, a pattern of scars burned into his broad back to look like a spreading tree. He was putting on quite the performance, lean muscles flexing as he stretched, twisted, touched his toes.

Raith just stood there, scratching at a nick out of his ear. 'Thought we were climbing, not dancing.'

'So did I.' Koll grinned. 'Might be we were misinformed.'

'My name's Raith.' And Raith held out a friendly hand.

The minister's boy smiled back. 'Koll.' And he took it. Just like Raith had known he would, 'cause weak men are always eager for the friendship of strong ones. His smile faded quick enough when he found he couldn't tug his hand free again. 'What're you—'

Queen Laithlin rang the bell.

Raith jerked the lad close and butted him in the face.

He could climb but Raith had no doubts these other two were better at it. If he wanted to win, and he always did, best make the contest about something else. At butting folk in the face he was a master, as Koll now discovered.

Raith punched him in the ribs three times, doubled him up gurgling with blood pattering from his smashed mouth, then caught his shirt and flung him upside down across a table where some of the Gettlanders were sitting.

He heard the chaos behind him, the crowd bellowing curses, but by that time the blood was roaring in his ears and his mind was on the tree. Soryorn was already dragging his great long body into the branches and if he got a good start Raith knew he'd never catch him.

He took a pounding run, sprang onto the lowest branch and swung himself up, jumped to a higher, twigs thrashing from his weight. At the next spring, full stretch, he caught Soryorn by the ankle and dragged him down, a broken stick scratching him all the way up his scar-marked back.

Soryorn kicked out and caught Raith in the mouth, but he'd never been put off by the taste of his own blood. He growled as he hauled himself on, no thought for the scraping branches, no thought for the aching through his left hand, caught Soryorn's ankle again, then his belt, and finally his garnet studded thrall-collar.

'What're you doing?' snarled the standard-bearer, trying to elbow him away.

'Winning,' hissed Raith, hauling himself up level.

'Gorm wants me to win!'

'I serve Skara, remember?'

Raith punched Soryorn right between the legs and his eyes bulged. Raith punched him in the mouth and snapped his head back. Raith bit his clutching hand hard and with a wheezing cry Soryorn lost his grip and went tumbling down through the branches, his head bouncing off one, another folding him in half, a third spinning him over and over till he crashed to the ground.

Which was a shame, but someone had to win, and someone had to fall.

Raith shinned up further to where the branches grew sparse. He could see over the walls of the citadel from here. Mother Sea glittering, the forest of masts on the dozens of ships crowded into Thorlby's harbour, the salt breeze kissing his sweating forehead.

He twitched the armring from the topmost branch. He'd have put it on his wrist but it was sized for Skara's twig of an arm and there was no way it'd fit. So he stuffed it into the pouch at his belt and started slithering down.

The wind blew up and made the whole tree sway, branches creaking, needles brushing Raith all over as he clung on tight. He caught a flash of white out of the corner of his eye, but all he could see when he peered down was Soryorn, trying and failing to drag himself up into the lowest branches. No sign of the minister's boy. More'n likely crept off to cry over his broken face. Might be a fine climber but he'd no guts at all, and to climb into Bail's Point alone, a man would need guts.

Raith swung free and dropped to the ground.

'You little bastard!' snarled Soryorn, clinging to a low branch. He must have hurt his leg when he fell, he was holding it up gingerly, toes trailing.

Raith laughed as he passed. Then he sprang in and drove a shoulder into Soryorn's ribs, ramming him so hard into the tree his breath was all driven out in a flopping wheeze.

'You big bastard,' he tossed out as he left Soryorn groaning in the dirt. The standard-bearer had always been a good friend to Raith.

So he really should've known better than to leave his side open like that.

'Princess Skara.'

She gave Raith what she hoped was a disapproving look. 'I would hardly call that a fair contest.'

He shrugged, looking her straight in the eye. 'You think Bright Yilling loses much sleep over what's fair?'

Skara felt herself blush. He had the manners of a stump, treated her with not the slightest deference. Mother Kyre would have been outraged. Maybe that was why Skara found it so hard to be. She was not used to bluntness and there was something refreshing in it. Something appealing in it, even. 'So I should send a dog to catch a dog?' she asked.

Raith gave a harsh little chuckle at that. 'Send a killer to kill a killer, anyway.' He reached for his pouch, and his smile vanished.

That was when Koll came strolling around the side of

the cedar, stopping a moment to help Soryorn up. His lip was split and his nose was swollen and bloody, but he was smiling.

'Lost something, friend?' he asked as Raith patted at his clothes. With a flourish of his spindly fingers he produced, apparently from nowhere, the armring Bail the Builder once wore into battle. He bowed in an entirely proper manner. 'I think this is yours, princess.'

Raith gaped. 'You thieving—'

Koll showed his bloody teeth as he smiled wider. 'You think Bright Yilling loses much sleep over thieving?'

Raith made a grab for the armring but Koll was too quick, flipped it glittering into the air. 'You lost the game.' He snatched the armring right out of Raith's clutching fingers, tossed it nimbly from left hand to right and left Raith grabbing at nothing. 'Don't lose your sense of humour too!'

Skara saw Raith clenching his fists as Koll flicked the armring up one more time.

'Enough!' She stepped between the two of them before any more harm could be done and plucked the armring from the air. 'Gettland is the winner!' she called, as she slipped it back over her wrist and up her arm.

The Gettlanders burst into cheering. The Vanstermen were a good deal quieter as they watched Soryorn hop away, leaning hard on Mother Scaer's shoulder. As for Skara's own little entourage, Raith looked as if he had swallowed an axe and Blue Jenner was in tears, but only because he was laughing so hard.

Thorn Bathu cupped her hands to shout over the noise.

'I guess all that time spent up the mast wasn't wasted after all!'

'A man can learn more up a mast than in any minister's chamber!' called Koll, basking in the applause and blowing kisses to his friends.

Skara leaned close to him. 'You realize you've won the chance to climb alone into an impregnable fortress full of enemies?'

His smile wilted as she took his wrist and raised his limp hand in triumph.

FIRST MAN IN

The walls of Bail's Point were frozen in another flash of lightning, the battlements black teeth against a brilliant sky. Gods, they looked a long way up.

'Is it too late to say I don't like this plan?' shrieked Koll over the howling of the wind, the hissing of the rain, the hammering of Mother Sea against their little boat.

'You can say it whenever you like,' Rulf bellowed back at him, his bald pate running with wet. 'Long as you climb up there afterward!'

The wind swept up and lashed spray into the faces of the struggling crew. Thunder crackled loud enough to make the world tremble, but Koll could hardly have been trembling more as they jerked and wobbled closer to the rocks.

'These skies don't strike me as a fine omen!' he called.

'Nor these seas neither!' shouted Dosduvoi, wrestling with his oar as if it was a horse that needed breaking. 'Bad luck all round!'

'We all have luck, good and bad!' Thorn weighed the grapple in her hand. 'It's how you meet it that matters.'

'She's right,' said Fror, his misshapen eye white in his tar-blacked face. 'He Who Speaks the Thunder is on our side. His rain will keep their heads indoors. His grumbling will muffle the sounds of our coming.'

'Provided his lightning doesn't fry you to a cinder.' Thorn slapped Koll on the back and nearly knocked him out of the boat.

The base of the wall was made from ancient elf-stone but buckled and broken, rusted bars showing in the cracks, coated in limpet, weed and barnacle. Rulf leaned low, teeth bared as he dragged hard on the steering oar, hauling them side on.

'Easy! Easy!' Another wave caught them, brought Koll's stomach into his mouth and carried them hard against stone, wood grating and squealing. He clung to the rail, sure the boat would break her back and Mother Sea come surging in, ever hungry for warm bodies to drag into her cold embrace, but the seasoned timbers held and he muttered thanks to the tree that had given them.

Thorn tossed the grapple and it caught first time among those ancient rods. She braced her legs on the strakes beside Koll, teeth gritted as she hauled the boat close.

Koll saw the two buttresses Princess Skara had spoken of. Man-built from rough-hewn blocks, mortar crumbled from years of Mother Sea's chewing. Between them was a shadowy cleft, stone shining slick and wet.

'Just imagine it's another mast!' roared Rulf.

'Masts often have angry seas at the bottom,' said Thorn, tar-blacked sinews flexing in her shoulders as she wrestled with the rope.

'But rarely angry enemies at the top,' muttered Koll, staring up towards the battlements.

'You sure you don't want tar?' asked Fror, offering out the jar. 'They see you climbing up—'

'I'm no warrior. They catch me I've a better chance talking than fighting.'

'You ready?' snapped Rulf.

'No!'

'Best go unready, then, the waves'll smash this boat to kindling soon enough!'

Koll clambered up onto the rail, one hand gripping the prow, the other jerking some slack into the rope he had tied across his chest and coiled up between the sea-chests. Wet it was some weight, and it'd only get heavier the higher he climbed. The boat yawed, grinding against the foot of the buttress. Angry water clapped between rock and wood and fountained up, would've soaked Koll through if rain and sea hadn't soaked him through already.

'Hold her steady!' shouted Rulf.

'I would!' called Dosduvoi, 'but Mother Sea objects!'

The wise wait for their moment, as Father Yarvi was always telling him, *but never let it pass*. Another wave lifted the boat and Koll muttered one more prayer to

Father Peace that he might live to see Rin again, then sprang.

He'd been sure he'd plunge scrabbling and wailing straight through the Last Door, but the chimney between the two buttresses was deeper than a man was tall and just the right width. He stuck there so easily it was almost a disappointment.

'Ha!' he shouted over his shoulder, delighted at his unexpected survival.

'Don't laugh!' snarled Thorn, still struggling with the grapple. 'Climb!'

The crumbling mortar offered foot and hand holds in plenty and to begin with he made quick progress, humming away to himself as he went, imagining the song the skalds would sing of Koll the Clever, who swarmed up the impenetrable walls of Bail's Point as swiftly as a gull in flight. The applause he'd won in the yard of Thorlby's citadel had only given him a taste for more. To be loved, and admired, and celebrated seemed to him no bad thing. No bad thing at all.

The gods love to laugh at a happy man, however. Like a good mast the buttresses tapered towards their tops. The chimney between them grew shallower, wind and rain lashing into it and giving Koll such an icy buffeting he couldn't hear himself hum any longer. Worse still it grew wider, so he was reaching further for handholds until there was no choice but to give up one buttress and climb in the angle between the other and the wall itself, the stone ice-cold and moss-slick so he had to keep stopping to scrape the wet hair from his face, wipe his battered hands and blow life back into his numb fingers.

The last few strides of sheer man-built stone took longer than all the rest combined. There was a deadly length of rain-heavy rope dragging at his shoulder now, weightier than a warrior's armour, whipping and snapping about the chimney as the wind took it. It was as hard a test as he'd faced in his life, muscles twitching, trembling, aching past the point of endurance. Even his teeth were hurting, but to turn back would've been more dangerous than to go on.

Koll picked his holds as carefully as a ship-builder his keel, knowing one mistake would see him smashed to fish-food on the rocks below, squinting in the moonlight and the storm-flashes, scraping mossy dirt from between the stones, crumbly here as old cheese. He tried not to think about the yawning drop below, or the angry men who might be waiting above, or the—

A stone burst apart in his numb fingers and he lost his grip, whimpering as he swung away, every stretched-out sinew in his arm on fire, clawing and scrabbling at old ivy until finally he found a firm purchase.

He pressed himself to the wall, watched the gravel tumble away, bouncing down around his rope, down to the jagged elf-boulders and the boat tossed on the angry brine.

He felt his mother's weights pressing into his breast-bone, thought of her frowning up at him on the mast, finger wagging. *Get down from there before you break your head.*

'Can't stay wrapped in a blanket all my life, can I?' he whispered over the pounding of his heart.

It was with legendary relief he peered over the battlements and saw the rain-lashed walkway, wider than a road, deserted. He groaned as he dragged himself over, hauling the rope after him, rolled on to his back and lay, panting, trying to work the blood back into throbbing fingers.

'That was an adventure,' he whispered, slithering up onto hands and knees and staring out over Bail's Point. 'Gods . . .'

From up here it wasn't hard to believe that it was the strongest fortress in the world, the very key to the Shattered Sea.

There were seven vast towers with vast walls between, six elf-built, the perfect stone gleaming wet, one squat and ugly, built by men to plug a breach left by the Breaking of God. Five towers rose from Father Earth on Koll's left, but on his right two were thrust out beyond the cliffs into Mother Sea, chains strung between them feathering the waves, enclosing the harbour.

'Gods,' he whispered again.

It was crammed with ships, just as Princess Skara had said it would be. Fifty at least, some small, some very great. Bright Yilling's fleet, safe as babes within the mighty elf-stone arms of the fortress, bare masts scarcely shifting despite Mother Sea's fury beyond.

A long ramp led from the wharves, up the cliffside to the great yard. Buildings of a dozen different ages and designs were piled up about it, their roofs a mismatched maze of mossy thatch, cracked tile, rain-slick slate, broken gutters spurting water to spatter on the flagstones below. A city, almost, clinging to the inside of the great elf-walls, firelight spilling from around the edges of a hundred windows shuttered against the storm.

Koll squirmed free of his rope, cursing his clumsy cold fingers as he looped it about the battlements, dragged hard at the wet knots to make sure they were fast, and finally allowed himself a weary smile. 'That'll do it.'

But the gods love to laugh at a happy man, and his smile vanished the moment he turned.

A warrior was trudging down the walkway towards him, spear in one hand, flickering lantern in the other, rain-heavy cloak flapping about his hunched shoulders.

Koll's every instinct was to run, but he forced himself to turn his back on the guard, wedged one boot carelessly on the battlements, stared out to sea as though this was the place he felt most at home in all the world, and offered a silent prayer to She Who Spins Lies. One way or another, she got a lot of prayers from Koll.

When he heard boots scraping up he turned with a grin. 'Hey, hey! Nice evening to be on the walls.'

'Hardly.' The man squinted at him as he raised his lantern. 'Do I know you?'

He sounded like a Yutmarker, so Koll took a guess and trusted to his luck. 'No, no, I'm one of the Inglings.'

Serve a man one good lie, he might offer you the truth himself. 'One of Lufta's boys?'

'That's right. Lufta sent me to check the walls.'

'He did?'

If you can't fashion a good lie, the truth will have to serve. 'Aye, there's these two buttresses, see, and Lufta's got this worry someone might climb up between them.'

'On a night like this?'

Koll gave a little chuckle. 'I know, I know, it's mad as a hatful of frogs, but you know how Lufta gets . . .'

'What's that?' asked the man, frowning towards the rope.

'What's what what?' asked Koll, stepping in front of it, run out of lies and now of truths as well. 'What?'

'That, you—' His eyes bulged as a black hand clamped over his mouth and a black blade took him through the neck. Thorn's face appeared beside his, hardly more than a shadow in the rain, only her eyes standing out white from the tar-smeared skin.

She lowered the warrior's limp body gently onto the parapet.

'What do we do with the corpse?' muttered Koll, catching his lantern before it dropped. 'We can't just—'

Thorn took him by the boots and flipped him into space. Koll peered over, open-mouthed, watching the body plummet down, hit the walls near the base and flop off broken into the surging waves.

'That's what we do,' she said as Fror slipped over the wall behind her, dragged the axe from his back and tore away the rag he'd used to muffle the tar-smeared blade. 'Let's go.'

Koll swallowed as he followed them. He loved Thorn, but it scared him how easily she could kill a man.

The steps down to the yard were just where Skara had

told them, puddled with rainwater in their worn centres. Koll was just letting himself dream again of the harvest of glory he'd reap if this mad plan worked when he heard a voice echo from below, and pressed himself into the shadows.

'Let's go inside, Lufta. It's windy as hell out here!'

A deeper voice answered. 'Dunverk said guard the little gate. Now stop your bloody whining.'

Koll peered over the edge of the steps. A canvas awning flapped in the wind below them, firelight spilling from underneath.

'This little gate isn't so secret as we hoped,' Thorn whispered in his ear.

'Like maggots from apples,' he whispered back, 'secrets do have a habit of wriggling free.'

'Fight?' muttered Thorn. Always her first thought.

Koll smoothed the path for Father Peace, as a good minister should. 'We might rouse everyone in the fortress.'

'I'm not climbing back down that chimney,' said Fror, 'I can promise you that.'

'Lend me your cloak,' whispered Koll. 'I've an idea.'

'Are you sure now is the best time for ideas?' Thorn hissed back.

Koll shrugged as he drew the hood up and tried to shake loose muscles still trembling from the climb. 'They come when they come.'

He left them on the steps and trotted carelessly down, past a half-ruined stable, water dripping from its rotten thatch.

He saw the men, now, seven warriors squatting around their fire, flames torn flickering by the wind that slipped in under their flapping awning. He noted how the firelight fell over the heavy door in the corner behind them, a thick bar lowered across it, the name of She Who Guards the Locks scored deep into the wood. He blew out a misty breath, gathered his courage, and gave a jaunty wave as he walked up.

'Ach, but damn this weather!' Koll ducked under the dripping canvas, thrust his hood back and scrubbed his hands through his wet hair. 'I couldn't be wetter if I'd gone swimming!'

The men all frowned at him, and he grinned back. 'Still, I suppose it's no worse than summer in Inglefold, eh?' He slapped one on the shoulder as he worked his way towards the door and a couple of the others chuckled.

'Do I know you?' asked the big man near the fire. By his silver armrings and surly manner, Koll reckoned him the leader.

'No, no, I'm one of the Yutmarkers. Dunverk sent me. I've a message for you, Lufta.'

The big man spat, and Koll was pleased to find he'd reckoned right. 'Give it, then, before I go deaf from age. It runs in my family.'

Now for the gamble. 'Dunverk's heard tell of an attack. Vanstermen and Gettlanders together, trying to take the fortress and burn our ships.'

'Attack this place?' One of the men snorted. 'They must be fools.'

Koll nodded wearily. 'That was my very thought when I heard the plan and I haven't changed my mind.'

'Did it come from this spy?' asked Lufta.

Koll blinked. That was unexpected. 'Aye, this spy. What's their name now . . . ?'

'Only Bright Yilling knows that. Why don't you ask him for a name?'

'I've so great a respect for the man I couldn't bring myself to bother him. They're coming for the great gate.'

'Fools? They're madmen!' Lufta licked his teeth in some annoyance. 'You four, with me, we'll go over to the gate and see. You two, stay here.'

'I'll keep watch, don't worry!' called Koll as the men trudged off, one holding his shield up over his head against the rain. 'There'll be no Gettlanders getting past me!'

The two left behind were a sorry pair. One young but going bald in clumps, the other with a red patch like spilled wine across his face. He had a fine dagger, silver crosspiece all aglitter, shown off in his belt like a thing to be most proud of though he'd no doubt stolen it from some murdered Throvenman.

Soon as Lufta was out of earshot, that one set to complaining. 'Most of Yilling's boys are dragging in plunder all over Throvenland and here we are stuck with this.'

'Without doubt it's a great injustice. Still.' Koll pulled Fror's cloak off and made great show of shaking the rain from it. 'Reckon there's no safer place about the Shattered Sea for a man to sit.'

'Careful with that!' grunted Red Face, so busy slapping the cloak away as water flicked in his eyes Koll had no difficulty easing the dagger from his belt with his other hand. It's amazing what a man won't notice while he's distracted.

'So sorry, my king!' said Koll, backing away. He nudged Bald Patches in the ribs. 'Got some airs on him, your companion, don't he?' And under his flapping cloak, he slipped the dagger into this man's belt. 'Let me show you a wonderful thing!' He held his hand up before either of them could get a word in, flipping a copper coin back and forth over his knuckles, fingers wriggling, both men fixed on it.

'Copper,' murmured Koll, 'copper, copper, and . . . silver!'

He flipped his hand over, palming the copper in a twinkling and holding a silver coin up between finger and thumb, Queen Laithlin's face stamped on it glinting in the firelight

Bald Patches frowned, sitting forward. 'How d'you do that?'

'Ha! I'll show you the trick to it. Lend me your dagger a moment.'

'What dagger?'

'Your dagger.' Koll pointed at his belt. 'That one.'

Red Face sprang up. 'What're you doing with my damn knife?'

'What?' Bald Patches gaped at his belt. 'How—'

'The One God frowns upon stealing.' Koll held up his hands in a display of piety. 'That's a fact well known.'

Thorn's black hand clamped down on Red Face's mouth and her black knife stabbed through his neck. At almost the same moment Bald Patches' head jerked as Fror hacked his axe into the back of it, and his eyes went crossed, and he muttered something, drooling, then toppled sideways.

'Let's move,' hissed Thorn, lowering her man to the ground, ''fore those others join me in realizing what a double-tongued little weasel you are.'

'By all means, my Chosen Shield,' said Koll, and he slid the rune-marked bar from its brackets, and heaved the gate open.

THE KILLER

The faintest dot of light glimmered in the storm and like a blood-drunk hound let off the leash, Raith was away.

He sped across the wet grass, shield on one arm and his axe gripped so tight below the blade his knuckles ached.

Swords were no doubt prettier but pretty weapons, like pretty people, are prone to sulk. Swords need subtlety and when the battle joy was on him Raith could be less than careful. He'd once beaten a man's head with the flat of a sword until both sword and head were bent far past any further use. Axes weren't so sensitive.

Lightning lit the sky again, Bail's Point a brooding blackness above the sea, wind-driven raindrops frozen before the night closed in. He Who Speaks the Thunder bellowed his upset at the world, so close it made Raith's heart leap.

He could still taste his bite of the last loaf, bread baked with blood salty across his tongue. The Vanstermen thought that good weaponluck, but Raith had always reckoned luck less use than fury. He bit down hard on the old builder's peg between his teeth. Near chewed the end of his tongue off in a rage once and ever since he'd made sure to wedge his jaws when there was a fight coming.

There was no feeling like charging into battle. Gambling everything on your cunning, your will, your strength. Dancing at the threshold of the Last Door. Spitting in Death's face.

He'd left Grom-gil-Gorm, and Soryorn, and even his brother Rakki far behind in his eagerness, the rain-slick elf-walls and the one flickering light at their foot rushing up to meet him.

'In here!'

Father Yarvi's boy held up a lantern, shadows in the hollows of his gawping face, pointing through a doorway hidden in the angle of the tower beside him.

Raith tore through, bouncing off the walls, bounding up the steps three at a time, growling breath echoing in the narrow tunnel, legs on fire, chest on fire, thoughts on fire, the din of metal, swearing, screaming building in his head as he burst out into the yard above.

He caught a mad glimpse of bodies straining, weapons flashing, spit and splinters, saw Thorn Bathu's tarred snarl and went crashing past her at full tilt, into the midst of the fight.

His shield crunched into a warrior's teeth and flung him over, sword skittering from his hand. Another staggered back, the spear poised to stab at Thorn wobbling wide.

Raith hacked at someone and made him scream, raw and broken and sounding like metal. Shoved with his shield and it grated against another, hissing and slobbering around the peg in his jaws as he pushed, wild, savage, driving a man back, his bloody spit spraying in Raith's face, close enough to kiss. Raith heaved him back again, kneed at him, made him stumble. A hollow thud as Thorn's sword chopped deep into his neck, stuck there as he fell and she let it go, kicking him away pouring blood.

Someone went down all tangled with a flapping canvas awning. Someone shouted in Raith's ear. Something pinged off his helmet and everything was bright, too bright to see, but he lashed blindly over his shield, growling, coughing.

A man grabbed at him and Raith smashed the butt of his axe into his head, smashed him again as he fell and stomped on his clutching hand, slipped and almost went down, the cobbles slick with blood and rain.

Wasn't sure which way he was facing of a sudden. The yard pitched and tossed like a ship in a storm. He saw Rakki, blood in his white hair as he stabbed with his sword, anger burned up again and Raith pushed in beside him, locking shields with his brother, shoving, butting, hacking. Something smashed him sideways and he went stumbling through a fire, kicking sparks.

Metal flashed and he jerked away, felt a burning on his face, something scraping against his helmet and knocking it skewed. He pressed past the spear, tried to ram his shield into a snarling face, got all tangled and realized it was a broken wreck, two of the planks dangling from the bent rim.

'Die, you bastard!' he snarled, the words just meaningless spit around the peg, flailing away at a helmet until it was dented all out of shape. Came to him he was hitting a wall, carving grey gashes in the stone, arm buzzing from the blows.

Someone was dragging him. Thorn with her black face a mess of spatter. She pointed with a red knife and her red mouth made words but Raith couldn't hear them.

A great sword tore at the wet air, split a shield, flung the man who held it against the wall in a shower of blood. Raith knew it. He'd carried that blade for three years, held it close as a lover in the darkness, made it sing with his whetstone.

Grom-gil-Gorm stepped forward, huge as a mountain, the dozens of jewelled and gilded pommels on his long chain glittering, his shield black as the night and his sword bright as Father Moon.

'Your death comes!' he roared, so loud the deep-rooted bones of Bail's Point seemed to shake.

Courage can be a brittle thing. Once panic clutches one man it spreads faster than plague, faster than fire. The High King's warriors had been warm and happy behind strong walls, expecting nothing worse from the night than a stiff wind. Now the Breaker of Swords rose from the storm in his full battle glory, and all at once they broke and fled.

Thorn cut one down with her axe, Gorm caught another by the scruff of his neck and smashed his face into the wall. Raith ripped his knife out, sprang onto a warrior's back as he ran, stabbing, stabbing. He leapt after another but his foot went out from under him and he tottered a wobbling step or two, bounced off the wall and fell.

Everything was blurry. He tried to stand but his knees wouldn't have it so he sat down. The peg had fallen out and his mouth ached, tasting of wood and metal. Feet stamped past. A man lay laughing at him. He was caught by a flying boot and rolled flopping over. A dead man, laughing at nothing. Laughing at everything.

Raith squeezed his eyes shut, opened them.

Soryorn was stabbing the wounded with a spear, calmly as if he was planting seeds. Men were still clattering through the small gate, drawing weapons, stepping over bodies.

'Always have to be first in the fight, eh, brother?' Rakki. He undid the buckle and pulled Raith's helmet off, tilted his face to look at the new cut. 'Doing your best to make sure I stay the pretty one, eh?'

Words felt strange on Raith's sore tongue. 'You need all the help you can get.' He shrugged his brother off and fought his way to standing, trying to shake his wrecked shield from his arm, trying to shake the dizziness from his head.

Bail's Point was vast, a jumble of thatched and slated

buildings grown up all around the towering elf-walls. There was crashing and shouting everywhere, Gettlanders and Vanstermen rooting through the fortress like ferrets down a warren, dragging the High King's men from their hiding places, pouring down the long ramp that led to the harbour, gathering in a crescent about a pair of carved double doors, King Gorm and King Uthil among them.

'We will smoke you out if we must!' Father Yarvi shouted at the wood. Like the crows, ministers always arrived as the fighting was done, eager to pick over the results. 'You had your chance to fight!'

A voice came muffled from beyond the door. 'I was putting on my armour. It has fiddly buckles.'

'The little ones can trick a big man's fingers,' Gorm admitted.

'I have it on now, though!' came the voice. 'Are there storied warriors among you?'

Father Yarvi gave a sigh. 'Thorn Bathu is here, and the Iron King Uthil, and Grom-gil-Gorm, the Breaker of Swords.'

A satisfied grunt from behind the door. 'I feel less sour about defeat against such famous names. Will any of them consent to fight me?'

Thorn sat on some steps nearby, wincing as Mother Scaer squeezed at a cut on her shoulder and made the blood run. 'I've fought enough for one evening.'

'I too.' Gorm handed his shield to Rakki. 'Let the flames take this unready fool and his small-buckled armour.'

Raith's feet stepped forward. His finger lifted. His mouth said, 'I'll fight the—'

Rakki caught hold of his arm and dragged it down. 'No you won't, brother.'

'Death is life's only certainty.' King Uthil shrugged. 'I will fight you!'

Father Yarvi looked horrified. 'My king—'

Uthil silenced him with one bright-eyed look. 'Faster runners have stolen the glory, and I will have my share.'

'Good!' came the voice. 'I am coming out!'

Raith heard a bar rattle back and the doors were swung wide, shields clattering as the half-circle of warriors set themselves to meet a charge. But only one man stepped into the yard.

He was huge, with a swirling tattoo on one side of his muscle-heavy neck. He wore thick mail with etched plates at the shoulders, and many gold rings upon his bulging forearms, and Raith grunted his approval for this looked a man well worth fighting. He hooked his thumbs carelessly into his gold-buckled sword-belt and sneered at the crescent of shields facing him with a hero's contempt.

'You are King Uthil?' The man snorted mist into the drizzle from his broad, flat nose. 'You are older than the songs say.'

'The songs were composed some time ago,' grated the Iron King. 'I was younger then.'

Some laughter at that, but not from this man. 'I am Dunverk,' he growled, 'that men call the Bull, faithful to the One God, loyal to the High King, Companion to Bright Yilling.'

'That only proves your choice is equally poor in friends, kings and gods,' said Father Yarvi. The laughter was louder this time, and even Raith had to admit it was a decent jest.

But defeat surely dampens a sense of humour, and Dunverk stayed stony. 'We will see when Yilling returns, and brings Death to you oathbreakers.'

'*We* will see,' tossed out Thorn, grinning even as Mother Scaer was pushing the needle through the meat of her shoulder. 'You'll be dead, and will see nothing.'

Dunverk slowly drew his sword, runes etched into the fuller, the hilt worked in gold like a stag's head with its antlers making the crosspiece. 'If I win, will you spare the rest of my men?'

Uthil looked scrawny as an old chicken against Dunverk's brawn, but he showed no fear at all. 'You will not win.'

'You are too confident.'

'If my hundred and more dead opponents could speak they would say I am as confident as I deserve to be.'

'I should warn you, old man, I fought all across the Lowlands and there was no one who could stand against me.'

A twitch of a smile passed across Uthil's scarred face. 'You should have stayed in the Lowlands.'

Dunverk charged, swinging hard and high but Uthil dodged away, nimble as the wind, his sword still cradled in the crook of his arm. Dunverk made a mighty thrust and the king stepped contemptuously away, letting his steel drop down by his side.

'The Bull,' scoffed Thorn. 'He fights like a mad cow, all right.'

Dunverk roared as he chopped right and left, sweat on his forehead from wielding that heavy blade, men shuffling back behind their shields in case a stray backswing took them through the Last Door. But the Iron King of Gettland weaved away from the first blow and ducked under the second so Dunverk's sword whipped at his grey hair, steel flashing as he reeled away into space again.

'Fight me!' bellowed Dunverk, turning.

'I have,' said Uthil, and he caught the corner of his cloak, wiped the edge of his sword, and tucked it carefully back into the crook of his arm.

Dunverk snarled as he stepped forward but his leg buckled and he fell to one knee, blood welling over the top of his boot and spreading across the flagstones. That was when Raith realized Uthil had slit the great vein on the inside of Dunverk's leg.

There was a murmuring of awe from the gathered warriors, and from Raith as much as anyone.

'The Iron King's fame is well-deserved,' murmured Rakki.

'I hope Bright Yilling's sword-work is better than yours, Dunverk the Bull,' said Uthil. 'You have scarcely given this old man exercise.'

Dunverk smiled then, a far-off look in his glassy eyes. 'You all will see Bright Yilling's sword-work,' he whispered, his face turned waxy pale. 'You all will see.' And he toppled sideways into the widening slick of his own blood.

All agreed it had been an excellent death.

MY LAND

Mother Sun was a smudge on the eastern horizon, hiding her children the stars behind the iron-grey curtain of the dawn sky. The fortress loomed ahead, sombre as a funeral howe in the colourless dawn, hopeful crows circling above.

'At least the rain has stopped,' muttered Skara, pushing back her hood.

'He Who Speaks the Thunder has taken his tantrums off inland,' said Queen Laithlin. 'Like all boys, he makes a great fuss but it's soon over.' And she reached out and chucked Prince Druin under the chin. 'Shall I take him?'

'No.' Skara squeezed him tighter. 'I can hold him.' Having his little arms around her neck made her feel strong. And the gods knew, she had need of strength then.

Bail's Point, shining symbol of Throvenland united, was not what she remembered. The village in the shadow of the fortress, where she had once danced at the summer festival, lay in ruins, houses burned or abandoned. The orchard before the crumbling man-built stretch of wall was throttled with ivy, last year's fruit rotting in the weeds. The great gateway between two soaring elf-built towers had once been decorated with bright banners. Now a hanged man swung on a creaking rope from the battlements, his bare feet dangling.

His fine gold armrings, his shining mail, his gilded weapons had been stripped away, but Skara knew his face at once.

'One of Bright Yilling's Companions.' She gave a shiver in spite of the fur about her shoulders. 'One of those who burned Yaletoft.'

'Yet here he swings,' said Laithlin. 'It seems praying to Death does not put off a meeting with her.'

'Nothing puts off that meeting,' whispered Skara. Probably she should have revelled in his death, spat on his corpse, given thanks to Mother War that this splinter of Throvenland at least was freed, but all she felt was a sick echo of her fear when she last saw him, and a dread that she would never be free of it.

Someone had chopped down the great oak that once grew in the yard of the fortress, the buildings crowding within the ancient elf-walls bare and ugly without its shade. Warriors lounged on the buckled cobbles around the stump, most drunk and getting more drunk, comparing wounds and trophies, cleaning weapons, trading stories.

A would-be skald was composing a verse, shouting the same line over and over while others offered choices for the next word to gales of laughter. A prayer-weaver droned out an elaborate thanks to the gods for their victory. Somewhere, someone was howling in pain.

Skara wrinkled her nose. 'What is that smell?'

'Everything men contain,' murmured Sister Owd, watching a pair of thralls haul something past between them.

Skara realized with a cold shock that it was a corpse, and then to her horror that they were dragging it onto a whole heap of others. A pale tangle of bare limbs, stained and spattered, mouths lolling silent, eyes unseeing. A pile of meat which last night had been men. Men who had taken years of work to birth, and nurse, and teach to walk, speak, fight. Skara held Prince Druin close, trying to shield his eyes.

'Should he see this?' she murmured, wishing she had not seen it herself.

'He will be king of Gettland. This is his destiny.' Laithlin glanced dispassionately at the bodies, and Skara wondered if she had ever met so formidable a woman. 'He should learn to rejoice in it. So should you. This is your victory, after all.'

Skara swallowed. 'Mine?'

'The men will argue over whose was the hairiest chest and the loudest roar. The bards will sing of the flashing steel and the blood spilled. But yours was the plan. Yours was the will. Yours were the words that set these men to your purpose.'

Words are weapons, Mother Kyre had told her. Skara stared at the dead men in the yard of Bail's Point, and thought of the dead men in her grandfather's hall, and rather than a crime avenged she saw two crimes, and felt the guilt of one piled on the pain of the other.

'It does not feel like victory,' she whispered.

'You have seen defeat. Which do you prefer?' Skara remembered standing at the *Black Dog*'s stern, watching the gable of her grandfather's hall sag into the towering flames, and found she could not argue.

'I was very impressed with you at the moot,' said Laithlin.

'Truly? I thought . . . you might be angry with me.'

'That you spoke for yourself and your country? I might as well be angry at the snow for falling. You are eighteen winters old, yes?'

'I will be, this year . . .'

Laithlin slowly shook her head. 'Seventeen. You have a gift.'

'Mother Kyre and my grandfather . . . all my life they tried to teach me how to lead. How to speak and what to say. How to make arguments, read faces, sway hearts . . . I always thought myself a poor pupil.'

'I very much doubt that, but war can force strengths from us we never expected. King Fynn and his minister prepared you well, but one cannot teach what you have. You are touched by She Who Spoke the First Word. You have that light in you that makes people listen.' The queen frowned at Druin, who was staring at the carnage in wide-eyed silence. 'I have a feeling my son's future may hang on that gift.'

Skara blinked. 'My gifts beside yours are like a candle beside Mother Sun. You are the Golden Queen—'

'Of Gettland.' Her eyes flicked to Skara's, bright and sharp. 'The gods know I have tried to steer this alliance, first to counsel peace and then to urge action, but to King Uthil I am a wife and to King Gorm I am an enemy.' She pushed a strand of hair from Skara's face. 'You are neither. Fate has made you the balance between them. The pin on which the scales of this alliance hang.'

Skara stared at her. 'I do not have the strength for that.'

'Then you must find it.' Laithlin leaned close and took Prince Druin from her arms. 'Power is a weight. You are young, cousin, I know, but you must learn to carry it, or it will crush you.'

Sister Owd puffed out her cheeks, making her round face look even rounder as she watched the queen glide away, her thralls and servants and guards trailing after her. 'Queen Laithlin has always been a well of good humour.'

'Good humour I can live without, Sister Owd. What I need is good advice.'

It surprised her how glad she was to see Raith alive, but then as things stood he was one whole third of her household, and by far the best-looking third. He and his brother sat laughing beside a fire, and Skara felt a strange pang of jealousy, they seemed so utterly at ease with each other. For two men sprung at once from the same womb they were easily told apart. Raith was the one with the wrinkle to his lip and the fresh cut down his face. The one with a challenge in his eye, even when he met Skara's, that she could not seem to look away from. Rakki was the one who hardly met her eye at all, and scrambled to rise with the proper respect as she drew close.

'You've earned your rest,' she said, waving him down. 'I hardly deserve to be among such blood-letters.'

'You spilled a little blood yourself in that moot,' said Raith, glancing down at Skara's bandaged hand.

She found herself hiding it with the other. 'Only my own.'

'It's spilling your own takes the courage.' Raith winced as he prodded at the long scratch down his white-stubbled jaw. He looked no worse for the mark. Better, if anything.

'I hear you fought well,' she said.

'He always does, princess.' Rakki grinned as he punched his brother on the arm. 'First through the gate! Without him we might still be squatting outside.'

Raith shrugged. 'Fighting's no hardship when you love to fight.'

'Even so. My grandfather always told me those who fight well should be rewarded by those they fight for.' And Skara twisted one of the silver rings Laithlin had given her from her wrist and held it out.

Rakki and Raith both stared. The armring had been much pecked with a knife to test its purity some time in the past, but Skara had been taught well the value of things. She saw that neither brother wore ring-money and knew this was no light matter to them. Raith swallowed as he reached to take it, but Skara kept her grip. 'You fight for me, don't you?'

She felt a nervous tingle as their eyes met, their fingers almost touching. Then he nodded. 'I fight for you.' He was rough and he was rude, and for some reason she found herself wondering what it might be like to kiss him. She heard Sister Owd clear her throat, felt her face burning and quickly let go.

Raith squeezed the ring closed, his wrist so thick the ends barely met around it. A reward for good service. But also a sign that he served, and a mark of whom he served. 'I should have come to find you after the battle, but . . .'

'I needed you to fight.' Skara pushed thoughts of kissing away and put a little iron into her voice. 'Now I need you to come with me.'

She watched Raith give his brother a parting hug, then stand, her silver glinting on his wrist, and follow her. He might not truly be her man, but she began to understand why queens had Chosen Shields. There is nothing for your confidence like a proven killer at your shoulder.

When Skara played in the great hall of Bail's Point as a child it had seemed grand beyond reckoning. Now it was narrow, and dim, and smelled of rot, the roof leaking and the walls streaked with damp, three dusty shafts of light falling across the cold floor from windows looking over grey Mother Sea. The great painting of Ashenleer as warrior-queen that covered one wall was peeled and blistered, a bloom of mould across her mail and the adoring expressions of her hundred guards faded to smudges. A fitting image for the fallen fortunes of Throvenland.

Bail's Chair still stood upon the dais, though, made of pale oak-wood cut from a ship's keel, the twisted grain polished to a sheen by years of use. Kings had once sat there. Until Skara's grandfather's great-grandfather decided the chair was too narrow to hold all his arse, and the hall too narrow to hold all his boasting, and had a new chair made in Yaletoft, and began to build a fine new hall around it that would be the wonder of the world. It took twenty-eight years to finish the Forest, by which time he was dead and his son was an old man.

Then Bright Yilling burned it in a night.

'Seems the fighting's not quite done,' grunted Raith.

Gorm and Uthil glowered at each other over Bail's Chair, their ministers and warriors bristling about them. The brotherhood of battle had lasted no longer than the life of their last enemy.

'We could draw lots—' King Uthil grated out.

'You had the satisfaction of killing Dunverk,' said Gorm, 'I should have the chair.'

Father Yarvi rubbed at one temple with the knuckles of his shrivelled hand. 'For the gods' sake, it is a chair. My apprentice can carve you another.'

'It is not just any chair.' Skara swallowed her nerves as she stepped up onto the dais. 'Bail the Builder once sat here.' King Uthil and his minister stood frowning on her left, Gorm and his minister on her right. She was the balance between them. She had to be. 'How many ships did we take?'

'Sixty-six,' said Mother Scaer. 'Among them a gilded beast of thirty oars a side which we hear is Bright Yilling's own.'

Father Yarvi gave Skara an appreciative nod. 'It was a deep-cunning plan, princess.'

'I only sowed the seed,' said Skara, bowing low to the two kings. 'Your bravery reaped the harvest.'

'Mother War was with us and our weaponluck held good.' Gorm turned one of the pommels on his chain around and around. 'But this fortress is far from safe. Grandmother Wexen knows well its importance, in strategy and as a symbol.'

'It is a splinter pushed into her flesh,' said Uthil, 'and it will not be long before she tries to pluck it out. You should return to Thorlby with my wife, princess. You will be far from danger there.'

'My respect for you is boundless, King Uthil, but you are wrong. My father knew well the importance of this fortress too. So much so he died to defend it, and is buried in the barrows outside the walls, beside my mother.' Skara lowered herself into the chair where her forefathers had once sat, painfully upright, the way Mother Kyre had taught her. Her guts were churning, but she had to be strong. Had to lead. There was no one else. 'This is Throvenland. This is my land. This is the very place I should be.'

Father Yarvi gave a tired smile. 'Princess—'

'In fact, I am a queen.'

There was a silence. Then Sister Owd began to climb the steps. 'Queen Skara is quite right. She sits in Bail's

Chair as King Fynn's only living descendant. There is precedent for an unmarried woman to take the chair alone.' Her voice quavered under Mother Scaer's deadly glare but she went on, nodding up towards the faded painting that loomed over them. 'Queen Ashenleer herself, after all, was unmarried when she won victory against the Inglings.'

'Is there another Ashenleer among us, then?' sneered Mother Scaer.

Sister Owd stood at Skara's left hand where a minister belongs, and resolutely folded her arms. 'That remains to be seen.'

'Whether you are princess or queen will mean nothing to Bright Yilling,' rumbled Gorm, and Skara felt a surge of that familiar fear at the name. 'He kneels to no woman but Death.'

'He will already be on his way,' said Uthil, 'and with vengeance in mind.'

You can only conquer your fears by facing them. Hide from them, and they conquer you. Skara let them wait, taking a moment to settle her thumping heart before she answered. 'Oh, I am counting on it.'

II

WE ARE THE
SWORD

YOUNG LOVE

She pushed her hand into his hair, pulled him down so their foreheads were pressed hard together, quick breath hot on his face. For a long while they lay tangled with each other, the furs kicked down around their ankles, in silence.

Not one word spoken since Koll said his goodbyes to Thorn on the docks and strode up like a thief after a promising purse through the darkened city. In silence Rin had opened her door, taken him into her house, into her arms, into her bed.

Koll had always loved words, but to be a minister's apprentice was to drown in them. True words, false words, words in many tongues. Right words, wrong words, written and spoken and unspoken. For now silence suited him. To forget for a moment what he owed

Father Yarvi, and what he owed Rin, and how there was no way he could settle both debts. Whatever words he said, he felt like a liar.

Rin put one rough hand on his cheek, gave him a parting kiss and slithered out from under him. He loved to watch her move, so strong and sure, shadows shifting between her ribs as she fished his shirt from the floor and pulled it on. He loved it when she wore his clothes, not asking, not needing to ask. It made them feel so close together, somehow. That and he loved the way the hem only came halfway down her bare backside.

She squatted, the key she wore to her own locks swinging free on its chain, tossed a log on the fire, sparks drifting up and the light flaring on her face. Not one word spoken all that time but, like everything good, the silence couldn't last.

'You're back, then,' she said.

'Only for tonight.' Koll probed gently at the bridge of his nose, still not quite healed from its sharp meeting with Raith's head. 'The Prince of Kalyiv has come to Roystock. Queen Laithlin is sailing to an audience and needs a minister beside her. Father Yarvi's busy trying to bail out our foundering alliances, so . . .'

'She calls on the mighty Koll! Changing the world, just like you always wanted.' Rin drew his shirt tight about her, the flames reflected in the corners of her eyes. 'Minister to the Golden Queen and you never even took the Minister's Test.'

'No, but . . . I will have to. And swear the Minister's Oath too.'

That fell between them like gull's droppings from a great height. But if Rin was hurt she didn't show it. That wouldn't have been her way at all. He loved that about her.

'What was Bail's Point like?'

'It reminded me very much of a big elf-stone fortress by the sea.'

'You're almost as funny as you think you are. I mean, what was it like climbing into it?'

'Heroes never think about the danger.'

She grinned. 'So you pissed yourself?'

'I tried, but I was so scared my bladder clenched up tight as King Uthil's fist. Couldn't get a drip out for days afterward.'

'Koll the warrior, eh?'

'I thought it best to leave the fighting to others.' Koll tapped at his head. 'Half a war is fought up here, Queen Skara is always saying.'

'*Queen* Skara, now.' Rin snorted. 'I've yet to meet a man who isn't much taken with that girl's wisdom.'

'I expect a lot of it's in the, you know . . .' Koll waved a hand about. 'Jewellery and so on.'

Rin raised one brow at him. 'Oh, you expect that, do you?'

'No doubt she looks like something from the songs.' He put his arms over his head, quivering as he stretched out. 'But I reckon a stiff breeze could blow her away. I like a woman with both feet on Father Earth.'

'That's your notion of a compliment? Earthy?' She made a tube of her tongue and spat hissing into the fire. 'Some honeyed minister's mouth you have.'

His mother's weights clicked around his neck as Koll rolled onto one elbow. 'What makes a woman beautiful to me isn't her blood or her clothes but what she can do. I like a woman with strong hands who isn't afraid of sweat or hard work or anything else. I like a woman with pride, and ambition, and quick wit, and high skill.' Just words, maybe, but he meant them. Or half-meant them, anyway. 'That's why I never saw a woman anywhere so beautiful as you, Rin. And that's before I even get to your arse, which I can't imagine has an equal anywhere around the Shattered Sea.'

She looked back to the fire, lips curling at the corner. 'That's better, I'll admit. Even if it is all a hatful of winds.'

Koll was much pleased with himself. He loved it when he made her smile. 'Sweet smelling breezes at least, I hope?'

'Better than your usual farts. Will you be charming Prince Varoslaf's nose with your flattery?'

That dented his smugness considerably. By all accounts the Prince of Kalyiv's taste ran less to funny men and more to skinned ones. 'I doubt I'll comment on his arse, at least. I may keep my mouth shut altogether and leave the talking to Queen Laithlin. Silent men rarely cause offence.'

'You can probably find a way. What does Varoslaf want?'

'What the powerful always want. More power. Or so Thorn says. This trip to Roystock isn't to her taste at all. She wanted to fight.'

Rin stood up. 'She usually does.'

'She's in a bastard of a mood now. Wouldn't want to be Brand tonight.'

'He'll manage.' She slid back into the bed beside him, propping herself on one elbow, his shirt rumpled across her chest. 'They love each other.'

Rin's eyes, fixed on him so close, were making Koll quite uncomfortable. He felt cornered in that narrow bed. Trapped by the heat of her. 'Maybe.' He kicked over onto his back, frowning at the ceiling. He had great things to do. Stand at the shoulder of kings and so on. How could he change the world with Rin smothering him? 'Love's hardly the answer to every question, though, is it?'

She turned away, drawing the furs up to her waist. 'Certainly seems not.'

With so many men away there were more women working on the docks of Thorlby than usual, busy at nets and sorting through the morning's squirming catches. Fewer guards about too – older men, and boys Koll's age yet to take their warrior's tests, and some of the girls that Thorn had been training – but otherwise you might never have known there was any war at all.

Six battered ships had landed the night before from the long journey up the Divine, and their sunburned crews were bringing ashore silks, and wine, and all manner of fine curiosities from the south. Queen Laithlin's men were loading her four ships for the voyage to Roystock and the air rang with their cries, and the barking of a stray being beaten away from the fish, and the laughter of children ducking among the wagons, and the calls of the scavenging gulls as they drifted in lazy circles, watching for spilled grain.

Mother Sun was bright as ever in the east, and Koll shaded his eyes as he gazed off towards Roystock, and sucked in a long, salty breath through his nostrils.

'Smells like good luck!'

'That and fish.' Rin wrinkled her nose. 'Four ships? To carry one woman?'

'And her minister!' Koll puffed up his chest and jabbed at it with his thumb. 'A man of that stature must be properly attended.'

'They're going to lash two ships together just to carry his swollen head, are they?'

'That and the Chosen Shield's temper,' he muttered, as Thorn's angry orders came chopping through the hubbub. 'You can tell a woman's importance by the gifts she gives and the company she keeps. Queen Laithlin means to make a deep impression on Varoslaf by taking plenty of both.'

Rin glanced sideways. 'What does it say about me that I keep company with you?'

Koll slipped his arm about her waist, grinning at how well it seemed to fit there. 'That you're a woman of high taste and refinement, not to mention excellent luck, and— Gods!' As the crowd shifted Koll caught a glimpse of Brand, hefting a great crate as if it had nothing in it at all. He ducked behind a rack where fish big as boys had been hung glittering in the sunlight. One that still had a little life in it twitched about, seeming to give him a rather disapproving stare.

So did Rin, looking down with hands on hips. 'The conqueror of Bail's Point.' And she stuck her tongue between her lips and blew a long fart at him.

'Strong men are many, wise men are few. Did he see us?'

'If you climbed *inside* one of those fish I think you could make sure.'

'You're almost as funny as you think you are.' He pushed a fish aside with a fingertip to peer past. 'We'd best part now.'

'There's always a reason to rush the parting, isn't there? Young love. Not quite the joy they sing of.' She caught him by the collar and half dragged him up, gave him the quickest of kisses and left him frozen with lips puckered and eyes closed. When he opened them he was disappointed to see her already walking away, an unexpected twinge of guilt and longing making him suddenly, stupidly desperate to stretch the parting out.

'See you in a week or two, then!'

'If you're luckier than you deserve!' she called, without turning.

Koll stuck his thumbs carelessly in his belt and strolled down through the crowds, slipping around a wagon loaded with fleeces, old Brinyolf the Prayer-Weaver droning out a blessing over the voyage in the background.

He froze as a heavy arm fell across his shoulders. 'I need a word.' For a big man, Brand could sneak up well enough when he wanted to.

Koll sent up a quick prayer to She Who Judges for mercy he knew he didn't deserve. 'To me? Whatever about?'

'The Prince of Kalyiv.'

'Ah!' It said something that a man famous for skinning people alive was the preferable topic. 'Him!'

'Varoslaf is a bad man to cross,' said Brand, 'and Thorn's got a habit of crossing those kind of people.'

'True, though she's a pretty bad woman to cross herself.'

Brand stared back at him. 'Well there's a recipe for a famous bloodbath, then.'

Koll cleared his throat. 'I see your meaning.'

'Just keep her out of trouble.'

'She's a hard woman to keep out of anything, especially trouble.'

'Believe me when I say you're telling me nothing I don't know. Steer her away from trouble, then.'

Steering a ship through a tempest sounded lighter work but all Koll could do was puff out his cheeks. 'I'll do my best.'

'Steer yourself away from trouble too.'

Koll grinned. 'That I've always had a knack for.' He looked hopefully towards Brand's scarred and muscled arm. It did not move.

'I'm not the sharpest man in Thorlby, Koll, I know that. But how thick do you think I am exactly?'

Koll winced so hard he closed one eye and peered at Brand out of the other. 'Not my nose. It's still not right after that white-haired bastard butted it.'

'I'm not going to hit you, Koll. Rin can make her own choices. I reckon she made a fine one with you.'

'You do?'

Brand looked at him calm and level. 'Except you're

due to swear a Minister's Oath, and give up all your
family.'

'Ah. The Oath.' As though he'd hardly spared it a
thought till now, when in fact he'd spent hours practising
the words, thinking just how to say them, dreaming of
what he'd do afterward, the high folk who'd nod at his
wisdom, the grand choices he'd make, the greater good
and the lesser evil he'd choose—

'Yes, the Oath,' said Brand. 'Seems to me you're stuck
between Rin and Father Yarvi.'

'Believe me when I say you're telling me nothing I
don't know,' mumbled Koll. 'I've been praying to He Who
Steers the Arrow for a point in the right direction.'

'Finding him slow to reply?'

'Father Yarvi says the gods love those who solve their
own problems.' Koll brightened. 'You don't have an
answer, do you?'

'Only the one you've already got.'

'Ah.'

'To pick one or the other.'

'Ah. I don't much like that one.'

'No, but you're a man now, Koll. You can't just wait
for someone else to put things right.'

'I'm a man.' Koll's shoulders sagged. 'When did that
happen?'

'It just happens.'

'I wish I knew what it meant, being a man.'

'Guess it means something different for each one of
us. The gods know I'm no sage, but if I've realized
anything, it's that life isn't about making something

perfect.' Brand looked over at Thorn, busy shaking her fist in the face of one of the queen's warriors. 'Death waits for us all. Nothing's forever. Life's about making the best of what you find along the way. A man who's not content with what he's got, well, more than likely he won't be content with what he hasn't.'

Koll blinked. 'You're sure you're not a sage?'

'Just be honest with her. She deserves that.'

'I know she does,' muttered Koll, looking guiltily down at the planks of the wharf.

'You'll do the right thing. If not, well . . .' Brand drew him close. 'I can hit you then.'

Koll sighed. 'It's good to have something to look forward to.'

'I'll see you when you get back.' Brand saw him off with a slap on the shoulder. 'Till then, stand in the light, Koll.'

'You too, Brand.'

As he hopped aboard the queen's ship Koll thought to himself, and not for the first time, that he was nowhere near as clever as he'd supposed. Something to remember, next time he got to thinking how clever he was.

He grinned at that. So much like something his mother would've said he almost thought it in her voice, and he gripped those old weights about his neck and looked up at the masthead, thinking of her screaming at him as he teetered there. He'd always hated his mother's fussing. Now he'd have given everything he had to be fussed over again.

He turned to watch Queen Laithlin fussing over her

son, the heir to the throne seeming tiny surrounded by slaves and servants, two hulking Ingling bodyguards with silver thrall-collars looming over him.

She adjusted his tiny cloak-buckle, and smoothed his blonde hair, and kissed him on the head, then turned towards the ship, one of her slaves kneeling on the wharf to make a step of his back for her.

'All will be well here, my queen,' called Brinyolf the Prayer-Weaver, one hand on Druin's shoulder and the other raised in an elaborate blessing. 'And may She Who Finds the Course steer you safely home!'

'Bye bye!' called the prince, and while his mother was raising her arm to wave he slipped from under Brinyolf's hand and scurried off giggling towards the city, his attendants hurrying to catch him.

Laithlin dropped her hand and gripped tight to the rail. 'I wish I could take him, but I trust Varoslaf only a little less than a snake. I have lost one son to the sword and another to the Ministry. I cannot lose a third.'

'Prince Druin could not be safer, my queen,' said Koll, doing his best to say what Father Yarvi would have. 'Thorlby is far from the fighting and still well-guarded, her walls never conquered and the citadel impregnable.'

'Bail's Point was impregnable. You climbed in.'

Koll dared a grin. 'How fortunate that men of my talents are rare, my queen.'

Laithlin snorted. 'You have a minister's humility, already.'

Thorn was the last aboard. 'Be safe,' Brand called to her as she stomped past him down the wharf.

'Aye,' she grunted, swinging one leg over the rail. She froze as Queen Laithlin's shadow fell across her, stuck with one foot off the ship and one foot on.

'Young love is a treasure truly wasted on the young,' mused the queen, frowning up towards the city with her hands clasped behind her. 'It is my place to know the value of things, so take it from me you will have nothing in your life more precious. Soon enough the green leaves turn brown.' She peered down sternly at her Chosen Shield. 'I think you can do better than that.'

Thorn winced. 'You think I can, my queen, or you're ordering me to?'

'To a Chosen Shield, a queen's every whim is a decree.'

Thorn took a deep breath, swung her leg onto the wharf, and stomped back to Brand.

'Since my queen commands it,' she muttered, using her fingers like a comb to push the stray hair out of his face. She caught him behind the head and dragged him close, kissed him long and greedily, squeezing him so hard she lifted his toes off the wharf while the oarsmen sent up a cheer, and laughed, and thumped their oars.

'I hadn't marked you for a romantic, my queen,' murmured Koll.

'It seems I have surprised us both,' said Laithlin.

Thorn broke away, wiping her mouth, the elf-bangle at her wrist glowing golden. 'I love you,' Koll heard her grunt over the noise of the crew. 'And I'm sorry. For the way I am.'

Brand grinned back, brushing the star-shaped scar on her cheek with his fingertips. 'I love the way you are. Be safe.'

'Aye.' Thorn thumped him on the shoulder with her fist, then stalked back down the wharf and vaulted over the ship's rail. 'Better?' she asked.

'I am warmed all over,' murmured Laithlin, with just the hint of a smile. She took one last glance towards the citadel, then nodded to the helmsman. 'Cast off.'

QUEEN OF NOTHING

They filed into the hall, maybe three dozen, lean as beggars, dirty as thieves. A couple had swords. Others wood-axes, hunting bows, butcher's knives. One girl with half a hedge in her matted hair clutched a spear made from a hoeing pole and an old scythe-blade.

Raith puffed out his cheeks, making the cut on his face burn. 'Here come the heroes.'

'Some fighters have a sword put into their hand in the training square.' Blue Jenner leaned close to mutter in his ear. 'Bred to it all their lives, like you. Some have an axe fall into their hand when Mother War spreads her wings.' He watched the ragged company kneel awkwardly in a half circle before the dais. 'Takes courage to fight when you didn't choose it, weren't trained for it, weren't ready for it.'

'Wasn't no sword put in my hand, old man,' said Raith. 'I had to rip it from a hundred others by the sharp end. And it ain't lack of courage bothers me, it's lack of skill.'

'Good thing you've a thousand picked warriors waiting. You can send them in next.'

Raith scowled sideways, but had naught to say. Rakki was the talker.

'It ain't the courageous or the skilful Mother War rewards.' Jenner nodded towards the beggars. 'It's those who make the best of what they've got.'

Skara had a fine art at that. She smiled on her ragged recruits as gratefully as if it was the Prince of Kalyiv, the Empress of the South and a dozen dukes of Catalia pledging their aid.

'Thank you for coming, my friends.' She sat forward earnestly in Bail's Chair. Small though she was, she had a way of filling it. 'My countrymen.'

They couldn't have looked more grateful if it was Ashenleer herself they were kneeling to. Their leader, an old warrior with a face scarred as a butcher's block, cleared his throat. 'Princess Skara—'

'Queen Skara,' corrected Sister Owd, with a prissy little pout. Plainly she was getting to like being out from Mother Scaer's shadow. Raith rolled his eyes, but he hardly blamed her. Mother Scaer's shadow could be dreadful chilly.

'I'm sorry, my queen—' mumbled the warrior.

But Skara hardly cast a shadow at all. 'I am the one who should be sorry. That you have had to fight alone.

I am the one who should be grateful. That you have come to fight for me.'

'I fought for your father,' said the man in a broken voice. 'Fought for your grandfather. I'll fight to the death for you.' And the others all nodded along, heads bobbing.

It's one thing to offer to die, quite another to fling yourself on the sharpened steel, specially if the only metal you're used to wielding is a milking bucket. Not long ago Raith would've been sniggering with his brother over their fool's loyalty. But Rakki was elsewhere, and Raith was finding it hard to laugh.

He'd always been sure of the best thing to do before, and it mostly had an axe on the end. That was the way things got done in Vansterland. But Skara had her own way of doing things, and he found he liked watching her do it. He liked watching her a lot.

'Where have you come from?' she was asking.

'Most of us from Ockenby, my queen, or the farms outside.'

'Oh, I know it! There are wonderful oak trees there—'

'Till Bright Yilling burned 'em,' spat out a woman whose face was hard as the hatchet at her belt. 'Burned everything.'

'Aye, but we showed him some fire.' The warrior set his dirty hand on the shoulder of a young lad beside him. 'Burned some of his forage. Burned a tent with some of his men inside.'

'Should've seen 'em dance,' growled the woman.

'I got one of 'em when he went to piss!' shouted the boy in a voice cracking between high and low, then his face went bright red and he stared at the floor. 'My queen, that is . . .'

'You've all done brave work.' Raith saw the tendons stark on Skara's thin hands as she gripped at the arms of Bail's Chair. 'Where is Yilling now?'

'Gone,' said the boy. 'He had a camp on the beach at Harentoft, but they up and left overnight.'

'When?' asked Jenner.

'Twelve days ago.'

The old raider tugged unhappily at his straggling beard. 'That worries me.'

'We've got his ships,' said Raith.

'But the High King's got more. Yilling could be working mischief on any coast of the Shattered Sea by now.'

'You're a crowd of worries, old man,' grunted Raith. 'Would you be happier if he was still burning farms?'

'No, I'd be worried then too. That's what it is to be old.'

Skara held her hand up for quiet. 'You need food, and a place to sleep. If you still wish to fight, we have arms taken from the High King's men. Ships too.'

'We'll fight, my queen,' said the old warrior, and the rest of the Throvenlanders, however wretched, all showed their most warlike faces. No doubt they'd got courage, but as Sister Owd herded them out to be fed Raith pictured them facing the High King's countless warriors. The next picture wasn't a pretty one.

As the doors were shut Skara slumped back in her chair with a groan, one hand to her stomach. Plainly all that smiling took a toll. 'Is that six crews, now?'

'And all willing to die for you, my queen,' said Jenner.

Raith took a heavy breath. 'If the High King's army comes, dying's just what they'll be doing.'

Jenner opened his mouth but Skara held up her hand again. 'He's right. I may have a queen's chair, but without Gorm and Uthil camped outside my walls I'm queen of nothing.' She stood, the dangling jewels on her earring flashing. 'And Gorm and Uthil, not to mention their idle warriors, are back at one another's throats. I should see if they've made any progress.'

Raith wasn't hopeful. On Jenner's advice, Skara had finally talked the two kings into working on the defences: felling trees grown too close, shoring up the man-built stretch of wall and digging out the ditch. Getting them to agree to that much had been a whole day of minister's wrangling. Skara gathered her skirts and with a lazy wave let Raith know he should follow.

Still made him bristle to take orders from a girl, and Jenner must've seen it. The old raider caught his arm. 'Listen, boy. You're a fighter, and the gods know, we need some. But the man who finds fights everywhere, well . . . soon enough he'll find one fight too many.'

Raith curled his lip. 'Everything I've got, I had to beat from the world with my fists.'

'Aye. And what have you got?'

Might be the old man had some ghost of a point.

'Just keep her safe, eh?'

Raith shook him off. 'Keep worrying, old man.'

Outside in the sunlight Skara was shaking her head at the big stump in the yard. 'I remember when a great

Fortress Tree grew here. Sister Owd thinks it a bad omen that it was cut down.'

'Some folk see omens everywhere.' Most likely Raith should've been sticking *my queen* on the end of every-thing, but the words felt wrong in his mouth. He was no courtier.

'And you?'

'Always seemed to me the gods send luck to the man with the most fight and the least mercy. That's what I saw, growing up.'

'Where did you grow up? A wolf pack?'

Raith raised his brows. 'Aye, more or less.'

'How old are you?'

'Not sure.' Skara blinked at him, and he shrugged. 'Wolves don't count too well.'

She set off towards the gates, her thrall following them with her eyes on the ground. 'Then how did you come to be sword-bearer to a king?'

'Mother Scaer picked us out. Me and my brother.'

'So you owe her.'

Raith thought of the minister's hard eyes and hard lessons, hunched his shoulders at the memory of more than one whipping too. 'Aye, I reckon.'

'And you admire the Breaker of Swords.'

Raith thought of the slaps, and the orders, and the bloody work he'd done on the frontier. 'He's the greatest warrior about the Shattered Sea.'

Skara's sharp eyes darted sideways. 'So did he send you to guard me or spy on me?'

Raith was caught off-balance. Being honest, he hadn't

been on-balance since he was sent to serve her. 'I daresay some of both. But I'm far better at guarding than spying.'

'Or lying either, it would seem.'

'My brother's the clever one.'

'So the Breaker of Swords doesn't trust me?'

'Mother Scaer says only your enemies can never betray you.'

Skara snorted as they stepped into the gloom of the elf-cut entrance tunnel. 'Ministers.'

'Aye, ministers. But here's how I see it. Far as the guarding goes, I'll die for you.'

She blinked at that, and the muscles in her neck fluttered as she swallowed, and he thought that quite a wonderful thing.

'Far as the spying goes, I'm too blunt to cut too deep into your business.'

'Ah.' Her eyes flickered over his face. 'You're just a beautiful fool.'

Raith didn't blush often, but he felt the blood hot in his cheeks then. He could dive into a shield-wall bristling with steel but a glance from this twig of a girl had his courage crumbling. 'Er . . . beauty I'll leave to you, I reckon. The fool part I won't deny.'

'Mother Kyre always said only stupid men proclaim themselves clever.'

Raith's turn to snort. 'Ministers.'

Skara's laugh echoed in the darkness. For a small woman she had a big laugh, wild and dirty as some old warrior's at an ale-hall story, and Raith thought that quite a wonderful thing as well. 'Aye,' she said, 'ministers. So why did the Breaker of Swords pick you?'

He felt like a poor swimmer being lured into deep water. 'Eh?'

'Why send an honest idiot to do a clever liar's job?'

He frowned at that as they stepped out into daylight. Luckily, he was spared from giving an answer.

A crowd had gathered just outside the gates but there was no work being done. Unless you counted bristling, glaring, and shouting insults, which to be fair Raith always had. Vanstermen facing Gettlanders, as usual, such a wearisome pattern even he was tiring of it. Rakki and the old Gettlander with the face like a slapped arse, Hunnan, were facing each other in the midst, both puffed up like tomcats. Rakki had a pick in his hands, Hunnan a shovel, and from the looks of things they'd both set to swinging soon and not at the ground.

'Whoa!' roared Raith, charging over, and their heads snapped round. He slipped in between the two, saw Hunnan's jaw clenching, the shovel twitching back. Gods, the burning urge to butt him, punch him, seize hold of him and bite his face. Raith found he'd bared his teeth to do it. It was against his every hard-learned instinct, but he darted out a hand and grabbed the shovel instead. Then, before the old Gettlander had time to think, Raith hopped down into the ditch.

'Thought we were allies?' And he set to digging, showering Hunnan and Rakki with clods of soil and making them break apart. 'Am I the only one ain't scared of work?' Raith might be no thinker but he could see what was put in front of him, and if he'd learned one thing from Skara it was that you'll get more from warriors by shaming them than biting them.

So it proved. First Rakki jumped down into the ditch beside him with his pick. Then a few more Vanstermen followed. Not to be outdone, Hunnan spat into his palms, tore a shovel from the man beside him, clambered down and set to some furious work of his own. Wasn't long before the whole length of the ditch was busy with warriors competing to give Father Earth the sternest beating.

'When's the last time you broke a fight up?' muttered Rakki.

Raith grinned. 'I've broken a few up with my fist.'

'Don't forget who you are, brother.'

'I'm forgetting nothing,' grunted Raith, stepping back to let Rakki swing the pick at a clump of stubborn roots. He glanced towards the gate and saw Skara smiling, couldn't help smiling back. 'But every day finds you a new man, eh?'

Rakki shook his head. 'She's got you on a short leash, that girl.'

'Maybe,' said Raith. 'But I can think of worse leashes to be on.'

POWER

Sister Owd frowned into the night pot. 'This seems auspicious.'

'How is one turd more auspicious than another?' asked Skara.

'People lucky enough to produce auspicious turds always ask that, my queen. Is your blood coming regularly?'

'I understand once a month is traditional.'

'And is your womb minded to break with tradition?'

Skara gave Sister Owd the frostiest glare she could manage. 'My womb has always behaved entirely properly. You can rest easy. I've never so much as kissed a man. Mother Kyre made very sure of that.'

Owd delicately cleared her throat. 'I am sorry to pry, but your wellbeing is my responsibility, now. Your blood is worth more to Throvenland than gold.'

'Then Throvenland rejoice!' shouted Skara as she stepped from the bath. 'I'm bleeding regularly!'

Queen Laithlin's thrall gently rubbed her dry, took a bundle of twigs and flicked her with scented water blessed in the name of He Who Sprouts the Seed. He might stand among the small gods, but he loomed large indeed over girls of royal blood.

The minister frowned. Skara's minister, she supposed. Her servant, though it was hard not to think of her as a disapproving mistress. 'Are you eating, my queen?'

'What else would I do at mealtimes?' Skara did not add that what little she forced down she felt endlessly on the point of spewing back up. 'I've always been slight.' She snapped her fingers at the thrall to bring her hurrying with her dressing-gown. 'And I don't enjoy being examined like a slave at the flesh-dealer's.'

'Who does, my queen?' Sister Owd carefully averted her eyes. 'But I fear privacy is a luxury the powerful cannot afford.' Her mildness was, for some reason, more infuriating even than Mother Kyre's bullying used to be.

'No doubt you eat for both of us,' snapped Skara.

Sister Owd only smiled, soft face dimpling. 'I've always been solid, but the future of no nation rests upon my health. Luckily for all concerned. Bring the queen something.' She gestured to the thrall and the girl shrugged back her long braid and took up the tray with the morning food.

'No!' snarled Skara, stomach clenching at the slightest smell of it, snatching back her hand as if to dash the lot on the floor, 'take it away!'

The thrall flinched as if her anger was a raised whip and Skara felt an instant pang of guilt. Then she remembered Mother Kyre's words, after her grandfather sold Skara's nurse and she had cried for days. *Feelings for a slave are feelings wasted.* So she waved the girl impatiently away, just as she imagined Queen Laithlin might have. She was a queen now, after all.

Gods. She was a queen. Her stomach cramped again, sick tickled at the back of her raw throat and Skara gave a strangled cough, half burp, half growl of frustration. She bunched her fist as if to punch her own rebellious guts. How could she hope to bend kings to her will when her own stomach would not obey?

'Well, there is much to do before today's moot,' said Sister Owd, turning for the door. 'May I leave you for now, my queen?'

'You can't do so soon enough.'

The minister paused, and Skara saw her shoulders shift as she took a hard breath. Then she turned back, firmly folding her arms. 'You may speak to me here however you wish.' Sister Owd might have seemed soft as a peach at a first meeting, but Skara was beginning to remember that a peach holds a stubborn stone on which the unwary will break their teeth. 'But behaving in this manner ill befits a queen. Do it before Uthil and Gorm and you will undo all the progress you have made. Your position is not strong enough to show such weakness.'

Skara was clenching every muscle, fully prepared to explode with fury, when it came to her that Owd was right. She was acting the way she used to with Mother

Kyre. She was acting like a petulant child. Her grandfather, generous to all in wealth and in word, would have been less than impressed.

Skara closed her eyes and felt tears prickling at the lids, took a breath and let it sigh shuddering away. 'You're right,' she said. 'That was unworthy of a beggar, let alone a queen. I am sorry.'

Sister Owd slowly unfolded her arms. 'A queen need never be sorry, especially to her minister.'

'Let me at least be grateful, then. I know you did not ask for this, but you have been a staunch support so far. I always supposed that I would one day be a queen, and speak in halls with the great, and strike wise deals on behalf of my people . . . I just never dreamed it would be so soon, and with the stakes so high, and without my grandfather to help me.' She wiped her eyes on the back of her hand. 'Mother Kyre tried to prepare me for the burden of power but . . . I am finding it a weight one is never quite ready for.'

The minister blinked. 'Considering the circumstances, I think you bear it admirably.'

'I will try to bear it better.' Skara forced out a smile. 'If you promise to keep correcting me when I fall short.'

Sister Owd smiled back. 'It will be an honour, my queen. Truly.' Then she gave a stiff bow, and shut the door softly behind her. Skara glanced over at the thrall, and realized she did not even know the girl's name.

'I am sorry to you too,' she found she had muttered.

The thrall looked horrified, and Skara soon guessed why. If a slave is but a useful thing to her mistress, she is safe. If a slave becomes a person she can be favoured. She can even be loved, as Skara had once loved her nurse. But a person can also be blamed, envied, hated.

Safer to be a thing.

Skara snapped her fingers. 'Bring the comb.'

There was a thudding knock at the door, followed by Raith's rude growl. 'Father Yarvi's here. He wants to speak with you.'

'Urgently, Queen Skara,' came the minister's voice. 'On business that benefits us both.'

Skara set a hand on her belly in a futile effort to calm her frothing stomach. Father Yarvi had been kind enough, but there was something unnerving in his eye, as though he always knew just what she would say and already had the answer.

'The blood of Bail is in my veins,' she murmured to herself. 'The blood of Bail, the blood of Bail.' And she closed her bandaged fist until the cut burned. 'Show him in!'

Not even Mother Kyre could have found fault with Father Yarvi's behaviour. He came with his head respect-fully bowed, his staff of slotted and twisted elf-metal in his good hand and his withered one behind him in case the sight of it offended her. Raith slunk in after him with his forehead creased in that constant frown of his, white hair flattened against one side of his skull from sleeping in her doorway and his scarred hand propped on his axe-handle.

Skara had stopped wondering about kissing him. Now she found herself often occupied thinking about what they might do after the kissing . . . She jerked her eyes away, but they kept creeping back. After all, there was no harm in wondering, was there?

The Minister of Gettland gave a stately bow. 'My queen, I am honoured to be admitted to your presence.'

'We have a moot later. Can't we speak when I am dressed?' And she drew her gown tighter about herself.

Now he looked up. Cool as spring rain, his grey-blue eyes. 'You need not concern yourself there. I have sworn a Minister's Oath. I am not a man, in that sense.' And he glanced sideways at Raith.

His meaning was clear. Raith was, without doubt, a man in every sense. Skara felt his eyes on her from under his pale lashes, not caring in the least for what was proper. Barely even knowing the meaning of the word. The fitting thing for her to do was to order him out at once.

'You can both stay,' she said. With Raith and his axe lurking at Father Yarvi's shoulder her power was greater. Propriety was all-important to a princess, but to a queen power was more important still. And, perhaps, hidden deep down, there was some part of her that liked the way Raith looked at her. Liked that it was far from proper. 'Tell me what could be so urgent.'

If Gettland's young minister was surprised his smiling mask did not show a twitch of it. 'Battles are most often won by the side that comes first to the field, my queen,' he said.

Skara beckoned to her thrall and brought her hurrying forward with the comb and oil, letting Father Yarvi know he was not important enough to disrupt her morning routine. 'Am I a battlefield?'

'You are a valued and a vital ally on one. An ally whose support I sorely need.'

'As you needed my murdered grandfather's?' she snapped. Too harsh, too harsh, that showed weakness. She filed the edge from her voice. 'Mother Kyre thought you tricked King Fynn into an alliance.'

'I say I persuaded him, my queen.'

She raised an eyebrow at Yarvi in the mirror. 'Persuade me, then, if you can.'

His staff tapped gently against the floor as he came forward, so slowly and subtly he hardly seemed to move. 'Soon enough, the High King's army will be coming.'

'That is no deep-cunning, Father Yarvi.'

'But I know when and where.'

Skara caught her thrall's wrist before the comb reached her head and pushed it away, turning with her eyes narrowed.

'In six nights' time, he will try to bring his army across the straits from Yutmark at the narrowest point, just west of Yaletoft . . . of the ruins of Yaletoft, that is.'

Her breath caught at that. She remembered the city in flames. The fire lighting the night sky. The stink of smoke as her past life burned. No doubt he meant to put a spark to her fear, a spark to her anger. He succeeded.

Her voice had a keener edge than ever. 'How do you know?'

'It is a minister's place to know. Our alliance may be far outnumbered on land, but we have fine crews and fine ships and the best of the High King's sit captured in your harbour below. At sea we have the advantage. We must attack while they try to cross the straits.'

'With my six ships?' Skara turned back to the mirror, waved to the thrall to carry on, and the girl slipped her silver thrall-chain over one shoulder and stepped silently back with the comb.

'With your six ships, my queen . . .' Yarvi drifted a little closer. 'And your one vote.'

'I see.' Though in fact Skara had seen something of the kind the moment he was announced. Her title was smoke, her warriors six boats' worth of bandits, her lands no bigger than the walls of Bail's Point. Everything she had was borrowed – her thrall, her guard, her minister, her mirror, the very clothes she wore. And yet the vote was hers.

Father Yarvi let his voice drop to a warm whisper. The kind of whisper that urges you to lean closer, to be part of the secret. But Skara made sure she did not move, made sure she kept her thoughts close, made sure he had to come to her.

'Mother Scaer opposes everything I say because I say it. I fear Grom-gil-Gorm will be too cautious to seize this chance and we may not get another. But if *you* were to come forward with the strategy . . .'

'Huh,' grunted Skara. *Never make a hasty choice,* Mother Kyre used to tell her. *Even if you know your answer, to delay your answer shows your strength.* So she delayed, while Queen Laithlin's lent slave stepped carefully up onto a stool to gather Skara's hair, coil it and pin it with practised fingers.

'Circumstances have made you powerful, my queen.' Father Yarvi stepped closer still, and as his collar shifted Skara saw a scattering of faint scars up his neck. 'And you have taken to it like a hawk to flying. Can I count on your support?'

She looked at herself in the mirror. Father Peace, who was that woman with the sharp eyes, so gaunt, and proud, and flinty hard? A hawk indeed. Surely it could not be her, whose stomach boiled over with doubts?

Seem powerful and you are powerful, Mother Kyre used to say.

She pushed her shoulders back as the thrall fixed her earring, flaring her nostrils as she took a hard breath. She gave the briefest nod. 'This time.'

Yarvi smiled as he bowed. 'You are as wise as you are beautiful, my queen.'

Raith turned back into the room after he pushed the door shut. 'I don't trust that bastard.' It was so improper Skara could not help a snort of laughter. She had never known anyone who let as little slip as Father Yarvi, nor anyone who kept as little hidden as Raith. His every thought was plainly written on that blunt, scarred, handsome face.

'Why?' she asked, 'because he judges me wise and beautiful?'

Raith's eyes were still on her. 'Just 'cause a man tells two truths doesn't mean he's got no lies in him.'

So Raith found her wise and beautiful too. That pleased her a great deal, but it would not do to show it. 'Father Yarvi gives us a chance to strike at the High King,' she said. 'I do not mean to miss it.'

'You do trust him, then?'

'You do not have to trust a man to make use of him. My doorkeeper, after all, used to fill cups for Grom-gil-Gorm.'

Raith frowned harder than ever as he fiddled at that notch in his ear. 'You might be best not trusting anyone.'

'Good advice.' Skara met his eye in the mirror. 'You can leave, now.' And she snapped her fingers at the thrall to bring her clothes.

THE OPINIONS OF THE PIGS

It was two years since Koll visited Roystock, and the place had sprouted upwards and outwards from its boggy island like a tumour.

Wooden tentacles had shot across the water on rickety stilts, crooked piers with houses clinging to their sides like stubborn barnacles, sheds built on shacks at every angle but straight, a rotting forest of warped supports below and a hundred chimneys puffing a pall of smoke above. Little clumps of hovels had been flung out like spatters from spew, catching on every hump dry enough to hold a pile among the marshes at the wide mouth of the Divine.

Never in his life had Koll seen so much appalling carpentry gathered in one place.

'It's grown,' he said, wrinkling his nose. 'I guess that's progress.'

Thorn pinched hers closed entirely. 'The smell's progressed some, that's sure.' The heady mix of ancient dung and salt decay with an acrid edge of fish-smoking, cloth-dying and leather-tanning made the breath snag at the back of Koll's throat.

Queen Laithlin was not a woman to be put off business by an odour, however. 'The headmen of Roystock have grown fat on the trade coming up the Divine,' she said. 'Their city has bloated up with them.'

'Varoslaf has come for his mouthful of the meat.' Koll frowned towards the wharves as they grew closer. 'And he's brought a lot of ships.'

Thorn's eyes were narrowed to slits as she scanned across those long, lean, vessels. 'I count thirteen.'

'More than just a show of strength,' murmured Queen Laithlin. 'I think the Prince of Kalyiv means to stay.'

Mother Sun was warm outside, but in the hall there was a chill.

Prince Varoslaf sat at the head of a long table, so polished one could see another, blurry, Prince Varoslaf reflected in its top. One was more than enough to worry Koll.

He was not a large man, wore no weapon, had not a hair on his head, his jaw, even his brows. There was no wrath, no scorn, no brooding threat on his face, only a stony blankness somehow more troubling than any snarl. Behind him was gathered a crescent of fierce warriors, another of kneeling slaves with heavy thrall-chains dangling. Beside him stood a spear-thin servant, coins twinkling from a scarf across her forehead.

The nine headmen of Roystock sat on one side of the table between Varoslaf and Laithlin, boasting their best silks and richest jewels but with their nervousness written plainly on their faces. Like the crew of a rudderless ship, drifting in the northern ice, hoping they wouldn't be crushed between two mighty bergs. Koll had a feeling hope would get them nowhere in this company.

'Queen Laithlin, Jewel of the North.' Varoslaf's voice was as dry and whispery as the rustling of autumn leaves. 'I feel favoured by the gods to once again bask in the radiance of your presence.'

'Great prince,' answered Laithlin, her own entourage crowding with heads bowed into the hall behind her, 'the whole Shattered Sea trembles at your coming. I congratulate you on your famous victory over the Horse People.'

'If one can call it a victory over the flies every time the horse swishes his tail. The flies always return.'

'I have brought gifts for you.' Two of Laithlin's thralls, twins with braids so long they wore them wound around one arm, shuffled forward with boxes of inlaid wood, imported at daunting expense from far-off Catalia.

But the prince held up his hand, and Koll saw the deep groove across his calloused fingers left by constant prac-tice with a bow. 'As I have gifts for you. There will be time for gifts later. Let us first discuss the matter.'

The Golden Queen raised one golden brow. 'Which is?'

'The great Divine, and the money that flows along it, and how we should share it between us.'

Laithlin sent her thralls scuttling back with a waft of her finger. 'Do we not already have agreements that have profited us both?'

'Put plainly, I would like them to profit me more,' said Varoslaf. 'My minister has devised many ways of doing so.'

There was a pause. 'You have a minister, great prince?' asked Koll.

Varoslaf turned his chill gaze upon Koll and he could almost feel his balls retreating into the warmth of his stomach. 'The rulers of the Shattered Sea seem to find them indispensable. I thought I would buy one of my own.'

He made the slightest jerk of his bald head and one of the slaves stood, and pushed back her hood, and Koll heard Thorn give a low growl.

Apart from a thin braid above one ear the woman's hair had been clipped to yellow fuzz. She wore a thrall-ring of silver wire around her long, lean neck and another around her wrist, a fine chain between them not quite long enough for comfort. She had been tattooed on one cheek with a prancing horse, the prince's mark of ownership, but it seemed her hatred was still at liberty. Her pink-rimmed eyes, sunken in bruised sockets, blazed with it as she glared across the hall.

'Gods,' Koll murmured under his breath, 'this is ill

luck.' He knew that face. Isriun, daughter to King Uthil's treacherous brother Odem, who once had been Father Yarvi's betrothed, then Minister of Vansterland, but had taken too high a hand with the Breaker of Swords and been sold as a slave.

'Odem's brat dogs me once again,' hissed Queen Laithlin.

The foremost of the headmen, a sharp-eyed old merchant festooned with silver chains, cleared his throat. 'Most feared great prince.' His voice wobbled only a little as Varoslaf's eyes slid towards him. 'And most admired Queen Laithlin, these matters concern us all. If I may—'

'It is traditional for the farmer and the butcher to divide the meat without seeking the opinions of the pigs,' said Varoslaf.

For a moment the silence was absolute, then the Prince of Kalyiv's slender servant leaned slowly towards the headmen and gave a thunderous pig's oink. The nearest recoiled. Several flinched. All paled. They must have closed many fine deals at that finely polished table, but it was awfully plain they would be turning no profits today.

'What is it you want, great prince?' asked Laithlin.

Isriun leaned down to whisper in Varoslaf's ear, her braid brushing gently against his shoulder, her bright eyes flickering to Laithlin and back.

Her master's face remained an unknowable mask. 'Only what is fair.'

'There is always a way,' said the queen, dryly. 'We could

perhaps offer you an extra tenth part of a tenth part of every cargo . . ?

Isriun leaned down again, whispering, whispering, chewed-short fingernails fussing at the tattoo on her cheek.

'Four tenths of a tenth part,' droned Varoslaf.

'Four parts is as far from fair as Roystock is from Kalyiv.'

This time Isriun didn't bother to speak through her master, but simply snapped the rejoinder to Laithlin's face. 'The battlefield is not fair.'

The queen narrowed her eyes. 'So you came for a battle?'

'We are ready for one,' said Isriun, lip wrinkled with contempt.

As long as she was whispering poison in the prince's ear they would travel a stony path indeed. Koll remembered the skinned men swinging on the docks of Kalyiv, and swallowed. Varoslaf was not a man to be intimidated, nor tricked into a rage, nor swayed by flattery or bluster or jokes. Here was a man no man dared challenge. A man whose power was built on fear.

Laithlin and Isriun had fallen into a duel as savage and skilful as any in the training square. They slashed mercilessly at each other with portions and prices, stabbed with tithes and parried with fractions while Varoslaf sat back in his chair, his hairless face a mask.

Koll saw only one chance, and he put his fingers to the weights under his shirt. He thought of his mother, screaming at him to come down from the mast. No doubt you will be safer on the deck. But if you wish to change the world, you must take a risk or two.

'Oh, great prince!' He was surprised to find his voice as bright and easy as it might have been in Rin's forge. 'Perhaps you should retire to bed and leave your minister to make the arrangements.'

Maybe cowards handle great terrors better than heroes, for they face fear every day. Koll forced his feet forward, forced his face into a smile, flapped his hands about with carefree disrespect.

'I see your decisions are all made by King Uthil's niece. A snake that turned against her own family. A snake that still drips poison even collared and chained. Why waste all our time pretending otherwise? After all,' and Koll put one hand on his chest, 'it is traditional for the farmer,' and he held that hand out towards Isriun, 'and the butcher . . . to divide the meat without seeking the opinions . . .' And now he held both hands out towards Queen Laithlin and Prince Varoslaf. 'Of the pigs.'

There was a disbelieving silence. Then Varoslaf's guards bristled. One muttered a curse in the tongue of the Horse People. Another stepped forward, reaching for his curved sword. Then there was a sharp smack as Thorn hit Koll backhanded across the face.

He would've liked to say he went down on purpose, but in truth it was like being hit with a hammer. He struggled up onto one elbow, his face burning and his head reeling, to see Queen Laithlin glaring down.

'I will have you flogged for that.'

Varoslaf's grooved hand was held up lazily to hold his

warriors back, his gaze so cold Koll thought he could feel the piss freezing in his bladder. It was only a few days ago he'd been telling himself he was nowhere near as clever as he supposed. Some men never learn.

Isriun leaned towards Varoslaf's ear. 'You must demand his skin for that—'

It was cut off in a squawk as he dragged her down by her chain. 'Never tell me what I must do.' And he flung Isriun stumbling towards the door, while Thorn caught Koll under the arm with fearsome strength and dragged him cringing after.

'Nicely done,' she whispered. 'Didn't hurt you, did I?'

'You hit like a girl,' he squeaked, as she flung him bodily out into the anteroom and slammed the doors closed.

'You must be pleased,' snarled Isriun.

Koll slowly sat up, touched his fingertips to his lip and brought them away red. 'I'd be more pleased without the bloody mouth.'

'You can laugh!' Isriun bared her teeth, closer to a grimace of agony than a smile. 'The gods know I'd laugh, in your place. I was daughter to a king! I was a minister, at the side of Grandmother Wexen! Now . . .' She jerked her wrist so her chain snapped taut and the collar bit into her neck, but however she squirmed she couldn't quite get her arm straight. 'I'd laugh myself, in your place!'

Koll shook his head as he clambered up. 'Not me. I know what it is to be a slave.' He remembered the cellar where he and his mother had been kept. The darkness of it. The smell of it. He remembered the feeling of the collar, the feeling when Father Yarvi ordered it struck off. Not things easily forgotten. 'I'm sorry. It's worth nothing, but I'm sorry.'

The tattooed horse on Isriun's face shifted as she ground her teeth. 'I only did what I had to. Stood with those who stood with me. I tried to do my duty. I tried to keep my word.'

'I know.' Koll winced at the floor, feeling a long way from the best man he could be. 'But I have to do the same.'

It was some time later the doors opened and Queen Laithlin swept into the anteroom.

'Did you reach an agreement, my queen?' asked Koll.

'Once the poison was drawn from the wound. That was subtle thinking on your part. You will make a fine minister, I think.'

Koll felt such a warm glow at that he could hardly hide his smile. The praise of the powerful was an intoxicating draught indeed. He bowed low. 'You are too kind.'

'Needless to say, if you ever do such a thing again, I really will have you flogged.'

Koll bowed lower yet. 'You are far too kind.'

'There was only one point on which I and the prince could not agree.'

Thorn grinned over at Isriun. 'Your price.'

'Mine?' she muttered, eyes going wide.

'I offered a fine red jewel for you, and the girl who oils my hair.' Laithlin shrugged. 'But Varoslaf wanted a hundred pieces of silver too.'

Isriun's face twitched, caught between fear and defiance. 'Did you pay?'

'I could buy a good ship with that money, sail and all. Why pay it just to see some thrall drowned in the sewer? Your master is waiting, and not in the best of moods.'

'I'll be revenged on you!' snarled Isriun. 'On you and your crippled son! I've sworn it!'

Laithlin smiled then, a smile as cold as the utmost north where the snows never melt, and Koll wondered whether she or Varoslaf was the more ruthless. 'Enemies are the price of success, slave. I have heard a thousand such empty oaths. I still sleep soundly.' She snapped her fingers. 'Come, Koll.'

He took one last look back at Isriun, staring at the open door, winding the chain about her hand so tight the links dug into her fingers and turned them white. But Father Yarvi always said a good minister faces the facts, and saves what he can. Koll hurried after Laithlin.

'What did you give him, my queen?' he asked, as they walked down a curving hallway, Mother Sea stirring beyond the narrow windows.

'Varoslaf is no fool and that snake Isriun had counselled him well. He knows we are weak. He wants to extend his power north, up the Divine to the shores of the Shattered Sea.' She let her voice fall soft. 'I had to give him Roystock.'

Koll swallowed. None of this felt very much like Brand's idea of standing in the light. 'A princely gift. But is it ours to give?'

'It is Varoslaf's to take,' said Laithlin, 'if neither we nor the High King stop him.'

'We and the High King are a little busy with each other,' growled Thorn.

'The wise man fights no wars at all, but only a fool fights more than one at once.'

Thorn nodded to the warriors standing guard at the queen's chambers and pushed the door wide. 'I have a feeling Varoslaf will not stop at Roystock.'

As he stepped over the threshold Koll thought of the prince's dead stare and gave a shudder. 'I have a feeling Varoslaf would not stop at the edge of the world.'

'Get back!' snapped Thorn, barging the queen against the wall and whipping out her axe so quickly it nearly took off one of Koll's eyebrows.

In the shadows at the far end of the room, cross-legged upon a table, a figure sat, swathed in a cloak of rags with the hood drawn down. Koll nearly dropped his dagger on his foot his heart was beating so hard. Nimble fingers tend to fail you when Death's breath chills your neck.

Thorn, fortunately, was harder to rattle. 'Speak now,' she snarled, already in a fighting crouch between the queen and their visitor. 'Or I kill you.'

'Would you strike me with my own axe, Thorn Bathu?' The hood shifted, the gleam of an eye inside. 'You have grown, Koll. I remember you dangling from the mast-head of the *South Wind* while your mother screamed for you to come down. I remember you begging me to show you magic.'

Thorn's axe slowly drifted down. 'Skifr?'

'You could simply have knocked,' said Laithlin, guiding Thorn away and smoothing her dress back to its usual perfection.

'Knocking does not guarantee an audience, Golden Queen. And I have come a long road from the land of the Alyuks, up the Denied and Divine in the company of Prince Varoslaf. Not that he knew it.' Skifr eased her hood back and Koll gave a ragged gasp. Even in the shadows he could see the left side of her face was streaked with mottled burns, half her eyebrow was missing and her cropped grey hair scattered with bald spots.

'What happened?' said Thorn.

Skifr smiled. Or one half of her face did. The other creased and twisted like old leather. 'Grandmother Wexen sent men south, my dove. To punish me for stealing relics from the forbidden ruin of Strokom.' She glanced towards the elf-bangle on Thorn's wrist as it pulsed a bright blue-white. 'They burned my house. They killed my son and his wife. They killed my son's sons. But they found I am not easily killed.'

'Grandmother Wexen has a long memory for scores,' murmured Laithlin.

'She will discover she is not the only one.' Skifr tipped back her face, mottled burns seeming to glisten. 'Grandmother Wexen brought Death to me. It is only good manners that I return the favour. I have read the portents. I have watched the birds across the sky. I have deciphered the ripples in the water and you will take me back across the Shattered Sea to Thorlby. Do you still wish to see magic, Koll?'

'No?' But it often seemed people loved to ask him questions but hadn't much interest in his answers.

'I must speak to Father Yarvi.' Skifr curled back her lips to show her teeth and barked the words. 'Then I will go to *war*!'

ASHES

Uthil's fleet made ready to spit in the High King's face.

A red-haired Throvenlander stood tall on a rock, bellowing verses from the Lay of Ashenleer with little tune but lots of vigour, that old fighter's favourite where the queen's closest prepare to die gloriously in battle. All around men mouthed along with the often-mouthed words as they gave blades final licks with the whetstone, plucked at bowstrings and hauled buckles tight.

You'd think fighting men would prefer songs about warriors who lived gloriously through a battle to die old and fat and rich, but there's fighting men for you, not much they do makes sense, once you think on it. One reason Raith tried never to think if he could avoid it.

They'd stripped any useless weight from the ships, supplies left heaped on the shore to make space for more fighters. Some men had chosen to wear mail, for fear of blade or arrow. Some to leave it, for fear of being dragged down into Mother Sea's cold embrace. A bleak choice that, a madman's gamble with everything you'll ever have. But war's made of such choices.

Every man dug up his own courage his own way. They forced out under-funny jokes and over-ready laughter, or made bets on who'd make the most corpses, or set out how their goods should be shared if they went through the Last Door before nightfall. Some clutched at holy signs and women's favours, hugged each other, slapped each other, roared defiance and brotherhood in one another's faces. Others stood silent, staring out at glimmering Mother Sea where their dooms would soon be written.

Raith was ready. He'd been ready for hours. For days. Ever since they held the moot and Skara voted along with Uthil to fight.

So he turned his back on the men, frowning towards the charred ruins of the town above the beach and drawing in deep the smell of salt and smoke. Funny, how you never enjoy your breaths until you feel your last one coming.

'It was called Valso.'

'Eh?' asked Raith, looking round.

'The town.' Blue Jenner combed his beard over to the left with his fingers, then the right, then back. 'There was a good market here. Lambs in the spring. Slaves in the autumn. Sleepy most of the time, but it got rowdy when the men came back from raiding. Spent a few wild nights at a hall here.' He nodded towards a teetering chimney stack still standing among a mess of scorched beams. 'Think that might've been it. Sung some songs there with men mostly dead now.'

'Got a fine voice, do you?'

Jenner snorted. 'When I'm drunk I think I do.'

'Reckon there'll be no songs sung there now.' Raith wondered how many families had made their homes in those burned-out houses. In the ones he'd seen all down the coast of Throvenland as they'd sailed west. Farm after farm, village after village, town after town, turned to ghosts and ashes.

Raith worked the fingers of his left hand, feeling that old ache through the knuckles. The gods knew, he'd set some fires himself. He'd stared in awed joy as the flames leapt up into the night and made him feel powerful as a god. He'd boasted of it, puffed himself up with Gorm's approval. The ashes were one of the many things he chose not to think about. The ashes, and the folk who'd lost everything, and the folk dead and burned. You can't choose your dreams, though. They say the gods send you the ones you deserve.

'Bright Yilling surely loves to burn,' said Jenner.

'What can you expect?' grunted Raith. 'Worships Death, doesn't he?'

'It'd be a good thing to send him to meet her.'

'This is a war. Best leave good out of it.'

'You usually do.'

He grinned at the voice, so like his own, and turned to see his brother swaggering through the *Black Dog*'s crew. 'If it ain't the great Rakki, shield-bearer to Grom-gil-Gorm. Who's the king got carrying his sword now?'

Rakki had that crooked little grin Raith could never quite make, however much alike their faces might be. 'He finally found a man won't trip over his own feet in the charge.'

'Not you, then?'

Rakki snorted. 'You should leave the jokes to funnier men.'

'You should leave the fighting to harder ones.' Raith caught him, half-hug, half-grapple, and pulled him close. He'd always been the stronger. 'Don't let Gorm trample you, eh, brother? All my hopes have got you in 'em.'

'Don't let Uthil drown you,' said Rakki, twisting free. 'I brought you something.' And he held out a heel of reddish bread. 'Since these godless Throvenlanders don't eat the last loaf.'

'You know I don't believe too much in luck,' said Raith, taking a chew and tasting the blood in it.

'But I do,' said Rakki, starting to back off. 'I'll see you after we're done, and you can marvel at my plunder!'

'I'll marvel if you get any, skulking in last!' And Raith flung the rest of the bread at him, scattering crumbs.

'It's the skulkers who do best, brother!' called Rakki as he dodged it. 'Folk love to sing about heroes but they hate standing next to 'em!' And he was away among the crews, off to fight in battle beside the Breaker of Swords. To fight with Soryorn and the rest of Gorm's closest, men Raith had looked up to half his life and that the better half, and he clenched his fists, wishing he could follow his brother. Wishing he could watch over him. He'd always been the strong one, after all.

'Do you miss him?'

You'd have thought time would've made him more comfortable around her, but the sight of Skara's sharp-boned face still knocked all thought from Raith's head. She watched Rakki thread his way back through the warriors. 'You must have spent your whole lives together.'

'Aye. I'm sick of the sight of him.'

Skara looked less than convinced. She'd a knack for guessing what was going on in his head. Maybe his head wasn't much of a puzzle. 'If we win today, perhaps Father Peace can have his time.'

'Aye.' Though Mother War usually had other ideas.

'Then you can join your brother, and fill Gorm's cup again.'

'Aye.' Though the prospect gave Raith less joy than it used to. Being Queen Skara's dog might be slim on honour, but she was an awful lot prettier than the Breaker of Swords. And there was something to be said for not having to prove himself the hardest bastard going every moment. And for not being cuffed around the head when he didn't manage it.

The jewels in Skara's earring twinkled with the evening sun as she turned to Blue Jenner. 'How much longer do we wait?'

'Not long now, my queen. The High King has too many men and too few ships.' He nodded towards the headland, a black outline with the shifting water glimmering around its foot. 'They're dropping them bit by bit on the beach beyond that spur. When Gorm judges the time right, he'll give a blast on his horn and crush the ones who've landed. We'll already be rowing out, hoping to catch the ships fully loaded in the straits. That's Uthil's plan, anyway.'

'Or Father Yarvi's,' muttered Skara, frowning out to sea. 'It sounds simple enough.'

'Saying it's always simpler than doing it, sadly.'

'Father Yarvi has a new weapon,' said Sister Owd. 'A gift from the Empress of the South.'

'Father Yarvi always has something—' Skara flinched, touched one hand to her cheek and her fingers came away red.

A prayer-weaver was threading among the warriors with the blood of a sacrifice to Mother War, wailing out blessings in a broken voice, dipping his red fingers in the bowl and flicking weaponluck over the men.

'That's good fortune for the battle,' said Raith.

'I won't be there.' Skara stared out at the ruins of Valso, her mouth a flat, angry line. 'I wish I could swing a sword.'

'I'll swing your sword.' And before he really knew what he was doing Raith had knelt on the rocks and offered his axe up across both palms, like Hordru the Chosen Shield did in the song.

Skara looked down with one brow lifted. 'That's an axe.'

'Swords are for clever men and pretty men.'

'One of two isn't bad.' She had her hair bound in a thick, dark braid and she flicked it back over her shoulder and, like Ashenleer did in the song, leaned down with her eyes on his and kissed the blade. Raith couldn't have got a warmer tingle if she'd kissed him on the mouth. All foolishness, but men can be forgiven a little foolishness when the Last Door yawns wide before them.

'If you see Death on the water,' she said. 'Try to give her room.'

'A warrior's place is at Death's side,' said Raith as he stood. 'So he can introduce her to his enemies.'

Down, then, towards Mother Sea, the coming sunset glittering on the waves. Down towards the hundred ships shifting with the swell, their pack of prow-beasts silently snarling, hissing, screeching. Down, among a host of jostling brothers, only their skill and courage and fury standing between them and the Last Door, a tide of men washing out to meet the tide of water washing in.

Raith felt that heady brew of fear and excitement as he found his place near the prow, always among the first into the fight, the battle-joy already niggling at his throat.

'Wish you were beside the Breaker of Swords?' asked Jenner.

'No,' said Raith, and he meant it. 'A wise man once told me war's a matter of making the best of what you're given. No warrior more fearsome than the Breaker of Swords with his feet on Father Earth.' He grinned at Jenner. 'But you're an old bastard who knows his way around a boat, I reckon.'

'I can tell one end from the other.' Blue Jenner slapped

him on the shoulder. 'Glad to have you on the crew, boy.'

'I'll try not to disappoint you, old man.' Raith had meant it to drip scorn, the sort of manly jibe he'd have jabbed his brother with, but the words came out plain. Even a little cracked.

Jenner smiled, leathery face all creasing up. 'You won't. The king speaks.'

Uthil had climbed onto the steering platform of his ship, one arm cradling his sword, one boot on the curving top rail, one hand gripping the stern below its iron-forged prow-beast of a snarling wolf. He had no mail, no shield, no helm, the King's Circle glinting in his grey hair. He trusted in his skill and his weaponluck, and his scorn for Death made him feared by his enemies, and admired by his followers, and that was worth more than armour to a leader.

'Good friends!' he called out in a grinding voice, stilling the nervous muttering on the boats. 'Bold brothers! Warriors of Gettland and Throvenland! You have waited long enough. Today we give Mother War her due. Today will be a red day, a blood day, a day for the crows. Today we fight!'

Raith gave a growl in his throat, and all about him other men did the same.

'This is a day the ministers will write of in their high books,' called Uthil, 'and the skalds will sing of about the firepits. A day you will tell your grandchildren's children of and swell with pride at your part in it. We are the sword that will cut away Bright Yilling's smile, the hand that will slap Grandmother Wexen's face. Grom-gil-Gorm and his Vanstermen will crush the High King's men against unyielding Father Earth. We will drive them into the cold arms of Mother Sea.'

The king stood taller, the grey hair flicking about his scarred face, his fever-bright eyes. 'Death waits for us all, my brothers. Will you skulk past her through the Last Door? Or will you face her with your heads high and your swords drawn?'

'Swords drawn! Swords drawn!' And all across the water blades hissed eagerly from their scabbards.

Uthil grimly nodded. 'I am no minister. I have no more words.' He took the sword from the crook of his arm and thrust it towards the sky. 'My blade shall speak for me! Steel is the answer!'

A cheer went up, men hammering their oars with their fists, blunting carefully-sharpened weapons on their shield-rims, holding blades high to make a glittering forest over every ship and Raith shouted louder than anyone.

'Didn't think to hear you cheering for the King of Gettland,' murmured Jenner.

Raith cleared his sore throat. 'Aye, well. The worst enemies make the best allies.'

'Ha. You're learning, boy.'

A long quiet stretched out. The small sounds came thunderous. The gentle creaking of wood under Raith's boots and the slow breakers washing up the beach. The hissing of skin as Blue Jenner rubbed his calloused palms together and the mutter of a final prayer to Mother War.

The rattling of oars in their sockets and the croaking of a single gull as it curved low over the ships and away to the south.

'A good omen,' said King Uthil, then brought his sword chopping down.

'Heave!' roared Jenner.

And the men set to their oars, blood hot with fear and hate and the hunger for plunder, the thirst for glory. Like a hound off the leash the *Black Dog* sped out to sea, ahead of Uthil's grey-sailed ship, spray flying from the high prow and the salt wind rushing in Raith's hair. Wood groaned and water thundered against the ship's flanks, and over the noise he heard the bellowing of other helmsmen as they urged their crews to be the first into battle.

This was what he was made for. And Raith tipped back his head and gave a wolf's howl at the joy of it.

WATCHING

Skara's heart was thudding in her mouth as she caught a tree-root and dragged herself up towards the crest. Hardly the most regal of behaviour, as Sister Owd had been keen to point out, but Skara would not simply sit on the beach chewing her nails while the future of Throvenland was decided.

She might not be able to fight in the battle. She could at least watch it.

The ground was levelling out now and she crept upward, bent low. The ragged coast of Yutmark came into view to the south. The faint hills, then the grey beaches, then the sparkling water of the straits themselves and, finally, halfway across, ships.

'The High King's fleet,' whispered Sister Owd, her face even more than usually peach-like from the climb.

Dozens of ships, oars dipping. Some low and sleek and built for battle, some fat-bellied traders, no doubt crammed with warriors sent north by Grandmother Wexen. Warriors fixed on sweeping their alliance aside and crushing Skara's little pocket of Throvenland as a callous boy might crush a beetle.

The anger surged up hot and she clenched her fists, took the last few steps to the summit of the headland and stood between Father Yarvi and Mother Scaer, gazing westward, a long beach stretching away towards sinking Mother Sun.

'Gods,' she breathed.

The shingle crawled with men like ants seething from a broken nest, their shields painted dots, steel flashing and winking, coloured banners flapping in the wind to mark where crews should gather. Those of the High King's warriors who had already landed. Two full loads of those transports, maybe three. Hundreds of them. Thousands. It hardly seemed real.

'So many,' she whispered.

'The more we allow across,' said Mother Scaer, 'the more Grom-gil-Gorm will catch on the beach, the more we *kill*.'

The last word came harsh as a stabbing dagger and Skara felt a surge of nerves, clutching at one hand with the other. 'Do you think . . .' Her voice faded to a croak as she made herself speak the name. 'Bright Yilling is down there?' She saw that calm, soft face again, heard that high, soft voice, felt an echo of the terror of that night and was furious at her own cowardice. She was a queen, damn it. A queen cannot fear.

Father Yarvi looked across at her. 'Any true hero leads from the front.'

'He's no hero.'

'Every hero is someone's villain.'

'Hero or villain,' said Mother Scaer, her blue, blue eyes fixed on those men below, 'he has not made his warriors ready.'

She was right. They had formed a shield-wall in the dunes above the beach, facing inland towards the sullen forest, a high pole topped with the seven-rayed sun of the One God in their centre, but even Skara, whose experience of battle went little further than watching the boys in the training square behind her grandfather's hall, could tell it was an ill-made line, crooked and full of gaps.

'Grandmother Wexen has gathered men from many places,' said Father Yarvi. 'They are not used to fighting together. They do not even speak one tongue.'

King Uthil's fleet had rounded the headland, an arrow-shaped mass of ships, sea-birds circling above the white-frothed wake curving back towards the blackened ruins of Valso. The High King's fleet must have sighted them, some turning towards the threat, others away, others ploughing on towards the beach, oars tangling and boats clashing in the confusion.

'Surprise is on our side,' said Sister Owd, having finally got her breath back. 'Surprise is half the battle.'

Skara frowned sideways. 'How many battles have you fought in?'

'I have faith in our alliance, my queen,' said the minister, folding her arms. 'I have faith in the Breaker of Swords, and in King Uthil, and in Blue Jenner.'

'And Raith,' Skara found she had added. She had not even realized she had faith in him, let alone that she would ever say so.

Sister Owd raised one brow. 'Him somewhat less.'

A long, low horn blast throbbed out, so deep it seemed to make Skara's guts tremble.

Mother Scaer stretched up tall. 'The Breaker of Swords comes to the feast!'

All at once men spilled from the trees, surging onto the dunes above the beach. Skara supposed they were running at full tilt but they seemed to move slowly as honey in winter.

She found she had reached out to clutch at Sister Owd's shoulder with her bandaged hand. She had not felt so scared since the night the Forest burned, but now with the fear there was an almost unbearable thrill. Her fate, the fate of Throvenland, the fate of the alliance, the fate of the Shattered Sea itself all balanced on a sword's edge. She could hardly stand to watch, could not bear to look away.

A warrior had rushed out from the High King's men, was waving his arms frantically, trying to ready the shield-wall to meet the charge. Skara could hear his cracked screams, faint, faint on the wind, but it was too late.

The Breaker of Swords was upon them. She saw his black banner flying, steel glittering beneath it like the spray at the head of a wave.

'Your death comes,' she whispered.

Her face hurt she was grimacing so hard, her chest burned she was gasping in the air so fast. She sent up a prayer to Mother War, a cold and vicious prayer that these invaders might be driven from her land and into the sea. That she might spit on Bright Yilling's carcass before Mother Sun set, and so win her courage back from him.

It seemed her prayers were answered before her eyes.

In a black tide the Vanstermen swept down the grassy dunes, their war-cries echoing high and strange on the wind, and like a wall of sand before a great wave the centre of the High King's crooked shield-wall crumbled. She felt Sister Owd's hand on top of hers and gripped it tight.

Gorm's men crashed into the faltering line and Mother War spread her wings over the coast of Throvenland and smiled upon the slaughter. Her voice was a storm of metal. A clamour like a thousand smithies and a hundred slaughter-yards. Sometimes by some unknown chance the wind would waft some word, or phrase, or cry full-formed to Skara's ear, of fury or pain or begging fear, and make her startle as if it was spoken at her shoulder.

Father Yarvi stepped forward, knuckles white about his elf-metal staff and his eager eyes fixed on the beach. 'Yes,' he hissed. 'Yes!'

Now the right wing of the High King's men slowly

buckled and in an instant gave, men fleeing down the shingle, flinging their weapons away. But there was nowhere to run but into the arms of Mother Sea, and that was a comfortless embrace indeed.

On the higher dunes a few knots of the High King's warriors still held, striving to make a stand worth singing of, but they were islands in a flood. And Skara saw the ruin panic can work on a great army, and learned how a battle can turn on a single moment, and watched the gilded symbol of the One God topple and be crushed beneath the heels of Mother War's faithful.

In the wake of Gorm's charge the beach was left dotted with black shapes, like driftwood after a tempest. Broken shields, broken weapons. Broken men. Skara's wide eyes darted over the wreckage, trying to reckon the number of the dead, and she could hardly swallow for the sudden tightness in her throat.

'I did this,' she whispered. 'My words. My vote.'

Sister Owd gave her hand a reassuring squeeze. 'And you did right, my queen. Lives spared here would have cost lives later. This was the greater good.'

'The lesser evil,' muttered Skara, remembering Mother Kyre's lessons, but her borrowed minister had misunderstood. It was not guilt she felt, but awe at her own power. She felt like a queen at last.

'The pyre-builders will be busy tonight,' said Father Yarvi.

'And, in due course, the slave-markets of Vulsgard too.' For once Mother Scaer had a tone of grudging approval. 'So far, all proceeds according to your design.'

Father Yarvi stared out to sea, gaunt face squirming as he worked his jaw. 'So far.'

The battle on Father Earth was well won, but in the straits the spearhead of King Uthil's fleet was only now reaching the blunt tangle of the High King's ships. At the very front Skara saw a blue sail straining with the wind, and she tasted blood as she bit into the quick beneath her thumbnail.

THE KILLER

'Don't do nothing foolish, eh?' said Blue Jenner. Raith was thinking of the training square in Vulsgard. Dropping a lad twice his size he'd hit him so hard and so fast. Looking at him huddled on the ground. The shadow of his boot across the lad's bloody face. He remembered Grom-gil-Gorm's great hand falling on his shoulder.

What are you waiting for?

He fixed his eyes on the High King's fleet, a muddle of stretched rope and heaved oar, wind-whipped sailcloth and straining men. 'The only foolish thing in a fight is holding back,' he growled, and wedged that battle-scarred joiner's peg in his mouth, his teeth fitting the dents as neatly as the two halves of a broken bowl fit together.

The *Black Dog*'s swift-hauled keel plunged through a

wave and sent spray fountaining to spatter down on the grimacing oarsmen and the crouching warriors between them.

Raith glanced back towards land, coast bobbing as Mother Sea lifted the *Black Dog* and dropped her, wondered if Skara was watching, thought of her eyes, those big green eyes that seemed to swallow him. Then he thought of Rakki, alone in the fight with no one to watch his back and he gripped the handle of his shield so tight his battered knuckles burned.

The High King's ships were rushing up fast, he could see the painted shields: grey gate, boar's head, four swords in a square. He could see the straining faces of the oarsmen at the rails. He could see bows full-drawn as a boat tipped, and arrows came flickering across the water.

Raith dropped behind his shield, felt a shaft click against its face and spin away over his shoulder. Another lodged in the rail beside him. The breath was getting hot in his throat and he shifted the peg with his tongue and bit down harder.

He heard bowstrings behind him, saw shafts looping the other way, caught by the wind, flitting down among the High King's ships. He heard helmsmen of King Uthil's fleet roaring for more speed. He heard the clashing of weapons on shields and rails and oars as men gathered their courage, making ready to kill, to die, and Raith heaved in another breath and did the same, knocking his axe tap, tap, tap against the rail in time to his pounding heart.

'Pull to the left!' roared Blue Jenner, picking out his

target. Had to be a Lowlander ship – no prow-beast, just a carved whirl. Its crew were struggling to come about to meet the *Black Dog* prow to prow, helmsman straining desperate at his steering oar, but the wind was against him.

'Heart of iron!' came a roar. 'Head of iron! Hand of iron!'

'Your death comes!' someone screamed, and others took up the shout, and Raith snarled it too but with the peg in his mouth it was only a slobbering growl. He felt his breath burning, burning, and hacked at the rail with his axe, woodchips flying.

More arrows whipped angry over the water, and a clamour of prayers and war-cries, the *Black Dog* ploughing on towards the Lowlander's ship, the men at her rail bulge-eyed as they scrambled back and Raith could smell their fear, smell their blood, and he stood tall and gave a great howl.

Keel struck timber with a shattering, shuddering crash, oars ripped up, snapping, splintering, sliding about the *Black Dog*'s prow like spears. The timbers trembled, warriors tottered and clutched, the Lowlander ship was tipped by the impact, men tumbling from their sea-chests and an archer fell and shot his arrow high, high towards sinking Mother Sun.

Grapples snaked out across the churning gap, iron fingers clutching. One hooked a Lowlander under the arm and dragged him whooping into the water.

'Heave!' roared Jenner and the ships were dragged together, a skein of rope and tangled oar between them, and Raith bared his teeth and planted one boot on the rail.

A rock tumbled from the air, bonked onto the head of the man beside Raith and knocked him flat, mouth yawning, a great dent in his helmet and the bloody rim jammed down over his nose.

What are you waiting for?

He sprang, cleared the frothing water and fell in the midst of men, a spear raking his shield, near twisting it from his hand.

Raith chopped with his axe, snarling, chopped again, slavering, shoved a man over backwards, saw another with a red beard just raising an axe of his own. He'd a jackdaw wing on a thong around his neck, a charm to make him fast. Didn't make him fast enough. An arrow stuck under his eye and he fumbled at the shaft.

Raith hit him in the head and ripped him off his feet. A wave struck the side of the ship, soaking friend and enemy. Sea-spray, blood-spray, men pushing, crushing, shoving, screaming. A stew of maddened faces. The swell lifted the back of the ship and Raith went with it, driving men back with his shield, snorting and howling, wolf voice, wolf heart.

All was a storm of splintering wood and clattering metal and broken voices that echoed in Raith's head until his skull rang with it, split with it, burst with it. The deck was sea-slippery, blood-slippery. Men staggered as the boat heeled and clashed grating against another, its prow-beast so prickled with arrows it looked like a hedgehog.

A man thrust at him with a spear but panic had the

Lowlanders and there was no heart in it. Raith was too fast, too eager, reeled around the stabbing point, his axe reeling after him in a shining circle and thudding into the man's shoulder so hard it sent him tumbling over the rail and into the heaving sea.

Mercy is weakness, Mother Scaer used to make them say before she'd give them their bread. *Mercy is failure.*

Raith rammed his left arm up and over and the edge of his shield caught an oarsman in the mouth and knocked him staggering, coughing, choking on his own teeth.

He saw Blue Jenner clinging to the prow, boot up on the rail, pointing with his weathered sword. He shouted words but Raith was the great dog now, and if he'd ever known the tongue of men it was long ago in another place.

The ship clashed into another. A man in the water gave a bubbling scream as he was crushed between the hulls. Fire flared, glinting on the blades, fearful faces jerking towards it.

Father Yarvi's southern weapon. A flaming pot tumbled in the air and smashed, fire blooming across a fat-bellied transport. Men toppled from the deck, burning, squealing, rigging turned to flaming lines, Mother Sea herself pooled with fire.

Raith felt Gorm's hand on his shoulder. *What are you waiting for?*

He chopped a man down, stomped on him as he fell, hacked another across the back as he turned to run. He'd fought his way down the ship, a tall warrior ahead of him with gold glinting on his face-guard, bright ring-money on his arms catching the sinking sun.

Raith slunk up growling in a crouch, his slobber spattering the deck, men and the shadows of men dancing about them, lit by gaudy flames.

They sprang together, axe shrieking against sword, sword clattering from shield, a kick and a stumble and a blow gouging the deck as Raith rolled away.

He circled, wet lips quivering, feeling out his balance, weighing his axe, until he saw his shadow stretch across the deck towards the captain. Knew Mother Sun was low, knew she'd take his eyes, and when she did he darted forward.

He hooked the captain's shield and ripped it down. He had the longer reach but Raith pressed close, butted him in the mouth just under his gilded face-guard.

He fell clutching at the rail, Raith's axe thudded into wood and the captain's fingers jumped spinning, sword tumbling over the side into the sea. Raith snarled, spraying pink drool, chopped low and caught the captain just below his flapping mail as he tried to stand. A crack as his knee snapped back the wrong way and he fell moaning onto his hands.

Raith felt Gorm's slap sting his face. *You are a killer!*

He gnawed at the peg as he hacked, and hacked, and hacked, snorting and slavering until he could swing no more and he lurched against the ship's rail, blood on his face, blood in his mouth.

Smoke rolled across the water, made Raith's eyes leak and his throat burn.

Here, at least, the battle was done. Men dead. Men

screaming. The water bobbed with floating bodies, nudging gently against the keel as the ship drifted. Raith's knees wobbled and he slumped down on his arse in the shadow of the whirl-carved prow.

More of Uthil's ships were cutting through the waves. Arrows flitting, grapples tumbling, men springing from one boat to another, men roaring and fighting and dying, black shadows in the fading light. Flames spread among the big trading ships and roared up into the dusk, oars a flaming tangle, giant torches on the water.

'That was some fighting, lad.' Someone set the captain's gilded helm on Raith's lap and gave it a pat. 'You got no fear in you at all, do you?'

Took an effort for Raith to unlock his aching jaw, to push the spit-slick peg out of his mouth with his sore tongue.

Sometimes felt like all he had in him was fear. Of losing his place. Of being alone. Of the things he'd done. Of the things he might do.

Fighting was the one thing didn't scare him.

VICTORY

The land was a black mystery when the ships began to plough ashore, the sky a dark blue cloth slashed with cloud and stabbed with stars. Out on the dark water, the scattered remnants of Grandmother Wexen's fleet were still burning.

The crews began to jump down, to flounder laughing through the surf, eyes shining with triumph in the light of a hundred bonfires set upon the beach.

Skara watched them, desperate to know who was living, who was wounded, who was dead, burning to run into the sea herself to find out sooner.

'There!' said Sister Owd, pointing, and Skara saw the prow-beast of the *Black Dog*, her crew trotting up the shingle. She felt a heady rush of relief when she saw Blue Jenner's smiling face, then the warrior beside him pulled off a gilded helmet and Raith grinned up towards her. Whether Mother Kyre would have considered it proper or not, Skara took off down the beach to meet them.

'Victory, my queen!' called Jenner, and Skara caught him, hugged him, seized his ears and pulled his head down so she could kiss him on his wispy pate.

'I knew you wouldn't let me down!'

Jenner was blushing red as he nodded sideways. 'Thank this one. He killed a captain, man against man. Never saw braver fighting.'

Raith's eyes were bright and wild and before Skara knew it she was hugging him too, her nose full of the sour-sweat smell of him, somehow anything but unpleasant. He jerked her into the air with easy strength, spun her about lightly as if she was made of straw, both of them laughing, drunk on victory.

'We've got prizes for you,' he said, upending a canvas bag, and a clinking mass of ring-money spilled onto the sand.

Sister Owd squatted to root through the gold and silver, round face dimpling as she grinned. 'This will do Throvenland's treasury no harm, my queen.'

Skara put her hand on her minister's shoulder. 'Now Throvenland has a treasury.' With this she could start to feed her people, maybe even begin to rebuild what Bright Yilling had burned, and be a queen rather than a girl with a title made of smoke. She raised one brow at Raith.

'I must confess I had no high hopes of you when you first sat beside me.'

'I'd no high hopes of myself,' he said.

Jenner grabbed him, scrubbing at his white hair. 'Who could blame you? He's an unhopeful-looking bastard!'

'You're one to talk, old man,' said Raith, slapping Blue Jenner's hand away.

'You both have proved yourselves great fighters.' Skara picked out two golden armrings and handed one to Jenner, thinking how proud her grandfather would have been to see her giving gifts to her warriors. 'And loyal friends.' She took Raith's thick wrist and slipped the other around it then, hidden in the darkness between them, let her fingers trail onto the back of his hand. He turned it over so she touched his palm, her thumb brushing across it one way, then the other.

She looked up and his eyes were fixed on hers. As if there was nothing else to look at in the world. Mother Kyre would certainly not have considered that proper. No one would. Perhaps that was why it gave Skara such a breathless thrill to do it.

'Steel was our answer!' came a roar and she jerked her hand free, turned to see King Uthil striding up the beach, Father Yarvi smiling at his shoulder. All about men held their swords, their axes, their spears high in salute, blades notched from the day's work catching the light of the bonfires and burning the colours of flame, so it seemed the Iron King and his companions stalked through a sea of fire.

'Mother War stood with us!' Grom-gil-Gorm loomed from the darkness in the dunes, a fresh wound added to his faceful of scars, his beard tangled with clotted blood. Rakki strode beside him with the king's great shield, scored with new marks of its own, Soryorn on the other side with an armful of captured swords. Mother Scaer stalked after him, thin lips ever-moving as she crooned a prayer of thanks to the Mother of Crows.

The two great kings, the two famed warriors, the two old enemies met, and eyed each other over a guttering fire. All across the crowded beach the laughter and the cheering faded, and She Who Sings the Wind sang a keening tune and tore bright sparks swirling down the shingle and out to sea.

Then the Breaker of Swords puffed out his great chest, that chain made from the pommels of his fallen enemies flashing, and spoke in a voice of thunder.

'I looked out to sea and I saw a ship speeding, fleet as a grey gull over the water, scattering the ships of the High King like starlings. Iron on the mast, in the hands of her warriors. Iron the eye of her merciless captain. Iron the slaughter she spread on the water. Corpses to sate even Mother Sea's hunger.'

An iron whisper went through the warriors. Pride at their strength and the strength of their leaders. Pride at the songs they would pass to their sons, more precious to them than gold. Uthil let his mad eyes widen, let the sword slide through the crook of his arm until it rested on its point. His voice came as harsh as the grinding of a whetstone.

'I looked back to land and I saw a host gather. Black was the banner the wind snapped above them. Black was the fury that fell on their foemen. Into the sea were the High King's men driven. Thunder of steel as helms split and shields riven. Red was the tide that washed over their ruin. Corpses to sate even Mother War's hunger.'

The two kings clasped hands over the fire and a mighty cheer went up, a din of metal as men smashed their notched weapons against their gouged shields, and thumped fists on the mailed shoulders of their comrades, and Skara clapped her hands and laughed along with them.

Blue Jenner raised his brows. 'Acceptable verses, at short notice.'

'No doubt the skalds can sharpen them later!' Skara knew what it was to win a great victory, and it was a feeling to sing of. The High King was driven from the land of her forefathers, and her heart felt light for the first time since she fled the burning Forest . . .

Then she remembered that bland smile, speckled with her grandfather's blood and shivered. 'Was Bright Yilling among the dead?' she called.

Grom-gil-Gorm turned his dark eyes upon her. 'I saw no sign of that Death-worshipping dog, nor his Companions. It was a rabble we butchered on the beach, weak-armed and weak-led.'

'Father Yarvi.' A boy slipped past Skara, catching the minister by his coat. 'A dove's come.'

For some reason she felt a weight of cold worry in her stomach as Father Yarvi tucked his elf-metal staff into the crook of his arm and turned the scrap of paper towards the firelight. 'Come from where?'

'Down the coast, beyond Yaletoft.'

'I had men watching the water . . .' He trailed off as his eyes scanned the scrawled letters.

'You have news?' asked King Uthil.

Yarvi swallowed, a sudden gust fluttering the paper in his fingers. 'The High King's army has crossed the straits to the west,' he muttered. 'Ten thousand of his warriors stand on the soil of Throvenland and are already marching.'

'What?' asked Raith, mouth still smiling but his forehead wrinkled with confusion.

Not far away men were still dancing clumsily to the music of a pipe, laughing, drinking, celebrating, but around the two kings the faces had turned suddenly grim.

'Are you sure?' Skara's voice had the pleading note of a pardoned prisoner who finds they are to die for some other crime.

'I am sure.' And Yarvi crumpled the paper in his hand and flung it in the fire.

Mother Scaer gave a bark of joyless laughter. 'This was all a ruse! A flourish of Grandmother Wexen's fingers to draw our eyes while she struck the true blow with her other hand.'

'A trick,' breathed Blue Jenner.

'She sacrificed all those men?' said Skara. 'As a *trick*?'

'For the greater good, my queen,' whispered Sister Owd. Further down the beach a few fires spluttered out as a cold wave surged up the shingle.

'She tossed away her leakiest ships. Her weakest fighters. Men she need no longer arm, or feed, or worry over.' King Uthil gave an approving nod. 'One must admire her ruthlessness.'

'I thought Mother War had smiled on us.' Gorm

frowned towards the night sky. 'It seems her favour fell elsewhere.'

As the news spread the music stuttered to a halt and the celebrations with it. Mother Scaer was scowling towards Yarvi. 'You thought to outwit Grandmother Wexen, but she has outwitted you and all of us with you. Arrogant fool!'

'I heard none of your wisdom!' Father Yarvi snarled back, shadows black in the angry hollows of his face.

'Stop!' pleaded Skara, stepping between them. 'We must be united, now more than ever!'

But a babble of voices had broken out. A clamour like the one she had heard outside her door the night the High King's warriors came to Yaletoft.

'Ten thousand men? That could be three times what we fought here!'

'Twice as many as we have!'

'There could be more flooding across the straits!'

'Plainly the High King has found more ships.'

'We must strike them now,' snapped Uthil.

'We must fall back,' growled Gorm. 'Draw them onto our ground.'

'Stop,' croaked Skara, but she could not seem to take a proper breath. Her heart was surging in her ears. Something clattered from the black sky and she gasped. Raith caught her by the arm and dragged her behind him, whipping free his dagger.

A bird, swooping from the night and onto Mother Scaer's shoulder. A crow, folding its wings and staring unblinking with yellow eyes.

'Bright Yilling has come!' it shrieked. And suddenly Skara was back in the darkness, the mad light of fires outside the windows, the white hand reaching out to touch her face. She felt her guts churn and her knees tremble, had to clutch at Raith's arm to stop herself from falling.

In silence Mother Scaer unpeeled the scrap of paper from her crow's leg. In silence she read the markings, her stony face growing stonier yet. In silence Skara felt the fear settling ever deeper on her like drifting snow, like a great stone crushing out her breath, acid tickling the back of her throat.

She remembered what her grandfather used to tell her. *Victory is a fine feeling. But always a fleeting one.*

Her voice was tiny in the night. 'What is it?'

'More dark news,' said Mother Scaer. 'I know where Bright Yilling has been.'

THE PRICE

Rulf always said there was no place to forget your troubles like the prow of a ship under full sail, where your worst enemy was the wind and your biggest worry the next wave but one. It surely seemed like wisdom to Koll as he clung grinning to the prow-beast, relishing the spray on his face and the salt on his lips.

But the gods love to laugh at a happy man.

A quick arm snaked around his shoulders. It might not have been as big an arm as Brand's but the strength in it was just as frightening, the dangling knuckles scabbed and scarred, the elf-bangle won from fighting seven men alone glowing a faint orange.

'Nearly back home.' Thorn took a long breath through her bent nose, and nodded towards the ragged line of

Gettland's hills just showing on the horizon. 'You'll be seeing Rin again, I reckon?'

Koll sighed. 'You can sheathe the threats. Brand already gave me the talk—'

'Brand doesn't talk loud enough. He's an easy-going man. The gods know he has to be, to put up with me. But I married Brand.' Thorn flicked at the red-gold key around her neck and set it swinging by its chain. 'So Rin's my sister too. And I'm not so easy-going. I've always liked you and I don't like anyone, but you see where I'm headed with this?'

'It hardly takes a far-sighted fellow.' Koll hung his head. 'Feel like I'm trapped in a shrinking room. Can't see how to do right by Rin and Father Yarvi both.'

'Can't see how to get what you want from both, do you mean?'

He glanced guiltily up at her. 'I want to be loved *while* I change the world. That so wrong?'

'Only if you end up doing neither and make a heap of wreckage getting there.' Thorn sighed, and gave his shoulder a sympathetic pat. 'If it's any consolation I know just how you feel. I swore an oath to Queen Laithlin to be her Chosen Shield and I made a promise to Brand to be his wife and . . . turns out they both deserve better.'

Koll raised his brows. It was an odd reassurance to know Thorn, who always seemed so certain, might have her own doubts. 'Not sure they'd agree.'

She snorted. 'Not sure they'd disagree. Feels like there's not enough of me to go around and what there is no one in their right mind would want. I never aimed to become . . . well . . .' She made a fist of her right hand and winced down at it. 'Some angry bastard.'

'You didn't?'

'No, Koll. I didn't.'

'What're you going to do, then?' he asked.

She puffed out her scarred cheeks. 'Try harder, I guess. What're you going to do?'

Koll puffed out his as he looked towards home. 'I've no bloody idea.' He frowned as he saw grey smudges against the sky. 'Is that smoke?' He slipped from under Thorn's arm, hopped onto a barrel and from there to the mast. The queen had come to stand at the rail, frowning off towards the west with her golden hair snatched and tossed in the wind.

'Dark omens,' Skifr murmured from inside her hood as she watched the birds circle in their wake. 'Bloody omens.'

Koll dragged himself onto the yard and hooked his legs over, one hand on the masthead, the other shading his eyes as he stared off towards Thorlby. At first he couldn't see much for the swaying of the ship, then Mother Sea calmed a moment and Koll caught a good glimpse. The docks, the walls, the citadel . . .

'Gods,' he croaked. There was a blackened scar down the hillside, right through the heart of the city.

'What do you see?' snapped out Queen Laithlin.

'Fire,' said Koll, the hairs on his neck prickling. 'Fire in Thorlby.'

Flames had swept through the docks. Where crowds had bustled and fishermen toiled and merchants called prices ghosts of dust whirled among scorched ruins. Scarcely a wharf was left standing, all fallen twisted into the water. The blackened mast of a sunken boat poked from the slapping waves, the forlorn prow-beast of another.

'What happened?' someone croaked against the stink of burned wood.

'Land us at the beach!' snarled Thorn, clinging so hard to the rail her knuckles were white.

In brooding silence they rowed, staring up towards the city, gaps torn from the familiar buildings on the steep hillside like teeth from a lover's smile, each an aching absence. Houses burned to shells, windows blank as corpse's eyes, charred skeletons of roof-beams stripped obscenely bare. Houses still coughing up a roiling of dark smoke, and above the crows circling, circling, cawing out gratefully to their iron mother.

'Oh, gods,' croaked Koll. Sixth Street, where Rin's forge had been, where they'd worked together, and laughed together, and lain together, was a streak of blackened wreckage in the shadow of the citadel. He went cold to the very tips of his fingers, the fear so savage a beast in his chest he could barely take a proper breath for its clawing.

The moment the keel ground on shingle Thorn sprang from the prow and Koll followed, hardly noticing the cold, nearly floundering into her on the sand she pulled up so quickly.

'No,' Koll heard her whisper, and she put the back of one hand to her mouth and it was trembling.

He looked up the slope of the beach towards the howes

of kings long dead. There was a gathering there on the dunes, among the thin grass lashed by the sea wind, a gathering of dozens, shoulders hunched and heads bowed.

A funeral gathering, and Koll felt the fear grip him tighter.

He tried to set a hand on Thorn's shoulder, for her comfort or his he couldn't have said, but she twisted away and ran on, sand kicking from her boot heels, and Koll followed.

He could hear a low voice droning out. Brinyolf the Prayer-Weaver, singing songs for Father Peace, for She Who Writes and She Who Judges, for Death who guards the Last Door.

'No,' he heard Thorn mutter as she struggled on up the dunes towards them.

Brinyolf's words stuttered out. Silence except for the wind fumbling through the grass, the faraway joy of a crow on the high breeze. The white faces turned towards them, gaunt with shock, glistening with tears, tight with anger.

Koll saw Rin and gave a gasp of relief, but his little prayer of thanks died as he saw her lips curl back and her face crush up and the tears wet on her cheeks. He followed Thorn towards her, his knees wobbly, at once desperate to see and desperate not to.

He saw the great pyre, wood stacked up waist high.

He saw the bodies on it. Gods, how many? Two dozen? Three?

'No, no, no,' whispered Thorn, edging towards the nearest one.

Koll saw the dark hair stirred by the wind, saw the pale hands folded on the broad chest, old scars snaking up the wrists. Hero's marks. Marks of a great deed. A deed that had saved Koll's life. He crept up beside Rin to look down at the face. Brand's face, pale and cold, with a dark little bloodless slit under one eye.

'Gods,' he croaked, not able to believe it.

Brand had always seemed so calm and strong, solid as the rock Thorlby was built on. He couldn't be dead. Couldn't be.

Koll squeezed his stinging eyes shut, and opened them, and there he lay still.

Brand was gone through the Last Door and that was all there was of his story. All there would ever be.

And Koll gave a silly snort, and felt the pain in his nose and the tears tickling his cheeks.

Thorn leaned down over Brand, the elf-bangle on her wrist gone dark and dead, and gently, so gently, brushed the strands of hair out of his face. Then she pulled off her chain, cradled Brand's head and slipped it over, tucked the golden key down inside his shirt. A best shirt he'd never worn because the time was never right, and she patted the front, smoothed it softly with trembling fingers, over and over.

Rin clung tight to him and Koll put his arm about her, limp, and weak, and useless. He felt her shuddering with silent sobs and he opened his mouth to speak but nothing came. He was supposed to be a minister's apprentice. He was supposed to have the words. But what could words do now?

He stood just as helpless as when his own mother died, and lay stretched out on the pyre, and Father Yarvi had spoken because Koll couldn't. Could only stand staring down, and think of what he'd lost.

The silent crowd parted to let Queen Laithlin through, her hair whipping about her face and her brine-soaked dress clinging to her. 'Where is Prince Druin?' she growled. 'Where is my son?'

'Safe in your chambers, my queen,' said Brinyolf the Prayer-Weaver, chin vanishing into his fat neck as he looked down sadly at the pyre, 'thanks to Brand. He set a bell ringing as a warning. Druin's guards took no chances. They dropped the Screaming Gate and sealed off the citadel.'

Laithlin's narrowed eyes swept across the corpses. 'Who did this?'

Edni, one of the girls Thorn had been training, a stained bandage around her head, spat on the ground. 'Bright Yilling and his Companions.'

'Bright Yilling,' murmured Laithlin. 'I have heard that name too often of late.'

Thorn slowly straightened. There were no tears on her face but Koll could hear her make a strangled moan with every breath. Rin plucked at her shoulder with one hand but Thorn didn't turn, didn't move, as though she stood in a dream.

'He came with two ships,' Edni was saying. 'Maybe three. In the night. Not enough to take the city, but enough to burn it. Some Throvenlanders had come the day before. Said they were merchants. We think they're the ones let him in. Then him and his Companions spread out and started setting fires.'

'Brand heard them,' mumbled Rin. 'Went to set a bell ringing. Said he had to warn folk. Said he had to do good.'

'Would've been worse without that,' said an old warrior with his arm in a sling, and when he blinked a long streak of tears was squeezed from his swimming eyes. 'First I knew of it was the bell. Then there were fires everywhere. All chaos, and Bright Yilling laughing in the midst.'

'Laughing and killing,' said Edni. 'Men, women, children.'

Brinyolf shook his head in disgust. 'What can one expect from a man who prays to no god but Death?'

'They knew just where the guards would be.' Edni bunched her fists. 'Which roads to take. Which buildings to burn. Knew where we were strong and where we were weak. They knew everything!'

'We fought, though, my queen.' The prayer-weaver put his fat hand on Edni's thin shoulder. 'You would have been proud of the way your people fought! Thanks to the favour of the gods we drove them off, but . . . the Mother of Crows ever takes a heavy toll . . .'

'This is Grandmother Wexen's debt,' muttered Koll, wiping his nose. 'And no one else's.'

'Thorn.' Queen Laithlin stepped forward. 'Thorn.' She took her by the shoulders and squeezed hard. 'Thorn!'

Thorn blinked at her as if waking from a dream.

'I have to stay,' said the queen, 'and try to heal Thorlby's wounds, and see to those who remain.'

Thorn's moaning breath had deepened to a jagged growling, the jaw muscles bunched hard on the sides of her scarred face. 'I have to fight.'

'Yes. And I would not stop you even if I could.' The queen lifted her chin. 'I release you from your oath, Thorn Bathu. You are my Chosen Shield no longer.' She leaned closer, voice sharp as a blade. 'You must be our sword instead. The sword that cuts vengeance from Bright Yilling!'

Thorn gave a slow nod, her hands clenched to quivering fists. 'I swear it.'

'My queen,' said Edni, 'we caught one of them.'

Laithlin narrowed her eyes. 'Where is he?'

'Chained and guarded in the citadel. He hasn't spoken a word. But from his armour and his ring-money we reckon him one of Bright Yilling's Companions.'

Thorn bared her teeth. The elf-bangle had started to glow again, but hot as a coal now, putting a red flush on the stark hollows of her face, sparking a bloody gleam in the corners of her eyes.

'He will speak to me,' she whispered.

III

WE ARE THE SHIELD

MONSTERS

'My allies,' Skara began. 'My friends.' As if by calling them friends she might make them feel less like her enemies. 'I thought it wise to call only the six of us together so we can discuss our situation without too many . . . interruptions.' Meaning the onslaught of petty arguments, insults and threats that strangled their full-scale moots.

King Uthil and King Gorm frowned at one another. Father Yarvi and Mother Scaer frowned at one another. Sister Owd sat back with arms grimly folded. A breeze sighed off the sea and stirred the long grass on the barrows, making Skara shiver even though the day was warm.

An intimate meeting out of doors, butterflies fluttering among the flowers that grew on the graves of the parents

Skara had hardly known. An intimate meeting of two kings, three ministers, and her. And with the wrath of Grandmother Wexen about to crash upon them.

'Our situation, then.' Mother Scaer turned one of her elf-bangles around and around on her thin wrist. 'Here is a pretty pickle.'

'Ten thousand of the High King's warriors descend upon us,' said Uthil. 'And with the banners of many storied heroes among them.'

'More swarm across the straits from Yutmark every day,' said Gorm. 'We must fall back. We must abandon Throvenland.'

Skara flinched. Abandon Bail's Point. Abandon her land and her people. Abandon her grandfather's memory. The thought made her sick. Or even sicker.

Uthil let his naked sword slide through his hand until its point was in the grass. 'I do not see victory that way.'

'Where do you see it?' pleaded Skara, struggling to sit straight and plaster a queen's dignity onto her face, even if she would far rather have curled up crying under her chair. But Uthil only twisted his sword gently, face as hard as the cliffs below them.

'I stand always ready to trust to my weaponluck, but I am not alone. I must think of my wife and my son. I must think of what I might leave them.'

Skara felt her gorge rising and fought it down. When even the Iron King could not say steel was the answer, things were truly desperate.

Mother Scaer turned her shaved head and spat over

her shoulder. 'Perhaps the time has come to send a bird to Grandmother Wexen.'

Father Yarvi snorted. 'Mother Adwyn made it very clear she will never make peace with me.'

'So you say.'

Yarvi narrowed his eyes. 'Do you think I lie?'

Scaer glared back. 'Usually.'

'King Fynn made peace with Grandmother Wexen,' said Skara, her voice cracking. 'Some good it did him!'

But the two kings sat in brooding silence as Mother Scaer leaned in, tattooed forearms resting on her knees. 'Every war is only a prelude to peace. A negotiation with swords instead of words. Let us go to Grandmother Wexen while we still have something to bargain with—'

'There'll be no bargains!' came a barking voice. 'There'll be no peace.'

Thorn Bathu stalked around the nearest howe. At first, Skara felt a rush of gladness at the sight of her. The very woman you needed when you faced impossible odds. Then Thorn jerked a chain and brought a prisoner staggering after her, hands bound behind him and a bloodstained bag over his face. Then Skara saw a figure following in a cloak of rags, hood drawn up. Finally she met Thorn's eyes, smouldering in blackened sockets with a fury almost painful to look upon.

'Bright Yilling attacked Thorlby,' she snarled, kicking her prisoner onto his knees before the three rulers and their three ministers. 'He burned half the city. Queen Laithlin is still there with her son, caring for the wounded.

He killed men, women, children. He killed—' She gave a strangled cough, and bared her teeth, and she mastered herself again and raised her sharp chin, eyes glistening. 'He killed Brand.'

Gorm frowned sideways at his minister. Uthil's fist whitened about the grip of his sword. Father Yarvi's eyes went wide, and he seemed to slump on his stool.

'Gods,' he whispered, all the colour drained from his face.

'I am . . . so sorry . . .' stammered Skara. She remembered how Thorn had held her when she was first brought to Thorlby. Wished she could do the same for her now. But her face was so twisted with anger Skara hardly dared look at her, let alone touch her.

The newcomer pushed back her ragged hood. A dark-skinned southerner, lean as a whip and with burns scattered across the left side of her face. They would have made Skara wince to look upon once, but she was growing used to scars.

'Greetings, great kings, great queens, great ministers,' she bowed, and showed burned bald patches in her cropped grey hair. 'In the Land of the Alyuks they call me Sun-nara-Skun. In Kalyiv they call me Scarayoi, the Walker in the Ruins.'

'What do they call you here?' snapped Mother Scaer.

'She is Skifr,' murmured Yarvi.

'The witch Skifr?' Scaer's lip twisted with disgust. 'The thief of elf-relics? The one denounced by Grandmother Wexen?'

'The very same, my dove.' Skifr smiled. 'Grandmother

Wexen burned my house and killed my kin, and so I am your bitter enemy's bitter enemy.'

'The best kind of ally.' The Breaker of Swords frowned at the chained man. 'And must we play a guessing game over this visitor?'

Thorn snorted, and ripped the bag from his head.

Skara was sickened at first to see his face. Battered shapeless, bloated with bruises, one eye swollen shut and the white of the other stained red. Then she realized she knew him. He was one of those who had stood in the Forest the night it burned. One of those who had laughed as King Fynn toppled into the firepit. She knew she should hate him, but all she felt at the sight of his ruined face was pity. Pity, and disgust at what had been done to him.

Be as generous to your enemies as your friends, her grandfather had always said. *Not for their sake, but for your own.*

Thorn's mood was anything but generous, however. 'This is Asborn the Fearless, Companion to Bright Yilling.' She dug her fingers into his blood-crusted hair and wrenched his face up towards her. 'He was caught in the raid on Thorlby, and he proves to have fear in him after all. Tell them what you told me, worm!'

Asborn's mouth lolled slack and toothless and broken words croaked out. 'A message . . . came to Bright Yilling. To attack Thorlby. When . . . and where . . . and how to attack.' Skara winced as his wet breath clicked and crackled. 'You have . . . a traitor among you.'

Father Yarvi sat forward, his withered hand clenched in a mockery of fist. 'Who is it?'

'Only Yilling knows.' His one bloodshot eye was fixed on Skara's. 'Perhaps they sit here now . . . among you.' His broken mouth curled into a red smile. 'Perhaps—'

Thorn struck him across his broken face, knocked him sideways, lifted her arm to hit him again.

'Thorn!' shouted Skara, clutching at her chest. 'No!' Thorn stared at her, face twisted with grief and fury at once. 'Please, if you keep hurting him, you hurt yourself. You hurt us all. I beg you, show some mercy!'

'Mercy?' Thorn spat, tears streaking her scarred cheek. 'Did they show Brand mercy?'

'No more than they showed my grandfather.' Skara felt her own eyes stinging as she leaned desperately forward. 'But we have to be better than them!'

'No. We have to be worse.' Thorn hauled Asborn savagely up by his chain, lifting her clenched fist, but he only smiled the wider.

'Bright Yilling comes!' he gurgled out. 'Bright Yilling comes and he brings Death with him!'

'Oh, Death is here already.' Skifr turned, raising her arm, a thing of dark metal gripped in her fist. There was a deafening crack that made Skara jolt in her chair, a red mist blew from the back of Asborn's head and he was flung twisted onto his side with his hair on fire.

Skara stared, wide-eyed, cold with horror.

'Mother War protect us,' whispered Gorm.

'What have you done?' shrieked Mother Scaer, springing up and sending her stool tumbling over in the grass.

'Rejoice, my doves, for I have brought you the means

of your victory.' Skifr held the deadly thing high, a wisp of smoke curling from a hole in its end. 'I know where more of these can be found. Relics beside which the power of this one would seem puny. Elf-weapons forged before the Breaking of God!'

'Where?' asked Yarvi, and Skara was shocked to see his eyes shining with eagerness.

Skifr let her head drop on one side. 'In Strokom.'

'Madness!' screeched Mother Scaer. 'Strokom is forbidden by the Ministry. Anyone who goes there sickens and dies!'

'I have been there.' Skifr raised a long arm to point at the elf-bangle burning orange on Thorn's wrist. 'I brought that bauble from within, and I still cast a shadow. No ground is forbidden to me. I am the Walker in the Ruins, and I know all the ways. Even those that can keep us safe from the sickness in Strokom. Say the word, and I will put weapons in your hands against which no man, no hero, no army can stand.'

'And curse us all?' snarled Mother Scaer. 'Have you lost your minds?'

'I yet have mine.' King Uthil had calmly risen, calmly walked to Asborn's corpse, calmly squatted beside it. 'The great warrior is the one who still breathes when the crows feast. The great king is the one who watches the carcasses of his enemies burn.' He pushed his little finger into the neat hole in Asborn's forehead, and the mad fire that had seemed burned out was bright again in his eyes. 'Steel must be the answer.' He pulled his finger free, red, and raised one brow at it. 'This is but another kind of steel.'

Skara closed her eyes, gripping tight to the arms of her chair. Tried to still her heaving breath and her churning stomach and smother her horror. Horror at seeing magic. Horror at seeing a prisoner murdered before her eyes. Horror that she was the only one who seemed to care. She had to be brave. Had to be clever. Had to be strong.

'I say it should stay sheathed lest it cut us all,' Gorm was saying.

'I say it should be sheathed in Bright Yilling's heart!' snarled Thorn.

'We can all see you are grief-mad,' snapped Mother Scaer. 'Elf-magic? Think what you are saying! We risk another Breaking of God! And with a traitor among us!'

'A traitor who made Thorlby burn,' barked Thorn, 'as you've dreamed of doing for years! A traitor working for the High King, who you'd make peace with!'

'Think carefully before you accuse me, you unnat-ural—'

Skara forced her eyes open. 'We all have made sacri-fices!' she shouted. 'We all have lost friends, homes, families. We must stand united or Grandmother Wexen will crush us each alone!'

'We have challenged the High King's authority,' said Father Yarvi, 'and that is all he has. All he is. He cannot turn back and neither can we. We have chosen our path.'

'You have chosen it for us,' snapped Mother Scaer. 'One bloody step at a time! And it leads straight to our destruction.'

Skifr barked out a laugh. 'You were fumbling your way

there well enough without me, my doves. Always there are risks. Always there are costs. But I have shown you forbidden magic and Mother Sun still rises.'

'We rule because men trust us,' said Gorm. 'What will this do to their trust?'

'You rule because men fear you,' said Father Yarvi. 'With weapons such as these their fear will be all the greater.'

Scaer gave a hiss. 'This is evil, Father Yarvi.'

'I fear it is the lesser evil, Mother Scaer. Glorious victories make fine songs, but inglorious ones are no worse once the bards are done with them. Glorious defeats, meanwhile, are just defeats.'

'We need time to consider,' said Skara, holding out her palms as if to calm a pack of fighting dogs.

'Not too long.' Skifr darted out one hand, catching a dried-up leaf as it whirled past. 'The sands slip through the glass and Bright Yilling marches ever closer. Will you do what you must to beat him? Or will you let him beat you?' She crushed the leaf as she turned away and, holding her hand high, let the dust blow on the breeze. 'If you ask me, my doves, that is no choice at all!'

'There'll be no peace,' growled Thorn Bathu, hauling the chain over her shoulder. 'Not while Bright Yilling and I both live. That I promise you!' And she turned to follow Skifr, the heels of Asborn's corpse leaving two grooves in the grass as she dragged the murdered man after her.

Gorm slowly stood, a heavy frown on his battle-worn face. 'Let us have a great moot at sunrise tomorrow, then, where we will decide the future of our alliance. The future of the whole Shattered Sea, perhaps.'

King Uthil was the next to rise. 'We have much to discuss, Father Yarvi.'

'We do, my king, but I must speak to Queen Skara first.'

'Very well.' Uthil twitched his naked sword up into the crook of his arm. 'While I try to stop Thorn Bathu killing every Vansterman in the world searching for traitors. Send a bird to Queen Laithlin. Tell her to kiss my son from me.' He turned away towards Bail's Point. 'Tell her I fear I will be late to dinner.'

Skara waited until King Uthil was gone and Mother Scaer had stalked away bitterly shaking her shaved head before she spoke. 'You knew this moment would come.' She carefully turned the pieces about until they fitted together in her mind. 'That is why you wanted me to summon only the six of us here. So that this business of elf-relics could not leak out.'

'Not everyone is as . . . considered as you, my queen.' Flattery, flattery. She tried not to let it sway her. 'It is wise to keep the circle tight. Especially if there truly is a traitor amongst us.'

It all made fine sense, but Skara frowned even so. 'I could tire of finding myself dancing to your tune, Father Yarvi.'

'It is Grandmother Wexen's music we all dance to, and I have sworn to stop the piper. You have a great decision to make, my queen.'

'One follows hard upon another.'

'That is the cost of power.' Yarvi stared down at the bloodstained grass, and for a moment he seemed to be struggling with some sickness of his own. 'Forgive me. I just learned as good a man as I ever knew is dead. Sometimes it is hard . . . to pick the right thing.'

'Sometimes there is no right thing.' Skara tried to imagine what her grandfather would have done in her place. What advice Mother Kyre would have given her. But she had been taught no lessons for this. She was far out on uncharted seas, with a storm coming and no stars to steer by. 'What should I do, Father Yarvi?'

'A wise man once told me that a king must win, the rest is dust. It is no different for a queen. Take Skifr's offer. Without something to tip the scales, the High King will sweep us all aside. Grandmother Wexen will take no pity on you. The people of Throvenland will not be spared. Bright Yilling will not thank you for your forbearance. Ask yourself what he would do in your place.'

Skara could not stop herself from shuddering at that. 'So I must become Bright Yilling?'

'Let Father Peace shed tears over the methods. Mother War smiles upon results.'

'And when the war is over?' she whispered. 'What kind of peace will we have won?'

'You want to be merciful. To stand in the light. I understand it. I admire it. But, my queen . . .' Father Yarvi stepped close, and held her eye, and spoke softly. 'Only the victors can be merciful.'

There was no choice at all. She had known it since Skifr worked her magic. Looking into Father Yarvi's face she knew that he had known it too. He had seen it from far off, and twitched their course towards it so gently she had thought she held the steering oar. But she knew also that as the High King's army drew closer, her borrowed power was slipping away. This might be her last vote. She had to win something for her grandfather, for her people, for Throvenland. For herself.

'I have a price.' She looked towards the battlements of Bail's Point, black against the white sky. 'You must convince King Uthil to fight Bright Yilling here.'

Father Yarvi gave Skara a searching stare. As though he could dig out her intentions with his eyes. Perhaps he could. 'He will be reluctant to fight so far from home. Gorm even more so.'

'Then I will speak to Mother Scaer, and see what she can offer for a vote against you.' Skara waved one hand towards the elf-walls looming over her mother's howe. 'There is no stronger fortress anywhere. If we hold it, Bright Yilling will have to come to us. Because of his pride. Because he cannot march past and leave us free behind him. We will fix the High King's men here, all in one place. We will be the shield on which Grandmother Wexen's strength will break. You will be free to find your weapons . . .' She tried not to let her revulsion show as she glanced towards the bloodied grass where Asborn had fallen. 'When you return we can crush Bright Yilling's army in one throw.'

Yarvi considered her. 'There is wisdom in it, but warriors are rarely interested in wisdom.'

'Warriors like polished metal and tales of glory and

songs in which steel is the answer. I daresay you can sing the two kings one of those. Do you have a fine singing voice, Father Yarvi?'

He raised one brow. 'As it happens.'

'I will not abandon the fortress my father died for. I will not abandon the land my grandfather died for.'

'Then I will fight for it alongside you, my queen.' Yarvi glanced at Sister Owd. 'Have you anything to add?'

'I speak when Queen Skara needs my advice.' She gave the mildest of smiles. 'I feel she handled you perfectly well without me.'

Father Yarvi snorted, and strode off between the barrows towards King Uthil's camp.

'That is a deep-cunning man,' murmured Sister Owd, coming to stand beside Skara. 'A man who could make any course seem wise.'

Skara looked sideways. 'I need read no omens to sense the "but" coming.'

'His plan is desperate. He would step onto forbidden ground with this witch Skifr to guide the way.' Sister Owd let her voice drop softer. 'He would step into hell with a devil to point out his path, and he would have us follow. If they cannot find these elf-relics? We will be left penned up in Bail's Point surrounded by ten thousand warriors. If they can?' A whisper now, and a fearful one. 'Will we risk another Breaking of the World?'

Skara thought of the burned farms, the burned villages, her grandfather's hall in ruins. 'The world is already broken. Without these weapons the High King will win. Grandmother Wexen will win.' She felt the sickness at the back of her throat, and swallowed it. 'Bright Yilling will win.'

Sister Owd's shoulders slumped. 'I do not envy you your choice, my queen.' She frowned off after Father Yarvi. 'But I fear in destroying one monster you may make another.'

Skara took one last look at her father's howe. 'I used to think the world had heroes in it. But the world is full of monsters, Sister Owd.' She turned away from the dead, back towards Bail's Point. 'Perhaps the best we can hope for is to have the most terrible of them on our side.'

LIES

Rin never did things by halves. Koll had always loved that about her.

The moment they arrived in Bail's Point she'd sought out the forge, found a space in the warren of cellars, laid out her tools in orderly rows, and set to work. No shortage of work for a smith at a time like that, she told him.

She'd been down in the hot, coal-smelling darkness ever since, hammering, and sharpening, and riveting. He was starting to worry about her. Even more than he was worried about himself, and that didn't happen often.

He gently put his hand on hers to still it. 'No one'll blame you if you stop.'

She shook him off and carried on polishing. 'If I stop I'll have to think. I don't want to think.'

He reached for her again. 'I know, but Rin—'

She shook him off again. 'Stop fussing.'

'I'm sorry.'

'Stop saying sorry.'

'All right, I'm not sorry.'

She stopped to frown up. 'Definitely stop joking.'

He risked a grin. 'I'm sorry.'

She gave the faintest flicker of a smile, then it was gone. He loved making her smile, but he doubted he'd coax another from her today. She propped her fists on the bench, shoulders hunched around her ears, staring down at the scarred wood.

'I keep thinking of things I want to tell him. I open my mouth to talk. I turn to call him over.' She bared her teeth as if she was about to cry, but she didn't. 'He's gone. He's gone and he's never coming back. Every time I remember it, I can't believe it.' She shook her head bitterly. 'He always had a kind word and a kind deed for everyone. What good did it do him?'

'It did them good,' said Koll. 'They won't forget it. I won't forget it.' Brand had saved his life, and asked one thing of him. That he do right by Rin. 'I've stood where you stand now . . .' His cracked voice almost vanished altogether. 'Losing someone.'

'And I've stood where you stand now. Trying to comfort someone. When your mother died.'

That was how things had started between them. Not in a great flash like lightning, but grown up slowly like a deep-rooted tree. Rin's arm around his shoulders when Father Yarvi said the words at his mother's funeral. Rin's hand in his when they howed her up. Rin's laughter when he came to sit in the forge, just to be near someone. She'd been there. The least he could do was the same for her. Even if he felt as if he was suffocating.

'What can I do?' he asked.

Rin set her face, took up her stone again. Gods, she was tough. She might only have been a year older than he was but sometimes she seemed a dozen.

'Just be here.' She set to polishing again, sweat glistening on her face. 'Just say you'll be here.'

'I'll be here,' he forced out, even though he was desperate to leave and breathe the free air and disgusted with himself because of it. 'I promise . . .'

He heard a heavy tread on the stairs and was pitifully glad of the distraction. Until he saw who ducked under the low doorway. None other than Grom-gil-Gorm's white-haired cup-filler, Raith, whose forehead had greeted Koll's nose so rudely beneath the cedar in Thorlby.

'You,' he said, bunching his fists.

Raith winced. 'Aye. Me. Sorry. How's your nose?' Maybe that was meant to be an apology, but all Koll saw in it was his own hurt.

'Bit dented,' he snapped. 'But less than your pride, I reckon.'

Raith shrugged. 'That was a ruin already. Knew you were twice the climber I was or I'd never have had to butt you. Climbed right in here, didn't you? Hell of a climb, that.'

The compliment gave Koll nothing to be angry about,

and that made him angrier than ever. 'What the hell do you want with me?' His voice broke at the end and went piping high, made him seem even more like a puppy picking a fight with a full-grown wolf.

'Nothing.' Raith glanced over at Rin, eyes lingering on the sweat beading her bare shoulders, and Koll didn't like the way he looked at her at all. 'Are you the blade-maker from Sixth Street?'

Rin wiped her forehead on her apron and gave him a long stare of her own. Koll didn't like the way she looked at him either, if it came to that. 'Bright Yilling burned my forge and most of Sixth Street too. Guess I'm the blade-maker downstairs at Bail's Point now.'

'Bail's Point is the better for it.' A far lighter tread on the steps and Queen Skara glided into the smithy. She looked even thinner than the last time Koll saw her, collarbones standing painfully stark, as out of place in the grime and sweat of the forge as a swan in a pigsty.

Koll raised his brows and Rin did the same. 'My queen,' he murmured.

Skara's big green eyes were fixed on Rin. 'I am so sorry for the death of your brother. Every word I hear is that he was a good man.'

'Aye, well.' Rin frowned down at her bench. 'It's them Mother War takes first.'

'We can all pray Father Peace gets his turn soon,' said Koll.

Queen Skara glanced sideways, every bit as scornful of that pious effort as Thorn Bathu might have been. 'As long as Bright Yilling is dead and rotting first.'

'I'm not much for prayers but I'll pray for that,' said Rin.

'I hear you make swords. The best in the Shattered Sea.'

'I made King Uthil's. I made Thorn Bathu's.' Rin unwrapped the bundle on her bench to show the last one she'd worked on. The one she and Koll had worked on together. 'Made this for a man died last week in Thorlby.'

'Did you carve the scabbard too?' Raith ran his thick fingertips down the wood. 'It's beautiful.'

'I work the metal,' said Rin. 'Koll works the wood.'

Raith looked round at him. 'You've a gift to be proud of, then. Wish I could make things.' He winced as he made a fist. As if it hurt him to do it. 'Always been better at breaking.'

'That takes less effort,' muttered Koll.

'I need a sword,' said Skara. 'And mail that fits me.'

Rin gave the young queen a doubtful look up and down. She hardly looked strong enough to stand in armour, let alone fight in it. 'Are you going into battle?'

Skara smiled. 'Gods, no. But I want to look like I might.'

TOO MANY MINISTERS

'Mother Scaer, what a pleasure.'

One glance at Gorm's minister told Skara her visit would not be much of a pleasure for anyone. She was always a woman of edges and angles, but now her face was as sharp as a chisel, and just as humourless.

'I am sorry for the state of my chambers, we have had to start rather from scratch.' The furniture had been scrounged up from anywhere, the hangings were captured battle-flags, and Blue Jenner would not say where the goose-feather mattress had come from. But these were the rooms Skara had been born in, the three great arched windows looking out over the yard of her own fortress. She was going nowhere.

'Will you have some wine?' She turned to beckon her thrall, but Mother Scaer stopped her dead.

'I have not come for wine, my queen. I have come to discuss your vote for Father Yarvi.'

'I vote in the interests of Throvenland.'

'Will Throvenland benefit from a second Breaking of God?' Scaer's voice was sharp with anger. 'What if Father Yarvi cannot control this magic? Or if he can control it, what then? Do you think he will give it up?'

'Would it benefit Throvenland more to have the High King's army ranging unchecked?' Skara felt herself getting shrill, struggled to keep calm and failed. 'To have Bright Yilling burn what little is left unburned?'

Mother Scaer's eyes were narrowed to deadly slits. 'You do not want to do this, my queen.'

'It seems everyone but me knows what I want to do.' Skara raised a brow at Sister Owd. 'Has one queen ever been blessed with the advice of so many ministers?'

'There at least I can lighten your burden,' said Scaer. 'If you mean to join in Father Yarvi's madness I must keep a close eye upon him. My king must have a minister at his side in the meantime.' She held out one long, tattooed arm, and beckoned with her crooked forefinger. 'Playtime is over, Sister Owd. Get back to your place and look to my crows.'

Owd's round face fell, and Skara had to make an effort to stop hers doing the same. She had not realized until that moment how much she had come to rely on her minister. How much she had come to trust her. To like her. 'I am not minded to give her up—'

'Not minded?' Scaer snorted. 'She is my apprentice,

lent, not given, and in case you were too foolish to realize it, *my queen*, she has been telling me everything. Who you speak to and what you say. Your every request and desire. The size of each morning turd, for that matter. I understand that, like she that produces them, they are a little . . . *thin*.'

Owd was staring stricken at her feet, face turned redder than ever. Skara should have known. Perhaps she had. But it still cut her deep. She was speechless for a moment. But only a moment. Then she thought of how her grandfather might have answered, had he been treated with such scorn in his own land, his own fortress, his own chambers.

As Sister Owd took a reluctant step towards the door Skara put out an arm to stop her.

'You misunderstand me! I am not minded to give her up because only this morning she swore her oath to me as Mother Kyre's successor. Mother Owd is the new Minister of Throvenland, and her only place is beside me.'

She was pleased to see Scaer look suitably astonished at the news. The only person who looked more so was Owd herself.

She stared from her old mistress to her new, then back, eyes round as cups. But she was too sharp to stay off-balance long. 'It is true.' Owd pushed her shoulders back and stretched out her neck. A posture Mother Kyre would have thoroughly approved of. 'I have sworn to serve Queen Skara as her minister. I was going to tell you—'

'But you spoiled our surprise,' said Skara, smiling sweetly. A smile costs nothing, after all.

'Oh, there will be a price for this,' said Mother Scaer, nodding slowly. 'Of that I assure you.'

Skara was out of patience. 'Wake me when it's time to pay. Now are you walking from my chambers or shall I have Raith toss you from the window?'

Gorm's minister gave one final hiss of disgust then stalked from the room, slamming the door behind her.

'Well.' Skara took a ragged breath and put one hand on her chest, trying to calm her hammering heart. 'That was bracing.'

'My queen,' whispered Sister Owd, eyes turned mortified to the floor. 'I know I do not deserve your forgiveness—'

'You cannot have it.' Skara put a calming hand on her shoulder. 'Because you have done nothing wrong. I have always known you are loyal. But I have always known your loyalties were divided. Mother Scaer was your mistress. Now you have chosen me. For that I am grateful. Very grateful.' And Skara squeezed her shoulder firmly, stepping closer. 'But your loyalties must be divided no longer.'

Sister Owd stared back, and dashed a little wetness from her lashes. 'I swear a sun-oath and a moon-oath, my queen. I shall be a loyal minister to you and to Throvenland. I shall have a greater care for your body than for my own. I shall have a greater care for your interests than for my own. I shall tell your secrets to no one and keep no secret from you. I am yours. I swear it.'

'Thank you, Mother Owd.' Skara let go of her with a parting pat. 'The gods know I have never been in sorer need of good advice.'

LOYALTY

Raith wove between the campfires, around the tents, among the gathered warriors of Vansterland. He'd done the same a hundred times, before duels, before raids, before battles. This was where he was happiest. This was home to him. Or it should've been. Things weren't quite what they used to be.

The men were tired, and far from their fields and their families, and knew the odds they faced. Raith could see the doubt in their firelit faces. Could hear it in their voices, their laughter, their songs. Could smell their fear.

He wasn't the only one wandering through the camp. Death walked here too, marking out the doomed, and every man felt the chill of her passing.

He struck away towards a low hill with a single fire on top, strode up towards the summit, the chatter fading behind him. Rakki knelt on a blanket by the fire, Gorm's shield between his knees, frowning as he polished the bright rim with a rag. Gods, it was good to see him. Like a sight of home for a man a long time gone.

'Hey, hey, brother,' said Raith.

'Hey, hey.' When Rakki looked around it was like staring in a mirror. The magic mirror Horald brought back from his voyages, that showed a man the better part of himself.

Sitting down beside him was as comfortable as slipping on a favourite pair of boots. Raith watched his brother work in silence for a moment, then looked down at his own empty hands. 'Something's missing.'

'If it's your brains, your looks or your sense of humour, I've got 'em all.'

Raith snorted. 'I was thinking of a sword for me to work on.'

'Queen Skara's scabbard doesn't need a polish?'

Raith glanced across and saw that crooked little smile on Rakki's mouth. He snorted again. 'I'm standing ready, but no royal invitation yet.'

'I wouldn't hold your breath, brother. While you're waiting you could always eat.' And Rakki nodded towards the old grease-blackened pot over the fire.

'Rabbit?' Raith closed his eyes and dragged in a long sniff. Took him back to happier times, sharing the same meals, and the same hopes, and the same master. 'I do love rabbit.'

'Course. Know each other better'n anyone, don't we?'

'We do.' Raith gave Rakki a sideways glance. 'So what do you want?'

'I can't just cook for my brother?'

'Course you can, but you never do. What do you want?'

Rakki put Gorm's great shield aside and fixed him with his eye. 'I see you with the young Queen of Throvenland, and that broken-down pirate of hers, and that chubby excuse for a minister, and you look happy. You never look happy.'

'They're not so bad,' said Raith, frowning. 'And we're all on the same side, aren't we?'

'Are we? Folk are starting to wonder whether you even want to come back.'

Rakki had always known just how to sting him. 'I never chose a bit of this! All I've done is make the best of where I was put. I'd do anything to come back!'

The answer came from behind him. 'That is good to hear.'

He was no helpless child any more but that voice still made him cringe like a puppy expecting a slap. He forced himself to turn, forced himself to look straight into Mother Scaer's blue, blue eyes.

'I have missed you, Raith.' She squatted in front of him, bony wrists on her knees and her long hands dangling. 'I think it high time you returned to your rightful place.'

Raith swallowed, his mouth suddenly dry. To fill his king's cup, carry his king's sword, fight at his brother's

side? To go back to being the fiercest, the hardest, the
bloodiest? To go back to burning, and killing, and to one
day be weighed down with a chain of pommels of his
own? 'That's all I want,' he croaked out. 'All I've ever
wanted.'

'I know,' said the minister, that soothing tone that
scared him more even than the harsh one. 'I know.' And
she reached out, and scrubbed at his hair like you might
scrub a puppy between the ears. 'There is just one service
your king needs you to perform.'

Raith felt a cold shiver between his shoulders at her
touch. 'Name it.'

'I fear Father Yarvi has a ring through the young Queen
Skara's pretty nose. I fear he leads her where he pleases.
I fear he will lead her to her doom, and drag all of us
along in a stumbling procession behind.'

Raith glanced at his brother, but there was no help
there. There rarely was. 'She's got her own mind, I reckon,'
he muttered.

Mother Scaer gave a scornful snort. 'Father Yarvi plans
to break the most sacred laws of the Ministry, and bring
elf-weapons out of Strokom.'

'Elf-weapons?'

She leaned hissing towards him and Raith flinched back.
'I have seen it! Blinded by his own arrogance, he plans to
unleash the magic that broke God. I know you are not
the clever one, Raith, but do you see what is at stake?'

'I thought no one can enter Strokom and live—'

'The witch Skifr is here, and she can, and she will. If
that little bitch gives Yarvi her vote.'

Raith licked his lips. 'I could talk to her . . .'

Scaer darted out a hand and he couldn't help cringing, but she only placed her cool palm ever so gently on his cheek. 'Do you think I would be so cruel as to pit you in a battle of words against Father Yarvi? No, Raith, I think not. You are no talker.'

'Then . . .'

'You are a killer.' Her brow creased, like she was disappointed he hadn't seen it right off. 'I want you to kill her.'

Raith stared. What else could he do? He stared into Mother Scaer's eyes, and felt cold all over. 'No . . .' he whispered, but no word had ever been spoken so feebly. 'Please . . .'

Pleading had never won anything from Mother Scaer. It only showed her his weakness.

'No?' Her hand clamped painful tight about his face. 'Please?' He tried to pull away but there was no strength in him and she dragged him so close their noses almost touched. 'This is no request, boy,' she hissed, 'this is your king's command.'

'They'll know I did it,' he whined, scrabbling for excuses like a dog for a buried bone.

'I have done the thinking for you.' Mother Scaer slid out a little vial between two long fingers, what looked like water in the bottom. 'You were a king's cup-filler. Slipping this into a queen's cup can be no harder. One drop is all it will take. She will not suffer. She will fall asleep and never wake. Then there can be an end to this elf-madness. Perhaps even peace with the High King.'

'King Fynn thought he could make peace—'

'King Fynn did not know what to offer.'

Raith swallowed. 'And you do?'

'I would start with Father Yarvi, in a box.' Mother Scaer let her head drop on one side. 'Along with, perhaps, the southern half of Gettland? Everything north of Thorlby should be ours, though, don't you agree? I feel confident Grandmother Wexen could be persuaded to listen to that argument . . .'

Mother Scaer took Raith's limp wrist, and turned his hand over, and dropped the vial into his palm. Such a little thing. He thought of Skara's words, then. *Why send an honest fool to do a clever liar's job?*

'You sent me to her because I'm a killer,' he muttered.

'No, Raith.' Mother Scaer caught his face again, tilted it towards her. 'I sent you because you are *loyal*. Now claim your reward.' She stood, seeming to tower over him. 'This time tomorrow, you will be back where you belong. At the king's side.' She turned away. 'At your brother's side.' And she was gone into the night.

Raith felt Rakki's hand on his shoulder. 'How many people have you killed, brother?'

'You know I'm not much at counting.'

'What's one more, then?'

'There's a difference between killing a man who'd just as soon kill you first and killing someone . . .' Someone who's done you no harm. Someone who's been kind to you. Someone you—

Rakki dragged him close by his shirt. 'The only differ-ence is there's far more to gain now, and far more to

lose! If you don't do it . . . you'll be on your own. We'll
both be on our own.'

'What happened to sailing off together down the wide
Divine?'

'You told me to thank Mother War that we stand with
the winners, and you were right! Let's not pretend you've
only killed warriors. How much have I gone along with
for your sake? What about that woman at that farm, eh?
What about her children—'

'I know what I've done!' The fury boiled up and
Raith closed his aching fist tight around the vial and
shook it in his brother's face. 'Did it for us, didn't I?'
He caught Rakki by the collar, made him stumble,
knocking the pot off the fire and spilling stew across
the grass.

'Please, brother.' Rakki held him by the shoulders, more
hug than clinch. The more Raith hardened, the more he
softened. Knew him better than anyone, didn't he? 'If we
don't look out for each other who will? Do this. For me.
For us.'

Raith looked into his brother's eyes. Didn't seem to
him they looked much alike, right then. He sucked in
air, and slowly breathed it out, and all the fight went
with it.

'I'll do it.' He hung his head, staring at the little vial
in his palm. How many people had he killed, after all?
'I was trying to think of a good reason not to, but . . .
you're the clever one.' He closed his fist tight. 'I'm the
killer.'

*

Rin was mostly silent, lengths of wire held in her mouth as she frowned down at her work. Maybe it was having a girl her age around, or the excitement of the coming moot, but Skara talked for both of them. About her youth at Bail's Point and her few memories of her parents. About the Forest in Yaletoft, and how it burned, and how she hoped to rebuild it better. About Throvenland and her people, and how with the gods' help she'd deliver them from the tyranny of the High King, claim vengeance on Bright Yilling and protect the legacy of her murdered grandfather. Sister Owd, now Mother Owd and with a frown to match her station, nodded along approvingly.

Raith didn't. He would've loved to be part of that fine future, but he'd seen what life was. He hadn't been brought up in a fortress or a king's hall with slaves hanging on his every whim. He'd clawed himself up with no one but his brother beside him.

He put one hand to his shirt, felt the lump of the little vial under the cloth. He knew what he was. Knew what he had to do.

Then Skara smiled at him, that smile that made him feel like Mother Sun had picked him alone to shine upon. 'How do you fight in this?' she said, shaking herself and making the mail rattle. 'The weight of it!'

Raith's resolve melted like butter on a hearthstone. 'You get used to it, my queen,' he croaked.

She frowned at him. 'Are you ill?'

'Me?' he stammered. 'Why?'

'When did you learn manners? Gods, it's hot.' She

tugged at the collar of the mailshirt and the padded jacket underneath. She'd never looked more alive – flushed, eyes bright and the faintest sheen on her face. She snapped her fingers at her thrall. 'Bring me some wine, would you?'

'I'll do it,' said Raith, stepping quickly over to the jug.

'Might as well be served by the best.' Skara nodded towards him, grinning at Rin. 'He was a king's cup-bearer.'

'Was,' muttered Raith. And would be again. If he could do this one thing.

He could hardly make out Skara's words over the thudding of his heart. Slowly, carefully, trying to make sure his shaking hands didn't give him away, he poured the wine. It looked like blood in the cup.

He'd wanted to be a warrior. A man who stood by his king and won glory on the battlefield. And what had he become? A man who burned farms. Who betrayed trust. Who poisoned women.

He told himself it had to be done. For his king. For his brother.

He could feel Mother Owd's eyes on his back as he took the sip the cup-filler takes to make sure the wine's safe for better lips than his. He heard her take a step towards him, then Skara said, 'Mother Owd! You knew Father Yarvi before he was a minister, didn't you?'

'I did, my queen, briefly. He could be ruthless even then . . .'

Raith heard the minister turn away, and without daring even to breathe he slipped Mother Scaer's vial from his shirt, eased the stopper out and let one drop fall into the cup. One drop was all it would take. He watched the ripples spread, and vanish, and tucked the vial away. His knees felt weak of a sudden. He leaned on his fists.

He told himself there was no other way.

He took the cup in both hands and turned.

Skara was shaking her head as she watched Rin tucking the mail at her waist, folding it with quick fingers to fit her, fixing it with twisted wire.

'I swear, you're as nimble with steel as my old dress-maker was with silk.'

'Blessed by She Who Strikes the Anvil, my queen,' muttered Rin, stepping back to consider the results of her work. 'Don't feel too blessed lately, though.'

'Things will change. I know they will.'

'You sound like my brother.' Rin gave a sad little smile as she walked around behind Skara. 'Reckon we're done. I'll unlace it and make the adjustments.'

Skara drew herself up as Raith came close with the wine, setting one hand on the dagger at her belt, mail gleaming in the lamplight. 'Well? Would I pass for a warrior?'

Gods, he could hardly speak. His knees were trembling as he knelt before her, the way he used to before Gorm, after every duel and battle. The way he would again. 'If every shield-wall looked like that,' he managed by some great effort to say, 'you'd have no problem getting men to charge at the bastards.' And he lifted the cup in both hands towards her.

He told himself he had no choice.

'I could get used to handsome men kneeling at my feet.' She gave that laugh. That big, wild laugh she had. And she reached for the cup.

DEALS

'Where is she?' muttered Father Yarvi, glancing towards the door again.

Koll wasn't used to seeing his master nervous and it was making him nervous too. As if he wasn't nervous enough already, what with the fate of the world to be decided and all.

'Maybe she's dressing,' he whispered back. 'Strikes me as the sort of person who'd take a long time dressing for this sort of thing.'

Father Yarvi turned to glare at him and Koll found himself wilting into his chair. 'She strikes me also as the sort of person who would account for the time it takes to dress for this sort of thing.' He leaned closer. 'Don't you think?'

Koll cleared his throat, glancing towards the door again. 'Where is she?'

Over on the other side of Bail's Hall at Grom-gil-Gorm's shoulder, Mother Scaer was beginning to look distinctly pleased with herself. It was as if she and Yarvi sat on a giant set of scales – one couldn't fall without hoisting the other up.

'There is a war to be fought!' she called, and around her the warriors of Vansterland grumbled their annoyance. 'Bright Yilling will not wait for the young queen, on that we can depend. We must choose our course soon or we will drift to disaster.'

'We are well aware of that, Mother Scaer,' grated out King Uthil, then leaned close to Father Yarvi. 'Where is she?'

One half of the double doors creaked open a crack and Mother Owd slipped through, froze as all eyes turned to her, flustered as a duck who'd lost her ducklings.

'Well?' snapped Yarvi.

'Queen Skara . . .'

Gorm narrowed his eyes. 'Yes?'

'Queen Skara . . .' Mother Owd leaned to the door to peer through, and stepped back with evident relief. 'Is here.'

The doors were flung wide and Mother Sun burst into the gloom, every man left blinking stupidly as the Throvenlanders marched into the hall.

Queen Skara strode at the front, head high and with her hair loose like a dark cloud. The dawn struck fire from the red stone on her armring, from the jewels in her earring, from her glittering coat of mail, for she came in full battle-gear, a dagger at her side and a gilded helm under her arm. Raith walked behind her, white head bowed, the sword Rin had forged cradled in the scabbard Koll had carved, which looked quite a marvellous piece of work, it had to be said.

Rin had surpassed herself. Skara surely looked a warrior-queen, even if she was absurdly slight for the job and all that hair would've been a fatal encumbrance in a fight. With harness jingling she marched between the delegations of Vansterland and Gettland, deigning to look neither right nor left and with her warriors tramping after.

Mother Scaer's smile had vanished. Father Yarvi had pilfered it from her. Grom-gil-Gorm was staring at the young queen, scarred face slack. King Uthil raised his iron brows a fraction. Koll had never seen him look so astonished.

Sister Owd and Blue Jenner sat to either side of Queen Skara but she ignored Bail's Chair, tossing her gilded helmet on the table and planting her iron-knuckled fists beside it, her warriors forming a crescent behind her. Raith went down on one knee, sliding the sword up his arm so he offered her the hilt.

They all knew Skara would never draw that sword. It was pure theatre, almost ridiculous. Almost, but not quite. For looming over them on the wall was the painted image of Ashenleer victorious, dressed in mail with hair unbound and her sword-bearer kneeling at her side, and Koll looked from the queen of legend to the queen of now and found them uncannily alike.

Father Yarvi's smile grew wider. 'Oh, that's nice.'

Mother Scaer was less impressed. 'You certainly like to make an entrance,' she sneered.

'Forgive me,' said Skara. 'I was getting ready to *fight*!' She might have been a small woman but she had the voice of a hero. She barked the last word with as much violence as Thorn might have and even Mother Scaer flinched at it.

Koll leaned close to Father Yarvi. 'I think she's arrived.'

'My allies!' called Skara, voice ringing out in the silence, bright and confident as if she was born to be there. 'My guests. Kings, ministers and warriors of Gettland and Vansterland!'

Raith risked a glance at those he'd always counted his friends. The Breaker of Swords himself had his eyes fixed on Skara, but Mother Scaer was staring straight at Raith with the most murderous look he'd ever seen on her, and he'd seen some deadly ones. Soryorn had a bitter twist of hatred to his lip. But it was Rakki's eye he could hardly bear to meet. No anger, just disappointment. The look of a man betrayed by the one he trusted most. Raith looked down at the floor, the breath crawling in his throat.

'We have a great decision to make today!' Skara was saying. 'Whether to use forbidden weapons against the High King's army or to fall back before him.'

Raith was hardly listening. He was thinking about last night. He'd knelt before her, ready to do it. Then he'd heard her laugh, and his fingers had betrayed him. The cup had dropped, and the poisoned wine had spattered across the floor, and Skara had passed it off with a joke about the quality of king's cup-fillers, and he'd lain outside her door staring into the darkness all night like the faithful hound he was.

Lain awake, thinking on how he'd doomed himself.

'I am the Queen of Throvenland!' called Skara. 'The blood of Bail flows in my veins. Others might like to run from the High King, but I never will again. I have sworn vengeance against Bright Yilling and I mean to rip it from his carcass. I mean to scream defiance with my last breath! I mean to fight with every weapon.' She glared across at Mother Scaer. '*Every* weapon. And I mean to fight here. I will not abandon Throvenland. I will not abandon Bail's Point.'

All Raith ever wanted was to serve his king, to fight beside his brother, and he'd thrown it away, and could never have it back. He was on his own, like Rakki said. Sword-bearer to a girl without the strength to even draw a sword.

'What say you, King Uthil?' she called.

'I say there cannot be a warrior here not humbled by your resolve, Queen Skara.' The Iron King smiled, a sight Raith had never thought to see. 'Death waits for us all. I will be honoured to face her at your side.'

Raith saw Skara swallow as she turned to the Vanstermen.

'What say you, King Gorm?'

The weight of the mail was crushing her. The heat of it was baking her. Skara had to force herself to stand straight, stand proud, clamp the haughty challenge to her face. She was a queen, damn it. She was a queen, she was a queen, she was a queen . . .

'Humbled by your resolve?' snarled Mother Scaer. 'There cannot be a warrior here not disgusted by your play-acting. As if you ever drew a sword, let alone swung one in anger! And now you would have us give our lives for your empty kingdom, your empty pride, your—'

'Enough,' said Gorm, softly. His dark eyes did not seem to have left Skara since she first entered the hall.

'But, my king—'

'Sit,' said the Breaker of Swords. Mother Scaer ground her teeth with fury, but she dropped down on her stool.

'You wish me to fight for your fortress,' said Gorm mildly, in his sing-song voice. 'To gamble with my life and the lives of my warriors far from home. To face the High King's numberless army on the promise of elf-magic from a bald witch and a one-handed liar.' He gave an open, friendly smile. 'Very well.'

'My king—' hissed Mother Scaer, but he raised his hand to quiet her, eyes still on Skara.

'I will fight for you. Every man of Vansterland will kill for you and die for you. I will be your shield, today, tomorrow, and every day of my life. But I want something in return.'

It was silent as death in the hall. Skara swallowed. 'Name your price, great king.'

'You.'

She felt sweat prickle under her borrowed mail. She felt her gorge rising, wanted nothing more than to spray the table with sick, but she doubted Mother Kyre would have considered that the proper response to a king's proposal of marriage.

'For a long time I have been searching for a queen,' said the Breaker of Swords. 'A woman my equal in cunning and courage. A woman who can make the coins in my treasury breed. A woman who can give me many children to be proud of.'

Skara found herself glancing at Raith, and he stared back, mouth hanging open, but had no more to offer than a sword she could barely lift.

Father Yarvi had turned pale. Plainly this was one development he had not foreseen. 'Someone who can give you Throvenland,' he snapped.

Gorm's chain of dead men's pommels rattled faintly as he shrugged his great shoulders. 'Someone who can join Throvenland to Vansterland and help guide both to glory. I want your hand, your blood and your wits, Queen Skara, and in return I offer you mine. I think it a fair trade.'

'My queen—' hissed Mother Owd.

'You can't—' said Blue Jenner.

But it was Skara's turn to still her advisors with a gesture.

It was a shock, but a queen cannot allow a shock to last long. She was not a child any more.

With the Breaker of Swords beside her she might hold Bail's Point. She might claim vengeance for her grandfather. She might see Bright Yilling dead. With the key of Vansterland around her neck she might win security for her people, might rebuild Yaletoft, might forge a future for Throvenland.

She was sick of coaxing, wheedling, playing one rival off against another. She was tired of her title dangling by a thread. Skara was far from eager to share Grom-gil-Gorm's bed. But sharing his power, that was something else.

He might be more than twice her size. He might be more than twice her age. He might be scarred, fearsome, ruthless, and as far as it was possible to be from the husband she had dreamed of as a girl. But dreamers must wake. She reckoned it a match Mother Kyre would have approved of. The world is full of monsters, after all. Perhaps the best one can hope for is to have the most terrible on your side.

And it was hardly as if she had a choice. She made herself smile.

'I accept.'

CHOICES

'Are you ready?' asked Father Yarvi, stacking books in a chest. Those favourite books of his, forbidden writings on elf-ruins and elf-relics. 'We must leave on the next tide.'

'Entirely ready,' said Koll. Meaning he was packed. This was a voyage he'd never be ready for.

'Talk to Rulf. Make sure we have plenty of ale to shore up the crew's courage. Even with a favourable wind it will be five days down the coast to Furfinge.'

'One cannot count on a favourable wind,' murmured Koll.

'No, indeed. Especially when we cross the straits to Strokom.'

Koll swallowed. He would have liked to put it off until the end of the world, but it would only make

things worse, and he did that enough. 'Father Yarvi . . .'
Gods, he was a coward. 'Perhaps . . . I should stay
behind.'

The minister looked up. 'What?'

'While you're gone King Uthil might need—'

'He will not be negotiating a trade deal, spinning
a coin trick or carving a chair. He will be fighting.
Do you think King Uthil needs your advice on how
to fight?'

'Well—'

'Mother War rules here.' Yarvi shook his head as he
went back to his books. 'Those of us who speak for Father
Peace must find other ways to serve.'

Koll made another effort. 'Honestly, I'm afraid.' A good
liar weaves as much truth into the cloth as he can, after
all, and there had never been a truer word spoken than
that.

Father Yarvi frowned at him. 'Like a warrior, a minister
must master their fear. They must use it to sharpen their
judgment, rather than let it become a fog that blinds
them. Do you think I am not afraid? I am terrified.
Always. But I do what must be done.'

'Who decides what must be done, though—'

'I do.' Father Yarvi slammed the lid of his chest and
stepped close. 'We have a great opportunity! A minister
is a seeker of knowledge, and you more than most. I
have never known a more curious mind. We have the
chance to learn from the past!'

'To repeat the mistakes of the past?' Koll muttered,

and instantly regretted it as Father Yarvi caught him by the shoulders.

'I thought you wanted to change the world? To stand at the shoulder of kings and guide the course of history? I'm offering you that chance!'

Gods, he did want that. Father Koll, feared and admired, never talked down to, never taken lightly, and certainly never butted in the face by some white-haired thug. He forced it away. 'I'm grateful, Father Yarvi, but—'

'You made a promise to Rin.'

Koll blinked. 'I . . .'

'You are not too hard a book to read, Koll.'

'I made a promise to Brand!' he blurted out. 'She needs me!'

'I need you!' snapped Father Yarvi, gripping at his shoulders. His hand might have been withered, but it could still squeeze hard enough to make Koll squirm. 'Gettland needs you!' He mastered himself, let his hands fall. 'I understand, Koll, believe me, no one better. You want to do good, and stand in the light. But you are a man now. You know there are no easy answers.' Yarvi winced down at the floor, as if in pain. 'When I brought you and your mother out of slavery I never expected anything in return—'

'Why bring it up so often, then?' snapped Koll.

Father Yarvi looked up. Surprised. Even a little hurt. Enough to give Koll a familiar surge of guilt. 'Because I made Safrit a promise. To see you become the best man you could be. A man she could be proud of.'

A man who does good. A man who stands in the light. Koll hung his head. 'I keep thinking about all the things I could have done differently. I keep thinking . . . about the offer Mother Adwyn made—'

Yarvi's eyes went wide. 'Tell me you did not speak of it to my mother!'

'I've told no one. But . . . if we had, perhaps she might have found a way to peace . . .'

Father Yarvi's shoulders seemed to sag. 'The price was too high,' he muttered. 'You know that.'

'I know.'

'I could not risk fracturing our alliance. We had to have unity. You know that.'

'I know.'

'Grandmother Wexen cannot be trusted. You know that.'

'I know, but . . .'

'But Brand might be alive.' Father Yarvi looked far older than his years, of a sudden. Old, and sick, and bent under a weight of guilt. 'Do you suppose I do not have a thousand such thoughts every day? It is a minister's place always to doubt, but always to seem certain. You cannot let yourself be paralysed by what might be. Even less by what might have been.' He made a fist of his shrivelled hand, mouth twisting as though he might hit himself with it. Then he let it fall. 'You must try to pick the greater good. You must try to find the lesser evil. Then you must shoulder your regrets, and look forward.'

'I know.' Koll knew when he was beaten. He had known

he was beaten before he opened his mouth. In the end, he had wanted to be beaten.

'I'll come,' he said.

He didn't need to tell her, which was just as well. He doubted he'd have had the courage.

Rin looked up at him, and that was all it took. She turned back to her work, jaw set tight.

'You've made your choice, then.'

'I wish I didn't have to choose,' he muttered, guilty as a thief.

'But you do and you have.'

He would've preferred her to break down in tears, or come at him in a rage, or beg him to think again. He'd worked out a cowardly little plan to twist any of those back on her. But this chilly indifference he had no answer to.

Dribbling out, 'I'm sorry,' was the feeble best he could manage. He wondered if his mother would've been proud of this, and didn't much care for the answer.

'Don't be. We've wasted enough time on each other. And I've only myself to blame. Brand warned me this would happen. He always said you were too full of your own hopes to hold anyone else's.'

Gods, that hit like a punch in the balls. He opened his mouth to blurt it wasn't fair, but how could he defend himself against a dead man's judgment? Especially when he was busy proving it true.

'I always knew best.' Rin gave a hiss through gritted teeth. 'Guess Brand gets the last laugh, eh?'

Koll took a shuffling step towards her. Maybe he couldn't give her what she wanted, couldn't be what she needed, but he could see her safe at least. He owed her that much. Owed Brand that much.

'Bright Yilling might be here in a few days,' he muttered. 'And thousands of the High King's warriors with him.'

Rin snorted. 'You always did like to frame common knowledge as deep-cunning. Used to find that endearing but, I have to say, it's wearing thin.'

'You should go back to Thorlby—'

'For what? My brother's dead and my home's a burned-out shell.'

'It's not safe here . . .'

'If we lose here how safe do you think Thorlby will be? I'd rather stay, do what I can to help. That's what Brand would've done. That's what he did do.' Gods, she had courage. So much more than he did. He loved that about her.

He found himself reaching for her shoulder. 'Rin—'

She slapped his hand away, fist clenched as if she was about to hit him. He knew he deserved it. But she was in no mood to make things easy. She turned away in disgust. 'Just go. You've made your choice, Brother Koll. Get on and live with it.'

What could he say to that? He needn't have worried she'd cry. He was the one sniffing back tears as he skulked from the forge, feeling as far from the best man he could be as he ever had in his life.

There was a thin rain falling on the elf-built quay of Bail's Point. A spitting rain that drew a gloomy curtain across the world to match Koll's mood, that clung like dew to the fur on Rulf's shoulders where he stood frowning on the steering platform, that stuck the oars-men's hair to their hard-set faces as they loaded the stores. He wished Fror was with them, or Dosduvoi, but the crew Koll sailed with down the wide Divine were scattered to the winds. These were mostly men he hardly knew.

'Why the funeral face, my dove?' asked Skifr, worming one long finger out of her cloak to pick carefully at her nose. 'You once asked me if you could see magic, did you not?'

'I did, and you told me I was young and rash, and that magic has terrible risks and terrible costs, and that I should pray to every god I knew of that I never saw it.'

'Huh.' She raised her brows at the result of her rummaging, then flicked it towards Gorm's ships, and Uthil's ships, and the captured ships of Bright Yilling rocking on the tide. 'That was dour of me. Did you pray?'

'Not hard enough, it seems.' He glanced sideways at her. 'You told me you knew enough magic to do much harm, but not enough to do much good.'

'This is a war. I came to do harm.'

'That isn't very reassuring.'

'No.'

'Where did you learn magic?'

'I cannot say.'

'Cannot or will not?'

'Cannot and will not.'

Koll sighed. Every answer she gave seemed to leave him knowing less. 'Can you really take us safely into Strokom?'

'Take you into Strokom? Yes. Safely?' She shrugged her shoulders.

'That isn't very reassuring either.'

'No.'

'Will we find weapons there?'

'More than Mother War herself could make use of.'

'And if we use them . . . do we risk another Breaking of God?'

'As long as we break Grandmother Wexen, I will be satisfied.'

'That's less reassuring than ever.'

Skifr stared out towards the grey sea. 'If you suppose I came here to reassure you, you are very much mistaken.'

'Why is nothing ever easy?' Father Yarvi was frowning at the long ramp of pitted elf-stone that led to the yard of the fortress. A lean figure was coming down it. A tall, shaven-headed figure with elf-bangles stacked up her tattooed arm. 'Mother Scaer, what a surprise! I thought you wanted no part of this madness?'

The Minister of Vansterland turned her head and spat. 'I want no one to have any part of this madness, but my king has chosen his path. My place is to make sure he walks it to victory. That is why I am coming with you.'

'Your company will be a delight.' Yarvi stepped close to her. 'As long as you mean to help me. Stand in my way, you will regret it.'

'We understand one another, then,' said Mother Scaer, curling her lip.

'We always have.'

Koll sighed to himself. What better foundation for an alliance than mutual hatred and suspicion?

'To your oars, then!' called Rulf. 'I'm getting no younger!'

GUDRUN'S EXAMPLE

It was a beautiful morning in late summer, Mother Sun making last night's rain glitter like jewels in the grass.

'This is our weakest point,' said Raith.

It took no great warrior to see that. The northeastern corner of the fortress had been sliced away by the Breaking of God as if by a giant knife, and kings of the distant past had built a tower to plug the gap. It was an ill-made and neglected thing, its roof fallen in and birds swarming on the dropping-caked rafters, the man-built stretch of wall beside it bowing outwards, shored up with crumbling bastions.

'Gudrun's Tower,' murmured Skara.

'How did it get the name?' asked Mother Owd.

Skara had been greatly annoyed when Mother Kyre

taught her the story but, like most of the minister's lessons, she found she remembered it well enough. 'Princess Gudrun was the granddaughter of a king of Throvenland.'

'A poor start,' grunted Mother Owd. She tended to be grumpy in the mornings. 'Still, I know a few of those who turned out well.'

'Not this one. She fell in love with a stable-boy.'

'That was rash.'

'I suppose love falls where it falls.'

Mother Owd raised one brow. 'Generally one can see it toppling from afar, and make an effort to get out of the way.'

'Well Gudrun didn't. Throvenland had three kings in those days, and her grandfather promised her to one of the others. She tried to run away, so he hung her lover from that tower and locked her in the top of it until she learned her duty.'

Mother Owd scratched at the loose bun her hair was gathered into. 'I'm having trouble seeing where the happy ending will come from.'

'It won't. Gudrun flung herself from the battlements and died in the ditch.'

'Let's hope we don't all end up following her example,' said Raith.

'Killing ourselves for love?' asked Skara.

'Dying in the ditch.'

Raith had seemed grim lately, even for him, and though she hardly needed to look further than the approach of ten thousand armed enemies to explain anyone's bad mood, Skara wondered if her deal with Gorm could be behind it. She was far from all delight at that herself, but there was nothing to be done. She gave a weary sigh. There were bigger things to worry about than anyone's feelings, even her own.

The sound of hoofbeats drew her eyes and she saw riders spilling from the gate. Two hundred or more horses in a fast-moving column, earth showering as they thundered past the men still digging the ditch deeper and across the muddied ground where Gorm and Uthil's camps had been pitched.

Blue Jenner was striding up the gentle rise towards them and Skara called out to him. 'Whoever doesn't want to stay for what's coming?'

'Thorn Bathu,' said Jenner, turning to watch the riders pass. 'But only because Bright Yilling isn't getting here fast enough for her taste. She's taking two hundred of Gettland's bloodiest to hurt him however she can.'

'That could be quite a lot of hurt,' murmured Skara, watching the riders stream out of the long shadow of Bail's Point, through the deserted village and away to the north.

'We've no fodder for the horses in any case, my queen.' Jenner stopped beside them, hands planted on his hips. 'There isn't too much fodder for the men. Bright Yilling burned most of the farms within a hundred miles and picked clean most of the rest. Uthil and Gorm reckon only a thousand men can stay. Those with families to worry over and harvests to bring in will be taking ship north to Thorlby and beyond.'

Skara blinked at that. 'We'll be outnumbered ten to one.'

'The longer the odds the greater the glory,' muttered Raith. 'Or so I've heard . . .'

'It'll be picked warriors who remain.' Jenner tried as usual to plot an optimistic course. 'And plenty to man the walls until Father Yarvi comes back. Four hundred Vanstermen, four hundred Gettlanders, a hundred smiths, cooks, servants. A hundred of ours.'

'We have that many willing to stay?'

'There's five times that many willing to die for you, my queen, and I can pick a hundred who'll kill a few of the High King's men doing it.'

'I'm humbled,' said Skara, 'truly. But you shouldn't be one of them. You've already done far more than—'

Blue Jenner snorted. 'Oh, I'm staying and that deal's done. I've promised my crew a hell of a pay-off when you beat the High King. If I don't deliver I'll look quite the fool. You should go, though.'

Her turn to snort. 'How can I expect others to risk their lives if I won't?'

'My queen,' said Mother Owd, 'your blood is worth more to Throvenland than—'

'I am a queen in my own fortress. The only person who can give me orders is the High King, and since I am in open rebellion against him, you are out of luck. I stay, and that is all.'

'Then I stay too.' Mother Owd sighed. 'A healer's place is among the wounded. A minister's place is beside her queen.'

Skara felt a rush of gratitude that almost brought tears to her eyes. They were hardly the advisors she would have picked but she would not have traded them for anyone now. 'The gods may have taken my grandfather.' Skara put one arm around Mother Owd, and one around Blue Jenner, and hugged them tight. 'But they sent me two pillars to lean upon.'

Mother Owd frowned down at herself. 'I am a little squat for a pillar.'

'You hold me up admirably even so. Now go.' Skara pushed them off towards the fortress. 'Pick me the hundred warriors who'll kick Bright Yilling hardest in his balls.'

'We'll pick 'em, my queen,' said Blue Jenner, grinning back. 'And find 'em the heaviest boots we can.'

Skara was left standing on the sward with Raith. The birds continued to twitter. The calls of the labourers in the ditch floated towards them. The breeze fumbled across the grass. Skara did not look sideways. But she liked knowing he was there, at her shoulder.

'You can go,' she said. 'If you want to.'

'I said I'd die for you. I meant it.'

He had some of that old swagger as she looked around, daring and dangerous and making no apologies, and she smiled to see it. 'No need quite yet. I still need someone to threaten my visitors with.'

'I can do that too.' He smiled back. That hard and hungry smile that showed all his teeth. Long enough for it to be no accident. Long enough for that warm nervousness to set her skin tingling.

There was a part of her that would have liked to follow Gudrun's example. To piss on the proper thing and go rolling in the hay with her stable-boy. At least to know what it felt like.

But there was a much larger part of her that laughed at the notion. She was no romantic. She could not afford to be. She was a queen, and promised to Grom-gil-Gorm, the Breaker of Swords. A nation relied on her. However she had railed at and complained to and rebelled against Mother Kyre, after all, in the end she had always done her duty.

So instead of clutching hold of Raith like a drowning girl to a log and kissing him as if the secret of life was in his mouth, she swallowed, and frowned back at Gudrun's Tower.

'It means a lot,' she said. 'That you'd fight for me.'

'Not that much.' The sun had been covered by cloud for a moment and the jewels in the grass were turned to cold water. 'Every good killer needs someone to kill for.'

THE THOUSAND

S oryorn was a grand archer and cut a hero's figure
against the bloody sunset, one foot up on the battlements at the top of Gudrun's tower, back curved
as he bent his great bow, the light from the flaming arrow
shifting on his hard-set face.

'Burn it,' said Gorm.

The eyes of the thousand picked warriors of
Throvenland, Vansterland and Gettland followed the
streak of fire as the shaft curved through the still evening
and thudded into the deck of Bright Yilling's ship. Blue
flame shot from it as the southern oil caught with a gentle
whomp. In a moment the whole boat was alight in a
blaze Raith could almost feel the heat of, even up here
on the wall.

He glanced sideways and saw the warm glow light up

Skara's smile. It had been her idea. A warrior's ship is his heart and his home, after all.

It had been a bastard of a job hauling it out of the harbour and on rollers up the long ramp to the yard. Raith's back was aching and his hands raw from his part in it. Queen Skara had given the gilded weathervane to Blue Jenner, King Gorm had torn out the silver fittings to melt down and make cups, King Uthil had taken the red-dyed sail to spare the women of Gettland some weaving. They'd pulled the mast down to fit it through the entrance passage and they'd gouged the fine carvings when it got wedged in the gateway, but they'd got it outside in the end.

Raith hoped Bright Yilling would appreciate the effort they'd made to welcome him to Bail's Point. But either way the defenders enjoyed the sight of his ship in flames. There was cheering, there was laughter, there were insults spat at Yilling's scouts, sat calmly on horseback far out of bowshot. The high spirits were shortlived, though.

Grandmother Wexen's army was beginning to arrive.

They tramped down the road from the north in an orderly column, an iron snake of men with the High King's great standard at their head, the seven-rayed sun of the One God bobbing here and there above the crowd, and the marks of a hundred heroes and more hanging limp in the evening stillness. On they came, through the ruins of the village, more, and more, stretching away into the haze of distance.

'When do they stop coming?' Raith heard Skara

whisper, one arm across her chest to nervously twist her armring.

'I'd been hoping the scouts got their numbers wrong,' muttered Blue Jenner.

'Looks like they did,' grunted Raith. 'They guessed too few.'

Up on the walls mocking laughs became grim smiles, then even grimmer frowns as that mighty snake of men split, flowed about the fortress like flooding water about an island, and the warriors of the Lowlands, and Inglefold, and Yutmark encircled Bail's Point from the cliffs in the east to the cliffs in the west.

No need for shows of defiance on their side. Their numbers spoke in thunder.

'Mother War spreads her wings over Bail's Point,' murmured Owd.

A fleet of wagons came now, groaning with forage, and after them an endless crowd of families and thralls, servants and merchants, priests and profiteers, diggers and drovers with a lowing and bleating herd of sheep and cows that put any market Raith had ever seen to shame.

'A whole city on the move,' he muttered.

Darkness was closing in and the rearguard were only just arriving in a river of twinkling torches. Wild-looking men, their bone standards lit by flame, their bare chests marked with scars and smeared with war-paint.

'Shends,' said Raith.

'Aren't they sworn enemies of the High King?' asked Skara, her voice more shrill than usual.

Mother Owd's mouth was a hard line. 'Grandmother Wexen must have prevailed upon them to be our enemies instead.'

'I hear they eat their captives alive,' someone muttered.

Blue Jenner gave the man a glare. 'Best not get captured.'

Raith worked his sweaty palm around the handle of his shield and glanced towards the harbour, where plenty of ships were still gathered behind the safety of the chains to carry the thousand defenders away . . .

He bit his tongue until he tasted blood and forced his eyes back to the host gathering outside their walls. He'd never felt scared of a fight before. Maybe it was that the odds had always been stacked on his side. Or maybe it was that he'd lost his place, and his family, and any hope of getting them back.

They say it's men with nothing to lose you should fear. But it's them who fear most.

'There,' said Skara, pointing out at the High King's ranks.

Someone was walking towards the fortress. Swaggering the way you might to a friend's hall rather than an enemy's stronghold. A warrior in bright mail that caught the light of the burning ship and seemed to burn itself. A warrior with long hair breeze-stirred and an oddly soft, young, handsome face, who carried no shield and propped his left hand loose on his sword's hilt.

'Bright Yilling,' growled Jenner, baring all the teeth he still had.

Yilling stopped well within bowshot, grinning up

towards the crowded battlements, and called out high and clear. 'I don't suppose King Uthil's up there?'

It was some comfort to hear Uthil's voice just as harsh and careless whether he faced one enemy or ten thousand. 'Are you this man they call Bright Yilling?'

Yilling gave an extravagant shrug. 'Someone has to be.'

'The one who killed fifty men in the battle at Fornholt?' called Gorm, from the roof of Gudrun's tower.

'Couldn't say. I was killing, not counting.'

'The one who cut the prow-beast from Prince Conmer's ship with a single blow?' asked Uthil.

'It's all in the wrist,' said Yilling.

'The one who murdered King Fynn and his defenceless minister?' barked Skara.

Yilling kept smiling. 'Aye, that one. And you should have seen what I did to my dinner just now.' He happily patted his belly. 'There was a slaughter!'

'You are smaller than I expected,' said Gorm.

'And you are larger than I dared hope.' Yilling wound a strand of his long hair around one finger. 'Big men make a fine loud crash when I knock them down. I am dismayed to find the Iron King and the Breaker of Swords penned up like hogs in a sty. I felt sure you would be keen to test your sword-work against mine, steel to steel.'

'Patience, patience.' Gorm leaned on the battlements, his hands dangling. 'Perhaps when we are better acquainted I can kill you.'

Uthil gave a stiff nod. 'A good enmity, like a good friendship, takes time to mature. One does not start at the end of a story.'

Yilling smirked the wider. 'Then I will bide my time and earnestly hope to kill you both in due course. It would be a shame to deny the skalds as fine a song as that would make.'

Gorm sighed. 'The skalds will find something to sing about, either way.'

'Where is Thorn Bathu?' asked Yilling, glancing about as though she might be hiding in the ditch. 'I've killed some women but never one of her fame.'

'No doubt she will introduce herself presently,' said Uthil.

'No doubt. It is the fate of every strong warrior to one day cross the path of a stronger. That is our great blessing and our great curse.'

Uthil nodded again. 'Death waits for us all.'

'She does!' Yilling spread his arms wide, fingers working. 'Long have I yearned to embrace my mistress, but I have yet to find a warrior skilful enough to introduce us.' He turned to the blazing ship. 'You burned my boat?'

'A gracious host gives guests a place at the fire,' called Gorm, and a gale of mocking laughter ran along the battlements. Raith forced up a jagged chuckle of his own, even though it took a hero's effort.

Yilling only shrugged, though. 'Bit of a waste. It was a fine ship.'

'We have more ships than we know what to do with since we captured all of yours,' growled Gorm.

'And you have so few men to put in them, after all,' said Yilling, dampening the laughter again. He sighed at the flames. 'I carved the prow-beast myself. Still, what's burned is burned, say I, and cannot be unburned.'

Skara clutched at the battlements. 'You've burned half of Throvenland to no purpose!'

'Ah! You must be the young Skara, queen of the few unburned bits.' Yilling pushed out his plump lips and squinted up. 'Make me your villain if you please, my queen, blame me for all your woes, but I have broken no oaths, and have a noble purpose in my burning. To make you kneel before the High King. That . . . and fire is pretty.'

'It takes a moment to burn what takes a lifetime to build!'

'That's what makes it pretty. You'll be kneeling to the High King soon enough, either way.'

'Never,' she snarled.

Yilling wagged a finger. 'Everyone says that till the tendons in their legs are cut. Then, believe me, they go down quick enough.'

'Just words, my queen,' said Blue Jenner, easing Skara back from the parapet. But if words were weapons, Raith felt Yilling had the best of that bout.

'Are you just going to stand and blather?' Gorm stretched his arms wide and gave a showy yawn. 'Or have a go at our walls? Even little men make a fine loud crash when I knock them down from this height, and I fancy some exercise.'

'Ooh, that's a worthy question!' Yilling peered up at the bruising sky, and then back towards his men, busy surrounding Bail's Point in an ever-thickening ring of sharpened steel. 'I find myself in two minds . . . let's toss for it and let Death decide, eh, Queen Skara?'

Skara's pale face twitched, and she gripped tight to Jenner's arm.

'Heads we come for you, tails we stay!' And Yilling flicked a coin high into the air, flickering orange with the light of his burning ship, and let it fall in the grass, hands on hips as he peered down.

'Well?' called Gorm. 'Heads or tails?'

Yilling gave a burst of high laughter. 'I'm not sure, it rolled away! So it goes sometimes, eh, Breaker of Swords?'

'Aye,' grunted Gorm, somewhat annoyed. 'So it goes.'

'Let's leave it till tomorrow. I've a feeling you'll still be here!'

The High King's champion turned, the smile still on his soft, smooth face, and sauntered back towards his lines. At twice bowshot from the walls they'd started hammering stakes into ground.

A circle of thorns, facing in.

THE FORBIDDEN CITY

No fevered imagining, no night-time foreboding, no madman's nightmare could have come close to the reality of Strokom.

The *South Wind* crawled across a vast circle of still water. A secret sea miles across, ringed by islands, some mere splinters of rock, some stretching out of sight, all sprouting with buildings. With torn cubes and broken towers and twisted fingers of crumbling elf-stone and still-shining elf-glass. More jutted half-drowned from the dark waters. Thousands upon thousands upon thousands of empty windows glowered down and Koll tried to reckon up how many elves might have lived and died in this colossal wreck, but could not find the numbers to begin.

'Quite a sight,' murmured Father Yarvi in the greatest understatement ever uttered.

All was silent. No birds circled overhead. No fish flickered in their wake. Only the creaking of the rowlocks and the muttered prayers of the crew. Long-tested oarsmen missed their strokes and tangled their oars with each other for gazing about in awestruck horror, and Koll didn't doubt he was the most awestruck and horrified of the whole crowd.

The gods knew, he'd never laid claim to being a brave man. But it seemed cowardice could land you in more trouble than courage.

'She Who Sings the Wind is angry,' murmured Mother Scaer as she peered up at the tortured sky, a giant spiral of bruised purples and wounded reds and midnight blacks where no star would ever show. A weight of cloud to crush the world.

'Here the wind is just the wind.' Skifr took off the tangle of holy signs, talismans, blessed medallions and lucky teeth she always wore and tossed them aside. 'Here there are no gods.'

Koll far preferred the notion of angry gods to the notion of none at all. 'What do you mean?'

Skifr stood tall by the prow and spread her arms, her ragged cloak flapping as if she was some huge, unnatural bird, some madman's prow-beast pointing the way to doom.

'This is Strokom!' she shrieked. 'Greatest ruin of the elves! You can cease your prayers, for here even the gods fear to tread!'

'I'm not sure you're helping,' growled Father Yarvi.

The crew gazed up at her, some hunching as though

they could vanish into their own shoulders. Tough and desperate warriors, every one, but there was no battle, no hardship, no loss that could prepare a man for this.

'We shouldn't be here,' grunted one old oarsman with a squinting eye.

'This place is cursed,' said another. 'Folk who tread here sicken and die.'

Father Yarvi stepped in front of Skifr, as calm as a man at his own firepit. 'One stroke at a time, my friends! I understand your fears but they are empty! The money-boxes Queen Laithlin will give you when you return, on the other hand, will be brimming full. The elves are thousands of years gone, and we have the Walker in the Ruins to show us the safe path. There is no danger. Trust me. Have I ever steered you wrong?' The warnings withered to grumbles, but even the promise of riches couldn't coax out a single smile.

'There!' called Skifr, pointing towards a set of slanted steps rising from the water, big enough to have been made for the feet of giants. 'Put us ashore.'

Rulf called for slow strokes, and leant upon the steering oar, and brought them smoothly in, gravel grating against the keel. 'How can the waters be so calm?' Koll heard him mutter.

'Because all things here are dead,' said Skifr. 'Even the waters.' And she sprang across to the steps.

As Father Yarvi put one hand on the rail, Mother Scaer caught his withered wrist. 'It is not too late to give up on this madness. One foot on this cursed ground and we break the most sacred law of the Ministry.'

Yarvi twisted free. 'Any law that cannot bend in a storm is destined to be broken.' And he leapt down.

Koll took a deep breath and held it as he vaulted over the side. He was much relieved not to be instantly struck down when his boots hit the stone. It seemed, in fact, just ground like any other. Ahead, in the shadowy valleys between the mountainous buildings nothing moved, except maybe some loose panel or dangling cable shifting in the ceaseless wind.

'No moss,' he said, squatting at the water's edge. 'No weed, no barnacle.'

'Nothing grows in these seas but dreams,' said Skifr. She fished something from inside her cloak of rags. A strange little bottle, and when she tipped it out five things lay on her pink palm. They looked like grubby beans, one half white, the other red, and peering closely Koll could see a faded inscription written upon each in tiny letters. Elf-letters, it hardly needed to be said, and Koll was about to make a holy sign over his chest when he remembered the gods were elsewhere, and settled for pressing gently at the weights under his shirt. That was some small comfort.

'Each of us must eat a bean,' said Skifr, and tossing her head back flicked one into her mouth and swallowed it.

Mother Scaer frowned down at them with even more than her usual scorn. 'What if I do not?'

Skifr shrugged. 'I have never been foolish enough to refuse my teachers' solemn instruction always to eat one when I pass through elf-ruins.'

'This could be poison.'

Skifr leaned close. 'If I wanted to kill you I would simply cut your throat and give your corpse to Mother Sea. Believe me when I say I have often considered it. Perhaps there is poison all around us, and this is the cure?'

Father Yarvi snatched his from Skifr's palm and swallowed it. 'Stop moaning and eat the bean,' he said, frowning off inland. 'We have chosen our path and it winds long ahead of us. Keep the men calm while we are gone, Rulf.'

The old helmsman finished tying off the prow-rope to a great boulder and swallowed his bean. 'Calm might be too much to ask.'

'Then just keep them *here*,' said Skifr, thrusting her palm and the thing upon it towards Koll. 'We will hope to be back within five days.'

'Five days out there?' asked Koll, the bean frozen halfway to his mouth.

'If we are lucky. These ruins go on for miles and the ways are not easy to find.'

'How do you know them?' asked Scaer.

Skifr let her head drop on one side. 'How does anyone know anything? By listening to those who went before. By following in their footsteps. Then, in time, by walking your own path.'

Scaer's lip wrinkled. 'Is there more to you than smoke and riddles, witch?'

'Perhaps, when the time is right, I will show you more. There is nothing to fear. Nothing but Death, anyway.' She leaned close to Mother Scaer, and whispered. 'And is she not always at your shoulder?'

The bean was uncomfortable sliding down Koll's throat, but it tasted of nothing and left him feeling no different. Plainly it was no cure for soreness, guilt, and a crushing sense of doom.

'What about the rest of the crew?' he whispered, frowning back towards the ship.

Skifr shrugged. 'I have only five beans,' and she turned towards the ruins with the ministers of Gettland and Vansterland at her heels.

Gods, Koll wished now he'd stayed with Rin. All the things he loved about her came up in a needy surge. He felt then he'd rather have faced ten of the High King's armies by her side than walked into the cursed silence of Strokom.

But, as Brand always used to say, you'll buy nothing with wishes.

Koll shouldered his pack, and followed the others.

WOUNDS

Men lay on the floor, spitting and writhing. They begged for help and muttered for their mothers. They swore through gritted teeth, and snarled, and screamed, and bled.

Gods, a man held a lot of blood. Skara could hardly believe how much.

A prayer-weaver stood in the corner, droning out entreaties to He Who Knits the Wound and wafting about the sweet-smelling smoke from a cup of smouldering bark. Even so there was a suffocating stink, of sweat and piss and all the secrets that a body holds and Skara had to press one hand over her mouth, over her nose, over her eyes almost, staring between her fingers.

Mother Owd was not a tall woman but she seemed a towering presence now, less like a peach than the

deep-rooted tree that bore them. Her forehead was
furrowed, stray hairs stuck with sweat to her clenched
jaw, sleeves rolled up to show strong muscles working
in her red-stained forearms. The man she was tending
to arched his back as she probed at the wound in his
thigh, then started to thrash and squeal.

'Someone hold him!' she growled. Rin brushed past
Skara, caught the man's wrist and pressed him roughly
down while Sister Owd plucked a bone needle from her
loose bun, stuck it in her teeth so she could thread it,
and began to sew, the man snorting and bellowing and
spraying spit.

Skara remembered Mother Kyre naming the organs,
describing their purpose and their patron god. *A princess
should know how people work*, she had said. But you can
know a man is full of guts and still find the sight of them
a most profound shock.

'They came with ladders,' Blue Jenner was saying. 'And
bravely enough. Not a task I'd fancy. Reckon Bright
Yilling promised good ring-money to any man could
scale the walls.'

'Not many did,' said Raith.

Skara watched flies flit about a heap of bloody bandages.
'Enough to cause this.'

'This?' She hardly knew how Jenner could chuckle
now. 'You should see what we did to them! If this is the
worst we suffer before Father Yarvi gets back I'll count
us lucky indeed.' Skara must have looked horrified,
because he faltered as he caught her eye. 'Well . . . not
these boys, maybe . . .'

'He was testing us.' Raith's face was pale and his cheek scraped with grazes. Skara did not want to know how he got them. 'Feeling out where we're weak.'

'Well it's a test we passed,' said Jenner. 'This time, anyway. We'd best get back to the walls, my queen. Bright Yilling ain't a fellow to give up at the first stumble.'

By then they were hauling another man up onto Sister Owd's table while the minister rubbed her hands clean in a bowl of thrice-blessed water already pink with blood. He was a big Gettlander not much older than Skara, the only sign of a wound a dark patch on his mail.

Owd had a rattling set of little knives strung on a cord around her neck, and she used one now to slit the thongs that held his armour, then Rin dragged it and the padding underneath up to show a little slit in his belly. Mother Owd bent over it, pressed at it, watched blood leak out. He squirmed and his mouth opened but he made only a breathy gasp, his soft face shuddering. Sister Owd sniffed at the wound, muttered a curse, and stood.

'There's nothing I can do. Someone sing him a prayer.'

Skara stared. That easily, a man condemned to death. But those are the choices a healer must make. Who can be saved. Who is already meat. Mother Owd had moved on and Skara forced herself up beside the dying man on trembling legs, her stomach in her mouth. Forced herself to take his hand.

'What is your name?' she asked him.

His whisper was hardly more than a breath. 'Sordaf.'

She tried to sing a prayer to Father Peace to guide him to an easy rest. A prayer she remembered Mother Kyre singing when she was small, after her father died, but her throat would hardly make the words. She had heard of men dying well in battle. She could no longer imagine what that meant.

The wounded man's bulging eyes were fixed on her. Or fixed beyond her. On his family, maybe. On things left undone and unsaid. On the darkness beyond the Last Door.

'What can I do?' she whispered, clutching at his hand as hard as he clutched at hers.

He tried to make words but they came out only squelches, blood speckling his lips.

'Someone get some water!' she shrieked.

'No need, my queen.' Rin gently prised Skara's gripping fingers from his. 'He's gone.' And Skara realized his hand was slack.

She stood.

She felt dizzy. Hot and prickly all over.

Someone was screaming. Hoarse, strange, bubbling screams, and in between she heard the burbling of the prayer-weaver, burbling, burbling, begging for help, begging for mercy.

She tottered to the doorway, nearly fell, burst into the yard, was sick, nearly fell in her sick, clawed her dress out of the way as she was sick again, wiped the long string of bile from her mouth and leaned against the wall, shaking.

'Are you all right, my queen?' Mother Owd stood wiping her hands on a cloth.

'I've always had a weak stomach—' Skara coughed, retched again, but all that came up was bitter spit.

'We all have to keep our fears somewhere. Especially if we cannot afford to let them show. I think you hide yours in your stomach, my queen.' Owd put a gentle hand on Skara's shoulder. 'As good a place as any.'

Skara looked towards the doorway, the moans of the wounded coming faint from beyond. 'Did I make this happen?' she whispered.

'A queen must make hard choices. But also bear the results with dignity. The faster you run from the past, the faster it catches you. All you can do is turn to face it. Embrace it. Try and meet the future wiser for it.' And the minister unscrewed the cap from a flask and offered it to Skara. 'Your warriors look to you for an example. You don't have to fight to show them courage.'

'I don't feel like a queen,' muttered Skara. She took a sip and winced as she felt the spirits burn all the way down her sore throat. 'I feel like a coward.'

'Then act as if you're brave. No one ever feels ready. No one ever feels grown up. Do the things a great queen would do. Then you are one, however you feel.'

Skara stood tall, and pushed her shoulders back. 'You are a wise woman and a great minister, Mother Owd.'

'I am neither one.' The minister leaned close, rolling her sleeves up a little further. 'But I have become quite good at pretending to be both. Do you need to be sick again?'

Skara shook her head, took another burning sip from the flask and handed it back, watched Owd take a lengthy swig of her own. 'I hear I have the blood of Bail in my veins—'

'Forget the blood of Bail.' Owd gripped Skara's arm. 'Your own is good enough for anyone.'

Skara took a shuddering breath. Then she followed her minister back into the darkness.

SPROUTED A CONSCIENCE

Raith stood on the man-built stretch of wall near Gudrun's Tower, staring across the scarred, trampled, arrow-prickled turf towards the stakes that marked the High King's lines.

He'd hardly slept. Dozed outside Skara's door. Dreamed again of that woman and her children, and started up in a chill sweat with his hand on his dagger. Nothing but silence.

Five days since the siege began and every day they'd come at the walls. Come with ladders, and wicker screens to guard them from the shower of arrows, the hail of stones. Come bravely, with their fiercest faces and their fiercest prayers, and bravely been beaten back. They hadn't killed many of the thousand defenders but they'd made their mark even so. Every warrior in Bail's Point was pink-eyed from sleeplessness, grey-faced from fear. Facing Death for a wild moment is one thing. Her cold breath on your neck day in and day out is more than men were made to bear.

Great humps of fresh-turned earth had been thrown up just out of bowshot. Barrows for the High King's dead. They were still digging now. Raith could hear the scraping of distant shovels, some priest's song warbled in the southerner's tongue to the southerner's One God. He lifted his chin, winced as he scratched at his neck with the backs of his fingernails. A warrior should rejoice in the corpses of his enemies, but Raith had no rejoicing left in him.

'Beard bothering you?' Blue Jenner strolled up yawning, smoothing down his few wild strands of hair and leaving them wilder than before.

'Itchy. Strange, how little things still find a way to niggle at you, even in the midst of all this.'

'Life's a queue of small irritations with the Last Door at the end. You could just shave.'

Raith kept scratching. 'Always pictured myself dying with a beard. Like most things long anticipated, turns out rather a disappointment.'

'A beard's just a beard,' said Jenner, scratching at his own. 'Keeps your face warm in a snowstorm and catches food from time to time, but I knew a man grew his long and got it caught in his horse's bridle. Dragged through a hedge and broke his neck.'

'Killed by his own beard? That's embarrassing.'

'The dead feel no shame.'

'The dead feel no anything,' said Raith. 'No coming back through the Last Door, is there?'

'Maybe not. But we always leave a bit of ourselves on this side.'

'Eh?' muttered Raith, not caring much for that notion.

'Our ghosts stick in the memories of those that knew us. Those that loved us, hated us.'

Raith thought of that woman's face, lit by flames, tears glistening, still so clear after all this time, and he worked his fingers and felt the old ache there. 'Those that killed us.'

'Aye.' Blue Jenner's eyes were fixed far off. On his own tally of dead folk, maybe. 'Them most of all. You all right?'

'Broke my hand once. Never quite healed.'

'Nothing ever quite heals.' Blue Jenner sniffed, hawked noisily, worked his mouth, and sent spittle spinning over the walls. 'Seems Thorn Bathu introduced herself in the night.'

'Aye,' said Raith. There was a charred scar through one side of Bright Yilling's camp, and by the faint smell of burning straw it seemed she'd done for a good deal of his fodder. 'Reckon it was an even more painful experience than my first meeting with her.'

'A good friend to have, that girl, and a bad, bad enemy.' Jenner chuckled. 'Liked her since I first ran into her out on the Denied.'

'You've been down the Denied?' asked Raith.

'Three times.'

'What's it like?'

'It's very much like a big river.'

Raith was looking past Blue Jenner towards the crumbling doorway in the side of Gudrun's Tower. Rakki had just stepped out of it, his white hair ruffled by the breeze as he frowned towards Yilling's great gravedigging.

Jenner raised one grey brow. 'Anything I can do?'

'Some things you have to do alone.' And Raith patted the old raider on the shoulder as he walked past.

'Brother.'

Rakki didn't look at him, but a muscle at his temple twitched. 'Am I?'

'If you're not you look surprisingly like me.'

Rakki didn't smile. 'You should go.'

'Why?' But even as he said it Raith felt the great presence, and turned reluctantly to find the Breaker of Swords stooping through the doorway and into the dawn, Soryorn at his shoulder.

'Look who comes strolling,' sang Gorm.

Soryorn carefully adjusted his garnet-studded thrall-collar. 'It is Raith.' He'd always been a man of few words and those the obvious.

Gorm stood with eyes closed, listening to the distant songs of the One God priests. 'Can there be more soothing music of a morning than an enemy's prayers for his dead?'

'A harp?' said Raith. 'I like a harp.'

Gorm opened his eyes. 'Do you truly think jokes will mend what you have broken?'

'Can't hurt, my king. I wanted to congratulate you on your betrothal.' Though few betrothals could've delighted him less. 'Skara will be the envy of the world as a queen, and she brings all of Throvenland for a dowry—'

'Great prizes indeed.' Gorm raised an arm and swept it towards the warriors that encircled them on every side. 'But there is the small matter of defeating the High King before I claim them. Your disloyalty has forced me to gamble everything on Father Yarvi's cunning, rather than bartering a peace with Grandmother Wexen, as I and Mother Scaer had planned.'

Raith glanced at Rakki, but his eyes were on the ground. 'I didn't think—'

'I do not keep dogs to think. I keep them to obey. I have no use for a cur who does not come when he is whistled for. Who does not bite who I tell him to bite. There is no place in my household for such a wretched thing as that. I warned you that I saw a grain of mercy in you. I warned you it might crush you. Now it has.' Gorm shook his head as he turned away. 'All those eager boys who would have killed a hundred times for your place, and I chose you.'

'Disappointing,' said Soryorn, then with a parting sneer he followed his master down the walkway.

Raith stood there in silence. There'd been a time he admired Grom-gil-Gorm beyond all other men. His strength. His ruthlessness. He used to dream of being like him. 'Hard to believe I ever looked up to that bastard.'

'There's one difference between us,' muttered Rakki. 'I've always hated him. Here's another, though. I know I still need him. What's your plan now?'

'Can't say I've been working to a plan.' Raith frowned

at his brother. 'Ain't easy, killing someone who's done you no harm.'

'No one said it was easy.'

'Well it's easier if you're not the one has to do it. Seems it's always you that wants the hard thing done,' snapped Raith, trying to keep his voice down, and his fists down too, 'but it's me has to do it!'

'Well you can't help me now, can you?' Rakki stabbed towards Bail's Hall with one finger. 'Since you chose that little bitch over your own—'

'Don't talk about her that way!' snarled Raith, bunching his fists. 'All I chose was not to kill her!'

'And now look where we are. Some time to sprout a conscience.' Rakki looked back to the graves. 'I'll pray for you, brother.'

Raith snorted. 'Those folk on the border, I reckon they prayed when we came in the night. I reckon they prayed hard as anyone can.'

'So?'

'Their prayers didn't save them from me, did it? Why would yours save me from some other bastard?' And Raith stalked off down the walls, back to Blue Jenner.

'Problem?' asked the old raider.

'Hatful of 'em.'

'Well, family's family. Daresay your brother will come around.'

'He might. I doubt the Breaker of Swords will be so giving.'

'He doesn't strike me as a giver.'

'I'm done with him.' Raith spat over the walls. 'I'm done with me too, the way I was.'

'Did you like what you were?'

'Plenty at the time. Now it seems I was more than a bit of a bastard.' That woman's face wouldn't leave him alone, and he swallowed and looked down at the old stones under his feet. 'How does a man know what's right to do?'

Jenner puffed out his cheeks. 'I've spent half my life doing the wrong thing. Most of the rest trying to work out the least wrong thing. The few times I've done the right thing it's mostly been by accident.'

'And you're about the best man I know.'

Blue Jenner's eyebrows shot up. 'I thank you for the compliment. And I pity you.'

'So do I, old man. So do I.' Raith watched the little figures moving in Bright Yilling's camp. Men crawling from their beds, gathered about their fires, picking at their breakfasts, maybe somewhere an old man and a young, looking up to where they stood on the walls and talking about nothing. 'Reckon they'll come again today?'

'Aye, and that concerns me somewhat.'

'They'll never get over these walls with ladders. Not ever.'

'No, and Yilling must know it. So why waste his strength trying?'

'Keep us nervous. Keep us worried. It's a siege, isn't it? He wants to get in somehow.'

'And in such a way as will burnish his fame.' Jenner nodded out towards the graves. 'After a battle, do you dig big howes for every man?'

'Most of 'em we'd burn in a heap, but these One God-worshippers got odd ways with their dead.'

'Why so close to our walls, though? You hide your hurts from an enemy. You don't shove your losses under his nose, even if you can afford them.'

Raith reached up and rubbed at that old notch out of his ear. 'I'm taking it you've got some clever explanation?'

'You're getting to know and admire me, I see.' Jenner pushed his chin forward to scratch at his neck. 'It had occurred to me Yilling might be ordering these mad attacks just so he's got bodies to bury.'

'He's what?'

'Worships Death, don't he? And he's got men to spare.'

'Why kill men just to bury them?'

'So we'd think that's all he's doing. But I don't reckon Bright Yilling's digging graves all night, just out of bowshot from where we're weakest.'

Raith stared at him a moment, and then out towards those brown humps, and felt a cold shiver up his back. 'They're digging under the walls.'

DUST

For a boy who was reluctantly starting to consider himself a man, Koll had seen a few cities. Stern Vulsgard in spring and sprawling Kalyiv in summer, majestic Skekenhouse in its elf-walls and beautiful Yaletoft before they burned it. He'd made the long journey down the winding Divine, over the tall hauls and across the open steppe, finally to gape in wonder at the First of Cities, greatest settlement of men.

Beside the elf-ruins of Strokom they were all pinpricks.

He followed Skifr and the two ministers down black roads as wide as the market square in Thorlby, bored into the ground in echoing tunnels or stacked one upon the other on mighty pillars of stone, tangled up into giant madman's knots while broken eyes of glass peered sadly down on the ruin. In silence they walked, each of them alone with their own worries. For the world, for those they knew, for themselves. Nothing lived. No plant, no bird, no crawling insect. There was only silence and slow decay. All around them, for mile upon mile, the impossible achievements of the past crumbled into dust.

'What was this place like when the elves lived?' whispered Koll.

'Unimaginable in its scale and its light and its noise,' said Skifr, leading the way with her head high, 'in its planned confusion and its frenzied competition. All thousands of years silent.'

She let her fingertips trail along a crooked rail then lifted them, peered at the grey dust that coated them, tasted it, rubbed it against her thumb, frowned off down the cracked and buckled roadway.

'What do you see?' asked Koll.

Skifr raised one burned brow at him. 'Only dust. There are no other omens here, for there is no future to look into but dust.'

From a high perch between two buildings a great snake of metal had fallen to lie twisted across the road.

'The elves thought themselves all-powerful,' said Skifr, as they picked their way over it. 'They thought themselves greater than God. They thought they could remake all things according to a grand design. Look now upon their folly! No matter how great and glorious the making, time will unmake it. No matter how strong the word, strong the thought, strong the law, all must return to chaos.'

Skifr jerked her head back and sent spit spinning high into the air, arcing neatly down and spattering on rusted metal. 'King Uthil says steel is the answer. I say his sight is short. Dust is the last answer to every question, now and always.'

Koll gave a sigh. 'You're a tower of laughs, aren't you?'

Skifr's jagged laughter split the silence, bouncing back from the dead faces of the buildings and making Koll jump. A strange sound here. It made him absurdly worried she'd somehow cause offence, though there'd been no one to offend for a hundred hundred years.

The old woman clapped him on the shoulder as she walked after Father Yarvi and Mother Scaer. 'That all depends on what you find funny, boy.'

As the light faded they crept between buildings so high the street was made a shaded canyon between them. Spires that pierced the heavens even in their ruin, endless planes of elf-glass still winking pink and orange and purple with the darkly reflected sunset, twisted beams of metal sprouting from their shattered tops like thorns from a thistle.

That brought Thorn to Koll's thoughts and he muttered a prayer for her, even if the gods weren't here to listen. When Brand died, it seemed as if something had died in her. Maybe no one comes through a war quite as alive as they were.

The road was gouged and slumping, choked with things of crumpled metal, their blistered paint flaking. There were masts as tall as ten men, festooned with skeins of wires that hung between the buildings like the cobwebs of colossal spiders. There were elf-letters everywhere, signs daubed on the roads, twisted about poles, banners proudly unfurled over every broken window and doorway.

Koll stared up at one set blazoned wide across a building, the last man-high letter fallen down to swing sadly from its corner.

'All this writing,' he murmured, neck stiff from staring up at it.

'The elves did not limit the word to the few,' said Skifr. 'They let knowledge spread to all, like fire. Eagerly they fanned the flames.'

'And were all burned by them,' murmured Mother Scaer. 'Burned to ashes.'

Koll blinked up at the great sign. 'Do you understand it?'

'I might know the characters,' said Skifr. 'I might even know the words. But the world they spoke of is utterly gone. Who could plumb their meaning now?'

They passed by a shattered window, shards of glass still clinging to its edge, and Koll saw a woman grinning at him from inside.

He was so shocked he couldn't even scream, just stumbled back into Skifr's arms, pointing wildly at that ghostly figure. But the old woman only chuckled.

'She cannot hurt you now, boy.'

And Koll saw it was a painting of amazing detail, stained and faded. A woman, holding up her wrist to show a golden elf-bangle, smiling wildly as though it gave her impossible joy to wear such a thing. A woman, long and thin and strangely dressed, but a woman still.

'The elves,' he muttered. 'Were they . . . like us?'

'Terribly like and terribly unlike,' said Skifr, Yarvi and Scaer coming to stand beside her, all gazing at that faded face from beyond the long fog of the past. 'They were far wiser, more numerous, more powerful than us. But, just like us, the more powerful they became, the more powerful they wished to become. Like men, the elves had holes in them that could never be filled. All of *this* . . .' And Skifr spread her arms wide to the mighty ruins, her cloak of rags billowing in the restless breeze. 'All of this could not satisfy them. They were just as envious, ruthless and ambitious as us. Just as greedy.' She raised one long arm, one long hand, one long finger to point at the woman's radiant smile. 'It is their greed that destroyed them. Do you hear me, Father Yarvi?'

'I do,' he said, shouldering his pack and, as always, pressing onwards, 'and could live with fewer elf-lessons and more elf-weapons.'

Mother Scaer frowned after him, fingering her own collection of ancient bangles. 'I say he could use the opposite.'

'What happens after?' called Koll.

There was a pause before Father Yarvi looked back. 'We use the elf-weapons against Bright Yilling. We carry them across the straits to Skekenhouse. We find Grandmother Wexen and the High King.' His voice took on a deadly edge. 'And I keep my sun-oath and my moon-oath to be revenged upon the killers of my father.'

Koll swallowed. 'I meant after that.'

Master frowned at apprentice. 'We can ford that river when we reach it.' And he turned and carried on.

Quite as if he hadn't spared it a thought until now. But Koll knew Father Yarvi was not a man to leave the field of the future unsown with plans.

Gods, was Skifr right? Were they the same as the elves? Their little feet in mighty footprints, but on the same path? He thought of Thorlby made an empty ruin, a giant tomb, the people of Gettland burned away to leave only silence and dust, perhaps some fragment of his carved mast left, a ghostly echo for those who came long after to puzzle over.

Koll took one last glance back at that gloriously happy face thousands of years dead, and saw something glint among the shattered glass. A golden bangle, just like the one in the painting, and Koll darted out a hand and slipped it into his pocket.

He doubted the elf-woman would miss it.

FATHER EARTH'S GUTS

'It will be dangerous,' said Skara, grimly.

An apt moment for Raith to puff himself up with some hero's bluster. There'd been a time he was an ever-gushing fountain of it, after all. *That's what I'm counting on,* or *danger's my breakfast,* or *for our enemies, maybe!* But all he could manage was a strangled, 'Aye. But we have to stop that mine before it gets under the walls . . .'

No need to say more. They all knew what was at stake. Everything.

Raith glanced about at the volunteers, their faces, their shield-rims, their weapons all smeared with ashes to keep them hidden in the night. Two dozen of the fastest Gettlanders, two dozen of the fiercest Vanstermen, and him.

The Breaker of Swords had drawn lots with King Uthil for the honour of leading them, and won. Now he stood smiling as they waited for their moment, savouring each breath as if the night smelled of flowers. The man showed no fear, not ever, Raith had to give him that. But where it used to feel like bravery, now it looked like madness.

'No one will think less of you if you stay,' said Skara.

'I'll think less of me.' If that was even possible. Raith met his brother's eye for an instant before Rakki looked away, ash-dark face fixed hard. Desperate to prove he could be the tough one, even if they both knew he couldn't. 'Got to watch my brother's back.'

'Even if he doesn't want your help?'

'Specially then.'

Rakki had one of the big clay jars over his shoulder that held Father Yarvi's southern fire, Soryorn another. Raith thought of how that stuff had burst blazing over the High King's ships, burning men toppling into the sea, then he thought of smearing it on timbers deep under the ground and setting a torch to it, and his courage took another hard knock. He wondered how many more it'd stand. Time was nothing scared him. Or had he always been pretending?

Gods, he wished they could go. 'It's the waiting hurts worst,' he muttered.

'Worse than being stabbed, or burned, or buried in that mine?'

Raith swallowed. 'No. Not worse than those.'

'You need not fear for me, my queen.' Gorm had strode over with his thumbs wedged into his great belt, keen to make it all about him. There's kings for you. Their towering opinions of themselves are generally both their making and their downfall. 'Mother War breathed on me in my crib,' he said, a tiresome refrain if ever there was one. 'It has been foreseen no man can kill me.'

Skara raised a brow. 'What about a vasty weight of dirt falling on your head?'

'Oh, Father Earth fashioned me too large to squeeze into Yilling's mine. Others will go delving while I guard the entrance. But you must learn to rejoice at the risks.'

Skara looked more likely to be sick at them. 'Why?'

'Without Death, war would be a dull business.' Gorm slipped his great chain over his head and offered it to her. 'Would you honour me by keeping this safe until the task is done? I would hate for its rattling to catch Death's ear.'

As their owner swaggered away Skara blinked down at the pommels draped over her hands, silver and gold and precious stones shining with the torchlight.

'Each of these is a dead man, then,' she murmured, pale as if she stared into their faces. 'Dozens of them.'

'And that's not counting all those he's killed that didn't have swords. Or all those that had no weapons at all.'

Time was Raith had looked at that chain and swelled with pride that he followed so great a warrior. Time was he'd dreamed of forging his own. Now he wondered how long a chain he might've forged already, and the thought made him feel almost as queasy as Skara seemed when she looked up.

'I didn't choose this.'

Gods, she was beautiful. It was like there was a light in her, and the darker things got the brighter she seemed to shine. He wondered, and not for the first time, what might've happened if they were different people, in a different place, at a different time. If she wasn't a queen and he wasn't a killer. But you can't choose who you are.

'Who'd choose this?' he croaked out.

'It's time.' Gorm took a prim little nibble from the last loaf, passed it on and stooped to fit his great frame into the narrow passageway.

Each man took his own bite as he followed, each no doubt wondering if it truly would be his last. Raith came at the back, took his mouthful and crumbled the rest in his fist, tossed it behind him as a gift for Mother War's children, the crows. He might be no great believer in luck, but he knew they'd need every bit they could get.

Down the passage through the elf-walls, echoing with their quick breath. The same one Raith had come charging up a few weeks before with no doubts and no fears, burning with battle-joy. Blue Jenner stood beside the hand-thick door, ready to triple bolt it after them, slapping each man on the back as they slipped past.

'Come back alive,' hissed the old raider. 'That's all that matters.' And he pushed Raith through the archway and out into the chill night.

A shroud of fog had drifted in from Mother Sea and Raith muttered his thanks to her. He reckoned it a gift that tripled his chances of living out the night. The fires of Bright Yilling's men were gloomy smears in the murk on their left. The walls of Bail's Point a black mass on their right.

They wore no mail so they'd run the swifter, all bent double and black as coal, ghosts in the darkness, quick and silent. Raith's every sense was sharpened double-keen by the whetstone of danger, every grunt and footfall seeming loud as a drum-beat, his nose full of the damp night and the distant campfires.

One after another they slid into the ditch, picking their way along the boggy bottom. Raith's boot hit something hard and he realized it was a corpse. They were every-where, unclaimed, unburned, unburied, tangled with the shattered remains of ladders, rocks flung from above, dead men's fallen shields.

He saw Gorm's smiling teeth in the darkness, leaning towards Soryorn, heard him whisper, 'Here was Mother War's good work done.'

The last loaf had left Raith's mouth sour and he spat as they struggled up from the ditch, men silently offering their hands to help each other climb, hissing curses as they slipped and slid, boots mashing the earth to sticky mud.

On they went, over ground prickled everywhere with arrows, the harvest of Bright Yilling's failed attacks, dense as the wind-slanted sedge on the high moors of Vansterland. Raith heard shouting in the distance as they left the fortress behind, the clashing of steel. King Uthil was sallying from the main gate, hoping to draw Bright Yilling's attention from his mine.

Shapes shifted in the mist, whipped into tricking

shadows by the hurrying men. Snakes, twisting together and breaking apart. Wolf faces. Man faces. The faces of those he'd killed, shrieking silently for vengeance. Raith wafted them away with his shield but they formed anew. He tried to tell himself the dead are dead, but he knew Jenner had been right. Their ghosts stick in the minds of those that knew them, loved them, hated them. Those that killed them most of all.

The sharpened stakes loomed from the murk and Raith slipped sideways between them and crouched in the darkness beyond, straining into the night.

He saw the humps of the fresh barrows, or at any rate the spoil of Yilling's mines, firelight at their edges. Gorm pointed with his sword and the men split, scuttling silently around the nearest hillock. Not a word spoken. Not a word needed to be spoken. They all knew their work.

Two men sat beside a campfire. The way Raith and Rakki used to sit. One working on a belt with a needle, the other with a blanket around his shoulders, frowning off towards the faint sounds of Uthil's diversion. He turned as Raith rushed up.

'What are—'

Soryorn's arrow took him silently through the mouth. The other man started to scramble up, tangled with his belt. Gorm's ash-black blade hissed and the warrior's head spun away into the darkness.

Raith sprang over his body as it toppled, slithered down into a trench between heaps of spoil, squatting beside a dark entrance flanked by torches.

'Go!' whispered Gorm, as his warriors spread out to form a crescent. Rakki muttered a quick prayer to She Who Lights the Way, then he was down into Father Earth's guts with the jar of southern fire over his shoulder, Soryorn and Raith just behind him.

Darkness, and the flickering shadows of the crooked logs that held up the earth above, roots brushing at Raith's hair. He was no miner but he could tell it had been dug hastily, trickles of soil falling as they worked their way down the passage, his eyes fixed on Soryorn's bent back.

'Gods,' he whispered, 'this is apt to fall without our help.'

Hot, and growing hotter, sweat trickling from Raith's brows, sticky under his clothes as he laboured on. He slid his axe through the loop at his belt and drew his dagger. If it came to a fight down here there was no room to swing. They'd settle it close enough to smell your enemy's breath.

They scrambled into a chamber lit by one guttering lamp. The earthen floor was scattered with picks and shovels and barrows, roof held up with a clumsy tangle of timbers, others stacked in heaps. Two more shadowy tunnels went deeper, towards the roots of Gudrun's Tower, no doubt, and Raith hurried over to one, peering into the darkness.

Could he hear scraping somewhere in there? Digging? Rakki was already fumbling the stopper from his jar, starting to slosh what was inside over anything made of wood.

'Careful o' that flame!' snapped Raith at Soryorn, who'd

brushed the flickering lamp and set it swinging on its hook. 'One slip and we're all buried.'

'Fair point,' croaked out the standard-bearer, tipping up his own deadly jar in the crook of one long arm, other hand across his face. Gods, the stuff stank in the stillness, a burning stink that set them all to coughing. Raith stumbled to the other tunnel, rubbing the tears from his stinging eyes on his forearm, looked up to see two men staring at him. One held a pick, the other a shovel, both stripped to the waist and smeared with grime.

'Are you the new diggers?' said one, frowning at Raith's shield.

The best fighters don't think too much. Not much before the fight, not much after, and not at all during. Tends to be the one strikes first that still stands in the end. So Raith knocked the man's pick away with his shield and stabbed him in the neck, blood spraying across the passageway.

The other miner swung his shovel but Raith was carried forward, stumbling into him, shrugging the blow off his shield, shoving the man against the wall so they were left snarling in one another's faces, so close Raith could have stuck his tongue out and licked him. He stabbed under the rim of his shield, wild, vicious, punches with steel on the end, and the digger gurgled and snorted with each one until Raith stepped back and let him drop, left him sitting with his hands clutched to his ripped-up belly and his blood black on Raith's shield, on his fist, on his dagger.

Rakki was staring, mouth hanging open, the way he always did when Raith set to killing, but there'd be time to pile the regrets up later.

'Finish it!' Raith scuttled to the passage they came in by to snatch a breath of clean air. His head was spinning from the reek. He could hear the sounds of fighting coming faint from outside. 'Now!'

Rakki tipped up the jar, coughing, soaking the props, the walls, the ground. Soryorn tossed his jar down, oil still gurgling from it across the floor, pushed past Raith and into the passageway, the shouts coming louder from above.

'Gods!' he heard Rakki croak, and spun around.

One of the miners was staggering across the room, mad eyes bulging, still clutching at his torn guts with one red hand. He caught Rakki with the other, growling through his clenched teeth, spraying red spit.

By every rule he should've been gone through the Last Door. But Death is a fickle mistress and has her own rules. Only she could say why it pleased her to give him a few more moments.

Rakki's jar tumbled down as he wrestled with the wounded miner, shattered against a timber, oil spattering the pair of them as they stumbled back.

Raith took a step, jaw dropping, but he was too far away.

They blundered into one of the props, and Rakki pulled his arm back for a punch, and his elbow clipped the lamp and knocked it from its hook.

It fell so slow, leaving a bright smear across Raith's

sight, and not a thing he could do. He heard his own breath whoop in. He saw the light from that little flame bright across the oily floor. He saw Rakki turn, caught one glimpse of his face, eyes wide.

Raith dropped down huddled behind his shield. What else could he do?

Then the narrow chamber was brighter than day.

BRAVE WORK

No doubt a woman should be tearful with relief when her betrothed comes back alive from battle, but Skara found herself dry-eyed when the Breaker of Swords was the first through the little gate.

His great shield had a broken shaft stuck in it near the rim, but otherwise he was unhurt. He slapped the arrow out, looked around as if for someone to hand the shield to, then frowned.

'Huh.' And he set it down against the wall.

Skara forced a smile onto her face. 'I am glad to see you returned, my king.' Though there were others she would rather have greeted.

'In truth I am glad to be back, Queen Skara. Fighting at night is little fun. We brought down their mine, however.'

'Thank the gods. What happens now?'

He smiled, teeth white in his ash-blacked face. 'Now they dig another.'

Men were straggling back into the fortress. All exhausted. Several hurt. Mother Owd started forward to help, Rin squatting beside her with some heavy pincers, already cutting a man's bloody jerkin open around a wound.

'Where is Raith?'

'He was with his brother in the tunnel when the oil caught fire.' A thrall had brought Gorm water and he was wiping the ash from his face.

Skara could hardly speak her throat was suddenly so closed up. 'He's dead?'

Gorm gave a grim nod. 'I taught him to fight, and kill, and die, and now he has done all three.'

'Only two,' she said, with a surge of relief that made her head spin.

Raith came shuffling from the shadows, his hair caked with dirt and his bloody teeth gritted, one arm over Blue Jenner's shoulder.

'Huh.' Gorm raised his brows. 'He always was the tough one.'

Skara darted forward, caught Raith by his elbow. His sleeve was ripped, scorched, strangely blistered. Then she realized to her horror it was not his sleeve, but his skin. 'Gods, your arm! Mother Owd!'

Raith hardly seemed to notice. 'Rakki's dead,' he whispered.

A slave had brought Gorm a bowl of meat fresh off

the spit. The similarity between it and Raith's arm as Mother Owd peeled the burned cloth away made Skara's gorge rise.

But if the Breaker of Swords had any fears at all, he did not keep them in his stomach. 'Fighting always gives me quite an appetite,' he said around a mouthful of meat, spraying grease. 'All in all, Mother War favoured us tonight.'

'What about Rakki?' snarled Raith, Owd hissing with annoyance as he jerked his half-bandaged arm from her hands.

'I shall remember him fondly. Unlike others, he proved his loyalty.'

Skara saw the tendons starting from Raith's fist as it clenched around his axe-haft, and she slipped quickly in front of him.

'Your chain, my king.' Lifting that rattling mass of dead men's pommels up was such an effort her arms trembled.

Gorm stooped to duck his head inside and it brought them closer than they had ever been, her hands behind his neck, almost an awkward embrace. He had a damp-fur smell like the hounds her grandfather had kept.

'It has grown long over the years,' he said as he straightened.

This close he seemed bigger than ever. The top of her head could scarcely have reached his neck. Would she need to carry a step with her to kiss her husband? She might have laughed at the thought another time. She did not feel much like laughing then.

'It was an honour to hold it.' She wanted very much to

back away but knew she could not, dropped her hands to arrange the gaudy, ghastly mementoes on his chest.

'When we are married, I will cut off a length for you to wear.'

She blinked up at him, cold all over. A chain of dead men to be forever tethered with. 'I have not earned the right,' she croaked out.

'No false modesty, please! Only half a war is fought with swords, my queen, and you have fought the other half with skill and courage.' He was smiling as he turned away. 'There will be hundreds dead for your brave work.'

Skara jerked awake, clutching at the furs on her bed, ears straining at the silence.

Nothing.

She hardly slept now. Two or three times every night Bright Yilling's warriors would come.

They had tried to swim into the harbour, brave men fighting the surging waves in the darkness. But sentries on the towers above had riddled them with arrows, left their bodies tangled on the chains across the entrance.

They had charged up with a felled tree shod in iron as a ram, brave men holding shields above, and made a din upon the gates to wake the dead. But the gates had hardly been scratched.

They had shot swarms of burning arrows over the walls to fall on the yard like tiny shooting stars in the night. They had bounced harmless from flagstones and slates but some had caught among the thatch. Skara's chest was sore from the billowing smoke, her voice cracked from shrieking orders to soak the roofs, her hands raw from dragging buckets from the well. The stables where she had first saddled a pony as a girl were a scorched shell, but they had managed to stop the fire from spreading.

In the end she had climbed to the walls, soot-smudged but triumphant to shriek, 'thanks for the arrows!' at the High King's retreating bowmen.

By fire or by water, over the walls or under, nothing had worked. Bail's Point was the strongest fortress in the Shattered Sea, its defenders the picked warriors of three warrior nations. Bright Yilling lost twenty to every one of theirs.

And yet the reinforcements kept coming. Every morning Mother Sun rose upon more warriors of Yutmark, Inglefold and the Lowlands. More mad-eyed, bone-pierced, painted Shends. More ships outside the harbour, stopping any help from coming to the defenders. Their spirits might be buoyed by little victories, but the terrible arithmetic had only worsened. Mother Owd's cellars overflowed with wounded. Twice they had sent boats drifting out with crews of dead to burn upon the water.

Skara felt as if they were digging ditches to stop the tide. You might keep out one wave. You might keep out ten. But the tide always wins.

She gave an acid burp, choked back sick and swung her legs from the bed, pushed her head into her hands and gave a long growl.

She was a queen. Her blood worth more than gold.

She had to hide her fear and show her deep-cunning. She could not use a sword, so she had to fight the other half of the war, and fight it better than Bright Yilling. Better than Father Yarvi and Mother Scaer too. There were people looking to her. People who had gambled their futures on her. She was hedged in by the hopes and needs and expectations of the living and the dead as if she slipped through a maze of thorns. A dozen opinions to consider and a hundred lessons to remember and a thousand proper things that had to be done and ten thousand improper ones she could never contemplate . . .

Her eyes slid to the door. On the other side, she knew, Raith would be sleeping. Or lying awake.

She did not know what she felt for him. But she knew she had never felt it for anyone else. She remembered the cold shock when she had thought him dead. The warm relief when she had seen him living. The spark of heat when their eyes met. The strength she felt when he was beside her. Her head knew he was a wretched match in every possible way.

But the rest of her felt otherwise.

She stood, heart thudding as she padded across the floor, stone cold against her bare feet. She glanced towards the little room where her thrall slept, but she would have better sense than to meddle in her mistress's business.

Her hand froze just short of the door, fingertips tingling.

His brother was dead. She told herself he needed her,

when she knew she needed him. Needed to forget her duty. Needed to forget her land and her people and have something for herself. Needed to know what it felt like to be kissed, and held, and wanted by someone she chose, before it was too late.

Mother Kyre would have torn her hair out at the thought of it, but Mother Kyre was gone through the Last Door. Now, in the night, with Death scratching at the walls, what was proper no longer seemed so important.

Skara slid the bolt back with trembling fingers, biting at her lip with the need to stay silent.

Gently, gently, she eased open her door.

NO LOVER

Raith kept his eyes closed afterwards, and breathed. He just wanted to hold someone, and be held, and he slid his bandaged hand up her bare back and pressed her tight against him.

Rakki was dead.

He kept realizing it fresh. Kept seeing that last glimpse of his face before the fire, and the earth fell.

She kissed him. Wasn't harsh or hurried, but he could tell it was a parting kiss, and he strained up to make it last. Hadn't done enough kissing in his life. Might not get the chance to do much more. All the time he'd wasted on nothing, now every moment past seemed an aching loss. She put a hand on his chest, pushing gently. Took an effort to let go.

He stifled a groan as he swung his legs onto the rush

matting, holding his ribs, his side one great ache. He watched her dress, black against the curtain. Caught little details in the faint light. The shifting muscles in her back, the veins on her foot, a glow down the side of her face as she turned away from him. He couldn't tell whether she was smiling or frowning.

Rakki was dead.

He looked down at his bandaged arm. He'd forgotten the pain for a moment but it was coming back now twice as bad. He winced as he touched it, remembering that last glimpse of his brother's face, so like his own and so different. Like two prow-beasts on the same ship, always facing different ways. Only now there was only one, and the ship was adrift with no course to hold to.

She sat beside him. 'Does it hurt?'

'Like it's still burning.' He worked his fingers and felt the fire all the way to his elbow.

'Can I do anything?'

'No one can do anything.'

They sat silently, side by side, her hand resting on his arm. Strong, her hands, but gentle. 'You can't stay. I'm sorry.'

'I know.'

He gathered up his scattered clothes, but while he was putting them on he started to cry. One moment he was fumbling at his belt, burned hand too clumsy to fasten it, then his sight started to swim, then his shoulders were shaking with silent sobs.

He'd never cried like that. Not ever in his life. All the

beatings taken, all the things lost, all the hopes failed, he'd always had Rakki beside him.

But Rakki was dead.

Now he'd started crying he couldn't seem to stop. No more than you can rebuild a burst dam when the flood's still surging through. That's the problem with making yourself hard. Once you crack, there's no putting yourself back together.

She took him around the head, pressed his face against her shoulder, rocked him back and forward.

'Shhh,' she whispered in his ear. 'Shhh.'

'My brother was the only family I had,' he whispered.

'I know,' she said. 'Mine too.'

'Does it get easier?'

'Maybe. Bit by bit.'

She did his belt up for him, dragging the scarred leather through the scarred buckle while he stood with his hands dangling. Never thought much about having a woman fastening his belt, but he found he liked it. Never had anyone to take care of him. Except Rakki, maybe.

But Rakki was dead.

When she looked up her face was tear-streaked too and he reached out to wipe it, tried to be as gentle as she'd been. Didn't feel like those aching, crooked, scabbed and battered fingers of his had any tenderness left in them. Didn't feel like his hands were good for aught but killing. His brother had always said he was no lover. But he tried.

'I don't even know your name,' he said.

'I'm Rin. You'd better go.' And she pulled back the curtain of the little alcove her cot was in.

He limped up the steps from the forge, one hand on the wall. Past a domed oven where three women were baking bread, men gathered waiting with their platters in a hungry crowd. He limped across the yard, lit silver by high, fat Father Moon, and past the burned-out stables. As burned-out as he was.

Raith heard someone laugh, jerked his head towards it, starting to smile. Rakki's voice, surely?

But Rakki was dead.

He hugged himself as he trudged on past the dead stump of the Fortress Tree. Wasn't a cold night but he felt cold then. Like his torn clothes were too thin. Or his torn skin was.

Up the long stairway, his feet scraping in the darkness, down the long hallway, windows looking out over glimmering Mother Sea. Lights moved there. The lamps on Bright Yilling's ships, watching to make sure no help came to Bail's Point.

He groaned as he lowered himself slowly as an old man beside Skara's door, everything aching. He drew his blanket across his knees, let his skull fall back against the cold elf-stone. He'd never been interested in comforts. Rakki had been the one to dream of slaves and fine tapestries.

But Rakki was dead.

'Where have you been?'

He jerked around. The door was open a crack and Skara was looking out at him, hair a mass of dark curls, wild and tangled from her bed like it had been the first day he saw her.

'Sorry,' he stammered out, shaking off his blanket. He gave a grunt of pain as he stood, clutching at the wall to steady himself.

Suddenly she'd slipped into the corridor and taken his elbow. 'Are you all right?'

He was a proven warrior, sword-bearer to Grom-gil-Gorm. He was a killer, carved from the stone of Vansterland. He felt no pain and no pity. Only the words wouldn't come. He was too hurt. Hurt to his bones.

'No,' he whispered.

He looked up then and saw she was wearing just her shift, realized with the torchlight he could see her lean shape through it.

He forced his eyes up to her face but that was worse. There was something in the way she was looking at him, fierce and fixed as a wolf at a carcass, made him suddenly hot all over. He could hardly see for her eyes on him. He could hardly breathe for the scent of her. He made the feeblest effort to pull his arm away and only pulled her closer, right against him. She pressed him back, sliding one hand around his sore ribs and making him gasp, putting the other on his face and pulling it down towards her.

She kissed him and not gently, sucking at his mouth, her teeth scraping his split lip. He opened his eyes and she was looking at him, like she was judging the effect she'd had, her thumb pressing hard at his cheek.

'Shit,' he whispered. 'I mean . . . my queen—'

'Don't call me that. Not now.' She slipped her hand up behind his head, gripping him tight, brushed her nose up along the side of his, down the other, kissed him again and left his head light as a drunkard's.

'Come with me,' she whispered, breath burning on his cheek, and she drew him towards her door, nearly dragged him right over, blanket still tangled around his legs.

Rakki had always told him he was no lover. Raith wondered what he'd have to say when he heard about this—

But Rakki was dead.

He stopped short. 'I need to tell you something . . .' That he'd just been crying in someone else's bed? That she was promised to Grom-gil-Gorm? That he'd nearly killed her a few nights before and still had the poison in his pocket? 'More'n one thing, really—'

'Later.'

'Later might be too late—'

She caught a fistful of his shirt and dragged him towards her, and he was helpless as a rag doll in her hands. She was far stronger than he'd thought. Or maybe he was just far weaker. 'I've done enough talking,' she hissed at him. 'I've done enough of the proper thing. We might all be dead tomorrow. Now come with me.'

They might all be dead tomorrow. If Rakki had one last lesson to teach him, surely that was it. And men rarely win fights they want to lose, after all. So he pushed his fingers into the soft cloud of her hair, kissed at her, bit at her lips, felt her tongue in his mouth, and nothing else seemed all that pressing. He was here and she was here, now, in the darkness. Mother Scaer, and the

Breaker of Swords, and Rin, and even Rakki seemed a long way off with the dawn.

She kicked his blanket against the wall, and pulled him through her door, and slid the bolt.

RELICS

'This is the place,' said Skifr.

It was a wide hall with a balcony high up, scattered with broken chairs, dim for the dirt crusted to the windows. A curved table faced the door with a thing above it like a great coin, ringed by elf-letters. There had been a wall of glass beyond but it was shattered, splinters crunching under Koll's boots as he stepped towards an archway, one door fallen, the other hanging by broken hinges. The hall beyond was soon lost in darkness, water dripping in the shadows.

'We could use some light,' he murmured.

'Of course.' There was a click, and in an instant the whole chamber was flooded with brightness. There was a hiss as Father Yarvi whipped out the curved sword he wore and Koll shrank against the wall, feeling for his knife.

But Skifr only chuckled. 'There is nothing here to fight but ourselves, and in that endless war blades cannot help.'

'Where does the light come from?' murmured Koll. Tubes on the ceiling were burning too bright to look at, as though pieces of Mother Sun had been caught in bottles.

Skifr shrugged as she sauntered past him into the hall. 'Magic.'

The ceiling had collapsed, more tubes hanging by tangled wires, light flickering and popping, flaring across the tight-drawn faces of the two ministers as they crept after Skifr. Paper was scattered everywhere. Sliding piles of it ankle deep, sodden but unrotted, scrawled with words upon words upon words.

'The elves thought they could catch the world in writing,' said Skifr. 'That enough knowledge would set them above God.'

'Look upon the wages of their arrogance,' muttered Mother Scaer.

They passed through an echoing hall filled with benches, each with a strange box of glass and metal on top, drawers torn out and cabinets thrown over and more papers vomiting from them in heaps.

'Thieves were here before us,' said Koll.

'Other thieves,' said Scaer.

'There is no danger in the world so fearsome that someone will not brave it for a profit.'

'Such wisdom in one so young,' said Skifr. 'Though I think all these thieves stole was death. This way.'

Stairs dropped down, lit in red, a humming from far

below. A chilly breath of air upon his face as Koll leaned over the rail and saw their square spiral dropping into infinite depth. He leaned away, suddenly giddy. 'A long way down,' he croaked.

'Then we had better begin,' said Father Yarvi, taking the steps two at a time, his withered hand hissing upon the rail.

They did not speak. Each of them too crowded by their own fears to make space for anyone else. The deeper they went the louder their heavy footsteps echoed, the louder that strange humming within the walls, within the very earth, until it made Koll's teeth rattle in his head. Down they went, and down, into the very bowels of Strokom, past warnings painted on the smooth elf-stone in red elf-letters. Koll could not read them, but he guessed at their meaning.

Go back. Abandon this madness. It is not too late.

He could hardly have said how long they went down, but the stairs ended, as all things must. Another hallway stretched away at the bottom, gloomy, chill and bare but for a red arrow pointing down the floor. Guiding them on towards a door. A narrow door of dull metal, and beside it on the wall a studded panel.

'What is this place?' murmured Mother Scaer.

Something in the terrible solidity of that door reminded Koll of the one in Queen Laithlin's counting house, behind which she was said to keep her limitless wealth. 'A vault,' he murmured.

'An armoury.' And Skifr began to sing. Soft and low, to begin with, in the tongue of elves, then higher, and faster,

as she had on the steppe above the Denied when the
Horse People came for their blood. Father Yarvi's eyes
were hungry-bright. Mother Scaer turned her head and
spat with disgust. Then Skifr made a sign above the panel
with her left hand, and with her right began to press the
studs in a pattern not even Koll's sharp eyes could follow.

A green jewel above the door suddenly burned bright.
There was a clunk as of bolts released. Koll took a step
back, almost stumbled into Mother Scaer as the door
came ajar with a breath of air like a long-sealed bottle
opened. Smirking over her shoulder, Skifr hauled it wide.

Beyond was a hallway lined with racks. They reminded
Koll of the ones he'd made to hold spears in the citadel
of Thorlby. Upon the racks, gleaming darkly in the half-
light, were elf-relics. Dozens of them. Hundreds.
Hundreds upon hundreds, racks stretching away into the
distance as more lights flared up, one by one.

'Elf-weapons,' said Skifr, 'just as I promised.'

'Enough to fit an army for war,' breathed Father Yarvi.

'Yes. They were forged for a war against God.'

Next to their craftsmanship Koll and Rin's proud efforts
seemed the mud-daubs of primitives. Every weapon was
the twin of the one beside it, beautiful in its clean
simplicity. Every weapon thousands of years old but
perfect as the day it was made.

Koll crept through the doorway, staring at the works
of the elves in awe and wonder and not a little fear. 'Are
these as powerful as the one you used on the Denied?'

Skifr snorted. 'That one beside these is a child's needle
beside a hero's spear.'

In a few moments on the wind-blown steppe that one
had left six men ripped open and burning and a few
dozen more running for their lives. 'What might these
do?' Koll whispered as he gave one the gentlest, hesitant
touch with his fingertips, its perfect surfaces more like
a thing grown than forged, neither rough nor smooth,
neither cold nor warm.

'With these, a chosen few could lay waste to Grandmother
Wexen's army,' said Skifr. 'To ten such armies. There are
even things here that can make that staff you carry send
Death.' She tossed a flat box to Father Yarvi and as he
snatched it from the air it rattled as if full of money.

'The staff of Gettland's minister?' Koll blinked at her.
'That's a weapon?'

'Oh, the irony!' Skifr gave a joyless chuckle as she
plucked one of the relics from the rack. 'It is strange
the things deep-cunning folk miss under their very
noses.'

'Are they dangerous now?' asked Koll, jerking his hand
away.

'They must be made ready but I can teach you the
rituals, as I was taught them, as my teacher was taught
them. One day with the *South Wind*'s crew and they can
be prepared. A sword takes years to master, and in those
years the pupil learns respect for the weapon, restraint
with the weapon, but this . . .' Skifr pressed the relic's
blunt end against her shoulder so she peered down its
length, and Koll saw the slots and holes were grips,
sculpted for hands to fit as snugly as a sword's hilt. 'A
man who holds this, be he never so weak, is in an instant

made a greater warrior than King Uthil, than Grom-gil-Gorm, than Bright Yilling himself.'

'That is halfway to being a god,' murmured Mother Scaer, bitterly shaking her head. 'The elves could not control that power. Should a man be given it?'

'We must take it regardless.' Father Yarvi carefully lifted one of the relics from the rack. As if he did not mean to put it back.

Skifr propped her weapon on her cocked hip. 'As the name of God has seven letters, so we should take only seven weapons.'

Father Yarvi lifted the relic, pointing it off down those endless racks. 'There is no god here, remember?' His withered left hand did not fit the grip so well as Skifr's, but it held the ancient weapon iron steady even so. 'We'll take all we can carry.'

THE KILLER

F ather Earth trembled and Raith felt fear stab him, scrambled up, fumbling his bowl and spraying soup across the yard.

Bright Yilling was bringing down his mine.

They'd all known it was coming. Ever since Rakki was buried in the last mine and the High King's men made no secret of digging another.

King Uthil had made sure the defenders weren't idle. He'd ordered a new wall built inside the fortress. A wall of worm-riddled beams torn from the low buildings, of strakes and masts from broken-up ships, of barnacle-crusted timbers from broken-up wharves, of roof joists and wagon wheels and barrel staves and dead men's shields. A wooden crescent not much higher than a man, running from elf-walls on one side to elf-walls on the other and with a meagre walkway where folk could stand, and fight, and die. Not much of a wall to keep out ten thousand warriors.

But a long stride better than nothing if Gudrun's Tower came down.

Most of the thousand defenders still able to run were running towards it now, barging into each other, shouting over each other, drawing weapons as they went, and Raith was carried by the tide. Blue Jenner offered his hand, helped him clamber onto the walkway, and as he stood at the parapet the ground shivered again, harder even than before.

Everyone gaped at the ugly mass of Gudrun's Tower and the crumbling man-built stretch of wall beside it. Willing it to hold firm. Praying it might. Raith wished he knew the right gods to plead with, settled for clenching his aching fist and hoping. Some birds flapped from the broken roof, but that was all. As tense a silence as Raith ever knew stretched out.

'It's held!' someone shouted.

'Quiet!' roared Gorm, holding up the sword Raith used to carry.

As if that was a signal there was a cracking bang, men cringing as dust and chunks of stone flew from the back of Gudrun's Tower, a rock big as a man's head bouncing across the yard and hammering against the wooden wall near Raith.

There was an almighty groaning and the ivy that covered the tower seemed to twist, cracks shooting through the stonework, the roof leaning sideways, birds showering up into the sky.

'Gods,' whispered Raith, his jaw dropping. With awful slowness the whole tower began to fold in on itself.

'Get down!' bellowed Blue Jenner, hauling Raith onto the walkway beside him.

It sounded as if the whole world was shaking itself apart. Raith squeezed his eyes shut, stones pattering on his back like hail. He was ready to die. Just wished he'd died with Skara.

He opened his eyes but all was murk. A ship in fog.

Something plucked at him and he slapped it clumsily away.

He saw Blue Jenner's lined face, all pale, all ghostly, shouting something but Raith couldn't hear him. His ears were ringing.

He dragged himself up by the parapet, coughing as he stared into the man-made fog. He could see the faint shape of the elf-built tower on the left, of the elf-built wall on the right, but in between, where Gudrun's Tower had stood, there was only a great gap. A broken mass of boulders and shattered beams, the yard between it and the wooden wall littered with rubble.

'Least it fell outwards,' he muttered, but he couldn't even hear his own voice.

He realized he'd left the fine helmet he took from that ship's captain outside Skara's door, but there was no going back for it. He'd just have to ask nicely that no one hit his head. Such a fool's notion he nearly laughed.

Then he saw shapes in the gloom. Shadows of men. The High King's warriors, clambering over the fallen ruins and through the breach. Dozens of them, painted shields turned dusty grey, swords and axes dulled in the gloom, mouths yawning in silent war-cries. Hundreds of them.

Arrows flitted into that heaving mass of men. From the crescent of defenders, from the elf-walls high above. Arrows came from all around them, and struggling over that broken rubble they couldn't have formed a decent shield-wall if they'd wanted. Men fell in the yard, fell among the boulders, crawled, and rolled and sat down staring. He saw a big old warrior shambling on with four or five shafts lodged in his mail. He saw a red-haired man who'd got his boot wedged between two rocks tear off his helmet and fling it away in frustration. He saw a warrior with golden armrings limping along using his sword like a crutch.

They kept coming, battle-cries a faint burble over the ringing in Raith's ears, surging to the foot of the wooden wall. They kept coming, as men above stabbed with spears, flung rocks down, leant out to hack with axes. They kept coming, some kneeling with shields above their heads as steps while others clawed their way up the timbers of the makeshift wall. Would've been bravery to admire if it hadn't all been bent on getting Raith killed.

He shut his eyes, wedged that battered old peg in his jaws, but no battle-joy surged up now. Used to be Raith had a thirst for violence felt like it'd never be satisfied. Seemed he'd finally drunk his fill, but Mother War kept on pouring. He thought of Skara looking down. Thought of her laugh. To hear that one more time seemed something worth fighting for. He forced his eyes open.

The High King's warriors were swarming over the wall, half the walkway seething with struggling men. One was lifting his sword to chop at Jenner and Raith hit him on the side of the head with his axe, left a great dent in his helmet and sent him sprawling. A hand clutched at the parapet and Raith hacked it in half, punched a man in the mouth with the rim of his shield and flung him back, dagger spinning from his fingers as he tumbled off the wall.

He saw Jenner's eyes go wide, spun around to see a big Lowlander bearing down on him, a great axe held in both fists and the One God's seven-rayed sun bouncing on a thong around his neck. Sometimes the best thing you can do with danger is run straight at it. Raith dived at him, the axe-haft catching on his shoulder and the blade just grazing his back, jarring from the Lowlander's hands and clattering into the yard below.

They grappled, waddled, clawing and spitting at each other. Raith dropped his axe, forced his burned arm down, fumbling for the grip of his knife. The Lowlander butted at him, caught him in the jaw, made enough room to bring his fist back for a punch, but enough for Raith to jerk his knife free too.

There might be no joy in it, but he wasn't lying down for anyone.

He dipped his chin so the Lowlander's fist caught him on the forehead instead of the nose, a trick he'd learned fighting boys way bigger than him. The peg was jolted out of his mouth, his ears ringing all the louder, but he felt the crunching of the man's handbones. Raith stabbed him in the side, blade scraping against mail, not going through, but still a hard enough poke to double the Lowlander up wheezing. He pawed at Raith's arm with his broken hand but Raith tore free of it and rammed the knife under the rim of his helmet, just below his ear.

The Lowlander looked quite surprised as his blood poured over the holy symbol he wore. Probably been sure he'd got the right god, the right king, the right cause. Everyone finds a way to make their side the right one, after all. Now, as he stumbled back trying to hold his neck together, he found it's not the righteous win, but them who strike first and strike hardest.

Raith ducked, caught him between the legs and hefted him over the parapet, knocking another man sprawling among the corpses on the way. No doubt they'd all thought they were on the right side too.

Raith stood staring, trying to catch his breath. He saw Mother Owd behind the wall, dragging a wounded man away. He saw Blue Jenner trying to untangle his sword from a dead man's bloody hair. He saw Grom-gil-Gorm send a man flying with a sweep of his shield. The High King's warriors had been driven off the wooden wall, but more were still pouring through the breach.

Then Raith saw something tumble from the walls above, and flinched as liquid fire showered the men crammed into that narrow space. He felt the heat of it across his face, remembered the heat of it underground. Even through the ringing in his ears he could hear the screams.

Another clay jar fell, another burst of flame, and the

High King's men crumbled and fled. No one stays brave forever, no matter how right they think they are. Gettlanders were cheering, and Vanstermen jeering, and Throvenmen whooping, chanting the names of King Uthil and King Gorm and even Queen Skara in celebration. Raith kept quiet. He knew they'd be back soon enough.

'You all right?' he heard Blue Jenner ask.

'Aye,' muttered Raith, but the truth was he was sick. Sick of fighting and he wanted to be back in Skara's bed.

There were corpses everywhere, and a stink of oil and cooking meat, and wounded men squealing for help that wasn't coming. In place of the settling dust smoke drifted, and from the murk a high voice came calling.

'Well that was quite a start to the day! That surely got the blood flowing!'

Something edged into the breach. A door with a splintered corner and the hinges still hanging off. Three knocks rang out, then Bright Yilling's soft face appeared around one side. 'Might I come in and talk without being pricked full of arrows?' He gave his bland little smile. 'That would make a poor song, after all.'

'Reckon Skara would sing it happily enough,' Raith muttered, and he'd have hummed along himself with few regrets.

But Gorm was more interested in glory. 'Come forward, Bright Yilling! We will listen.'

'You are most gracious!' The High King's champion let his door topple down the hill of smoking masonry and sprang nimbly after it, into that stained, ruined, arrow-strewn corner of the yard.

'What brings you here?' called Uthil. 'Do you want to surrender?' There was some laughter at that, but Yilling only grinned up alone at the crescent of frowns. They said he worshipped Death. Certainly seemed he'd no fear of meeting her.

'I want what I wanted when we first spoke. To fight.' Yilling took his sword by the crosspiece and drew it, scratching daintily at his top lip with the pommel. 'Will one of you two kings test his sword-work against mine?'

There was a pause, while nervous muttering spread down the length of the wooden walls. Uthil raised one brow at Gorm, grey hair flicking about his scarred face with the breeze, and Gorm raised one brow back, slowly turning a pommel on his chain around and around. Then he gave an extravagant yawn, and waved Bright Yilling away. 'I have better things to be about. My morning turd will not make itself.'

Yilling only grinned the wider. 'We must wait to put that famous prophecy of yours to the test. At least until my men kick over your wall of twigs. What of you, Iron King? Is your taste for turds or sword-work?'

Uthil frowned down at Yilling for a long, tense moment. Long enough for the muttering to swell into eager chatter. Two such famous warriors meeting in a duel was a thing a man might see only once in his lifetime. But the King of Gettland didn't mean to be hurried. He peered at his sword, licked his little finger, gently rubbed some tiny blemish from the blade.

'It has been a while since I was tested,' said Yilling. 'I

visited Thorlby hoping for a fight, but there was no one there to kill but women and boys.'

Uthil gave a sad smile, then. As if he would've liked to give a different answer, but knew there could be only one. 'That jewel you have for a pommel will make a fine bauble for my son to play with. I will fight you.' He handed his sword to Master Hunnan, clambered somewhat stiffly over the parapet and slid down to the yard below.

'That is the best news I have had all month!' Yilling gave a childish little caper. 'Shall I fight you with my right hand or my left?'

'Whichever causes you to die most quickly,' said Uthil, plucking his blade from the air as Hunnan tossed it down. 'Your attack interrupted my breakfast and there is a sausage I am keen to get back to.'

Yilling spun his sword about in his left hand as nimbly as a dress-maker might her needle. 'Old men are particular about their mealtimes, I understand.'

As if the whole business had been arranged for years, the two famed warriors began to circle each other.

'This will be one for the songs,' breathed Jenner.

Raith worked his aching hand. 'I'm less keen on songs than I used to be.'

Fast as a snake Yilling darted in, blade a bright blur. Raith's own arm twitched as he thought how he'd have blocked, how he'd have struck back. Then he saw he'd have been dead.

Bright Yilling twisted with inhuman speed, sword whipping in a low cut. But Uthil was equal to it. Steel scraped as he parried, stepped effortlessly around the blade, slashed back. As quickly as they'd come together they broke apart, Yilling grinning with his arms spread wide, Uthil frowning, sword dangling by his side.

'Whoever wins,' croaked Raith, eyes rooted to the duel, 'the war goes on.'

'Aye,' said Jenner, twitching with the movements of the fighters. 'None of us have any other choice.'

Another exchange, steel darting faster than Raith could follow, thrust, thrust, slash and parry, and both men spun away into space, picking their way between the bodies, the rubble, the scattered rubbish.

'All this just for the fame of it?'

'Fame's worth more to some men than anything.'

Slow silence, and the slow walking, slow prowling, slow circling around each other. Yilling crouched low, flowing like Mother Sea into different stances, different shapes, chuckling at every exchange like it was a fine new joke. Uthil stood stiff upright, solid as Father Earth, frowning as if he circled a funeral. They watched each other, feeling out the moment, riddling out the opponent, the silence stretching until it seemed it had to snap. Then with no warning the clash and ring and scrape of steel, Death lurking at both men's shoulders, clinging to the edges of both men's blades, the steel question asked and the steel answer given then the quick breaking apart and the slow prowling, slow circling, slow silence.

'It is a great shame that one of us must lose.' Yilling dodged a high cut, eyes slightly crossed as he watched

Uthil's point flicker past his nose. 'There is much I could learn from you.'

'I fear we have time for only one lesson. Death waits for us all.' Yilling sprang forward as the king was still speaking but Uthil was ready, steering the thrust away, twisting his wrist so his sword raked down the sleeve of Yilling's mail and across the back of his hand.

Yilling jerked back, blood pattering on the already-bloody stones of the yard. With a carefree chuckle he tossed his sword across to his right hand.

Someone screamed, 'Bleed, you bastard!' from the tower above and suddenly everyone was shouting, hooting, roaring their insults and their defiance. They smelled victory. They smelled blood.

Uthil came on, metal twinkling as his sword caught the sun. Deadly thrusts no mail could have stopped. Yilling dodged, twisted, steel screeching as he pushed Uthil's blade just wide on one side, turned so it whipped past him on the other, tottering back, off-balance.

Uthil sprang forward for the finishing blow and his foot twisted on a stone. The slightest stumble before his sword came hissing down. The slightest stumble, but long enough for Yilling to drop onto his knees, jerking away so the king's blade left a cut down his smooth cheek and clanged into the stones just beside him.

Yilling's own sword was left straight through Uthil's body, most of the blade sticking bloody from his back.

The cheering stuttered out to leave a dumbstruck silence.

'A stone,' grunted Uthil, frowning at the sword-hilt

pressed against his chest. 'Poor weaponluck.' And all of a sudden he fell, Bright Yilling jumping to catch him as he whipped his sword free.

'No,' muttered Jenner, slapping at the parapet with his palm.

All along the wooden crescent there were curses, hisses, groans of dismay as Bright Yilling lowered Uthil to the dusty ground, settling his arm so that the Iron King of Gettland clutched his sword to his chest, steel his answer in death as it had been in life.

'A good death,' murmured Blue Jenner.

Raith tossed his shield clattering down on the walkway. 'A death, anyway.'

Mother Sun broke through the clouds as Bright Yilling wiped his sword, making the diamond pommel flash, the blood on his face glisten. He looked like Death's chosen indeed, smiling among a harvest of corpses with Uthil's body at his feet.

'I will come back for the rest of you!' he called as he turned towards the breach.

So that was the end to the day's murder.

DREAMS

Skara liked sharing her bed.

Considering the fuss that had always been made of it, she wasn't sure how much she enjoyed the coupling. It seemed to her messy, strange and uncomfortable. Faintly ridiculous, even. She might have laughed the first time had he not been taking it so seriously. Some sticky fumbling. Some awkward grunting. Some clumsy peeling and unpeeling of skin with no grace or romance in it. In her dreams they had both known just what to do. In reality she hardly knew what she wanted, let alone what he did.

But she liked his body beside hers afterward. She liked the strength, and the roughness, and the warmth of him. She liked the way her chest fitted against his broad back, the way her legs twined with his, the way his ribs swelled against hers when he breathed. She liked the way he twitched and shuddered in his sleep, like the dogs used to by the firepit in her grandfather's hall. She liked the sour-sweat stink of him, even, which had no business being pleasant but for some reason she could never breathe in deeply enough.

She liked not being alone.

She touched his shoulder. Felt the rough skin of a scar under her fingertip. Followed it down to where it met another, then another, then another.

'So many scars,' she whispered.

'In Vansterland we call 'em warrior's rewards,' she heard him say. Not asleep, then. She would have been surprised if anyone in Bail's Point was. Why sleep through your last night alive, after all?

'They feel like whip marks.'

He was silent, and she wondered if she should have said nothing. She had no notion what the rules were between them any more, but she was learning that baring your body to someone didn't make baring your heart any easier. Harder than ever, maybe.

Raith's shoulders shifted as he shrugged. 'Before I was Gorm's servant, I was bad. After, I wasn't always bad enough.'

'I'm sorry,' she muttered. Sorry that he'd been whipped. Sorry that she hardly knew what to say about it. They were so different, in every way. It made no sense that they could fit together. But when she slid her arm over his side and he slipped his fingers through hers they fitted together well enough. Maybe any living hand fits when Death is offering you hers.

'What are we doing?' he asked.

'Holding hands.'

'Tonight we are. What about tomorrow?'

'I didn't think you were much worried about tomorrow. It's one of the things I like about you.'

'Tomorrow used to seem a long way off. It got close of a sudden.'

The truth was she had no idea what they were doing, now or tomorrow. She had spent a lot of thought on what it might be like to have him. None at all on what she might do once she got him. It was like that puzzle box an emissary from Catalia had brought as a gift for her grandfather. Four days it had taken her to get it open and, once she had, there was another box inside.

In spite of Raith's warmth she gave a shiver, whispered the words into his battered ear. 'Do you think Bright Yilling will come tonight?'

'He's in no rush. Reckon he'll wait for dawn.'

She thought of the blood tapping from the point of Yilling's sword in the darkness and pressed herself tighter to Raith's back.

'King Uthil's dead,' she muttered. He had seemed a man forged from iron, indestructible. But she had seen him laid out pale and cold before Bail's Chair.

'Death waits for us all,' said Raith. 'All it takes is a stray pebble and no skill, no name, no fame can shield you from her.'

Skara glanced towards the door, torchlight around its edge. Out there, she had to be strong. Had to show no fear and no doubt. But no one can stay strong all the time. 'We're doomed,' she whispered.

Finally he rolled towards her, but in the darkness she could hardly tell more from his face than from his back. Just the faint gleam of his eyes fixed on her, the hard set of his cheek. He didn't speak. He didn't deny it.

She gave a ragged sigh. 'I missed my chance to jump off Gudrun's Tower.'

'I'll admit it's a lot lower than it was.'

She touched his chest, ran her fingertip through the few pale hairs there. 'I suppose I should be ready to jump off one of the others.'

He caught her hand in his bandaged one. 'Might be Blue Jenner could get you away. Like before.'

'So I can be the one who always runs? A queen with no country? An object of contempt?'

'Not to me. You're about the best thing ever happened in my life.'

From the little he'd told her, his life had been horrible. 'What comes second?'

She could just see his smile. 'Rabbit stew, probably.'

'Flatterer.'

His smile slowly faded. 'Might be Blue Jenner could get both of us away.'

'Gudrun and the stable-boy, living out their lives herding goats by a mountain stream?'

He shrugged again. 'I've always liked goats.'

'You've got a lot in common.' She gripped his hand, looked into his eyes, trying to explain it to him. Trying to explain it to herself. 'I am a queen, whether I feel like one or not. I can't just be whoever I want to. I have to lead. I have to stand for Throvenland. The blood of Bail is in my veins.'

'So you keep saying.' He rubbed at the faint scar on her palm with his thumb. 'I'd like to see it stay there.'

'So would I. But my father died defending this place.' She pulled her hand free of his. 'I won't run.'

'I know. Nice to dream, though.' He gave a weary groan as he started to sit up. 'I should go.'

She caught him first, dragging him close, heard him sigh and felt all the resistance sag out of him. She liked the power she had over him. Not a queen's power. Just her own.

'You don't want to stay?' she whispered in his ear.

'Can't think of a queen whose bed I'd rather be in.' He turned his head to look up at her. 'Well, Laithlin is a damn handsome woman— ah!'

She caught him by the shoulder and pushed him down, slipping her leg over his hips so she straddled him. She kissed him, slow kisses while they still had time, while they still had breath, easing away a little with each one, smiling as she felt him straining up to meet her—

'My queen!'

She could not have sprung from the bed more quickly had it been on fire, staring towards the door as it rattled from heavy knocks outside.

'What is it?' she called, getting her elbow caught in her shift and nearly tearing it in her hurry to pull it on.

'My queen!' Blue Jenner's voice. 'There are ships off the coast!'

*

'Where the hell's Raith?' snapped Jenner as he followed Skara down the walls, her hood up against the drizzle.

'Hiding in my bed,' was most likely not the best answer, but a good liar mixes in truth wherever possible, and Skara was getting to be a better liar every day. 'He hasn't always been at my door the past few nights,' she said, offhand. 'I have a feeling he's finding comfort with a girl.'

Jenner grunted. 'Guess I can't blame him.'

'No.' Skara hurried up the steps towards the roof of the Seaward Tower. 'We have to take whatever comfort we can get.'

'They were Gettlanders.' Master Hunnan stood at the battlements, frowning into the night. 'Six ships.'

'Were?' snapped Skara, stepping up beside him and staring out to Mother Sea, trying not to think of the long, long drop to the waves. Off to the north she saw lights on the water. Whoever they were, they had lamps burning, but they were already drifting away into the darkness. She felt her shoulders slump.

'They tried to break through to the fortress but they were soon driven off,' growled Hunnan. 'They're rowing back north fast as ever they can with a dozen of the High King's ships following tight as hounds on a fox.'

Hope died like embers doused with ice, and Skara propped her fists on the battlements and frowned into the black sea, the smallest glimmer of moonlight on the waves.

'Queen Laithlin's ships, I reckon.' Blue Jenner tugged thoughtfully at his beard. 'But if their aim was to slip in why are they lit so brightly?'

Skara glimpsed a shadow flitting on the dark water and the embers of hope suddenly flared brighter than ever. 'Because they were only a distraction. There!' She threw an arm around Jenner's shoulders, pointing with the other. She could see oars dipping now, a ship driving straight and swift towards the harbour.

'I think she has doves for prow-beasts,' murmured Hunnan.

'It's the *South Wind*!' Skara hugged Blue Jenner tight. 'Order the chains dropped!'

'Drop the chains!' roared the old sailor, hugging her every bit as hard. 'Father Yarvi's back!'

IV

SUN-OATH,
MOON-OATH

DAWN

The hinges groaned, a crack of light showing down the middle of the gates, then widening. Dawn fell on the hard faces in the entrance passage. On Gorm's scars. On Rulf and Jenner's weather-battered cheeks. On Father Yarvi's gaunt frown. It glinted at the corners of Skara's eyes, the cords in her neck shifting as she swallowed.

'You should stay here,' said Raith, knowing she'd never agree.

She didn't. 'If we plan to surrender, I should be there.'

Raith glanced at Mother Scaer, hunched in the shadows, something bulky held under her coat, a gleam of dull metal showing as she shifted from one foot to the other.

'We don't plan to surrender,' he said.

'But we must seem to. And anyway.' Skara set her thin

shoulders under the weight of her mail, narrowing her eyes against the glare. 'I mean to look Bright Yilling in the face when he dies.'

Raith could've told her there were no secrets worth learning in the face of a dying man, not even your bitterest enemy. Only pain and fear. A glimpse of the pain and fear you'd feel when your turn came. And everyone's turn would come soon enough. But those who knew it didn't want to hear it, and those who didn't had to learn it for themselves. So Raith kept silent.

The gate stood wide open, now, the boot-scarred, wreckage-strewn, arrow-wounded ground stretching away, cold and empty, dew glittering in the grass. Far off, just showing in the dawn haze, were the sharpened stakes that marked the High King's lines.

Blue Jenner cleared his throat. 'We sure about this plan?'

'Bit late to think up another,' said Rulf.

'We have waded into the swamp to our necks,' Mother Scaer snarled through clenched teeth, and she twisted her head in a circle and made her neck-bones click. 'The only way out is through.'

'We are sure.' Father Yarvi showed no sign of second thoughts, the tapping of his staff echoing from the elf-stone walls as he set off down the entrance passage. Strolling towards the Last Door with elf-magic their only hope of victory. Everything gambled on one last, mad cast of the runes. The gods knew Raith had never been much for prayers, but he mouthed a quick one then.

'Stay close,' he muttered over his shoulder.

Skara's eyes were fixed ahead. 'I know where to be.'

As they stepped into the dawn they spread out to make an arrowhead. Father Yarvi went at the point, head high. Raith, Jenner and Rulf took the left, Gorm, Soryorn and Hunnan the right, all six of them carrying the biggest shields they could find and wishing they were bigger. Skara and Mother Scaer walked behind. Dosduvoi came last, a dove prow-beast mounted on a pole and held high above them, to show they came in peace.

Even if there'd never been a bigger lie.

Koll stood above the gate, frowning into the wind. Frowning down at the ten tiny figures creeping out across no-man's land. Frowning at the few men of the *South Wind*'s crew scattered on the walls, clinging to the relics they brought out from Strokom. Frowning towards the High King's army, surrounding Bail's Point on every side, like the jaws of a world-swallowing wolf about to snap shut.

Everywhere the glint of metal caught the dawn. The banners of heroes stirred in the breeze. The greatest warriors of Yutmark, Inglefold and the Lowlands. The fiercest of the Shends. The most ruthless mercenaries, dragged from every corner of the world by the promise of plunder. All the High King's matchless power, gathered by Grandmother Wexen in one place and with one purpose. The greatest host assembled since the elves made war on God, and fixed on Koll's destruction.

Well, not just his, but if things went ill for Father Yarvi the future for his apprentice did not exactly burn bright.

Koll realized he was clutching tight at the battlements and made his aching hands unclench. He hadn't felt this scared since . . . the last time he felt this scared. Not long ago, now he thought about it. There had been Strokom, and before that Prince Varoslaf, and before that the climb up the walls not far from where he stood.

'Gods,' he muttered to himself, watching those ten little figures halt on a hump of ground to await the inevitable. 'I need to learn courage.'

'Or better yet,' murmured Skifr, 'avoid danger.'

He glanced down at the old woman, sitting cross-legged, her head tipped back against the chill stone, her hood of rags drawn over her face so all he could see was her mouth, twisted faintly in a smile.

'Can we really beat all these men?' he whispered, tugging nervously at one hand with the other.

Skifr unfolded her long limbs and stood, twitching back her hood. 'All these? Hah!' She rummaged in her nose with one long finger, then neatly flicked the results over the walls towards the High King's men. 'I almost wish there were more.' She held out her hand and, ever so gingerly, as though afraid it might burst into flames, which indeed he was, Koll handed her the first of the drums. 'No host of men can stand against the power of the elves.' Skifr tapped the drum against the side of her head then slotted it into the blunt elf-relic she carried, knocked it home with a click, spun it so it gave a whirring rattle and the letters written upon it became a blur. 'You will see.'

'Do I want to see?'

'All will see, whether they wish to or no.' And Skifr planted one boot on the battlements, elbow propped on her knee so that her elf-weapon pointed at the grey sky. High above them, birds were gently circling. Sensing a meal would soon be served, perhaps. 'Be happy, boy, if you know how.' Skifr took a long breath through her nose, and smiling blew it out. 'The signs are auspicious.'

Soft and low, in the language of the elves, she began to chant.

Skara saw them now, and her heart began to beat even faster. A group of warriors, forming a loose arrowhead like theirs, striking out from the High King's lines across the open ground towards them. Time crawled. She burned to run, to fight, to scream, to do anything but stand still and wait.

No ordinary warriors, these. Their fame was displayed for the world to see in the bright ring-money on their arms and their fingers. Their victories boasted of by the gold on their sword-hilts, the amber on their shield-rims, the engraved patterns on their high helmets.

'Pretty bastards,' snarled Raith through tight lips.

'More jewels between 'em than a royal wedding,' grunted Blue Jenner.

They all smiled. Just as they had smiled when they killed the people she loved. Just as they had smiled when they burned the hall, the city, the country she grew up in, and Skara felt her stomach give a painful squeeze, sweat prickling under the weight of her mail.

'How many of them?' she heard Gorm mutter.

'I count twenty-five,' said Rulf. 'And a minister.'

'Mother Adwyn,' growled Scaer. 'Grandmother Wexen's errand-girl.' Somewhere behind them, faint on the breeze, Skara could hear chanting.

'Twenty or twenty thousand,' Father Yarvi shifted his grip about his elf-staff, 'this will end the same way.'

Skara wondered what way that would be as she watched Bright Yilling amble forward at the head of his Companions.

Apart from the fresh cut Uthil had given him, it was the same face she had seen when her grandfather died. The same bland smile he had worn when he cut off Mother Kyre's head. The same dead eyes that had looked into Skara's in the darkness of the Forest. She felt her gorge rising, clenched her fists, clenched her jaw, clenched her arse, as Yilling swaggered to a stop a few strides from Father Yarvi.

'A shame,' he said. 'I was looking forward to coming in there for you.'

'We have saved you the trouble,' snapped Skara.

'No trouble, Queen Skara.' She felt her breath catch as Yilling's eyes met hers, and he gave a puzzled little frown. 'Wait, though . . . have we met before?' He jumped up in a boyish little caper of excitement. 'I know you! The slave in King Fynn's hall!' He slapped at his thigh in delight. 'You surely outwitted me that night!'

'And will again,' she said.

'I fear that time has passed.' Yilling's eyes wandered on. 'Have you come to fight me, Breaker of Swords, as Uthil did?'

Gorm shook his head as he watched Yilling's companions, hands loose on sword-hilts, axe-handles, spear-hafts, all confident menace. 'I fear that time has passed too,' he said.

'A shame. I had hoped to send Death another famed warrior, and add your song to mine and so make a greater.' Yilling squinted over his shoulder at Mother Sun, and gave a smoky sigh. 'Perhaps Thorn Bathu will step from the shadows now. She killed my favourite horse in one of her raids, you know.' He raised a brow at the man beside him. A tall man with a horn at his belt. 'Rude of her, eh, Vorenhold?'

Vorenhold's teeth showed white in his beard. 'That is her reputation.'

'Warriors.' Bright Yilling puffed out his smooth cheeks. 'Obsessed with their fame. You must be Father Yarvi.'

'He is.' Adwyn's purple-stained lips were twisted with contempt. 'And I am surprised to see you here. I felt sure you had wriggled away as soon as the fighting started.'

Gettland's minister shrugged. 'I wriggled back.' The blood was thumping in Skara's skull. Mother Scaer shifted her shoulders, something moving beneath her coat.

Bright Yilling kept smiling. 'I am glad to finally meet you in person. You are a young man, to have caused so much trouble.'

'One could say the same of you,' said Yarvi. The chanting was growing louder. One of the Companions was frowning up towards the gatehouse. 'Is it true that after you killed King Bratta you made a cup from his skull?'

'I did.' Yilling gave a happy shrug. 'But the wine leaked out of the nose-holes.'

'There is a lesson there,' said Yarvi, and Skara saw he gripped his staff so tight the tendons stood stark from the bloodless back of his hand. 'Things do not always go the way we hope.'

'A lesson you should have learned,' snapped Mother Adwyn. 'Not long ago, Grandmother Wexen gave you another chance, but you slapped her hand away.' Skara bared her teeth at that. She remembered no chances, only the corpses on the floor of the Forest. Only Yaletoft burning on the black horizon. 'You have nothing left to bargain with. You will all be led to Skekenhouse in chains to face the judgment of the One God.'

'Judgment is coming!' Skara remembered her grand-father toppling into the firepit. The blood pit-pattering from the point of Yilling's sword. Her heart was beating so hard it almost strangled her voice. 'But not from the One God. And not to us!'

The smiles of the Companions were fading, their hands straying towards their weapons. Bright Yilling tidied a strand of hair behind one ear. 'She looks well but she talks too much.' And he peered up towards the walls of the fortress, where the strange wailing was growing too loud to ignore.

Mother Adwyn was glaring at Yarvi. 'You and Queen Laithlin stand accused of using elf-magic, and must answer for your crimes!'

'Must I?' Father Yarvi barked out a laugh. 'Let me show you what elf-magic looks like.'

He jerked his staff up so it rested on his withered hand, the end pointed towards Bright Yilling's chest.

The High King's champion had an expression between puzzled and bored. He lifted his hand towards Yarvi, as though to brush aside this minister's blather.

'Greet your mistress!' screamed Skara.

There was a sharp pop. Something flew from the top of Yarvi's staff. Yilling's fingers vanished and his face was spattered with blood.

He took a drunken step back, frowning down. He pawed at his chest with his ruined hand. Skara saw a little hole in his bright mail there. It was already turning dark with blood.

'Uh,' he grunted, brows high with surprise, and toppled backwards.

Someone said, 'Gods.'

A sword hissed as it was drawn.

A shield-rim caught the sun and flashed in Skara's eyes.

She was knocked sideways as Mother Scaer elbowed past her, shrugging her coat off one shoulder.

She heard wing beats as somewhere in the grass a bird took to the skies.

Vorenhold lifted his spear, bridge of his nose creasing with rage. 'You treacherous—'

Mother Scaer stepped between Gorm and Soryorn as they raised their shields, the sinews in her tattooed arm flexing as she lifted the great elf-relic to her shoulder.

'No!' screamed Mother Adwyn.

ANOTHER KIND OF STEEL

R aith was throwing up his arm to block that gilded spear when the shield of the man who held it was ripped apart, the iron rim flopping. He was flung back as if by a giant's hammer, his fine green-dyed cloak on fire and his broken spear tumbling away end over end.

Then came the thunder.

A noise like the Breaking of God, a rattling boom fast as a woodpecker strikes. Mother Scaer's elf-weapon jerked in her grip like a thing alive, her whole body shaking with its mad fury, her scream turned to a jagged warble, shards of metal showering from its top and fire spitting from its mouth.

Before Raith's smarting eyes Bright Yilling's

Companions, storied warriors every one, were in the space of a snatched breath all smashed like beetles on an anvil, mown down like corn before the scythe, blood and splinters and mail-rings showering and their bent and shattered weapons spinning and their ruined limbs flying one from another like straw in a mad gale.

Even as his jaw was dropping Raith heard more cracks behind them, fire stabbing from the walls of the fortress. He flinched at a flash in the High King's lines, a monstrous blooming of fire, broken stakes and earth and armour and men and the parts of men thrown high into the air. The ground shook, Father Earth himself trembling at the power of the elves released.

His axe seemed a pointless little thing now and Raith let it fall, caught Skara's arm and dragged her down behind his shield, Blue Jenner locking with him on one side and Rulf on the other to form a feeble little wall, huddling in terror while the ministers sent Death across the ruined fields before Bail's Point.

There was a great thud as the weapon jolted in Skifr's hands again, a trail of fog curving down through the air towards the High King's lines. It touched the earth among some penned-up horses. Koll gasped as fire shot up in clawing fingers, clapped his hands over his ears at the shuddering boom.

Horses were flung into the air like the toys of a bad-tempered child, others reared on fire, or charged off, dragging burning wagons. Koll gave a kind of moan of horror and dismay. He hadn't known what the elf-engines would do, but he hadn't dared guess it might be this.

The gods knew he was no lover of fighting, but he could understand why bards sung of battles. The matching of warrior against warrior. Of skill against skill and courage against courage. There was no skill or courage here. Nothing noble in this blind destruction.

But Skifr wasn't interested in nobility, only vengeance. She slapped the side of her weapon and the drum dropped out, tumbling down the outside of the wall to bounce in the ditch. She held out her hand.

'More.'

Everywhere elf-relics clattered, stuttered, stabbed, battering Koll's hearing so he could hardly think.

'I . . .' he stammered, 'I . . .'

'Pfft.' Skifr dug her hand into his bag and pulled out another drum. 'You told me once you wanted to see magic!' She locked it into the smoking slot where the first had been.

'I changed my mind.' Wasn't that what he did best, after all? But over the noise of screaming weapons, screaming men, screaming beasts, no one could have heard him, let alone taken the slightest notice.

He blinked out over the parapet, nose almost on the stone, trying to make sense of the chaos. Over to the north there seemed to be fighting. Steel glinting through drifting smoke. Signs of bone and hide bobbing over a seething throng.

Koll's eyes widened even further. 'The Shends have turned on the High King!'

'Just as Father Yarvi told them to,' said Skifr.

Koll stared at her. 'He never told me.'

'If you have not learned that Father Yarvi is a man who says as little as possible, there is no help for you.'

To the east the High King's men were struggling to form a shield-wall. Koll saw a warrior running forward, holding up his sword. Great bravery, but it was a wall of cobwebs. There was a barking clatter from the little knot of shields around the *South Wind*'s prow-beast and the would-be hero fell, shields knocked from the line beyond him like coins flicked over.

'That won't do,' said Skifr, pressing the elf-weapon to her cheek. Koll wanted to weep as he pushed his fingers into his ears. Another thud. Another trail of fog. One more earth-shaking boom, a vast hole ripped from the line. How many men gone in an instant? Burned away as though they had never been or flung ruined like sparks whirling from Rin's forge?

They crumbled, of course. How could men fight the power that broke God? Swords and bows were useless. Mail and shields were useless. Courage and fame were useless. The High King's invincible army streamed down the road and across the fields in a mad confusion, not caring where they ran as long as it was away from Bail's Point, trampling through their camps and flinging away their gear, driven by the screaming Shends and the merciless elf-weapons, turned from men with one purpose to animals with none in their panic.

Squinting into the dawn haze, Koll saw more

movement beyond them – horses spilling from the trees near the abandoned village.

'Riders,' he said, pointing.

Skifr lowered the elf-weapon and snapped out a laugh. 'Hah! Unless my eye for portents deceives me, that is my finest pupil at work. Thorn never was one to miss out on a fight.'

'It's not a fight,' murmured Koll. 'It's a slaughter.'

'Thorn never was one to miss out on a slaughter either.'

Skifr stood tall, burns creasing on her neck as she stretched up to look about her. Everywhere, Grandmother Wexen's mighty host was being scattered like chaff on the wind, Thorn's horsemen moving among them, steel flashing as they cut them down, harrying them through the blackened ruins of the village and off to the north.

'Huh.' She pulled the drum from her elf-weapon and tossed it back to Koll, made him juggle it in a panic before he clutched it desperately to his chest. 'It seems the day is ours.'

Slowly, weakly, hesitantly as a moth breaking from its cocoon, Skara pushed Raith's limp arm away and, using the rim of his shield like a crutch, wobbled to her feet.

The sounds all seemed strange. Screaming, and shouts, and the calls of birds. Now and again the stuttering bark of elf-weapons. But all far away, as though it happened in another time and place.

Mother Scaer stood rubbing her bruised shoulder.

With a grimace of disgust she tossed her still-smoking relic to the ground.

'Are you hurt, my queen?' Blue Jenner's voice. It took Skara a moment to realize he was talking to her. She looked stupidly down at herself. Her mailshirt was all twisted and she tried to drag it straight, brushed mud from her side.

'Dirty,' she mumbled, as though that mattered, her tongue clumsy in her dry mouth as she blinked across the battlefield. If it could be called a battle.

The line of stakes was buckled and torn, great pits dug from it and broken earth and broken gear and broken bodies flung into smouldering heaps. The High King's army, so terrible a few moments before, was burned away like the morning fog before Mother Sun.

Father Yarvi gazed down at the shattered bodies of Yilling's Companions, his elf-staff, his elf-weapon, tucked under one arm. Not frowning or smiling. Not weeping, or laughing. A studied calmness on his face. A craftsman well-satisfied with his morning's work.

'Up, Mother Adwyn,' he said.

From among the corpses the minister lifted her head, red hair plastered to her scalp with clotted blood.

'What have you done?' She stared at Yarvi in slack disbelief, tear-streaks on her mud-spattered face. 'What have you done?'

Yarvi twisted his withered hand in her coat and dragged her up by it. 'Exactly what you accused me of!'

he snarled. 'Where is your court for this? Where is the jury? Who will judge me now?' And he rattled his elf-staff, his elf-weapon, in her face, and threw her down cringing among the bodies.

One of them had somehow staggered up, blinking about him like a man woken from a dream. Vorenhold, though Skara hardly recognized him now. His mail was as tattered as a beggar's coat, his shield hanging in splinters from its bent rim, one earless side of his face all scored and bloody and the arm that had held a spear gone at the elbow.

He fumbled the horn from his belt, lifted it as though to give a blast, then saw the mouthpiece was broken off. 'What happen?' he mumbled.

'Your death.' Gorm put a hand on his shoulder and pushed him gently down to his knees, then with a sweep of his sword sent his head spinning away.

'Where is Yilling?' murmured Skara, tottering to the corpses. Gods, she could hardly tell one from another. Those who had stood so proud a few moments before, made butcher's offal. Perhaps she should have felt triumph, but all she felt was terror.

'This is the end of the world,' she whispered. The end of the world she had known, anyway. What had been strong was strong no longer. What had been certain was wreathed in a fog of doubt.

'Careful, my queen,' Raith muttered, but she hardly heard him, let alone marked him.

She had seen Bright Yilling's body, wedged among the

others, arms flung wide, one leg folded beneath him, mail soaked dark with blood.

She crept closer. She saw the smooth cheek, the long scratch Uthil had given him.

Closer yet, fascinated, fearful. She saw the bland little smile on the plump lips, even in death.

She leaned down over him. The same blank eyes that had haunted her dreams ever since that night in the Forest. The night she had sworn vengeance.

Did his cheek twitch?

She gasped as his eyes flicked to hers, gave a squawk of shock as his hand clutched her mail and dragged her down. So her ear was pressed to his face. So she heard his rasping breath. But not just breath. Words too. And words can be weapons.

Her hand was on her dagger's grip. She could have drawn it. Could have sent him through the Last Door with a flick of her wrist. She had dreamed of it often enough. But she thought of her grandfather, then. *Be as generous to your enemies as your friends. Not for their sake, but for your own.*

She heard Raith growl, felt his shadow fall across them, stabbed her palm out behind her to stop him. Bright Yilling's hand fell, and she pulled away from him to see his red-spotted face.

He pressed something weakly into Skara's palm. A leather pouch, and inside she saw slips of paper. Slips like the ones Mother Kyre used to unfold from the talons of Grandmother Wexen's eagles.

She leaned down over Bright Yilling, the fear gone,

and the hate gone too. She took his hand in hers, slipped her other around the back of his head and gently lifted it towards her.

'Tell me the name,' she murmured, and turned her ear to his lips. Close enough to hear his final breath. His final word.

THE DEAD

I t was a great affair.

Many powerful Gettlanders who had not gone to war would be angered that King Uthil was howed up at Bail's Point, denying them the chance to have their importance noted at an event that would live so long in the memory.

But Laithlin forced through clenched teeth, 'Their anger is dust to me.' Her husband's death had made her queen-regent, the young King Druin clinging to her skirts and her power greater than ever. Thorn Bathu hovered at her shoulder with an eye so vicious and vengeful only the bravest dared meet it even for a moment. Once Laithlin spoke it was a thing already done.

And, after all, there was no shortage of famed figures to attend the Iron King's funeral.

There was the young Queen Skara of Throvenland, lately a pitiful refugee, now celebrated for her courage, her compassion, and her deep-cunning most of all, her white-haired bodyguard frowning silent behind her chair.

There was her betrothed, Grom-gil-Gorm, the Breaker of Swords and Maker of Orphans, his chain of pommels grown longer than ever, his feared minister Mother Scaer brooding at his side.

There was the infamous sorceress Skifr, who had killed more warriors in a few moments than King Uthil in a bloody lifetime, sitting with her cloak of rags drawn tight about her, reckoning the omens in the dirt between her crossed legs.

There was Svidur, a high priestess of the Shends, a green elf-tablet on a thong around her neck. It turned out Father Yarvi had once begged guest-right at her fire after a storm, then convinced her to make an alliance with Grandmother Wexen, then, when it suited him, to break it.

There was the deep-cunning Minister of Gettland himself, of course, who had brought elf-weapons from the forbidden depths of Strokom, and used them to destroy the High King's army, and changed the Shattered Sea for ever.

And there was his apprentice, Koll, whose coat was too thin for the season, and so sat cold and mournful in the sea wind feeling as if he had no business being there.

The king's ship, the best in the crowded harbour of Bail's Point, twenty-four oars upon a side, was dragged by honoured warriors to the chosen place, keel grinding against the stones in the yard of the fortress. The same ship in which King Uthil had sailed across the Shattered Sea on his famous raid to the Islands. The same ship which had wallowed low in the water with slaves and plunder when he returned in triumph.

On its deck they laid the body of the king, wrapped in the captured standard of Bright Yilling, rich offerings arranged about him in the manner Brinyolf the Prayer-Weaver judged the gods would most appreciate.

Rulf laid a single arrow beside the body, and Koll reckoned he was struggling to keep back tears. 'From nothing, to nothing,' he croaked out.

Father Yarvi laid his withered hand on the old helmsman's arm. 'But what a journey in between.'

Queen Laithlin put a cloak of black fur over the dead king's shoulders, and helped her little son wedge a jewelled cup in his fists, then she placed one hand upon his chest, and stood looking down, her jaw clenched tight, until Koll heard Father Yarvi lean close to her and murmur, 'Mother?'

She turned without a word and led the mourners to their chairs, the sea wind catching the battered grass on which the battle had been fought, or the slaughter perpetrated, and setting it thrashing about their feet.

Three dozen captured horses were led onto the ship, hooves clattering at the timbers, and slaughtered so that their blood washed the deck. All agreed Death would show King Uthil through the Last Door with respect.

'The dead will tremble at the news of his coming,'

murmured the Breaker of Swords, and gave a great sniff, and Koll saw tears glistening on his grizzled cheeks.

'Why do you cry?' asked Skara.

'The passing of a fine enemy through the Last Door is as great a sorrow as the passing of a fine friend. Uthil was both to me.'

Father Yarvi helped the young King Druin set a torch to the pitch-soaked kindling. In a moment the ship was all ablaze, a sorrowful moan drawn from the warriors gathered in a great half-circle. They told sad tales of Uthil's prowess, and sung sad songs of his high weapon-luck, and spoke of how the like of his sword-work would never be seen again.

His heir, not even three years old, sat dwarfed in a great chair with his feet dangling, the sword that Rin had forged and that his father had carried with him always laid naked across his knees, beaming at the procession of warriors who shuffled past to offer sorrow and loyalty and grave-gifts but lately stolen from the High King's fallen. He said 'hello' to every one, and ate cakes given to him by his mother until there was honey smeared all around his mouth.

Father Yarvi glanced sideways at him. 'Two years old, and he handles this with better grace than I did.'

'Perhaps.' Queen Laithlin ruffled Druin's pale blonde hair. 'He sits straighter, but he has not sworn so fine an oath as you did.'

'He does not have to.' Yarvi's jaw worked as he looked back to the fire. 'Mine still binds us all.'

They sat, cold and silent, as Father Moon rose and his

children the stars showed themselves, and the flames of the burning ship, and the burning goods, and the burning king lit up the faces of the hundred hundred mourners. They sat until the procession of warriors was over, and the boy-king was snoring gently in Queen Skara's arms. They sat until the flames sank to a flickering, and the keel sagged into whirling embers, and the first muddy smear of dawn touched the clouds, glittering on the restless sea and setting the little birds twittering in the grass.

Queen Skara leant sideways, and laid her hand gently on Queen Laithlin's, and Koll heard her murmur, 'I am sorry.'

'Don't be. He died as he would have wanted to, with steel in his hand. The Iron King! And yet . . . there was so much more in him than iron. I only wish . . . that I had been beside him at the end.' Laithlin shook herself, pulled her hand free of Skara's to briskly wipe her eyes. 'But I know what things are worth, cousin, and you will buy nothing with wishes.'

Then the queen-regent clapped her hands and the slaves with clinking collar-chains began to dig the earth over the still-smouldering pyre, raising a great howe that would stand tall beside that of Queen Skara's father, killed in battle, and her great-grandfather Horrenhod the Red, and kings and queens of Throvenland, the descendants of Bail the Builder himself, dwindling away into the mist of history.

Laithlin stood, adjusting the great key of Gettland's treasury, and spoke in a voice that betrayed neither doubt nor sorrow. 'Gather the men. We sail for Skekenhouse.'

Away down the road, the High King's captured warriors were still heaping the High King's fallen warriors on poorer pyres. Pyres for a dozen, pyres for a hundred, their smoke smudging the sky for miles around.

Koll had become a minister to learn, not to kill. To change the world, not to break it. 'When does it end?' he muttered.

'When I fulfil my oath.' Father Yarvi's eyes were dry as he stared out towards grey Mother Sea. 'Not a moment before.'

Until he reached the bottom step, Koll was still arguing with himself over whether to go down.

He could hear the tapping of Rin's hammer. Her tune-less humming under her breath as she worked. Time was that seemed a welcome as he stepped through her door. A song sung just for him. Now he felt like an eaves-dropper, prying on a private conversation between her and the anvil.

She was frowning as she worked, a warm yellow glimmer across her face, mouth pressed into a firm line and the key she wore tossed over her shoulder so the chain was tight around her sweaty neck. She never did things by halves. He'd always loved that about her.

'You took to working gold?' he said.

She looked up, and when her eyes met his they seemed to steal his breath. He thought how much he'd missed her. How much he wanted to hold her. Be held by her. He'd always thought, hating to admit it to himself, that maybe she wasn't pretty enough. That maybe someone prettier would trip and fall into his arms. Now he couldn't believe he'd ever felt that way.

Gods, he was a fool.

'King Druin's head is smaller than his father's.' Rin held up the resized King's Circle in her pliers, then set it back and carried on tapping.

'I thought you were only interested in steel?' He tried to wander into the forge the same carefree way he used to, but every step was a nervy challenge. 'Swords for kings and mail for queens.'

'After what those elf-weapons did, I've a feeling swords and mail might not be quite so popular. You have to change. Make the best of what life deals you. Face your misfortunes with a smile, eh?' Rin snorted. 'That's what Brand would've said.'

Koll flinched at the name. At the thought he'd let Brand down, who'd treated him like a brother.

'Why did you come here, Koll?'

He swallowed at that. Folk always said he'd a gift with words. But the truth was he'd a gift with ones that meant nothing. At saying what he actually felt he'd no gift at all. He pushed his hand into his pocket, felt the cool weight of the golden elf-bangle he'd taken from Strokom. A peace offering, if she'd have it.

'I guess I've been thinking . . . maybe . . .' He cleared his throat, mouth dry as dust as he glanced up guiltily at her. 'I made the wrong choice?' He'd meant it to be a firm admission. An open confession. Came out a self-justifying little squeak.

Rin looked less than impressed. 'Did you tell Father Yarvi you made the wrong choice?'

He winced down at his feet but his shoes didn't have the answers. Shoes don't tend to. 'Not yet . . .' He couldn't get the breath to say he would do, if she asked him to.

She didn't. 'Last thing I want to do is upset you, Koll.' He winced harder at that. Something folk only say when upsetting you is their first priority. 'But I reckon whatever choice you make, you soon get to thinking you made the wrong one.'

He would've liked to say that wasn't fair. Would've liked to say he was so caught up between what Father Yarvi wanted, and what Rin wanted, and what Brand would've wanted, and what his mother would've wanted, he hardly knew what he wanted at all any more.

But all he managed was to croak out, 'Aye. I'm not proud of myself.'

'Nor am I.' She tossed her hammer down, and when he met her eye she didn't look angry. Sad. Guilty, even. He was starting to hope that might mean she'd forgive him when she said, 'I laid with someone else.'

Took him a moment to catch up, and when he did he wished he hadn't. His fist closed painful tight around the elf-bangle in his pocket. 'You . . . Who?'

'What does it matter? It wasn't about him.'

He stood staring at her, suddenly furious. He felt ambushed. Wronged. He knew he had no right to feel that way, and that only made him feel worse. 'You think I want to hear that?'

She blinked, caught somewhere between guilt and anger. 'I hope you hate to hear it.'

'That why you did it?'

Anger won. 'I did it because I needed to you selfish prick!' she barked. 'Not everything's about you and your great big talents and your great big choices and your great big bloody future.' She stabbed at her chest with her finger. '*I* needed something and you chose not to be here!' She turned her back on him. 'No one'll complain if you choose not to be here again.'

The tapping of her hammer chased him back up the steps. Back to the courtyard of Bail's Point, and the war, and the smoke of dead men.

DIGGING

Raith's back ached, and his chest was sore, and his long-broken hand and his newly-burned hand both stung in their own ways from the work. He'd dug ten graves' worth of mud already, and found no sign of Rakki, but he kept digging.

He'd always fretted over what his brother might do without him. Never thought about what he'd do without his brother. Maybe he'd never really been the strong one after all.

Spade up, spade down, and the calm thud, thud of the blade in the soil, and the steady heaping of the earth to either side. It spared him from having to think.

'Looking for treasure?'

A long figure stood at the lip of the pit with Mother Sun behind, hands on hips, gold and silver glinting on

the unshaved side of her head. The last person he'd hoped
to run into out here. But so it goes, with hopes.

'Digging for my brother's body.'

'What's that worth now?'

'It's worth something to me.' He flung soil so it scattered
across her boots, but Thorn Bathu wasn't one to be put
off by a little dirt.

'You'll never find him. Even if you do, what then?'

'I build a proper pyre, and I burn him proper, and I
bury him proper.'

'Queen Skara was thinking of burying Bright Yilling
proper. She says you have to be generous to your
enemies.'

'And?'

'I bent his sword in half and buried that. His carcass
I cut up and left for the crows. I reckon that more
generous than he deserved.'

Raith swallowed. 'I try not to think about what men
deserve.'

'The dead are past help, boy.' Thorn closed one nostril
with her finger and blew snot onto Raith's diggings
through the other. 'All you can do is take a price from
the living. I'll be heading to Skekenhouse in the morning.
Take a price from the High King for my husband.'

'What price will pay for that?'

'His head'll make a start!' she snarled at him, spit
flecking from her twisted lips.

Being honest, her fury scared him a little. Being honest,
it excited him a lot.

Reminded him of his own. Reminded him of a simpler

time, when he knew who he was. When he knew who his enemies were, and all he wanted was to kill them.

'Thought you might want to come along,' said Thorn.

'Didn't think you liked me much.'

'I think you're a bloody little bastard.' She poked a stone with her toe and it rolled down into the pit. 'That's just the kind of man I'm after.'

Raith licked his lips, that old fire flickering up in him like Thorn was the sparking flint and he was the ready tinder.

She was right. Rakki was dead, and no amount of digging would help him.

He chopped the shovel hard into the soil. 'I'm with you.'

Skara was changed. Or perhaps she'd been changing bit by bit, and he hadn't seen it till now.

She'd given up the mail, and looked less like the great painting of Ashenleer behind her. But she still wore the long dagger at her belt, and the armring with the red stone Bail the Builder once wore into battle. She still had the sword Rin made, though some boy from among the burned-out farmers knelt beside her with it in Raith's place.

A queen indeed, and with learned advisors at her side. Blue Jenner hadn't lost his raider's slouch, but he'd cut back his wispy hair, and trimmed close his beard, and gained a fine fur and a gold chain to sit on top of it. Owd had shed weight and heaped on dignity since she was Mother Scaer's apprentice, a disapproving frown on her sharpened face as she watched Raith skulk into the audience chamber, his stolen helmet clutched under his arm.

Skara looked down at him, chin high and shoulders back so her neck seemed to go on a mile, quite at home in Bail's great chair and seeming as lofty as Laithlin ever had. Could it really be the same girl whose bed he'd shared a few nights before? Whose fingers had trailed across the scars on his back? Whose whispers had tickled at his ear? Seemed a dream now. Maybe it had been.

He wobbled out a bow. Felt quite the fool, but what else could he do? 'I've, er, been thinking—'

'*My queen* would be the proper opening,' said Mother Owd, and Skara made no effort to put her right.

Raith winced. 'My queen . . . I've been offered a place on Thorn Bathu's crew. To lead the attack on Skekenhouse.'

'You minded to take it?' asked Jenner, bushy brows high.

Raith made himself look right in Skara's eyes. As if it was just the two of them, alone. Man and woman rather than killer and queen. 'If you can spare me.'

Perhaps there was the faintest flicker of hurt in her face. Perhaps he just wanted to see one. Either way, her voice stayed smooth as glass. 'You are a Vansterman. You have sworn me no oaths. You are free to go.'

'I have to,' said Raith. 'For my brother.'

It actually hurt in his chest, he hoped so hard she'd say, *No, stay, I need you, I love you.*

But Skara only nodded. 'Then I thank you for your faithful service.' Raith couldn't stop his cheek from twitching. Faithful service, that was all he'd given her. The same as any dog. 'You will be much missed.'

He tried to find some sign in her face that he'd be missed at all, but it was a mask. He glanced over his shoulder, saw a messenger from the Prince of Kalyiv waiting, fur hat clutched in eager hands, impatient for her moment.

Mother Owd was frowning down mightily at him. 'If there is nothing else?' No doubt she guessed some part of what had gone on and was keen to see his back. Raith could hardly blame her.

His shoulders slumped as he turned away. Felt like he'd outwitted himself altogether. Used to be the only thing moved him was the chance at punching folk in the head. Skara had showed him a glimpse of something better, and he'd traded it for a vengeance he didn't even want.

Blue Jenner caught up to him in the doorway. 'Do what you have to. There'll always be a place for you here.'

Raith wasn't so sure. 'Tell me, old man . . . if you've done evil things . . . does that make you evil?'

Jenner blinked at him. 'Wish I had the answers, boy. All I know is there's no changing yesterday. You can only look to do better tomorrow.'

'Aye, I reckon.' Raith wanted to give the old raider a parting hug, but that gold chain made him seem too grand. So he settled for just an awkward grin down at his boots, dirty from digging, and skulked away.

HEAD AND HEART

The dawn was crisp and clear, and Skara's breath, and Laithlin's breath, and Druin's breath, and the breath of their gathered guards and slaves and attendants made a gently rising cloud of smoke as they looked down from the ramp leading to the harbour.

King Uthil was ashes and King Druin too young for the task, so it fell to Father Yarvi to lead the fleet to their reckoning with the High King in Skekenhouse. Standing for Father Peace did not prevent the young minister of Gettland from doing Mother War's work that morning, and as well as any warrior.

As Mother Sun showed herself bright over the looming walls of Bail's Point she cast long shadows from dozens of prow-beasts, lined up neatly as the heads of horses on parade, every oarsman calm and ready. Father Yarvi gave one grim wave to Queen Laithlin, then his high, hard call rang out across the silent harbour, and as though all those hundreds of men had one mind and one body, the ships began to move.

'It seems Father Yarvi has become our leader,' said Skara.

'War has a way of revealing things in people.' The pride was plain in Laithlin's voice as she watched the ships of Gettland glide out to sea, two by two. 'Some flourish and some falter. But I always knew Yarvi had resolve in him. Yours has surprised me more.'

'Mine?'

'Did you not stand firm here against the numberless armies of the High King? You are very much changed, cousin, from the girl brought wet-eyed and weary into my chambers.'

'We all are changed,' murmured Skara.

She saw Thorn Bathu stand scowling at the prow of her ship, one boot up on the rail as though she could not get to Skekenhouse fast enough. The boat had belonged to one of Bright Yilling's Companions, a golden ram for a prow-beast, but Thorn had charred it black so it better fitted her black mood and, if you stood on the High King's side, her black reputation. Skara's eyes moved down the crew on their sea-chests, dangerous men all bent on vengeance, until she saw a white head bobbing with the stroke and made herself look away.

Yesterday, in Bail's Hall, she had wanted to ask him to stay. To order him to stay. She had opened her mouth to do it, but at the last moment, she had let him go. She had made him go. She had not even been able to say a true goodbye. It would not have been proper.

She was not sure if you could call it love. It was nothing like the bards sing of. But whatever she felt was too powerful to risk having him outside her door every day, every night. That way she would have to be strong every moment, and sooner or later she would weaken. This way, she had to be strong only once.

It hurt her to push him away. It hurt her more to see how much she hurt him. But Mother Kyre had always told her hurts are part of life. All you can do is shoulder them, and carry on. She had her land, and her people, and her duty to think of. Taking him into her bed had been foolish. Selfish. A reckless mistake, and she could not afford to make another.

Blue Jenner gave Skara a nod from the steering platform of the *Black Dog*, and as she raised her arm in reply a rousing cheer went up from the crews of Throvenland. Men had been flooding into Bail's Point since the victory to kneel before her and swear loyalty, and though the ships might have been taken from the High King, the warriors were hers.

'You must have twenty crews, now, cheering for you,' said Laithlin.

'Twenty-two,' said Skara, as she watched her ships follow the Gettlanders out of the harbour.

'No meagre force.'

'When I came to you I had nothing. I will never forget how much I owe you.' Wanting to make some kind of gesture, Skara beckoned to her thrall. 'You should take back the slave you lent me—'

'Has she displeased you?'

Skara saw the fear in the girl's eyes. 'No. No, I just—'

'Keep her.' Laithlin waved her back. 'A gift. The first of many. You will soon be High Queen over the whole Shattered Sea, after all.'

Skara stared at her. 'What?'

'If the wind blows our way, Grandmother Wexen will be toppled from her high perch in the Tower of the Ministry. The priests of the One God will be driven back to the south. The High King will fall. Have you spared no thought for who will replace him?'

'I was a little distracted with getting through each day alive.'

Laithlin snorted as if that was a petty reason to ignore the turning of the wheels of power. Perhaps it was. 'The Breaker of Swords is the most famous warrior left alive. The one king never defeated in battle or duel.' She nodded towards the wharves, and Skara saw him striding up the long ramp towards them, men ducking out of his way like scattering pigeons. 'Grom-gil-Gorm will be High King. And you will be his wife.'

Skara put a hand on her churning stomach. 'I hardly feel ready to be queen of Throvenland.'

'Who is ever ready? I was a queen at fifteen. My son is a king at two.'

'It's sore,' piped Druin, jerking the King's Circle from his head.

'He feels its weight already,' murmured Laithlin, easing

it gently back down over his wispy yellow hair. 'I have buried two husbands. Those marriages began with what was best for Gettland, but they gave me my two sons. And, almost without realizing it, respect can develop. Liking. Even love.' Laithlin's voice seemed suddenly broken. 'Almost . . . without realizing it.'

Skara said nothing. To be High Queen, and wear the key to the whole Shattered Sea. To kneel to no one, ever. To have whole nations look to her for an example. A girl just turned eighteen who could scarcely make her own stomach obey. She tried to calm her nervous guts as the Breaker of Swords stopped before them. Puking over the boots of her husband-to-be would make a poor omen.

'Queen Laithlin,' he said, bowing awkwardly. 'Queen Skara . . . I wished to trade a few words, before I leave for Skekenhouse. We are . . .' He winced towards the jostling ships, one hand fussing at the grips of the daggers that bristled from his belt.

'To be married?' Skara finished for him. She had always known she would not get to choose her own husband but somehow, as a girl, she had fancied the perfect prince would be offered up and her head and her heart would be in blissful accord. Now she saw how naïve she had been. Her head knew Gorm was a good match. Her heart would have to make the best of it.

'Forgive me,' he said, 'if lover's words are . . . heavy in my mouth. I have always been more of a fighter.'

'That is no secret.' Strange how his nervousness made her feel calmer. 'It is not a chain of conquered ladies' keys you wear.'

'No, and nor will my wife.' The Breaker of Swords held up a chain, the low sun glinting on gold and silver, glittering on polished stones. 'The pommels of Bright Yilling and his Companions,' he said, as he lifted them over Skara's head. 'You have claimed a famous vengeance for your grandfather.' He settled the chain upon the fur on her shoulders, 'and deserve to wear them as proudly as I wear mine.'

Skara blinked down at the flashing jewel in the chain's centre, a diamond the size of an acorn in a claw of gold. She knew it well. Had seen it every night in her dreams. It had gleamed with reflected fire on the hilt of Bright Yilling's sword as he killed Mother Kyre and King Fynn.

She felt a shiver of disgust, wanted to tear the chain off and fling it in the sea along with the memories of that night. But for better or worse they were part of her, and she could not refuse the gift. She straightened, and worked her shoulders back, and wondered if she did not like the weight of the chain upon them after all.

To her, it murmured a reassurance. She had been through the fire, and like the best steel come out stronger.

To others, it spoke a threat. No matter your fame, make an enemy of this woman and you will end up one more lump of metal on her chain.

'A gift fit for a High Queen of the Shattered Sea,' she said, pressing it to her chest.

'I wished to set your mind at rest since I am . . . perhaps not the man you would have chosen. I wished to tell you that I mean to be a good husband. To defer to you in matters of the coin and the key. To give you sons.'

Skara swallowed at that, but it was a proper thing to say, and Mother Kyre would never have forgiven her if she had not made a proper reply. 'No less do I mean to be a good wife to you. To defer to you in matters of the plough and the sword. To give you daughters.'

Gorm's craggy face broke out in a strange grin. 'I hope so.' He glanced down at Druin, staring up at him from so far below. 'Small people, at your feet, to whom you can give the future. That seems a fine thing.'

Skara tried not to let her doubts show. Tried to give a winning, willing smile. 'We will find our way through it together, hand in hand.' And she held hers out to him.

It looked tiny, and white, and smooth in his great scarred paw. It looked like a child's hand. But its grip was the firmer. It seemed his trembled.

'I have no doubt you will make as fine a husband as you do a warrior,' she said, putting her other hand under his to still it.

'We will be as formidable together as Mother Sea and Father Earth.' He brightened as he moved to more familiar ground. 'And I will start by bringing you the High King's head as a wedding gift!'

Skara winced. 'I would prefer peace.'

'Peace comes when you have killed all your enemies, my queen.' Gorm took back his hand, bowed again, and strode off towards his ship.

'If that chain around his neck should have taught him anything,' murmured Laithlin, 'it is that there are always more enemies.'

THE MINISTER'S BATTLEFIELD

'You think you have so much time,' said Skifr, staring into the flames. 'So many brave prizes ahead, so many harvests to reap. Mark my words, my dove, before you realize it, your glorious future has become a set of tired old stories, and there is nothing ahead but dust.'

Koll puffed out his cheeks. The firelight on Skifr's face reminded him of the forgelight on Rin's, dragged their miserable last meeting to his mind. Two women could hardly have looked less alike, but when you're in a sorry mood, everything brings up a sorry memory.

'Have some tea, eh?' he ventured, trying and failing to sound perky as he pulled the pot off the fire. 'Perhaps things won't seem so dark afterward—'

'Seize life with both hands!' snapped Skifr, making

Koll jump and nearly upend the pot in his lap. 'Rejoice in what you have. Power, wealth, fame, they are ghosts! They are like the breeze, impossible to hold. There is no grand destination. Every path ends at the Last Door. Revel in the sparks one person strikes from another.' She huddled into her cloak of rags. 'They are the only light in the darkness of time.'

Koll dumped the pot back, making tea slop and hiss in the flames. 'Have some tea, eh?' Then he left Skifr alone with her darkness, and took his own out of the ruin and onto the hillside, staring down towards Skekenhouse, seat of the High King.

The Tower of the Ministry rose from the centre, perfect elf-stone and elf-glass soaring up and up, then sheared off by the Breaking of God, a crusting of man-made walls, towers, domes, roofs covering the wound like an unsightly scab. Specks circled those highest turrets. Doves, perhaps, like the ones Koll used to tend, bringing panicked messages from far-flung ministers. Or eagles sent out with Grandmother Wexen's desperate last orders.

The High King's vast new temple to the One God squatted in the elf-tower's shadow, a damned ugly thing for all the effort lavished upon it, still crusted with scaffolding after ten years of building, half the rafters bare like the rib-bones of a long-dead corpse. He'd built it to show men could make great works too. All he'd proved was how feeble their best efforts were beside the relics of the elves.

Roofs spread out around tower and temple in every direction, a maze of narrow streets between buildings of stone and buildings of wood and buildings of wattle and hide. Outside stood the famous elf-walls. Miles of them. Crumbling in places, shored up by man-built bastions and crowned by man-built battlements. But strong, still. Very strong.

'We need to get in,' Thorn was snarling, elf-bangle smouldering red as she glowered at the city like a wolf at a chicken coop. Koll wouldn't have been surprised to see her drooling like one, she was that hungry for vengeance.

'No doubt,' said Mother Scaer, eyes narrowed to their habitual slits. 'How, is the question?'

'We still have elf-weapons. I say we crack Grandmother Wexen's shell and prick her from the wreckage.'

'Even with elf-weapons it will take time to overcome those walls,' said Father Yarvi. 'Who knows what mischief Grandmother Wexen could cook up in the meantime?'

'We could shoot burning arrows over them,' offered Rulf, patting his black horn bow. 'Man-weapons will do for that, and we'd soon get a good blaze going.'

'This is my city now,' said Father Yarvi. 'I do not wish to see it burned to the ground.'

'*Your* city?' sneered Mother Scaer.

'Of course.' Yarvi took his eyes from Skekenhouse and turned them calmly upon her. 'I will be Grandfather of the Ministry, after all.'

Scaer gave a disbelieving snort. 'Will you indeed?'

'If Vansterland is to have the High King's chair, and Throvenland the High Queen's key, it seems only fair that Gettland should have the Tower of the Ministry.'

Mother Scaer narrowed her eyes even further, trapped on uncomfortable ground between suspicion at the thought of Yarvi raised up and ambition at the thought of Gorm enthroned. 'We should have a proper moot upon it.'

'Must people as wise as we really discuss the obvious? Must we hold a moot to establish that Mother Sun will follow Father Moon across the sky?'

'Only fools argue over what they don't have,' murmured Koll. He seemed to be the only minister trying to smooth the way for Father Peace, and he hadn't even sworn his Oath.

Rulf pushed his thumbs into his weathered sword-belt. 'For weeks they were stuck outside our elf-walls. Now we're stuck outside theirs.'

'Bright Yilling made the mistake of trying to climb over them or dig under them,' said Yarvi.

'What should he have done?' snapped Thorn.

Koll already knew the answer, even if he didn't much like it. 'Talked through them.'

'Precisely.' Father Yarvi took up his staff, and began to pick his way down the hillside. 'The warriors can stay here. You stand on the minister's battlefield now.'

'As long as there's vengeance to be found there!' growled Thorn at his back.

Yarvi turned, teeth bared. 'Oh, there will be vengeance enough for everyone, Thorn Bathu. I have sworn it.'

Before the gates of Skekenhouse the road was churned to a squelching bog, littered with trampled rubbish, with torn tents and broken furniture and dead animals. The possessions of folk who'd tried to crowd into Skekenhouse for safety. Or maybe those who'd tried to swarm out for it. Folly, whichever. When Mother War spreads her wings, there is no safe place.

Koll felt as if he had a rock in his throat. He'd hardly been more scared approaching Strokom. He kept finding himself creeping closer to Rulf and his shield, hunching down as the elf-walls loomed over them, the long banners of the High King and his One God hanging weather-stained from the battlements.

'Ain't you the one climbed into Bail's Point alone in bad weather?' grunted the helmsman from the side of his mouth.

'Yes, and I was properly terrified then too.'

'Madmen and fools feel no fear. Heroes fear and face the danger anyway.'

'Could I be none of the three and go home?' muttered Koll.

'There can be no going back,' snapped Mother Scaer over her shoulder, shifting the elf-relic under her coat.

'Have no fear, friend.' Dosduvoi hoisted the pole he carried a little higher, the *South Wind*'s prow-beast mounted at the top. 'We have a minister's dove to keep the shafts off.'

'A pretty enough piece of carving,' said Koll, flinching at a flicker of movement on the battlements, 'but a little slender for stopping arrows.'

'The purpose of a minister's dove,' hissed Father Yarvi

over his shoulder, 'is to stop the arrows being shot at all. Now be still.'

'Halt there!' came a shrill command, and their party clattered to a stop. 'Three dozen bows are upon you!'

Father Yarvi puffed out his chest as if offering it as a good home for arrows, though Koll noticed he kept his elf-metal staff gripped tight in his good hand.

'Put away your weapons!' His voice could not have been steadier if he was the one atop the wall. 'We are ministers, come to speak for Father Peace!'

'You have armed men with you too!'

'We will speak for Mother War if we must, and in voices of thunder.' Father Yarvi gestured towards the armed men spreading out through the muddy fields around the city. 'The warriors of Gettland and Throvenland surround your walls. The Breaker of Swords himself approaches from the sea. And behind us on the hill the sorceress Skifr watches. She whose magic laid low the High King's army. She waits for my word. That you will agree to terms, and can have peace.' Yarvi let his arms drop. 'Or that you will not, and can have what Bright Yilling had.'

When the voice came the challenge had all drained away. 'You are Father Yarvi.'

'I am, and I have Mother Scaer of Vansterland with me.'

'My name is Utnir. I am elected to speak for the people of Skekenhouse.'

'Greetings, Utnir. I hope we can save some lives between us. Where is Grandmother Wexen?'

'She has sealed herself in the Tower of the Ministry.'

'And the High King?'

'He has not been seen since news came of the defeat at Bail's Point.'

'Every victory is someone's defeat,' muttered Koll.

'Just as every hero is someone's villain,' said Rulf.

'Your leaders have abandoned you!' called out Mother Scaer.

'Best you abandon them,' said Father Yarvi, 'before they drag all of Skekenhouse through the Last Door with them.'

Another pause, perhaps the muttering of voices above, and a chill breeze whipped up and made the long banners flap against the elf-stone.

'There is a rumour you have made an alliance with the Shends,' came Utnir's voice.

'So I have. I am an old friend of their high priestess, Svidur. If you resist us, I will give the city to her, and when it falls its citizens will be slaughtered or made slaves.'

'We had no part in the war! We are not your enemies!'

'Prove yourself our friends, then, and play your part in the peace.'

'We hear you spoke fine words before Bright Yilling. Why should we trust you?'

'Bright Yilling was a mad dog who worshipped Death. He murdered King Fynn and his minister. He burned women and children in Thorlby. Over his end I shed no tears and harbour no regrets.' Father Yarvi lifted his withered hand, his voice firm and his face open. 'But I am a minister, and stand for Father Peace. If you wish to walk in his footsteps you will find me there beside you. Open the gates to us, and I swear a sun-oath and a moon-oath that I will do all I can to safeguard the lives and property of the people of Skekenhouse.'

After all the blood spilled it made Koll proud to see his master making of the fist an open hand. More voices whispered above, but finally Utnir seemed satisfied. Or satisfied he had no choice, at least. 'Very well! We will give the keys to the city into the hands of your men!'

'History will thank you!' called Father Yarvi.

Koll realized he'd been holding his breath, and let it out in a cheek-puffing sigh. Mother Scaer gave a grunt in her throat, and shrugged her coat closed. Dosduvoi leaned down to Koll, grinning. 'I told you the dove would keep the arrows off.'

'I think Father Yarvi's words were our shield today,' he answered.

The minister himself was drawing Rulf into a huddle. 'Gather your best-behaved men and take command of the gates.'

'I've not many left,' said Rulf. 'Some of those that were on the *South Wind* with us have fallen sick.'

'Those that rowed to Strokom?' muttered Koll.

Father Yarvi ignored him. 'Use what you have and see the defenders disarmed. I want good discipline and good treatment for all.'

'Yes, Father Yarvi,' said the old helmsman, turning to beckon men forward with one broad hand.

'Then give the city to the Shends.'

Rulf looked back at him, eyes wide. 'You're sure?'

'They demand vengeance for all the High King's raids upon them. I gave my word to Svidur that she could have the city first. But let Thorn Bathu and Grom-gil-Gorm have their pieces of it too. That is the lesser evil.'

'You swore an oath,' muttered Koll, as Rulf walked off to give the orders, shaking his bald head.

'I swore an oath to do all I can. I can do nothing.'

'But these people—'

Yarvi caught Koll's shirt with his withered hand. 'Did these people complain when Yaletoft burned?' he snarled. 'Or Thorlby? When King Fynn was killed? Or Brand? No. They cheered Bright Yilling on. Now let them pay the price.' He smoothed Koll's shirt gently as he let him go. 'Remember. Power means having one shoulder always in the shadows.'

END OF THE ROPE

Father Yarvi might've said no fires, but something was burning somewhere.

The smoke was a faint haze that turned day in the streets of Skekenhouse to muddy dusk. It scratched at Raith's throat. Made every breath an effort. Shapes moved in the murk. Running figures. The looters or the looted.

Strange how smells can bring the memories rushing up so clear. The stink of burning snatched Raith back to that village on the border between Vansterland and Gettland. Halleby, had they called it? That one they'd torched for nothing, and Raith drowned a man in a pig trough. It'd seemed a fine thing to do at the time. He'd boasted of it afterwards and Grom-gil-Gorm had laughed with his warriors and called him a bloody little bastard, and smiled to have so vicious a dog on his leash.

Now Raith's mouth was sour with fear and his heart thud-thudding in his aching head and his palm all tacky around the grip of his axe. He startled at a crash somewhere, a long scream more like an animal than a man, spun about straining into the gloom.

Maybe he should've been giving thanks to Mother War that he stood with the winners. That's what he used to tell his brother, wasn't it, when Rakki shook his head over the ashes? But if there was a right side, it was hard to imagine Thorn Bathu's crew of killers on it.

It was a vicious crowd he'd joined up with, bright-eyed like foxes, slinking like wolves, their persons neglected but their weapons lavished with gleaming care. Most were Gettlanders, but Thorn welcomed anyone with a score to settle and no qualms over how they went about it. Raith didn't even know the names of most of them. They were nothing to each other, bound together only by hate. Men who'd lost families or friends. Men who'd lost themselves and had nothing left but taking from others what'd been taken from them.

Some dragged folk from their houses while others crashed through inside, smashing chests and slitting mattresses and turning over furniture, supposedly to find hidden treasure but really just for the joy of breaking. The victims fought no more than sheep dragged to the slaughter-pen. Used to surprise Raith, that they didn't fight. Used to disgust him. Now he understood it all too well. He'd no fight left himself.

Folk aren't just cowards or heroes. They're both and neither, depending on how things stand. Depending on who stands with them, who stands against. Depending on the life they've had. The death they see waiting.

They were lined up on their knees in the street. Some were pushed down. Some were flung down. Most just joined the end of the line on their own, and knelt there, meek. A slap or a kick where one was needed to get them moving, but otherwise no violence. A beaten slave was worth less than a healthy one, after all, and if they weren't worth enough to sell, why waste even that much effort on 'em?

Raith closed his eyes. Gods, he felt weary. So weary he could hardly stand. He thought of his brother's face, thought of Skara's, but he couldn't get them clear. The only face he could see was that woman's, staring at her burning farm, calling her children's names, her voice gone all broken and grief-mad. He felt tears prickling under his lids and let his eyes flicker open.

A Vansterman with a silver ring through his nose was dragging a woman around by her armpit, laughing, but the laughter was all jagged and forced, like he was trying to convince himself there was something funny in it.

Thorn Bathu didn't look like laughing. The muscles working on the shaved side of her head, the scars livid on her pale cheeks, the sinews standing stark and merciless from the arm she gripped her axe with.

'Most o' these are hardly worth the taking,' said one of the warriors, a great big Gettlander with a lopsided jaw, shoving an old man down onto his knees at the end of the line.

'What do we do with 'em, then?' said another.

Thorn's voice came flat and careless. 'I've a mind to kill 'em.'

One of the women started sobbing a prayer and someone shut her up with a slap.

Here was the dream. To plunder a big city. To take whatever you saw for your own. To strut like the biggest dog down streets where you'd be sneered at in peacetime. To rule supreme just 'cause you had a blade and were bastard enough to use it.

Raith's eyes were watery. The smoke, maybe, or maybe he was crying. He thought of that farm burning. He felt crushed, as buried as his brother, could hardly breathe. Seemed like everything worth saving in him died with Rakki, or was left behind with Skara.

He fumbled at the strap on his helmet, pulled it off and tossed it down with a hollow clonk, watched it roll on its edge down the cobbles. He scrubbed hard at his flattened hair with his nails, hardly felt it.

He looked sideways at that row of people, kneeling in the road. He saw a boy clench his fist, clench a handful of dirt out of the gutter. He saw a teardrop dangling from a woman's nose. Heard the old man at the end wheezing fear with every breath.

Thorn's boots crunched as she walked over to him.

She took her time. Working up her courage, maybe. Enjoying getting there, maybe. Letting the haft of the axe slowly slide through her hand until she was gripping it by the palm-polished end.

The old man flinched as she set her feet behind him,

working them into the ground like a woodsman beside the chopping block.

She shook out her shoulders, cleared her throat, turned her head and spat.

She lifted the axe.

And Raith let his breath out in a shuddering sigh, and he stepped between Thorn and the old man and stood facing her.

He didn't say a word. He wasn't sure he could've got a word out, his throat was so raw and his heart going so hard. He just stood there.

Silence.

The warrior with the crooked jaw took a step towards him. 'Get your arse shifted, fool, before I—'

Without taking her eyes off Raith, Thorn held up one long finger and said, 'Sss.' That was all, but enough to stop the big man dead. She stared at Raith, eyes sunken in shadow, their corners just catching the angry red gleam from that elf-bangle of hers.

'Out of my way,' she said.

'I can't.' Raith shook the shield off his arm and let it drop. Tossed his axe clattering down on top of it. 'This ain't vengeance. It's just murder.'

Thorn's scarred cheek twitched and he could hear the fury in her voice. Could see her shoulders almost shaking with it. 'I won't ask again, boy.'

Raith spread his arms, palms towards her. He could feel the tears on his cheeks and he didn't care. 'If you're set on killing, you can start with me. I deserve it more'n they do.'

He closed his eyes and waited. He wasn't fool enough to think this made up for a hundredth part of the things he'd done. He just couldn't stand and watch no more.

There was a crunch and a white-hot þain in his face.

He stumbled over something and his head cracked on stone.

The world reeled. He tasted salt.

He lay there a moment, wondering if he was leaking all over the street. Wondering if he cared.

But he was breathing still, for all he was blowing bubbles from one nostril with each snort. He put one clumsy hand to his nose. Felt twice the size it used to. Broken, no doubt, from the sick feeling when he touched it. He grunted as he rolled onto his side, propping himself on an elbow.

Hard faces, scarred faces, swimming around him, looking down. The old man was still kneeling, lips moving in a silent prayer. Thorn still stood over him, axe in her hand, the elf-bangle smouldering red as a hot coal. From the smear of blood on her forehead Raith reckoned she must have butted him.

'Phew,' he grunted.

Took a hell of an effort to roll over, blood pattering from his nose onto the backs of his hands. Up onto one knee and he gave a wobble, threw one arm out to steady himself, but he didn't fall. The dizziness was fading, and he stumbled as he stood, but got there in the end. Back between Thorn and the old man.

'There we are.' He licked his teeth and spat blood, then

he held his arms out wide, and closed his eyes again, and stood swaying.

'Gods damn it,' he heard Thorn hiss.

'Is he mad?' said someone else.

'Just kill him and be done,' growled the one with the lopsided jaw.

Another pause. A pause seemed to go on forever, and Raith winced, and squeezed his eyes shut tighter. Each shuddering breath made a weird squeak in his broken nose, but he couldn't stop it.

He heard a slow scraping and prised one eye open. Thorn had slid her axe through the loop at her belt and was standing, hands on hips. He blinked stupidly at her.

Not dead, then.

'What do we do?' snapped the one with the ring through his nose.

'Let 'em go,' said Thorn.

'That's it?' The warrior with the crooked jaw sprayed spit as he snarled the words. 'Why should they be let go? Didn't let my wife go, did they?'

Thorn turned her head to look at him. 'One more word and you'll be the one kneeling in the street. Let 'em go.' And she dragged the old man up by his collar and shoved him stumbling off towards the houses.

Raith slowly let his arms fall, face one great throb.

He felt something spatter against his cheek. Looked round to see the big man had spat on him.

'You little bastard. You're the one should die.'

Raith gave a weary nod as he wiped away the spittle. 'Aye, probably. But not for this.'

THE TEARS OF FATHER PEACE

Father Yarvi strode at their head, the tapping of the elf-staff that had killed Bright Yilling echoing down the hallway. He went so swiftly Koll had to jog the odd step to keep up, Skifr's cloak of rags snapping about the elf-weapon she held down by her side, the gear of Rulf and his warriors rattling as they followed. Mother Adwyn stumbled at the back, her fin of red hair grown out into a shapeless mop, one hand trying to drag some slack into the rope around her chafed neck.

The hallway was lined with weapons, bent and rust-speckled. The weapons of armies defeated by High Kings of the past few hundred years. But there would be no victory for the High King today. From beyond the narrow windows, Koll could hear the sack of Skekenhouse. Could smell the burning. Could feel the fear, catching as the plague.

He put his head down, trying not to imagine what was happening out there. Trying not to imagine what might happen here, when Father Yarvi finally came face to face with Grandmother Wexen.

'What if she has fled?' snapped Skifr.

'She is here,' said Yarvi. 'Grandmother Wexen is not the fleeing kind.'

High doors of dark wood stood at the end of the hallway, carved with scenes from the life of Bail the Builder. How he conquered Throvenland. How he conquered Yutmark. How he climbed a hill of dead enemies to conquer the whole Shattered Sea. Another day Koll would've admired the craftsmanship, if not the conquest, but no one was in the mood for woodwork now.

A dozen guards blocked the way, mailed men with frowns fixed and spears levelled.

'Step aside,' said Father Yarvi, Rulf and his warriors spreading out across the width of the hallway. 'Tell them, Mother Adwyn.'

'Let them through, I beg you!' Adwyn spoke as though the words hurt her more than the rope, but she spoke even so. 'The city is fallen. Blood spilled now is blood wasted!'

Koll hoped they would listen. But you know how it goes, with hopes.

'I cannot.' The captain of the guards was a warrior of no small fame, his silver-studded shield painted with the eagle of the First of Ministers. 'Grandmother Wexen has ordered that these doors stay sealed, and I have sworn an oath.'

'Oaths,' muttered Koll. 'Nothing but trouble.'

Skifr nudged him aside as she stepped past, raising her elf-relic to her shoulder. 'Break your oath or meet Death,' she said.

'Please!' Mother Adwyn tried to duck in front of Skifr, but the warrior who held her rope dragged her back.

The captain raised his shield to look proudly over the rim. 'I do not fear you, witch! I—'

Skifr's weapon barked once, thunderously loud in the narrow space. Half the captain's shield blew apart, his arm flew off in a gout of fire and knocked over the man beside him. He was flung against the door, bounced off and crumpled on his face. One leg kicked a little then was still, blood spreading about the smouldering corpse, blood spattered across the fine carvings on the door. A little piece of metal fell, bounced, tinkled away into a corner.

'Does anyone else wish to stay loyal to Grandmother Wexen?' asked Yarvi.

As if by prior agreement the guards flung down their weapons.

'Merciful god,' whispered Mother Adwyn as Rulf stepped smartly over their dead leader, seized the iron handles and heaved on them to no effect.

'Locked,' he growled.

Skifr raised her elf-relic again. 'I have the key.'

Rulf flung himself to the floor. Koll clapped his hands over his ears as the weapon spat fire, blasting chunks from the beautiful woodwork where the two doors met, splinters flying in stinging clouds. Before the echoes faded Skifr stepped forward, raised her boot, and kicked the ruined doors shuddering open.

Even for a man who'd seen the wonders of Strokom the Hall of Whispers was dizzying, elf-stone and elf-glass soaring up into the distance, a ring-shaped balcony five times a man's height above them, another as far above that, another above that. It was all lit by a flickering madman's glare, for in the centre of the round expanse of floor a huge fire burned. A pyre of books, and papers, and scrolls as high as a king's barrow, the heat of the roaring flames sucking the sweat from Koll's brow.

Statues of the six Tall Gods loomed high, flames glimmering in their garnet eyes, and standing even taller a new statue of the One God, neither man nor woman, gazing down with bland indifference on the destruction. Smaller figures were picked out against the flames. Grey-robed Sisters of the Ministry, some staring in horror towards the door, some still frantically feeding the fire, half-burned papers floating high into the echoing space above, fluttering down like leaves in autumn.

'Stop them!' bellowed Yarvi, voice shrill over the roar of the flames. 'Collar them! Chain them! We will choose later who to spare and who to blame!'

Rulf's warriors were already spilling through the doors, their mail, and blades, and eager eyes shining with the colours of fire. A shaven-headed girl was dragged kicking past, blood on her bared teeth. An apprentice like Koll, only doing as she was ordered, and he rubbed at the old chafe-marks where his own thrall-collar had sat, long ago.

Some might think it strange that a man who'd suffered as a slave himself could be so quick to force slavery on others, but Koll knew better. We all teach the lessons we are taught, after all.

'Where is Grandmother Wexen?' snarled Skifr, spit flecking from her burned lips.

'Above!' squealed a cringing minister. 'The second balcony!' There was no loyalty left in Skekenhouse, only fire and chaos.

Across the wide floor to a narrow passageway, ash fluttering down around them like black snow. Up a curving stair, higher and higher, their breath echoing and their shadows dancing in the darkness. Past one doorway and out of another, into the garish light.

An old woman stood at the elf-metal rail in a robe that trailed the floor, white hair cut short, a great stack of books beside her, their spines marked with gold, set with gems. She snatched up an armful and flung them over the rail: years of work, decades of lessons, centuries of learning gone to the flames. But so it goes when Mother War spreads her wings. She rips apart in a gleeful moment what it takes her weeping husband Father Peace lifetimes to weave.

'Grandmother Wexen!' called Yarvi.

She froze, shoulders hunched, then slowly turned.

The woman who had ruled the Shattered Sea, chosen the fates of countless thousands, made warriors quail and used kings as puppets, was not at all what Koll had expected. No cackling villain. No towering evil. Only a motherly face, round and deeply lined. Wise-seeming.

Friendly-seeming. No gaudy marks of status. Only a fine chain about her neck, and strung upon it papers scrawled with writing. Writs, and judgments, and debts to be settled, and orders to be obeyed.

She smiled. Hardly the desperate prey, finally at bay. The look of a mentor whose wayward pupil has at last answered their summons.

'Father Yarvi.' Her voice was deep, and calm, and even. 'Welcome to Skekenhouse.'

'Burning books?' Yarvi eased ever so slowly towards his old mistress. 'I thought it was a minister's place to preserve knowledge?'

Grandmother Wexen gently clicked her tongue. The disappointment of the learned teacher at the rash pupil's folly. 'That you should lecture me on a minister's place.' She let a last armful of books fall over the balcony. 'You will not benefit from the wisdom I have gathered.'

'I do not need it.' He held up his elf-staff. 'I have this.'

'The elves had that, and look what became of them.'

'I have learned from their example. Not to mention yours.'

'I fear you have learned nothing.'

'Forget learning,' growled Skifr. 'You will bleed for the blood of my children you have shed, the blood of my children's children you have shed.' She levelled her elf-weapon. 'My one regret is that you can never bleed enough.'

Grandmother Wexen did not so much as flinch in the face of Death. 'You are deceived if you think the blood of your children is on my hands, witch. I heard you were seen in Kalyiv, and was happy that you were gone from the Shattered Sea, and more than content that you would never return.'

'You are made of lies, minister,' snarled Skifr, the sweat glistening on her furrowed forehead. 'You sent thieves and killers to pursue me!'

Grandmother Wexen gave a sorry sigh. 'Says the thief and killer who licks the feet of the prince of liars.' She swept Koll, and Skifr, and finally Yarvi with her eyes. 'From the moment when you kissed my cheek after your test, I knew you were a snake. I should have crushed you then, but I chose mercy.'

'Mercy?' Yarvi barked out a laugh. 'You hoped you could make me bite for you, rather than against.'

'Perhaps.' Grandmother Wexen looked with disgust at the elf-weapon Skifr cradled in her arms. 'But I never dreamed you would resort to *this*. To break the deepest laws of our Ministry? To risk the world for your ambitions?'

'You know the saying. Let Father Peace shed tears over the methods. Mother War smiles upon results.'

'I know the saying, but it belongs in the mouths of murderers, not ministers. You are *poison*.'

'Let us not pretend only one of us stands in the shadows.' Father Yarvi's eyes glittered with reflected fire as he eased forward. 'I am the poison you mixed with your own schemes. The poison you brewed when you ordered my father and brother killed. The poison you never supposed you would drink yourself.'

Grandmother Wexen's shoulders sagged. 'I am not

without regrets. That is all power leaves you, in the end. But Laithlin's arrogance would have dragged us into Mother War's embrace sooner or later. I tried to steer us clear of the rocks. I tried to choose the lesser evil and the greater good. But you demanded chaos.'

The First of Ministers ripped a paper from the chain around her neck and flung it at Yarvi so it floated down between them. 'I curse you, traitor.' She raised her hand, and tattooed upon her palm Koll saw circles within circles of tiny letters. 'I curse you in the name of the One God and the many.' Her voice rang out, echoing in the towering space of the Hall of Whispers. 'All that you love shall betray you! All that you make shall rot! All that you build shall fall!'

Father Yarvi only shrugged. 'There is nothing worth less than the curses of the defeated. If you had stood upon the forbidden ground of Strokom, you would understand. Everything falls.'

He took a sudden step forward, and shoved Grandmother Wexen with his withered hand.

Her eyes went round with shock. Perhaps, however wise we are, however wide the Last Door gapes, the crossing of the threshold always comes as a surprise.

She gave a meaningless squawk as she tumbled over the rail. There was an echoing crash, and a long shriek of horror.

Koll edged forward, swallowing as he peered over the balcony. The fire still burned below, smoke pouring up, the shimmering heat like a weight pressing on his face. The all-powerful First of Ministers lay broken at its edge, her twisted body seeming small from so high up. Everything falls. Mother Adwyn slowly knelt beside her, palm pressed to her purple-stained mouth.

'So I have kept my oath.' Father Yarvi frowned at his withered hand as though he could hardly believe what it had done.

'Yes.' Skifr tossed her elf-weapon rattling down on the balcony. 'We both have our vengeance. How does it feel?'

'I expected more.'

'Vengeance is a way of clinging to what we have lost.' Skifr leaned back against the wall, slid down it until she was sitting, cross-legged. 'A wedge in the Last Door, and through the crack we can still glimpse the faces of the dead. We strain towards it with all our being, break every rule to have it, but when we clutch it, there is nothing there. Only grief.'

'We must find something new to reach for.' Father Yarvi planted his shrivelled hand on the rail and leaned over. 'Mother Adwyn!'

The red-haired minister slowly stood, looking up towards them, the tears on her cheeks glistening in the firelight.

'Send eagles to the ministers in Yutmark and the Lowlands,' called Yarvi. 'Send eagles to the ministers of Inglefold and the Islands. Send eagles to every minister who knelt to Grandmother Wexen.'

Mother Adwyn blinked down at the corpse of her mistress, then up. She wiped her tears on the back of her hand and, it seemed to Koll, adjusted quite smoothly to the new reality. What choice did she have? What choice did any of them have?

'With what message?' she asked, giving a stiff little bow.

'Tell them they kneel to Grandfather Yarvi now.'

THE KILLER

The dead men lay in heaps before the doors. Priests of the One God, Raith reckoned, from their robes with the seven-rayed sun stitched on, each with the back of their heads neatly split. Blood curled from under the bodies, making dark streaks down the white marble steps, turned pink by the flitting drizzle.

Maybe they'd been hoping for mercy. It was well known the Breaker of Swords preferred to take slaves than make corpses. Why kill what you can sell, after all? But it seemed Gorm was in the mood for destruction, that day.

Raith sniffed through his broken nose, splinters crunching as he stepped over the shattered doors and into the High King's great temple.

The roof was half-finished, bare rafters showing against the white sky, rain pattering on a mosaic floor half-finished too. There were long benches, perhaps where the faithful had sat to pray, but there were no faithful here now, only the warriors of Vansterland, drinking, and laughing, and breaking.

One sat on a bench, boots up on another, a gilded hanging wrapped around his shoulders like a cloak, face tipped back, mouth open and tongue stretched out to catch the rain. Raith walked past him, between great pillars tall and slender as the trunks of trees, neck aching from looking up to the fine stonework high above.

A body was laid on a table in the middle of the vast chamber, swathed in a robe of red and gold that spilled across the floor, a jewelled sword clutched in hands withered to white claws. Soryorn stood beside him, frowning down.

'He is small,' said the standard-bearer, who seemed to have lost his standard somewhere. 'For a High King.'

'This is him?' muttered Raith, staring in disbelief at that pinched-in face. 'The greatest of men, between gods and kings?' He looked more like an old flesh-dealer than the ruler of the Shattered Sea.

'He's been dead for days.' Soryorn jerked the sword from the High King's lifeless hands leaving one flopping off the table. He set the blade on the floor and took out a chisel, meaning to strike off the jewel-studded pommel. Then he paused. 'Have you got a hammer?'

'I've got nothing,' said Raith, and he meant it.

The high walls at the far end of the hall had been painted in pink and blue and gold, scenes of winged women he couldn't make a start at understanding, the work of hours and days and weeks. Gorm's warriors chuckled as they practised their aim with throwing axes, smashing the plaster away, scattering it across the floor. Men Raith had laughed with once, as they watched farms burn up near the border. They hardly spared him a glance now.

At the back of the temple was a marble dais, and on the dais a great block of black stone. Grom-gil-Gorm stood with his fists upon it, frowning up towards a high window filled with chips of coloured glass to make a scene, a figure with the sun behind handing something down to a bearded man.

'Beautiful,' murmured Raith, admiring the way Mother Sun caught the glass and cast strange colours across the floor, across the block of stone and the candles, the cup of gold, the wine jug that stood upon it.

Gorm looked sideways. 'I remember when the only things beautiful to you were blood and glory.'

Raith could hardly deny it. 'I reckon folk can change, my king.'

'Rarely for the better. What happened to your face?'

'Said the wrong thing to a woman.'

'Her counter-argument was impressive.'

'Aye.' Raith winced as he touched one finger to his throbbing nose. 'Thorn Bathu is quite the debater.'

'Ha! You cannot say you were not warned about her.'

'I fear I'm prone to recklessness, my king.'

'The line between boldness and folly is a hard one even for the wise to find.' Gorm toyed thoughtfully with one of the pommels strung around his neck, and Raith wondered what dead man's sword it had balanced. 'I have been puzzling over this window, but I cannot fathom what story it tells.'

'The High King given his chair by this One God, I reckon.'

'You're right!' Gorm snapped his fingers. 'But it is all a pretty lie. I once met the man who carved that chair, and he was not a god but a slave from Sagenmark with the most awful breath. I never thought it fine craftsmanship and my opinion has not changed. Too fussy. I will have a new one made, I think.'

Raith raised his brows. 'A new one, my king?'

'I shall soon sit enthroned in the Hall of Whispers as High King over the whole Shattered Sea.' Gorm peered sideways, mouth pressed into a smug little smile. 'No man was ever favoured with greater enemies than I. The three brothers Uthrik, Odem and Uthil. The deep-cunning Queen Laithlin. Bright Yilling. Grandmother Wexen. The High King himself. I have prevailed over them all. By strength and cunning and weaponluck. By the favour of Mother War and the treachery of Father Yarvi.'

'The great warrior is the one who still breathes when the crows feast. The great king is the one who watches the carcasses of his enemies burn.' How hollow those words rang to Raith now, but Gorm smiled to hear them. Men always smile to hear their own lessons repeated.

'Yes, Raith, yes! Your brother may have spoken more, but you were always the clever one. The one who truly understood! Just as you said, Skara will be the envy of the world as a queen, and manage my treasury well, and bear me strong children, and speak fair-sounding words that will bring me friends across the sea. As it turns out, you were right not to kill her.'

Raith's knuckles ached as he bunched his fist. 'You think so, my king?' His voice almost croaked away to nothing, he was so sickened with jealousy, sickened with the unfairness of it, but Gorm took it for tearful gratitude.

'I do, and . . . I forgive you.' The Breaker of Swords smiled as though his forgiveness was the best gift a man could have, and certainly a better one than Raith deserved. 'Mother Scaer likes things that are constant. But I want men about me, not unquestioning slaves. A truly loyal servant must sometimes protect his master from his own rash decisions.'

'The gods have truly favoured you, my king, and given you more than any man could desire.' More than any man could deserve. Especially one like this. Raith stared up into that smiling face, scarred by a hundred fights, lit in garish colours from the window. The face of the man he'd once so admired. The face of the man who'd made him what he was.

A killer.

He snatched up the golden cup from the altar. 'Let me pour a toast to your victory!' And he tipped the jug so it slopped over, dark wine spattering red as blood-spots on the marble dais. He took the sip the cup-filler takes to make sure the wine's safe for better lips than his.

There was an echoing crash behind them, bellowed insults, and Gorm turned. Long enough for Raith to slip two fingers into his pouch and feel the cold glass between them.

The High King's stringy corpse had been knocked from its funeral table and flopped onto the floor while two of Gorm's warriors fought over his crimson shroud, fine cloth ripping as they dragged it between them like dogs over a bone.

'There is a song in that, I think,' muttered Gorm, staring at the naked body of the man who'd ruled the Shattered Sea, sprawled with scant dignity on his unfinished floor. 'But there will be many songs sung of this day.'

'Songs of the fall of cities and the death of kings,' said Raith. He knelt, offering the golden cup to his master. Just as he used to after every duel and battle. After every victory. After every burned farm. After every petty murder. 'A toast to the new High King!' he called. 'Drunk from the cup of the old!'

'I have missed you, Raith.' Gorm smiled as he reached for the cup, just as Skara had when she was fitted for her mail, but this time Raith's hands stayed firm. 'I have been ungenerous, and we can see what happens to an ungenerous king. You shall return to me, and carry my sword again, and my cup too.' And Grom-gil-Gorm lifted the drink to his lips.

Raith took a long breath and let it sigh away. 'That's all I ever wanted.'

'Ugh.' The Breaker of Swords wrinkled his nose. 'This wine has an ugly flavour.'

'Everything has an ugly flavour here.'

'Too true.' Gorm narrowed his eyes at Raith over the

cup's rim as he took another draught. 'You have changed a great deal. Your time beside my queen-to-be has taught you much of perception and patience.'

'Queen Skara has made me see things differently, my king. I should tell her I'm quitting her service to return to my right place. That'd be the proper thing.'

'The proper thing? I might almost call you house-broken!' Gorm drained his cup and tossed it rattling on the altar, wiping the stray drips from his beard. 'Go to the queen, then. She should be ashore by now. We are to be married in the morning, after all. She will be sad, I think, to lose her favourite dog.' And the Breaker of Swords reached down to scratch roughly at Raith's head. 'But I will be happy to have mine back.'

Raith bowed low. 'Not near so happy as the dog will be, my king.' And he turned and strutted down from the dais with some of his old swagger, nodding to Soryorn, who was just coming the other way with the High King's scarred pommel.

'Shall we burn this place, my king?' Raith heard the standard-bearer ask.

'Why burn what you can use?' said Gorm. 'A few strokes of the chisel will change these miserable statues into Mother War, and at once we have raised a mighty temple to her! A fitting gift for she that has given her favoured son the whole Shattered Sea . . .'

Raith stepped out smiling into the night. For once he had no regrets.

THE HAPPIEST DAY

Skara stared at herself in the mirror.

She remembered doing the same when she first came to Thorlby, a hundred years ago it seemed, after she fled from the burning ruins of her grandfather's hall. She had hardly recognized the brittle-looking girl in the glass then. She was not sure she knew the sharp-faced woman there now any better. A woman with a proud defiance in her eye, and a ruthless set to her mouth, and a dagger at her jewelled belt she looked more than willing to use.

Skara twisted the armring Bail the Builder had once worn, the red stone winking. She remembered her grandfather giving it to her, thought how proud he would have been to see her now, pictured his smiling face, then flinched at the thought of his body pitching in the firepit, had to swallow the familiar surge of sickness, shut her eyes and try to calm her thumping heart.

She had told herself that when she saw Bright Yilling dead she would be free. She felt her thrall gently arranging the chain of pommels around her neck, the chain the High Queen's key would soon hang from, and she felt the cold weight of it on her bare shoulders, the weight of things done and choices made.

Instead of banishing the ghosts of Mother Kyre and King Fynn she had added the ghosts of Bright Yilling and his Companions. Instead of freeing herself from the cold touch of his fingertips in the shadows of the Forest she had chained herself further with his death-gripping fist on the fields before Bail's Point.

Mother Owd had been right. The faster you run from the past, the faster it catches you. All you can do is turn and face it. Embrace it. Try and meet the future stronger for it.

There was a heavy knock at the door, and Skara took a long, sharp breath, and opened her eyes. 'Come in.'

Blue Jenner was due to take her father's place in the ceremony, which seemed apt, as he was the closest thing she had to family now. She felt a fresh surge of sickness at the sight of the sacred cloth over his shoulder. The one that would be wrapped around her hand and Gorm's to bind them together for a lifetime.

The old raider came to stand beside her, his battered features looking doubly battered in the mirror, and slowly shook his head. 'You look a High Queen indeed. How do you feel?'

'As if I'm going to puke.'

'I hear that's just how a girl's meant to feel on her wedding day.'

'Is everything ready?'

If she had been hoping a great flood had swept the guests far out to sea she was disappointed. 'You never saw the like! Queen Laithlin brought miles of white hangings with her, and the Hall of Whispers is all garlanded with autumn flowers and carpeted with autumn leaves. The statue of the One God lost its head and'll soon lose its body and the Tall Gods back in charge where they belong. Say what you will about Grandfather Yarvi, he's a man who gets things done.'

Skara puffed out her cheeks. 'Grandfather Yarvi, now.'

'Lot of people climbed up a way lately.'

'Climbed up a hill of corpses.' She adjusted the chain of pommels around her neck, Bright Yilling's diamond flashing on her breastbone. 'And none higher than me.'

Jenner was hardly listening. 'Folk have come from all across the Shattered Sea. From Gettland and Throvenland and Vansterland. From Inglefold and the Lowlands and the Islands. Shends and Banyas and the gods know where some of 'em hale from for I surely don't. I even saw some emissaries from Catalia, set out to speak to the High King and found there's a new one since they left.'

'How is the mood?'

'There's many raw wounds still, and always those who tend towards the sour, but mostly folk are happy Mother War's folding her wings and Father Peace is smiling again. There are plenty who despise Gorm, plenty more who mistrust Yarvi, but the love for you goes a long way.'

'For me?'

'Your fame's spread far and wide! The warrior-queen who fought for her land when there was no one else! The woman who laid Bright Yilling low but gave him succour as he died. Majesty and mercy combined, I heard. Ashenleer come again.'

Skara blinked at herself in the mirror. She remembered no succour between her and Yilling. Only that pouch of papers. She gave an acid burp, pressed her hand to her guts and wondered if Ashenleer had been plagued with fears in the stomach. 'The truth and the songs rarely sit close together, do they?' she muttered.

'Not even in the same hall, but truth-telling isn't what skalds are hired for.' There was a pause, and Blue Jenner looked up at her from under his brows. 'Are you sure you want to do this?'

She was very, very far from sure, but she did not need his doubts heaped on her own. 'I made a deal. I cannot turn back even if I wanted to.'

'But do you want to? Maybe there are worse men than the Breaker of Swords, but I think I know you, my queen. If you could pick anyone, I doubt he's the husband you'd choose . . .'

Skara swallowed. The girl she had been before the flames took her grandfather's hall might have longed to make a different choice. The girl who had pressed herself tight against Raith in the darkness, too. But she was not a girl any more.

She lifted her chin and regarded her advisor through narrowed eyes. She made herself look sure. 'Then you do not know me as well as you think, Blue Jenner. Grom-gil-Gorm shall be made High King today. He is the most famed warrior about the Shattered Sea. An alliance between Vansterland and Throvenland will make us strong, and our people strong, and never again will men bring fire to Yaletoft in the night!' She realized she was shouting, and forced her voice down. Forced her heart to be silent, and spoke with her head. 'Gorm is the husband I would choose. The husband I have chosen.'

Blue Jenner looked down at his boots. 'I never meant to doubt you—'

'I know what you meant.' Skara put her hand gently on his shoulder, and his eyes came up to hers, a little dewy. 'You stood for me when no one else did, and I know you still stand for me. I pray you always will. But this is my duty. I will not turn from it.' She could not. However much it hurt.

Blue Jenner gave that gap-toothed smile she had come to love, his weathered face filling with happy creases. 'Then let's get you married.'

They both turned as the door banged open. Mother Owd stood staring, her new robe too long and somewhat tangled with her feet, her chest heaving and a sheen of sweat on her pale forehead. One needed no great mind to see she was weighed down by heavy news.

'Out with it,' snapped Skara, sick tickling at the back of her throat.

'My queen . . .' Mother Owd swallowed, eyes round in her round face. 'Grom-gil-Gorm is dead.'

CHANGING THE WORLD

'I know it was you!' snarled Mother Scaer, her rage filling the Hall of Whispers to the top, echoing back so savagely Koll hunched into his shoulders, 'or that bitch of yours—'

'If you are talking of Queen Skara she is neither a bitch nor is she mine.' Grandfather Yarvi's smile was as unmarked by Scaer's fury as elf-stone by arrows. 'If you knew I was responsible you would be presenting evidence, but I know you have none because I know I had nothing to do with it.'

Scaer opened her mouth but Yarvi talked over her. 'We speak of Grom-gil-Gorm, Breaker of Swords and Maker of Orphans! He used to boast that no man had more enemies! Every pommel on that chain he wore was some-one's score in need of settling.'

'And, after all . . .' Koll spread his hands and tried to look as earnest as any man could. 'Sometimes . . . people just *die*.'

Mother Scaer turned her freezing glare on him. 'Oh, men will die over this, I promise you!'

Yarvi's guards shifted unhappily, their faces hidden behind gilded face-plates but their elf-weapons on conspicuous display. The men who'd rowed the *South Wind* to Strokom had sickened. Three had died already. It seemed without Skifr's magic beans the ruins were every bit as dangerous as the stories said. For now there would be no more relics brought from within, but Grandfather Yarvi found no shortage of men keen to carry the ones he had. The moment they took them up, after all, they were made stronger than any warrior in all the songs.

'Have you really nothing better to do, Mother Scaer, than toss empty threats at my apprentice?' Grandfather Yarvi gave a careless shrug. 'Gorm died without an heir. Vansterland could fall into chaos, every warrior vying to prove himself the strongest. You must keep order, and ensure a new king is found without too much blood spilled.'

'Oh, I shall find a new king.' She glowered at Yarvi and growled the words. 'Then I will dig out the truth of this and there will be a reckoning.' She pointed up towards the statues of the Tall Gods with a clawing finger. 'The gods see all! Their judgment is always waiting!'

Yarvi's brow furrowed. 'In my experience they take their time about it. Dig out whatever truth you please, but for now there shall be no High King. All the last one brought us was blood, and the Shattered Sea needs time to heal.' He put his withered hand reluctantly on his own chest. 'For now power shall rest with the Ministry, and Father Peace shall have his day.'

Mother Scaer gave a disgusted hiss. 'Not even Grandmother Wexen presumed to set herself so high.'

'This is for the greater good, not my own.'

'So say all tyrants!'

'If you despise my methods so, perhaps you should give up that elf-weapon you carry? Or is it not quite the evil you first feared?'

'Sometimes one must fight evil with evil.' Scaer looked towards Yarvi's guards, and shifted the relic she carried beneath her coat. 'If you have taught the world one lesson it is that.'

Yarvi's frown hardened. 'You should have the proper respect, Mother Scaer. For the office of Grandfather of the Ministry, if not the man who holds it.'

'Here is all the respect I have for you at once.' And she spat onto the floor at his feet. 'You have not heard the last from me.' And her footsteps clapped in the great space above as she stalked from the Hall of Whispers.

'A shame.' Yarvi wiped the spittle calmly away with his shoe. 'When we were always such good friends. Still.' And he turned to Koll with a grin at the corner of his mouth. 'Enemies are the price of success, eh?'

'So I'm told, Father Yarvi—' Koll quickly corrected himself. '*Grandfather* Yarvi, that is.'

'So it is. Walk with me.'

Though Mother Sun was high and bright there had been rain that morning, and the grey stones of Skekenhouse were dotted with puddles. The fires had all been put out but there was still the faintest tang of burning. The killing had been stopped but there was still an edge of violence on the air. The calls of the traders came muted, the eyes of the people were cast down. Even a dog's distant bark sounded somehow fearful. Mother War might have folded her wings but Father Peace was far from settled at his loom.

A crowd of supplicants had gathered in the long shadow of the Tower of the Ministry. Folk come to beg for some prisoner released or some indulgence granted. They knelt in the wet, cringing as Grandfather Yarvi swept past, implacable, and called out thanks to him for saving the city from the Shends.

None mentioned that he'd been the one who gave the city up to the Shends in the first place. Not to his face, anyway.

'Folk used to nod to you,' murmured Koll. 'Bow if they really wanted something. Now they kneel.'

'It is only proper that they kneel to the Grandfather of the Ministry,' he murmured, acknowledging the most servile efforts with a generous wave of his shrivelled hand.

'Aye, but do they really kneel to him, or to the elf-weapons his guards carry?'

'What matters is that they kneel.'

'Are fear and respect really the same?'

'Of course not,' said Yarvi, walking on and leaving

more of his many guards to clear away the crowd. 'Respect soon blows away in a storm. Fear has far deeper roots.'

Teams of thralls crawled among the ruins, struggling under the ready whips of chain-masters, working to restore the city to the way it had been before the sack. Some of them, Koll was sure, were folk who'd stood high in the favour of Grandmother Wexen. Now they found that the higher you climbed, the further there was to fall.

It made Koll wonder whether they'd really changed the world so much for all that blood shed. Different folk wearing the collars, maybe, and different folk holding the chains, but life was still life. Same questions. Same answers.

'You are unusually quiet,' said Grandfather Yarvi as they walked on towards the docks.

'Sometimes you work so hard for something that when it comes you hardly know what to do with it.'

'Victory rarely feels much of a victory, in the end.' Yarvi's eyes slid sideways and it seemed, as ever, that he could see straight into Koll's thoughts. 'Is that all, though?'

'There's something that's been . . . well . . . *bothering* me.' It had in fact been burning a hole through Koll's mind since the day it happened.

'You've never been one to keep your worries to yourself.'

Koll twisted his neck and felt the reassuring rattle of the storekeeper's weights under his shirt. 'My mother always told me honesty was a man's best shield.'

'Fine advice, as your mother's always was. Be honest, then.'

'Grandmother Wexen . . .' He picked at a fingernail. 'She said she didn't send the men who burned Skifr's family.'

Yarvi peered at Koll down his nose. He seemed to peer from a long way up, since he became Grandfather of the Ministry. 'A lie. Like the lie about there being a traitor within our alliance. Grandmother Wexen knew how to sow discord among her enemies. Now she does it from beyond the Last Door.'

'Maybe . . .' Koll pressed the tips of his forefingers together so they turned blotchy white. Every word was an effort. 'Ask who benefits, you always told me.'

Grandfather Yarvi came to a sudden halt and Koll heard the guards halt with him. He could see their shadows stretching out towards him on the cobblestones. The shadows of the elf-weapons they carried. 'And who benefits?'

'You do,' croaked Koll, not looking up from his fingers, and added in a rush, 'or we do. Gettland. All of us. Without that hall-burning Skifr would not have come north. Without Skifr there would have been no journey to Strokom. Without the journey to Strokom, no elf-weapons. Without elf-weapons, no victory at Bail's Point. Without victory at Bail's Point—'

The weight of Father Yarvi's bad hand on his shoulder put a stop to Koll's blathering. 'The future is a land wrapped in fog. Do you really think I could have planned all that?'

'Perhaps . . .'

'Then you flatter and insult me both at once. I have always said that power means having one shoulder in the shadows. But not both, Koll. Skifr was our friend. Do you really think I could send men to kill her? To burn her children?'

Looking into his pale eyes then, Koll wondered whether there was anything the First of Ministers would not do. But he had no more evidence than Mother Scaer, and even less chance of getting satisfaction. He forced a quick smile onto his face, and shook his head. 'Of course not. It just . . . bothered me, is all.'

Father Yarvi turned away. 'Well, you cannot be so easily bothered if you are to take my place as Minister of Gettland.' He tossed it out like a trainer might a bone and, sure enough, Koll chased after it like an eager puppy.

'Me?' He hurried to catch up, his voice gone high as a little girl's. 'Minister of Gettland?'

'You are the same age I was when I took up Mother Gundring's staff. I know you do not quite believe in yourself, but I believe in you. It is high time you took your test, and swore your oath, and became a minister. You will sit beside the Black Chair, and be Father Koll, and your birthright will be the plants and the books and the soft word spoken.'

Everything he'd wanted. Respect, and authority, and his talents put to use. Father Koll. The best man he could be. So why did the thought fill him with dread?

The docks crawled with humanity, people bargaining, arguing and threatening in six languages Koll knew and at least six he didn't, ships tangling at the wharves, tangling with each other as they came and went, oars clashing and scraping.

Many were leaving Skekenhouse in the murk of mistrust that had followed Gorm's death. The Shends had already cleared out with their plunder, grumbling at getting only a part of what they were promised. The Throvenmen were heading home to rebuild their broken farms, their broken towns, their broken country. Without the chain of Gorm's fame binding them the Vanstermen were splintering into factions already, racing back to safeguard what was theirs or set about taking what was someone else's before winter gripped the north.

'Lots of people leaving,' said Koll.

'True enough.' Father Yarvi gave a satisfied sigh as he watched the hubbub. 'But people arriving too.'

There were sharp-eyed merchant-women of Gettland, servants of the Golden Queen come to clamp levies on every ship that passed through the straits. There were zealous prayer-weavers fixed on driving out the One God and singing the songs of the many on every street-corner in Skekenhouse. And every day more landless warriors swaggered in, hired by Grandfather Yarvi from all across the Shattered Sea, the white eagle of the Ministry fresh-daubed on their shields.

'They're bringing plenty of swords with them,' murmured Koll.

'Indeed they are. We must keep Father Peace smiling for a while.'

'Since when did Father Peace smile at swords?'

'Only half a war is fought with swords, Koll, but only half a peace is won with ploughs.' Yarvi propped his withered palm on the hilt of the curved sword he still wore. 'A blade in the right hands can be a righteous tool.'

Koll watched a group of frowning warriors stroll past, weapons worn as proudly as a new wife might wear her key. 'Who decides whose hands are right?'

'We will. We must. It is the duty of the powerful to put aside childish notions and choose the lesser evil. Otherwise the world slides into chaos. You aren't still having doubts are you, Koll?'

'Doubts?' Gods, he was made of them. 'No, no, no. No.' Koll cleared his throat. 'Maybe. I know how much I owe you. I just . . . don't want to let you down.'

'I need you beside me, Koll. I promised your father I would free you, and I did. I promised your mother I would look after you, and I have.' His voice dropped softer. 'I have my doubts too and you . . . help me choose what is right.' There was a weakness there Koll hadn't heard before, had never expected to hear. A desperation, almost. 'Rulf has gone back to Thorlby to be with his wife. I need someone I can trust. Someone who reminds me I can do good. Not just greater good, but . . . *good*. Please. Help me to stand in the light.'

'I've so much still to learn—' blathered Koll, but however he twisted there was no slipping free.

'You will learn by doing. As I did. As every man must.' Yarvi snapped his fingers. 'Let us put aside the Test.'

Koll blinked up at him. 'Put it aside?'

'I am Grandfather of the Ministry, who will refuse me?

You can swear your oath now. You can kneel here, Koll the woodcarver, and rise Father Koll, Minister of Gettland!'

He might not have pictured it kneeling on the quayside, but Koll had always known this moment would come. He'd dreamed of it, boasted of it, eagerly learned the words by heart.

He wobbled slowly down and knelt, Koll the woodcarver, damp soaking through his trousers. Grandfather Yarvi towered over him, smiling. There was no need for him to threaten. The faceless guards still lurking at his shoulders did it for him.

Koll only had to say the words to be a minister. Not only Brother Koll, but Father Koll. To stand beside kings and change the world. To be the best man he could be, just as his mother had always wanted. To never be an outsider. To never be weak. To have no wife and no family but the Ministry. To leave the light, and have one shoulder always in the shadows. At least one.

All he had to do was say the words, and stand.

ONE VOTE

There was an overgrown courtyard at the heart of the house that Skara had taken for her own. It was choked with weeds and throttled with ivy but someone must have cared for it once, for late flowers were still blossoming in a sweet-smelling riot against the sunny wall.

Even though the leaves were falling and the year was growing cold, Skara liked to sit on a lichen-spattered stone bench there. It reminded her of the walled garden behind the Forest where Mother Kyre had taught her the names of herbs. Except there were no herbs. And Mother Kyre was dead.

'The atmosphere in Skekenhouse is . . .'

'Poisonous,' Mother Owd finished for her.

As usual, her minister chose an apt word. The citizens

were steeped in grudges and fear. The remains of the alliance were at one another's throats. Grandfather Yarvi's warriors were everywhere, the white dove of Father Peace on their coats but Mother War's tools always close to twitchy fingers.

'It is high time we left for Throvenland,' said Skara. 'We have much to do there.'

'The ships are already being fitted, my queen,' said Blue Jenner. 'I was going to offer Raith an oar—'

Skara looked up sharply. 'Has he asked for one?'

'He's not the kind to ask. But I heard it didn't work out too well for him with Thorn Bathu, and it's not as though he can carry Gorm's sword any more—'

'Raith made his choice,' snapped Skara, her voice cracking. 'He cannot come with us.'

Jenner blinked. 'But . . . he fought for you at the straits. Saved my life at Bail's Point. I said we'd always have a place for him—'

'You shouldn't have. It is not up to me to keep your promises.'

It hurt her, to see how hurt he looked at that. 'Of course, my queen,' he muttered, and walked stiffly into the house, leaving Skara alone with her minister.

The wind swirled up chill, leaves chasing each other about the old stones. A bird twittered somewhere in the dry ivy. Mother Owd cleared her throat.

'My queen, I must ask. Is your blood coming regularly?'

Skara felt her heart suddenly thudding, her face burning, and she looked down at the ground.

'My queen?'

'No.'

'And . . . might that be . . . why you are reluctant to give an oar to King Gorm's sword-bearer?' Blue Jenner might be baffled but plainly Mother Owd guessed the truth. The trouble with a shrewd advisor is they see through your own lies as easily as your enemy's.

'His name's Raith,' muttered Skara. 'You can use his name, at least.'

'He Who Sprouts the Seed has blessed you,' said the minister softly.

'Cursed me.' Though Skara knew she had no one else to blame. 'When you doubt you'll live through tomorrow you spare few thoughts for the day after.'

'One cannot do the wise thing every time, my queen. What do you want to do?'

Skara dropped her head into her hands. 'Gods help me, I've no idea.'

Mother Owd knelt in front of her. 'You could carry the child. We might even keep it secret. But there are risks. Risks to you and risks to your position.'

Skara met her eyes. 'Or?'

'We could make your blood come. There are ways.'

Skara's tongue felt sticky as she spoke. 'Are there risks to that?'

'Some.' Mother Owd looked evenly back. 'But I judge them less.'

Skara set her palm on her belly. It felt no different. No more sickness than usual. No sign of anything growing. When she thought of it gone it gave her nothing but relief, and a trace of queasy guilt that she felt nothing more.

But she was getting practised at storing away regrets. 'I want it gone,' she whispered.

Mother Owd gently took her hands. 'When we get back to Throvenland, I will make the preparations. Don't spare it another thought. You have enough to carry. Let me carry this.'

Skara had to swallow tears. She had faced threats, and rage, and even Death, with eyes dry, but a little kindness made her want to weep. 'Thank you,' she whispered.

'A touching scene!'

Mother Owd stood quickly, twisting around as Grandfather Yarvi stepped out into their little garden.

He still wore the same plain coat. The same worn sword. He still carried the elf-metal staff he used to, though it sent a very different message since he killed Bright Yilling with it. But he had around his neck the chain Grandmother Wexen once wore, a rustling mass of papers of his own already threaded on it. And his face had changed. There was a bitter brightness in his eye Skara had not seen before. Perhaps he had put on a ruthless mask, since he moved into the Tower of the Ministry. Or perhaps, no longer needed, he had let a soft mask fall away.

All too often when we topple something hateful, rather than breaking it and starting fresh, we raise ourselves up in its place.

'Even my battered little stone of a heart is warmed to see such closeness between ruler and minister.' And Yarvi gave a smile with no warmth in it at all. 'You are a woman who inspires loyalty, Queen Skara.'

'There is no magic to it.' She stood herself, carefully smoothing the front of her dress, carefully smoothing her face too, giving nothing away, the way Mother Kyre had taught her. She had a feeling she might need all of Mother Kyre's lessons and more in the next few moments. 'I try to treat people the way I would want to be treated. The powerful cannot only be ruthless, Grandfather Yarvi. They must be generous too. They must have some mercy in them.'

The First of Ministers smiled as if at the innocence of a child. 'Charming sentiments, my queen. I understand you will soon be leaving for Throvenland. I need to speak to you first.'

'Wishes for good weatherluck, most honoured Grandfather Yarvi?' Mother Owd folded her arms as she faced him. 'Or matters of state?'

'Matters best discussed in private,' he said. 'Leave us.'

She gave a questioning sideways glance, but Skara returned it with the faintest nod. Some things must be faced alone. 'I will be just inside,' said Mother Owd as she stepped through the door. 'If you need me for *anything*.'

'We won't!' The pale eyes of the First of Ministers settled on Skara, cold as new snow. The look of a man who knows he has won before the game is even played. 'How did you poison Grom-gil-Gorm?'

Skara raised her brows. 'Why would I? He suited me much better on this side of the Last Door. The one who gained most from his death is you.'

'Not every scheme is mine. But I'll admit the dice have fallen well for me.'

'A lucky man is more dangerous than a cunning one, eh, Grandfather Yarvi?'

'Tremble, then, when you see both together!' He smiled again, but there was something hungry in it that made every hair on her spine stand up. 'It is true that things have changed since we last negotiated, among the howes outside Bail's Point. Much . . . *simpler*. No need to talk any longer of alliances, or compromises, or votes.'

You can only conquer your fears by facing them, her grandfather used to say. *Hide from them, and they conquer you.* Skara tried to draw herself up proudly, the way he had, when he faced Death. 'Uthil and Gorm are both gone through the Last Door,' she said. 'There is only one vote, now, and it is—'

'Mine!' barked Yarvi, opening his eyes very wide. 'I cannot tell you how refreshing it is to talk to someone who sees straight to the heart of things, so I will not insult you by dithering. You will marry King Druin.'

Skara had been prepared for many things, but she could not quite smother a gasp at that one. 'King Druin is three years old.'

'Then you will find him a far less demanding husband than the Breaker of Swords would have been. The world is changed, my queen. And it seems to me now that Throvenland . . .' Yarvi lifted his withered hand and turned it around and around in the air. 'Serves little purpose.' He somehow managed to snap that one stubby finger with a sharp click. 'It shall be part of Gettland from now on, though I think it best if my mother continues to wear the key of the treasury.'

'And me?' Skara struggled to keep her voice level for the thumping of her heart.

'My queen, you look beautiful whatever you wear.' And Grandfather Yarvi turned towards the door.

'No.' She could hardly believe how utterly certain she sounded. A strange calm had come over her. The calm that Bail the Builder felt before a battle, perhaps. She might be no warrior, but this was her battlefield, and she was ready to fight.

'No?' Yarvi turned back, his smile fading. 'I came to tell you how things would be, not to ask for an opinion, but perhaps I overestimated your—'

'No,' she said again. Words would be her weapons. 'My father died for Throvenland. My grandfather died for Throvenland. I gave up everything to fight for Throvenland. While I live I will not see it torn apart like a carcass between wolves.'

The First of Ministers stepped towards her, gaunt face tight with anger. 'Do not presume to defy me, you puking waif!' he snarled, stabbing at his chest with his withered hand. 'You have no idea what I have sacrificed, what I have suffered! No idea of the fires I was forged in! You do not have the gold, or the men, or the swords—'

'Only half a war is fought with swords.' Mother Kyre had always said *a smile costs nothing,* so Skara showed the very sweetest one she could as she took the slip of paper from behind her back, folded between two fingers, and held it out. 'A gift for you, Grandfather Yarvi,' she said. 'From Bright Yilling.'

There might have been no man in the Shattered Sea

more deep-cunning than he, but Skara had been taught how to read a face, and she caught the twitch by his eye, and knew Yilling's final whisper on the battlefield before Bail's Point was true.

'To being a puking waif I freely confess,' she said as Yarvi snatched the paper from her fingers. 'I am told I keep my fears in my stomach. But I have seen some tempering myself over the last few months. Do you recognize the hand?'

He looked up, jaw clenched tight.

'I thought you might. It seems now great foresight on Mother Kyre's part that she taught me to read.'

His face twitched again at that. 'Far from proper, spreading the secret of letters outside the Ministry.'

'Oh, Mother Kyre could be far from proper when the future of Throvenland was at stake.' Now she put a little iron in her voice. She had to show her strength. 'And so can I.'

Father Yarvi crumpled the paper in his trembling fist, but Skara only smiled the wider.

'Keep that one, by all means,' she said. 'Yilling gave me a whole pouch full. There are seven people I trust scattered across Throvenland with one each. You will never know who. You will never know where. But if I should suffer some accident, trip one night and fall through the Last Door like my husband-to-be, messages will be sent, and the story told on every coast of the Shattered Sea . . .' She leaned close and murmured the words. 'That Father Yarvi was the traitor within our alliance.'

'No one will believe it,' he said, but his face had turned very pale.

'A message will find its way to Master Hunnan and the warriors of Gettland, telling them that it was you who betrayed their beloved King Uthil.'

'I don't fear Hunnan,' he said, but his hand was trembling on his staff.

'A message will find its way to your mother, the Golden Queen of Gettland, telling her that her own son sold her city to her enemies.'

'My mother would never turn against me,' he said, but his eyes were glistening.

'A message will find its way to Thorn Bathu, whose husband Brand was killed in the raid you made happen.' Skara's voice was cold, and slow, and relentless as the tide. 'But perhaps she is more forgiving than she appears. You know her much better than I.'

As a stick bent further and further snaps all at once, Grandfather Yarvi gave a kind of gasp and the strength seemed to go suddenly from his legs. He tottered back, stumbled into the stone bench and fell heavily upon it, elf-staff clattering from his good hand as he clutched out to steady himself. He sat, shining eyes wide, staring at Skara. Staring through her, as if his gaze was fixed on ghosts far beyond.

'I thought . . . I might sway Bright Yilling,' he whispered. 'I thought I might bait him with little secrets and hook him with one great lie. But it was he that hooked me at the straits.' A tear trickled from one of his swimming eyes and streaked his slack cheek.

'The alliance was faltering. King Uthil's resolve was waning. My mother saw more profit in peace. I could not trust Gorm and Scaer.' He made a crooked fist of his left hand. 'But I had sworn an oath. A sun-oath and a moon-oath. To be revenged on the killers of my father. I could not have peace.' He blinked stupidly, tears rolling down his pale face, and Skara realized, perhaps for the first time, how young he was. Only a few years older than she.

'And so I told Bright Yilling to attack Thorlby,' he whispered. 'To make an outrage from which there could be no turning back. I told him when and how. I did not mean for Brand to die. The gods know I did not mean it, but . . .' He swallowed, the breath clicking in his throat, his shoulders hunched and his head hanging as though the weight of what he had done was crushing him. 'A hundred decisions made, and every time the greater good, the lesser evil. A thousand steps taken and each one had to be taken.' He stared down at the elf-staff on the ground, and his mouth twisted with disgust. 'How could they lead me here?'

Skara felt no hate for him then, only pity. She was up to her neck in her own regrets, knew she could give him no worse punishment than he would give himself. She could give him no punishment at all. She needed him too badly.

She knelt before him, the chain of pommels rattling against her chest, and took his tear-stained face in her hands. Now she had to show her compassion. Her generosity. Her mercy. 'Listen to me.' And she shook his head so that his glazed eyes flicked to hers. 'Nothing is lost. Nothing is broken. I understand. I know the weight of power and I do not judge you. But we must be together in this.'

'As a slave is chained to his mistress?' he muttered.

'As allies are bound to each other.' She brushed away his tears with her thumb-tips. Now she had to show her cunning, and strike a deal the Golden Queen herself would be proud of. 'I will be Queen of Throvenland not only in name but in fact. I will kneel to no one and have the full support of the Ministry. I will make my own decisions for my own people. I will choose my own husband in my own time. The straits belong as much to Throvenland as to Yutmark. Half the levies your mother is collecting from the ships that pass through it shall go to my treasury.'

'She will not—'

Skara shook his face again, hard. 'One right word severs a whole rope of will-nots, you know that. Throvenland bore the worst of your war. I need gold to rebuild what Bright Yilling burned. Silver to buy my own warriors and my own allies. Then you shall be Grandfather of the Ministry, and your secrets just as safe in my hands as in yours.' She leaned down, took his staff from the ground, and offered it to him. 'You are a minister, but you have stood for Mother War. We have had blood enough. Someone must stand for Father Peace.'

He curled his fingers around the elf-metal, mouth scornfully twisting. 'So we will dance into your bright future hand in hand, and keep the balance of the Shattered Sea between us.'

'We could destroy each other instead, but why? If Grandmother Wexen has taught me one lesson, it is that you are a dire enemy to have. I would much rather be your friend.' Skara stood, looking down. 'You may need one. I know I will.'

The pale eyes of the First of Ministers were dry again. 'It is hardly as if I have a choice, is it?'

'I cannot tell you how refreshing it is to talk to someone who sees straight to the heart of things.' She brushed a few stray leaves from her dress, thinking how proud her grandfather would have been. 'There is only one vote, Grandfather Yarvi. And it is mine.'

NEW SHOOTS

R aith heard laughter. Skara's big, wild laughter,
and the sound alone made him smile.

He peered from the dripping doorway and
saw her walking, fine cloak flapping with the hood up
against the drizzle, Mother Owd beside her, guards and
thralls around her, an entourage fit for the queen she
was. He waited until they were passing before he eased
out, scraping back his wet hair.

'My queen.' He'd meant it to sound light-hearted. It
came out a needy bleat.

Her head snapped around and he felt the same breathless shock as when he first saw her face, only stronger
than ever and, soon enough, with a bitter edge too. She
cracked no delighted smile of recognition, no look of

haunted guilt even, only a pained grimace. Like he reminded her of something she'd much rather forget.

'One moment,' she said to Mother Owd, who was frowning at Raith as if he was a barrow full of plague corpses. The queen stepped away from her servants, glancing both ways down the wet street. 'I can't speak to you like this.'

'Maybe later—'

'No. Never.' She'd told him once words can cut deeper than blades, and he'd laughed, but that *never* was a dagger in him. 'I'm sorry, Raith. I can't have you near me.'

He felt like his belly was ripped open and he was pouring blood all over the street. 'Wouldn't be proper, eh?' he croaked.

'Damn "proper"!' she hissed. 'It wouldn't be *right*. Not for my land. Not for my people.'

His voice was a desperate whisper. 'What about for you?'

She winced. Sadness. Or maybe just guilt. 'Not for me either.' She leaned close, looking up from under her brows, but her words came iron-hard and, however eager he was to trick himself, they left no room for doubts. 'Best we think of our time together as a dream. A pleasant dream. But it's time to wake.'

He would've liked to say something clever. Something noble. Something spiteful. Something, anyway. But talk had never been Raith's battlefield. He'd no idea how to bind all this up into a few words. So in helpless silence he watched her turn. In helpless silence he watched her sweep away. Back to her thralls, and her guards, and her disapproving minister.

He saw how it was, now. Should've known how it was all along. She'd liked his warmth well enough in winter, but now summer came she'd shrugged him off like an old coat. And he could hardly blame her. She was a queen, after all, and he was a killer. It wasn't right for anyone but him. He would've felt lucky to have got what he had, if it hadn't left him so raw and hurting, and with no idea how he could ever feel any other way.

Maybe he should've made some vengeful scene. Maybe he should've airily strode off, as if he'd a hundred better women begging for his attentions. But the sorry fact was he loved her too much to do either one. Loved her too much to do anything but stand, nursing his aching hand and his broken nose and staring hungrily after her like a dog shut out in the cold. Hoping she'd stop. Hoping she'd change her mind. Hoping she'd just so much as look back.

But she didn't.

'What happened between the two of you?' Raith turned to see Blue Jenner at his shoulder. 'And don't tell me nothing, boy.'

'Nothing, old man.' Raith tried to smile, but he didn't have it in him. 'Thanks.'

'For what?'

'Giving me a chance to be better. More'n I deserve, I reckon.'

And he hunched his shoulders and pressed on into the rain.

Raith stood across the street from the forge, watching the light spill around the shutters, listening to the anvil music clattering from inside, wondering if it was Rin that swung the hammer.

Seemed wherever she went she soon found a place for herself. But then she was a good person to have around. Someone who knew what she wanted and was willing to work for it. Someone who made things from nothing, mended things that were broken. She was just what Raith wasn't.

He knew he'd no right to ask for anything from her, but she'd had some comfort for him after his brother died. The gods knew he needed some comfort, then. He didn't know where else to look for it.

He gave a miserable sniff, wiped runny snot from under his broken nose on his bandaged arm, and stepped across the street to the door. He lifted his fist to knock.

'What brings you here?'

It was the minister's boy, Koll, a crooked grin on his face as he ambled up out of the fading light. A crooked grin reminded Raith for a strange little moment of the one his brother used to have. He still had a twitchy way about him, but there was an ease there too. Like a man who'd made peace with himself. Raith wished he knew how.

He thought fast. 'Well . . . been thinking about getting a new sword. This is where that blade-maker's working now, right?'

'Rin's her name and, aye, this is where she's working.' Koll cocked one ear to the door, smiled like there was sweet singing on the other side. 'No one makes better swords than Rin. No one anywhere.'

'How about you?' asked Raith. 'Didn't mark you as the type for swords.'

'No.' Koll grinned even wider. 'I was going to ask if she'd marry me.'

Raith's brows went shooting up at that, and no mistake. 'Eh?'

'Should've done it long ago, but I never been too good at making choices. Made a lot of the wrong ones. Done a lot of dithering. I've been selfish. I've been weak. Didn't want to hurt anyone so I ended up hurting everyone.' He took a long breath. 'But death waits for us all. Life's about making the best of what you find along the way. A man who's not content with what he's got, well, more than likely he won't be content with what he hasn't.'

'Wise words, I reckon.'

'Yes they are. So I'm going to beg her forgiveness – on my knees if I have to, which knowing her I probably will – then I'm going to ask her to wear my key and I'm hoping a very great deal she'll say yes.'

'Thought you were headed for the Ministry?'

Koll worked his neck out, scratching hard at the back of his head. 'For a long time so did I, but there's all kinds of ways a man can change the world, I reckon. My mother told me . . . to be the best man I could.' His eyes were suddenly swimming, and he laughed, and tugged at a thong around his neck, something clicking under his shirt. 'Shame it took me this long to work out what she meant. But I got there in the end. Not too late, I hope. You going in then?'

Raith winced towards the window, and cleared his

throat. 'No.' He used to have naught but contempt for this boy. Now he found he envied him. 'I reckon your errand comes first.'

'Not going to butt me again, are you?'

Raith waved at his broken nose. 'I'm nowhere near so keen on butting as I was. Best of luck.' And he slapped Koll on the shoulder as he passed. 'I'll come back tomorrow.'

But he knew he wouldn't.

Evening time, and the shadows were long on the docks as Mother Sun slipped down over Skekenhouse. The last light glinted on glass in Raith's palm. The vial Mother Scaer had given him, empty now. It'd been foreseen no man could kill Grom-gil-Gorm, but a few drips in a cup of wine had got it done. Koll had been right. Death waits for us all.

Raith took a hard breath, made a fist of his hand and winced at that old ache through his broken knuckles. You'd think pain would get less with time, but the longer you feel it, the worse it hurts. Jenner had been right too. Nothing ever quite heals.

He'd been a king's sword-bearer and a queen's body-guard, he'd been the first warrior into battle and an oarsman on a hero's crew. Now he wasn't sure what he was. Wasn't even sure what he wanted to be.

Fighting was all he'd known. He'd thought Mother War would bring him glory, and a glittering pile of ring-money, and the brotherhood of the shield-wall. But she'd taken his brother and given him nothing but wounds.

He hugged his sore ribs, scratched at the dirty bandages on his burned arm, wrinkled his broken nose and felt the dull pain spread through his face. This was what fighting got you, if it didn't get you dead. Hungry, aching and alone with a heap of regrets head-high.

'Didn't work out, eh?' Thorn Bathu stood looking down at him, hands propped on her hips, the orange glory of Mother Sun's setting at her back, so all he could see was her black outline.

'How did you know?' he asked.

'Whatever it is, you don't look like a man it worked out for.'

Raith gave a sigh right from his guts. 'Did you come to mock me or kill me? Either way I can't be bothered to stop you.'

'Neither one, as it happens.' Thorn slowly sat, her long legs dangling over the side of the quay beside his. She was silent a while, a frown on her scarred face. A breeze blew up and Raith watched a pair of dried-up leaves go chasing each other down the quay. Finally she spoke again. 'Life ain't easy for the likes of us, is it?'

'Doesn't seem to be.'

'Those who are touched by Mother War . . .' She stared out towards the glittering horizon. 'We don't know what to do with ourselves when Father Peace gets his turn. Those of us who've fought all our lives, when we run out of enemies . . .'

'We fight ourselves,' said Raith.

'Queen Laithlin offered me my old place as her Chosen Shield.'

'Good for you.'

'I can't take it.'

'No?'

'I stay around here, all I'll ever see is what I've lost.' She stared off at nothing, a sad half-smile on her lips. 'Brand wouldn't have wanted me pining. That boy had no jealousy in him. He'd have wanted new shoots in the ashes.' She slapped the stones beside her. 'So Father Yarvi's giving me the *South Wind*.'

'Handsome gift.'

'Don't think he'll be sailing anywhere for a while. I've a mind to take her back down the Divine and Denied, all the way to the First of Cities and beyond, maybe. If I leave in the next few days, I reckon I can stay ahead of the ice. So I'm putting a crew together. Got my old friend Fror as helmsman, my old friend Dosduvoi as storekeeper, my old friend Skifr to pick the course.'

'You're surely blessed with friends for a woman as unfriendly as you are.' Raith watched the gold glint on the water as Mother Sun sank behind them. 'You'll row away, and leave your sorry self here on the docks, eh? I wish you luck.'

'I'm not a big believer in luck.' Thorn gave a long sniff and spat into the water. But she didn't leave. 'I learned something worth knowing, the other day.'

'My nose breaks easily as anyone's?'

'I'm someone who sometimes needs to be told no.' She looked sideways at him. 'That means I'm someone who needs someone around with the guts to tell me no. Aren't many of them around.'

Raith raised his brows. 'Fewer than there used to be, too.'

'I can always find a use for a bloody little bastard, and I've got a back oar free.' Thorn Bathu stood, and offered him her hand. 'You coming?'

Raith blinked at it. 'You want me to join the crew of someone I always hated, someone nearly killed me a couple of days back, to sail half the world away from all I've ever known or wanted on the promise of nothing but hard work and bad weather?'

'Aye, that's it.' She grinned down. 'Why, you beating away better offers?'

Raith opened his fist and looked down at the empty vial. Then he turned his palm over and let it fall into the water. 'Not really.'

He took Thorn's hand, and let her pull him to his feet.

THE RISE

'There!' bellowed Koll, stabbing his open palm towards the drover to halt the dozen straining oxen, the great chain creaking and twitching. There was a grinding, then a mighty clonk as the feet of the vast gable dropped into their stone-carved sockets.

'Stake it!' shouted Rin, and teams of carpenters who not long ago had been warriors, and not long before that farmers, began to hammer posts into the ground, hauling tight a web of ropes that would keep the great truss from falling.

Skara stared up, neck aching it reared so high above them. It stood over the ruined steps of different-coloured marble where Mother Kyre had once greeted visitors to Yaletoft. Just where the great gable of her grandfather's hall had stood. The one she had watched fall the night

Bright Yilling came. Could it only have been a few months ago? It felt a hundred years and more. It felt as if a different girl had watched it happen in a different world, and Skara had only heard the story.

Blue Jenner showed his gap-toothed smile as he stared up at it. 'Stands just where the old hall did.'

'But higher, and wider, and far more graceful,' said Skara. Each of the two posts and two rafters had been fashioned from a spear-straight pine-trunk, floated downriver from the high hills above Throvenland where the trees grew oldest and tallest, stripped to the pale wood and beautifully shaped. 'It's fine work.' And Skara set her gloved hand on Rin's shoulder. 'I swear I could not have found a better smith and carpenter anywhere in the whole Shattered Sea.'

Rin grinned over her shoulder. 'A well-known fact, my queen. You're lucky we were tired of making swords.'

'All this and modest too?' murmured Mother Owd.

Rin twitched her apron straight. 'Modesty's for folk with nothing to boast of.'

'Hold them here!' Koll called to the drovers, catching the long chain that linked their yoke to the very top of the truss and swinging underneath it.

Rin started towards him. 'Where the hell are you going, you fool?'

'Up!' he called, and swarmed off underneath the chain with his legs crossed over it, nimble and fearless as a squirrel, soon far overhead and swinging in the breeze.

Rin clutched at her head with both hands, hair sticking out between her fingers, the two keys she wore rattling together on her chest. 'Get down from there before you kill yourself!'

'This is an excellent chain!' called Koll as he climbed higher and higher. 'You should be proud!'

'Gods damn it!' Rin screamed up at him, near-jumping in the air to shake her fist, then giving Skara a begging look. 'Can't you order him to come down, my queen?'

'I could.' Skara watched him clamber onto the highest point of the truss where the two massive beams crossed, remembering Mother Kyre's words to her on this very ground. 'But the secret to keeping authority is to give only orders that you know will be obeyed.'

'The joints all look good!' Koll slapped happily at the smooth meeting of the two rafters. 'Your new bolts are all holding, Rin!'

'I'll bolt your bloody feet to the ground when you get back down here!'

'How will I carve the roof beams then?' he called, sliding his fingers over the pale wood. 'What do you fancy, my queen? Dragons?'

'Black dogs!' she called up, setting a hand on Blue Jenner's shoulder. 'Like the worn prow-beast on the ship that carried me away to safety, saw me through a storm and brought me home again!'

Blue Jenner set his hand on top of hers and gave it a pat, while a group of prayer-weavers gathered around the foot of the truss and droned out entreaties to She Who Shapes the Wood and He Who Shelters and She Who Raises High the Stones that this hall should never fall.

Koll caught one of the dangling ropes and slithered down. 'Black dogs it is!'

'Why didn't I marry a bloody farmer?' muttered Rin, scrubbing at her scalp with her fingernails.

Koll dropped the last few strides and ambled back towards them. 'You couldn't find one who'd take you?'

'How many of these will we need?' asked Mother Owd, peering up at the towering truss.

'Fifteen will make the skeleton,' said Koll, looking up and sketching the timbers in the air with jerky movements of his pointing fingers. The gods knew how he managed it, but he gave some sense of the building completed, the huge beams above, the vast space they would enclose, and Skara found herself smiling as she pictured the warm dimness within, the echoing of the skalds' voices, the women's oiled hair and the men's polished cloak-buckles gleaming in the light of the great firepit, just as it used to be in her grandfather's day.

Mother Owd gave a soft whistle as she considered the emptiness overhead. 'We could be here a while.'

'The Forest took twenty-eight years to build,' said Skara.

'I hope to be finished a *splinter* more quickly, my queen.' Koll gave a smoky sigh as he looked up proudly at the work done so far. 'But nothing worth building is ever built quickly.'

'Mother War strikes like lightning,' said Mother Owd. 'Father Peace grows like the sapling tree, and needs the same care.'

'Yaletoft grows more like mushrooms.' Blue Jenner

peered down from the steps and into the town. 'You wake up one morning after the rains and there they are.'

It was true, the new city sprang from the ashes of the old, the frames of fine new houses sprouting along the wide straight streets Mother Owd had laid out between the site of the hall and the sea, the saws and hammers and masons' shouts a constant chorus from dawn until dark.

More people flooded in every day. Some of them folk who had lived in Yaletoft and fled the burning, but Gettlanders and Yutmarkers, Inglings and Lowlanders, too. Folk from all across the Shattered Sea who had lost their old lives in the war. Folk looking for fresh starts and hearing that Queen Skara had honest silver for honest work.

'Some of what Bright Yilling burned can never be replaced,' murmured Mother Owd.

'Then we must remember it fondly and look forward to fresh glories. It is hard to lose something.' Skara turned back towards the towering truss. 'But it gives you the chance to make something better.'

Koll was laying out his plans with vast flourishes of his hands while Rin watched, arms folded and one sceptical brow arched high.

'I'll hope to have five of them up and braced together before winter comes. The rest will have to wait until spring. I'll need to go into the hills and pick out the right trees first, though.' He scratched innocently at the back of his head, sidling up towards her. 'Maybe my wife will come with me, keep me warm when the snows come?'

'The snows come three men high up there! We'll be trapped till spring.'

'Exactly,' he said, hooking the golden elf-bangle she wore on her wrist and gently easing her arms unfolded.

'You're mad.'

'I'm just trying to be the best man I can be.' He took her chain and ducked nimbly inside so it was around both their necks. 'Just trying to stand in the light.'

She laughed as he gathered her in his arms and held her tight, swaying from one foot to the other. Soon they were kissing shamelessly, eyes closed, his hand tangled in her hair, her hand up under his chin, their jaws working. Never mind seeing it, it was kissing one could hear from a few strides distant, and several of the waiting workmen tossed their tools down and wandered off, shaking their heads.

Mother Owd rolled her eyes. 'The one drawback of this particular smith and carpenter.'

'We all have our foibles.' Skara was glad for them, but watching made her sad for herself. She turned away and stared out towards the sea, and found she was thinking of Raith.

By now, if the *South Wind* had beaten the ice on the Divine, he would be rowing down the long Denied. She hoped he was happy, but he had always struck her as someone to whom happiness did not come easily. They had always had that much in common, if so little else. She thought of his face, forehead deep-furrowed and mouth pressed hard, the way it used to be. She thought of the warmth of him beside her. She wondered if he ever thought of her. She wondered if—

'An eagle came from Grandfather Yarvi,' said Mother Owd.

Skara shook herself. She had no time to waste on fancies. 'Good news?'

'The Vanstermen have a new king. Mother Scaer organized a trial by combat and this man drove every warrior before him. His name is Yurn-gil-Ram.'

Jenner scratched at his sparse hair. 'Means naught to me.'

'He is a chieftain from the utmost north where the snows never melt, and they call him The Ram because he breaks men with his head.'

Skara puffed out her cheeks. 'Charming.'

'He has declared himself the greatest warrior the Shattered Sea has ever seen, and offers to kill anyone who dares challenge him.'

'I am eighteen years old and already had my lifetime's fill of warriors' boasting.'

'They say he mixes blood with his beer and is making a chain from the fingerbones of his enemies.'

Blue Jenner gave Skara a wink. 'Sounds fine husband material, my queen.'

She snorted. 'Send him a bird to say Blue Jenner happily consents to wear his key.'

'Marriage is the last thing on his mind,' said Mother Owd, folding her arms tight. 'Grandfather Yarvi fears he is already planning raids over the border into Gettland.'

Jenner gave a disgusted shake of his head. 'Can the Vanstermen really be battle-hungry again? Aren't they scared of elf-magic?'

'Even as a bow only has so many arrows,' said Owd, 'it seems those elf-weapons can only send Death so many times. And with the witch Skifr gone to the south, Strokom is once again forbidden.'

Blue Jenner put his weathered face in his calloused hands and gave a groan. 'Seems the world hasn't changed as much as we thought.'

'In the ashes of every war the seeds of the next take root,' murmured Skara. She felt the old nerves bubbling up her throat, pressed a hand to her stomach and tried to swallow them back down again. 'Send a bird to Mother Scaer with our congratulations and a bird to Queen Laithlin with our sympathies.'

'And then?' asked Mother Owd.

'Watch carefully, speak softly, smile sweetly, gather our friends close, pray fervently to Father Peace for calm, and keep our swords handy.'

'Orders that suit any situation.'

'Might be wise to rebuild the walls of Bail's Point too,' said Jenner, 'and stronger than ever.'

'My queen!' A boy was hurrying up from the docks, his boots squelching in the half-frozen mud. 'There are three ships coming in! Their sails have the white horse of Kalyiv!'

'Duke Varoslaf's emissaries,' said Jenner. 'You want to greet them at the docks?'

Skara considered the message that would send. 'We must not seem over-eager. Set a chair here, beneath the gable. It would be proper for them to come to me.'

Mother Owd smiled. 'We must always think of what is proper.'

'We must. And then, where necessary, ignore it.'

'I'll carve you a better one in due course, my queen.' Koll thumped down one of the rough chairs the carpenters sat on while they ate. 'But this might have to serve for now.' And he flicked a little dirt from the seat with the side of his hand.

It was a simple old thing, and a little rickety, the wood blackened in places by fire.

'It is not the chair that makes the queen,' said Mother Owd. 'But the queen that makes the chair.'

'It must've come through the night Bright Yilling came,' murmured Blue Jenner, 'and survived.'

'Yes.' Skara smiled as she stroked its arm. 'But so has Throvenland. And so have I.'

She sat, facing the sea, with Mother Owd at her left hand and Blue Jenner at her right. Chest up, shoulders down, chin high, the way Mother Kyre had taught her. Strange, how what had seemed so awkward once could feel so natural now.

'Warn the emissaries my hall is still a little draughty,' said Skara. 'But the Queen of Throvenland is ready to receive them.'

ACKNOWLEDGEMENTS

As always, four people without whom:
Bren Abercrombie,
whose eyes are sore from reading it.
Nick Abercrombie,
whose ears are sore from hearing about it.
Rob Abercrombie,
whose fingers are sore from turning the pages.
Lou Abercrombie,
whose arms are sore from holding me up.

Then, because no man is an island, especially this one, my heartfelt thanks:
For planting the seed of this idea: Nick Lake.
For making sure the sprout grew to a tree: Robert Kirby.
For making sure the tree bore golden fruit: Jane Johnson.

Then, because the fruit metaphor has run its course, all those who've helped make, market, publish, publicize, illustrate, translate and above all *sell* my books wherever they may be around the world but, in particular: Natasha Bardon, Emma Coode, Ben North, Jaime Frost, Tricia Narwani, Jonathan Lyons, and Ginger Clark.

To the artists and designers somehow rising to the impossible challenge of making me look classy: Nicolette and Terence Caven, Mike Bryan and Dominic Forbes.

For endless enthusiasm and support in all weathers: Gillian Redfearn.

And to all the writers whose paths have crossed mine on the internet, at the bar, or in some cases even on the printed page, and who've provided help, advice, laughs and plenty of ideas worth the stealing.

You know who you are . . .